Gemma's Bluff

Karly Lane lives on the mid north coast of New South Wales. Proud mum to four beautiful children and wife of one very patient mechanic, she is lucky enough to spend her day doing the two things she loves most—being a mum and writing stories set in beautiful rural Australia.

Also by Karly Lane
North Star
Morgan's Law
Bridie's Choice
Poppy's Dilemma
Tallowood Bound

Karly
LANE
Gemma's Bluff

ARENA
ALLEN&UNWIN

This edition published in 2015
First published in 2014

Copyright © Karly Lane 2014

All rights reserved. No part of this book may be reproduced or transmitted in
any form or by any means, electronic or mechanical, including photocopying,
recording or by any information storage and retrieval system, without prior
permission in writing from the publisher. The Australian *Copyright Act 1968*
(the Act) allows a maximum of one chapter or 10 per cent of this book, whichever
is the greater, to be photocopied by any educational institution for its educational
purposes provided that the educational institution (or body that administers it) has
given a remuneration notice to the Copyright Agency (Australia) under the Act.

Arena Books, an imprint of
Allen & Unwin
83 Alexander Street
Crows Nest NSW 2065
Australia
Phone: (61 2) 8425 0100
Email: info@allenandunwin.com
Web: www.allenandunwin.com

Cataloguing-in-Publication details are available
from the National Library of Australia
www.trove.nla.gov.au

ISBN 978 1 76029 041 2

Set in Sabon LT Pro by Bookhouse, Sydney
Printed and bound in Australia by Griffin Press

10 9 8 7 6 5 4 3 2

MIX
Paper from
responsible sources
FSC® C009448

The paper in this book is FSC® certified.
FSC® promotes environmentally responsible,
socially beneficial and economically viable
management of the world's forests.

To my children—Jessica, Kaitlin, Rourke and Milly.
May you always follow your dreams,
but never lose your way back home.

Part 1

One

'Look out!'

A grey blur streaked past the front of the car and Gemma Northcote swerved, fighting the impulse to shut her eyes to block out the horror unfolding before her. Everything slowed down as the car spun out of control, then slammed to a sudden halt. Closing her eyes, Gemma heard the airbags detonate, and the impact slammed her back into her seat and knocked the breath from her chest. Then all she could hear was her own laboured breathing.

At a faint moan beside her, she snapped her eyes open. 'Jazz? Are you okay?'

'Oh my God. Are we dead?' Jazz asked, turning her head from side to side tentatively before undoing her seatbelt.

'I don't think so. I'm pretty sure I'm still a size twelve.' Gemma shakily followed Jazz's lead and fumbled for her seatbelt release. 'Are you alright? Can you move your arms and legs?'

'I think so. What about you?'

'Yeah, I'm okay,' Gemma said uncertainly.

'We should get out of the car. What if it blows up or something?'

'Don't you have to smell petrol before that happens?' Gemma asked, sniffing the air anxiously.

'Do you really want to wait and find out?'

Deciding not to argue the point, Gemma hunted around for the door handle beneath the now deflated airbag. The door stuck slightly and she had to use both hands to push it open. Looking down, she noticed that her hands had started to shake. She slowly eased herself out of the driver's seat and stepped from the car. Holding onto the doorframe, she looked around, trying to get her bearings. Jazz swore under her breath as she staggered up from the ditch her side of the car had ended up straddling.

Gemma's gaze fell on a lump in the middle of the bitumen. 'Oh no,' she whispered.

'You killed Skippy!' Jazz said reproachfully.

'You think it's dead?' asked Gemma, staring at the limp form of the big kangaroo.

'Pretty sure they don't normally lie that still. We should move it off the road. We can't just leave it there.'

Gemma edged towards the animal, her heart thudding. She'd never been so close to one before. Standing above it, she looked down and saw the soft, thick fur of the animal's underbelly. 'Aren't we supposed to check for babies in the pouch or something?'

'Don't look at me. I'm not sticking my hand inside a dead roo.' Jazz stood well back on the side of the road.

'We have to check,' Gemma insisted.

'Then may I suggest establishing if it's male or female before you go poking around looking for a pouch?'

'And how the hell do you tell that?'

'Um—lift up its tail?'

'I'm not lifting its tail! You do it.'

'You killed it,' Jazz pointed out.

Grimacing, Gemma crouched down behind the big animal and reached for the tail. 'How do I know what I'm looking for?'

'If it's male I can guarantee you'll work it out.'

Gemma put her hand gingerly around the tail and went to lift it, then tried with both hands. 'Man, this thing is heavy,' she panted.

'Gem, drop the tail.'

'You'll have to look,' said Gemma, craning her neck. 'I can't hold this thing up and bend down at the same time.'

'Gemma,' Jazz said more loudly. 'Drop the tail now!'

'Oh, for goodness sake, this was your id—' Gemma stopped mid-sentence as she looked up into two big brown eyes that seemed to be trying to focus on her face. Dropping the tail, she staggered back, just as the animal began kicking and clawing its way onto its feet.

The girls screamed, trying to scamper out of its path, but the enormous animal was obviously still stunned and lurched towards them, tripping and sliding. They ran for the car, then jumped into the back seat and slammed the doors behind them.

'You said it was dead!' Gemma yelled.

'Well, it didn't look too healthy.'

'It could have mauled me to death!'

'You *did* hit it with a car,' said Jazz. 'It probably had good reason to be pissed off at you.'

After the kangaroo had loped off unsteadily into the bush, Gemma pushed open the door and went around to look at the front of the car. As she stared at the cracked bumper and the steam billowing out from beneath the crumpled bonnet, her shoulders slumped. They were stranded on the side of the road in the middle of who knew where, heading to a tiny blip on the map called Bingorra. They'd set off at some ungodly hour this morning, leaving behind their comfortable Sydney life to undertake this six-week 'adventure', working as jillaroos on a station in northwest New South Wales. It was now close to four o'clock, and they still hadn't made their destination. This was the very last thing they needed.

Jazz came to stand beside her. 'Look on the bright side,' she said, wrapping an arm around Gemma's waist.

'And that would be?'

'At least you're not a roo murderer anymore. That's good news, right?'

Gemma stared at her best friend and shook her head in disbelief. Usually she found Jazz's Pollyannaish ways endearing, but right now she could have cheerfully strangled her. 'Look at the car, Jazz. It's totalled.'

'Well, that's what you paid an arm and a leg in insurance for. It's a car. It's replaceable. We're not, and luckily we're both okay.' Jazz shrugged. 'That's a win in my book.'

'I don't know what lame-arse book you're reading, but in mine, having a car we can't drive is not a win. It's a disaster!'

This was their worst idea ever, Gemma decided, and together she and Jazz had had—and acted on—their fair share of bad ideas. She should have known by now that nothing they planned would ever work out the way it was supposed to. She looked across at Jazz again and her frown deepened. Of course something like this wouldn't bother her; Jazz never had a plan for anything. She'd changed her major three times in the last four years and still didn't have a single degree to her name. She didn't even seem fazed that she had no idea what she was going to do with the rest of her life. Apparently after four years, Jazz had had enough of university and was going to venture forth without a degree of any sort, which she had decided 'were a waste of time having anyway'.

What had prompted Gemma to agree to Jazz's crazy plan had been more of a knee jerk reaction to discovering she could no longer shrug off the realisation that her entire life now stretched out before her in a predictable shade of blandness. While everyone around her was talking excitedly about what they would do next—big, bright, beautiful dreams of amazing career opportunities, of travel and endless possibilities—it had dawned on Gemma that her entire future had been meticulously planned out for her.

Not that this had ever been any great secret. But for some reason, at that particular instant, it had been like a light

7

bulb going on inside her brain, illuminating her life, and she suddenly saw it as if she was looking through someone else's eyes. And it looked . . . monotonous.

There had never been any other option for Gemma. Every member of the family had always gone into the business. Her great-grandfather had started Northcote & Sons, and from then on it had been assumed that each generation would naturally follow in their parents' footsteps. Everyone else in the family seemed to have found their own place within the company. Her father's expertise lay in architecture, while his elder brothers had specialised in law and finance, as had Gemma's cousins. She in turn had also been expected to align her study to some branch of the family firm. She'd chosen business as her major, for no other reason than she couldn't draw and had no interest in finance, law or accounting. For the most part, she'd enjoyed it—she found business inter-esting—but she didn't love it. Not the way her father loved architecture, or her cousins loved finance. They lived and breathed it, while she just . . . did it, obediently following the path that had been set out for her. She just wished she loved it as much as her father wanted her to.

So, late one afternoon over coffee in the student cafe, Gemma had found herself agreeing to Jazz's harebrained scheme for a working holiday in the back of beyond.

'It'll be just like *McLeod's Daughters*, with handsome cowboys on horseback, everywhere we turn,' Jazz had sighed wistfully.

The only experience Gemma had with horses had been when her parents had supplied pony rides at her fifth birthday party. She still sported the scar on her leg where one of the ponies had bitten her. Gemma was sure she also carried a little bit of emotional trauma around to this very day from that experience. She wouldn't be getting too close to any cowboys on horseback. Give her the bright city lights any day; she was a born and bred city girl. And now here they were on day one and everything had gone to hell.

'Well, at least we're off the road,' said Jazz. 'We should be safe here.'

'We need to call someone. Where's my phone?' Gemma opened the driver's side door and dug through her handbag, then realised that half its contents had spilled over into the passenger-seat footwell.

'I'm sure things can't get any worse than they are right now,' Jazz added comfortingly.

'I *hate* when people say that in movies, because you just know things are about to get a hell of a lot worse. Like now.' Gemma held up her phone grimly. 'There's no reception.'

'Ah.' Jazz's face fell.

Gemma swore long and hard inside her head. 'Okay, then we'll just wait here till a car comes along,' she said at last, trying to sound calm.

'How long since we saw another car, do you think?' Jazz asked nervously.

Now that she thought about it, she couldn't quite remember when the last one had been and she saw that Jazz was beginning to pace a little anxiously. 'Don't freak out on me, we need to stay calm. Someone will have to come along eventually,' Gemma said, hoping she didn't sound as scared as she was beginning to feel.

'Will they? *Will they, Gem?*' Jazz demanded, her tone bordering on frantic. 'We need to go and look for help.'

Gemma shook her head firmly. 'We stay with the car. In all the documentaries they always say to stay with the vehicle.'

'Oh, great idea! They'll find two skeletons inside the car. Besides, name one time leaving the car wasn't a good idea? I bet you can't! Because you always hear the survival stories of people staggering into campsites and *saving themselves*.'

Gemma folded her arms. 'Burke and Wills? That one didn't end too well, did it?'

Jazz set her mouth in a thin line. 'At least they had camels to eat,' she said, looking morosely in the direction the kangaroo had departed. 'Pity that roo wasn't dead.'

'Don't you think you're being just a tad melodramatic here? We're not lost in the Simpson Desert.'

'Melodramatic? Hello? We're in the middle of nowhere in a car we can't drive and it's almost dark.'

'Well, we have each other and we have shelter. Someone will come past.'

'I still say we should go looking for a house so we can call a tow truck.'

'Have you *seen* any houses?' Gemma asked, sighing impatiently as she began to lose her patience. On the other side of the road where the kangaroo had disappeared was thick, dense bushland, part of a national park, but behind them beyond the fence line were endless acres of . . . nothingness. A few scattered trees dotted the plains and straggled along the roadside, but they were mostly thin, shaggy saplings, with the occasional large gum.

'So they don't build close to the road,' said Jazz. 'It doesn't mean they're not there. Look, it'll be dark soon and people will start putting their lights on. That'll make it easier to find one.'

'And we're going to walk across paddocks in the dark with no torch? I don't think so. What if we tread on a snake? I don't have a snakebite kit in my handbag. Do you?' Gemma snapped.

'Why are you being so negative? I'm trying to get us out of here.'

'I'm not being negative,' Gemma said, exasperated.

'Stop getting angry at me. I'm trying to be practical about this. Going for help is better than standing around doing nothing.'

'Practical!' Gemma turned away from her friend to stare out at the empty road before her. 'Practical would have been us realising we weren't cut out for this trip *before* we took it.'

Jazz snorted. 'Wow, that didn't take long.'

'What didn't take long?'

'The time it took you to start playing the "this was all your idea" blame game.'

'This *was* all your idea!' Gemma said, throwing up her arms in exasperation. 'If you recall, I was the one who thought this was completely stupid!' She said giving up on trying to remain calm.

'And yet here you are.' Jazz shrugged.

Gemma gave a frustrated growl. This was the way it had been between them ever since primary school. Jazz would think up ludicrous ideas and Gemma would eventually give in to her pestering and go along with them, only realising once everything went wrong that she should have stuck to her guns. You'd think after all this time she'd have learnt.

Who was she kidding? Jazz Beadman had been her best friend since their first day at school, when Jazz had stood up to a bunch of girls laughing at Gemma's shiny black school shoes. Their personalities were so different it was sometimes hard even for Gemma to believe they were best friends. Blonde pixie Jazz was outgoing, confident and always the life of the party. Dark-haired Gemma, on the other hand, had always been shy and preferred to hide in the background, more so when they had been younger. Gemma always wondered why Jazz, who resembled a parrot with her brightly coloured clothes, would ever have wanted to befriend Gemma, who had been more like a little sparrow, nondescript and, well, boring. But for all Jazz's bravado, Gemma knew that deep down she wasn't as carefree as she liked everyone to believe.

'Okay,' Gemma said now. 'You're right. I did agree to come along, so it's me I should be angry with, not you. You don't know any better,' she added haughtily.

Jazz chuckled. 'I told you this trip was exactly what you needed, Northcote. You need to live on the edge, just once in your life. Take some risks.'

'I hate to point it out to you, Miss *Wild Thang*, but we could've been killed!'

'But we weren't. It's all good. Just a minor setback.'

Only Jazz could write off a near-death experience as a minor setback. Gemma turned on her heel and stared at the long, empty road ahead with a weary sigh. It looked about as optimistic as her future right now.

'Ha! I told you we'd be okay. Look!'

Gemma turned at her friend's gleeful outburst, and felt a rush of relief as she saw a set of headlights coming towards them. Jazz began jumping up and down excitedly, waving her arms above her head.

'Would you stop?' said Gemma. 'It's not like they won't realise we're in trouble, what with the car sticking out of a ditch and all!' Ignoring her, Jazz continued to wave her arms wildly as though trying to signal an aircraft from a deserted island in the middle of the Pacific Ocean.

To Gemma's relief, the big white four-wheel drive that pulled up looked perfectly respectable. The two girls exchanged a silent 'Would you look at that' as they watched a man climb from the driver's side of the vehicle and walk towards them.

He looked like he'd just stepped out of a RM Williams catalogue with his moleskin pants and blue and white checked button-up shirt. His brown leather boots looked brand new.

A quick glance at Jazz proved her friend was just as impressed by their good Samaritan as she was, and in no way embarrassed to hide her open appreciation.

'Hi there. I'm Jazz and this is my friend Gemma.'

'Mackenzie,' the man introduced himself. 'Most people call me Mack. Interesting parking technique you have there,' he said giving the car in the ditch a brief look.

'We had a bit of an accident,' Gemma murmured.

'I kinda figured,' he said moving towards the car. 'Everyone okay?'

'We're much better now that you've come along,' Jazz all but purred.

'Where you headed?' the stranger asked, his gaze lingering on Jazz.

'Bingorra. Do you know how far away it is?' Gemma asked.

'You're about half an hour out.'

'We haven't got any phone reception to call roadside service,' Gemma felt obliged to point out in case Jazz's eyelash-batting made him think they were completely useless.

'Yeah, there're a few black spots along this section. I can give you a lift into town, if you want?'

Gemma was about to refuse his offer, asking instead if he'd call a tow truck for them, when Jazz jumped in quickly. 'That would be fantastic.'

'You could just send someone back for us,' Gemma said, sending her friend a pointed stare. You don't just get in a stranger's car, even if he was drop-dead gorgeous.

'I really wouldn't hold my breath on the local towing mob getting out here too soon and I don't feel right leaving you two out here by yourselves once it got dark.'

'Ignore her. She's never really been out of the city before,' Jazz said, waving a hand in Gemma's direction. 'We'd love a lift into town.'

'I'll give you a hand to grab your gear.'

Heading back to his four-wheel drive with an armful of luggage, Gemma waited till he was out of earshot before grabbing Jazz's arm. 'He could be a serial killer.'

'Oh, please. You really want to stay out here in the dark?'

'Well, I'm sure I'd be completely safe with you out here to protect me, since you're *so much more experienced* with country life and all,' Gemma hissed sarcastically.

'My instincts are telling me we can trust this guy.'

'I think you're confusing your instincts with your libido,' Gemma muttered as she followed behind Jazz after locking the car and carrying the last of their luggage to Mack's car.

Two

The main street was tidy and wide, as was the fashion with many of the little towns they'd driven through, but there was a decided lack of amenities, with the few shops providing no more than the basics of groceries, petrol and farming supplies. Where did people go to shop? Gemma wondered. It was quaint. There really wasn't any other word to describe it.

After stopping by the local service station to organise a tow truck to pick up their car, Mack dropped them outside the only accommodation in town. The pub was a lovely-looking old building—the posts and wrought ironwork on the upstairs verandahs gave it a yesteryear kind of charm.

'It could be worse,' said Jazz, bouncing to test out the mattress on the single bed. The frame squeaked loudly as if laughing at their predicament.

First thing in the morning they'd have to try to call the car-rental company and sort out another car, but it had been a long day, and after scoffing down a counter meal, they paid for their room and took their luggage upstairs.

'I'm going for a shower,' Gemma said, grabbing pyjamas and a towel from her suitcase. She made her way along the hallway and found the ladies' bathroom. In one of the two shower stalls, she turned on the hot water tap and waited for it to heat up. Goose bumps broke out on her skin as she waited, and waited . . .

'That was quick,' said Jazz when Gemma walked back into the room a few minutes later.

'There's no hot water.' She dumped her toiletries bag into her suitcase and pulled back the covers of her own creaky bed.

'Everything will be better in the morning, Gem,' said Jazz. 'You'll see. Just get some sleep.'

Gemma closed her eyes and let her tired mind drift off, tossing and turning through the night as she dreamed of wild-eyed kangaroos with sharp teeth chasing her through the bush.

•

The girls spent the majority of the next morning on the phone to their hire-car company.

'Okay, so it looks like we won't be able to get a replacement for up to a week,' Jazz said, disconnecting the call after finally speaking to an operator.

'How are we going to get out to this place if we don't have a car? They were expecting us today.' The two girls swapped frowns as they pondered their next move. 'Maybe we can just call Brittany's brother and ask him to come and pick us up until we work out what to do with the car?' Gemma suggested after a while.

'We can't do that,' Jazz said, shaking her head adamantly.

'Why not?'

'Because if we can't even manage to get ourselves out to the property, we're going to look pretty silly.'

'I have a feeling looking pretty silly will be happening quite frequently while we're out there. You're *sure* Brittany told him we have no idea what we're doing?'

'Would you stop worrying about everything?'

'I can't believe he was fine with that.' Who knew how things worked out here, but from what Brittany had told Jazz, they were short-staffed and had a lot of work to do. Why would he agree to taking on two untrained girls from the city? Surely he'd prefer someone with experience so he didn't waste time showing them what to do all day?

'It'll be fine. How hard can it be?'

Jazz's words were anything but comforting. 'I could call my father,' Gemma said reluctantly. 'He'd send someone to come and get us.'

'We can't turn around now when we're this close. Besides, do you really want to call your father and listen to him remind you that he was right and you were wrong?'

Okay, so put like that, maybe it wasn't the best plan. 'Well, what would you suggest?'

Jazz's gaze had fallen on the bartender at the end of the long counter. 'Wait here. I have an idea.'

'Jazz!' Gemma tried to grab her friend's arm, but she

was too late. Great, just what they needed, another of Jazz's brilliant ideas.

•

An hour later, Gemma shook her head as they loaded their suitcases into the back of the ancient filthy ute. 'I can't believe we actually paid money for this piece of junk.'

Jazz's big idea had been to sweet-talk the publican into finding someone willing to sell them a car; as luck would have it, his cousin was trying to sell his ute. He'd seen them coming a mile off, Gemma thought bitterly.

'I thought you said it was white?' she muttered.

'That's what the rego papers say. Oh, look,' Jazz said with a grin as she picked at the flaky red paint with a nail. 'It's white under the rust!'

'They should have paid us to take it off their hands.'

'You'd rather call your dad, or tell our new boss we crashed our car and ask him to bail us out?' asked Jazz. At Gemma's wince, she nodded knowingly. 'That's what I figured. Come on, we need to get out there, we're already late.'

Under the circumstances, Gemma was sure their boss would understand if they were a little late. What was he going to do, fire them? He was getting free labour in exchange for fulfilling their city-girl dreams of adventure, and it was unlikely they'd lose a job they weren't even getting paid to do.

In typical Jazz fashion, this entire trip had been arranged in a beauty salon over a manicure. Jazz had been there with Brittany, a girl who shared some classes with her. Gemma knew Brittany didn't particularly like her: on the few occasions they'd met socially, she'd picked up on an undercurrent of hostility. She wasn't sure what she'd done to earn it, but from some sarcastic comments she'd overheard, she was pretty sure it had something to do with the fact Gemma came from a wealthier background than her own.

While their nails were being done, Brittany had complained about having to cancel her upcoming holiday to the Gold Coast and return to the family property in order to work over the summer break. Jazz, naturally, had pounced on the opportunity, revealing her long-held secret desire to work in the great outdoors as a jillaroo. By the time their top coats were dry, the two girls had hatched a plan. It was brilliant—Brittany could go to the Gold Coast and take her holiday, and Jazz would get to live out her fantasy of living and working on the land. To sweeten the deal, she had volunteered to bring Gemma along to help out—two workers for the price of one! And Jazz had assured Brittany that as long as food and board were included they didn't even need to be paid. In fact, Jazz told Gemma, *they* would be the ones getting the bargain: overseas tourists paid a lot of money to stay on a working station and toil alongside real jack- and jillaroos.

It took Jazz quite a while to talk Gemma round, considering she'd never had the slightest desire to leave the comforts of the city to work outside in the dirt and dust and whatever else they had out there. But knowing that Jazz was going with or without her, she had felt a certain sense of obligation to accompany her on this random escapade. How could she send her best friend out alone to the back of beyond? Who knew what kind of trouble Jazz would get herself into? Besides, maybe doing something completely out of character like this would help take her mind off her job, and the path that would take her down from which there would be no deviating.

•

'I miss air-conditioning,' Gemma sighed as she rolled up the window before the large road train rumbled past, billowing dust. The ute was like a furnace, and winding down the windows was the only way to stay cool.

So much for an early start and impressing their new boss with their punctuality. By the time they finished talking with the rental company and had dealt with the necessary paperwork for the dilapidated ute, it was mid-afternoon when they finally left Bingorra and headed out of town.

•

The driveway to the property was long and dusty. It was so long that after driving for five kilometres with no sign of a house, the girls began to worry they'd missed a turn somewhere.

'Are you sure this is the right place?' Gemma asked.

'The sign out the front said Dunoon,' Jazz said, tapping her finger on the steering wheel in time with the country song on the radio.

'Do you think the house is far enough away from the road?' Gemma asked sarcastically.

'Oh look! There it is,' cried Jazz.

Sure enough, the track crested a slight rise and up ahead they saw a low-set house with a wide wraparound verandah. The sloping tin roof seemed huge as it reflected the bright sunlight. The white timber weatherboards could have done with a new coat of paint, the fenced yard looked a bit untidy and no clothes hung on the old Hills hoist, but there was something welcoming about the homestead. Off to one side was a series of large silver sheds.

In the paddocks beside the driveway, brown and white cattle lazily pulled at grass; a few lifted their heads as the old ute rattled past. Gemma let her gaze drift across the wide brown land that stretched out towards a mountain range in the distance. The open space seemed strange to a girl who had only ever lived in the city. There was so much ... *nothing*. A shiver ran through her at the thought of wandering around out there. *Why had she agreed to this?* she asked herself again.

'Well, it's not exactly how I was picturing it,' Jazz said, looking doubtfully at the farmhouse. 'The way Brittany talked about it, I was picturing something ... fancier. But we're really doing this! We're on a real working property!'

They pulled up outside the house, but the sound of dogs barking made them wait inside the ute for a moment. Picturing giant Dobermans with bared teeth, Gemma hoped they weren't about to become lunch for some hungry guard dogs. But when there was no sign of the dogs, the girls opened the doors and climbed out.

'I don't think anyone's here,' Gemma said nervously as they looked around.

'Let's go and check the sheds.' Jazz was already crossing the dusty ground between the house and the big silver structures.

Gemma followed her inside the first one and stared around the cavernous space with its compacted dirt floor. It was obviously used to house some kind of large machinery.

'You'd think if they were expecting us today someone would be here,' she mused with a frown. She was hot and sweaty and more than a little tired, and could have done with a cup of coffee.

'Did you hear that?' Jazz asked, tilting her head to one side.

Listening for a few moments, Gemma heard a muffled mewing sound coming from somewhere in the shed, and joined Jazz in the search. It took them a while to locate the source of the pitiful meows. Eventually, Jazz climbed up onto a pile of hay stacked along the far wall of the shed and looked down into the small space behind it.

'Oh, the poor thing,' she called back to Gemma. 'It's a cat. I think it's fallen down and can't get back out.' She reached down behind the hay to try to grab it. 'I can't reach.'

'Are you sure it's stuck?' asked Gemma. 'I mean, cats can climb. Maybe if we leave it alone it'll come out by itself.' She'd never been overly fond of animals in general, but cats in particular always seemed so damn superior.

'It's definitely stuck. We can't just leave it there. I know what—come up here and I'll hold your feet and lower you down so you can grab it.'

'Are you *insane*?' cried Gemma. 'I'm not going down there. You won't be able to hold me—you'll drop me on my head.'

'I was on the damn rowing team; I have upper-body strength that'd make a footy player jealous. Come on! It's starting to cry louder. We have to get it out!'

Gemma swatted at her friend's hands. 'Don't push me!' She sighed as she climbed up onto the hay bales next to Jazz. 'I *cannot* believe I'm doing this. You better not drop me, Beadman.'

'I won't drop you, you big sook. Ready?'

No, she wasn't ready! Gemma just knew this was going to end badly for her. Why could she never seem to say no to Jazz? As she gingerly leaned down into the space, she spotted the bundle of ginger fur wedged in between the wall and the bales, and had to admit it did look rather stuck. The cat stared up at her furiously as it continued to utter frantic cries. Reaching down as far as she could, Gemma could only just touch the cat's fur with her fingertips. Cautiously she eased her torso lower behind the bales, the hay poking and scratching her as she went. For some reason she'd always assumed hay would be soft like grass, not this coarse, nasty-smelling stuff that made her itch.

Jazz stood on the lower bale, her arms locked tightly around Gemma's hips, helping to ease her forward while Gemma tried to grab hold of the animal. It was bigger than she'd first thought. 'Come here, you stupid cat!'

'Don't yell, you'll frighten it,' Jazz scolded.

'It keeps squirming and it's only getting more stuck. I can't reach it.'

'Here, lean down closer,' Jazz said, and instantly dropped Gemma lower, angling her further into the gap behind the hay bales.

Caught unaware, Gemma's panicked scream drowned out the cat's high-pitched meow, and the string of swearwords she produced concealed the sound of footsteps behind the two cat rescuers.

There was a deep clearing of a throat, Gemma froze. At the same time, she felt Jazz's fingers tighten convulsively before losing their grip and plunging her headfirst down the hole.

With her legs in the air and her hands trapped in front of her, Gemma was effectively stuck. She squeezed her eyes shut in frustration and humiliation. Jazz swore, then quickly grabbed hold of Gemma's thighs and pulled her backwards out of the small space. As she felt herself being dragged upwards, the hay scratching her exposed skin and snagging her hair, Gemma almost wished she could have stayed down there. She did *not* want to face whoever had just walked into the shed.

Three

'Can I help you?' The voice was deep, and relatively calm, considering that whoever had just walked in had been greeted by the sight of two women looking more than a little ridiculous—including one with her backside up in the air.

At the last minute Gemma had somehow managed to grab a fistful of fur, bringing the struggling, protesting cat with her. Once out of its prison, in a flash of ginger fur the cat was gone. Gemma found her footing and wiggled out of Jazz's grip, while her friend gave a cheerful hello as though nothing out of the ordinary had just happened.

Gemma took a minute to dust off her clothing and pick out some of the hay. She could imagine the sight she must look with her ponytail scraped backwards through a hay bale and her face streaked with dust. Not to mention the scratch marks she'd earned while face-planting the dirt next to a terrified cat.

'I'm Jasmine, but call me Jazz. And this is Gemma.'

Reluctantly, Gemma lifted her gaze to meet a pair of warm—if rather perplexed—brown eyes. 'Okay,' the man said slowly. 'And you'd be in my shed because . . . ?'

'Rescuing that—' Gemma waved in the general direction the cat from hell had run off in— 'stupid cat.' She rubbed the scratch marks irritably.

'I think I must be missing something. What are you *doing* here?'

As the puzzled expression deepened on the stranger's face, Gemma forgot the cat fiasco and a new concern began to flutter to life. Something was very wrong here.

'We're your new farmhands.' Jazz smiled up at him.

'Farmhands,' he repeated flatly.

'You *were* expecting us, weren't you?' she asked.

'No, I wasn't. I didn't hire any farmhands. You must have the wrong place.'

'Are you Nash Whittaker?' Jazz asked, unfazed by his fierce frown.

'Yes, but I didn't hire any farmhands,' he repeated.

'Brittany organised for us to come out and lend a hand.'

'My *sister* did this? Where is she?'

'My guess would be sitting in a spa somewhere on the Gold Coast. We said we'd come out here instead and use the experience as a working holiday,' Jazz prattled on, oblivious to the man's growing horror.

'Wait a minute,' Gemma cut in. 'Are you telling us you didn't know anything about this?'

'That's exactly what I'm telling you,' Nash said grimly. 'My sister was supposed to be arriving today to pull her share of the weight around here for a change.'

'Did you know she hadn't cleared this with anyone?' demanded Gemma, turning on her friend.

'Of course not!' Jazz replied, then gave a small wince.

Gemma narrowed her eyes.

'Alright, I didn't exactly *ask* if she'd checked. But how was I supposed to know she had to? I was under the impression you guys were joint owners of this place,' Jazz said, turning back to the tall, annoyed-looking man before them.

'Oh yeah, we're joint owners when it suits her,' he snapped. 'Look, it doesn't matter. You two can't stay here. I don't have time to babysit a pair of city girls all day.'

Jazz and Gemma exchanged glances. Jazz looked dismayed, but Gemma felt a flash of relief, part of her hoping she wouldn't have to do this after all.

'You can't do that!' said Jazz, rallying. 'We're not inexperienced, and you won't have to babysit us. Besides, I don't think you have much choice, do you? From the way Brittany spoke, you need a couple of extra sets of hands but you can't afford to hire any more staff. So, let's stop talking and get stuck into it.'

'You have experience with farm work?' he asked sceptically.

'Of course we do!' said Jazz. 'Do you think we'd drive all the way out here if we didn't have experience?'

Gemma concentrated on avoiding both pairs of eyes. Part of her was horrified that Jazz was telling such blatant lies to a complete stranger, while another part was too busy rolling around on the floor laughing hysterically at the thought of the two of them ever having worked on anything remotely farm-like in their lives. She couldn't help but be impressed by Jazz's bravado though—she sounded so convincing that for a moment she almost had Gemma believing it too.

She could see Nash trying to work out if Jazz was telling the truth; finally he seemed to give up, turning to walk away. 'I'll deal with this after I've tracked down my sister,' he said over his shoulder, his tone ominous.

As soon as he was out of earshot, Gemma grabbed Jazz's arm. 'Are you crazy?' she hissed. 'What will you do if he actually lets us stay? He'll be furious when he finds out we don't have a clue what we're doing.'

'Would you relax? We're two intelligent women. Surely between us we can figure out anything he wants us to do.'

'Oh, really? What, we're just going to google how to do it, are we?'

'Why not? Actually, what a brilliant idea. That's exactly what we're going to do! See, we've already figured this out!'

Gemma shook her head, defeated. 'We're doomed.'

'Nope. We've got this.' Grinning, Jazz turned to see that the cat had slunk back around the corner and was now stalking something in the corner of the shed. 'How's it feel to save an animal's life?' she asked brightly.

'It stings, actually. Quite a lot, in fact,' Gemma muttered, glowering at the cat.

'He needs a name.'

'It reminds me of that mean cat from *Footrot Flats*. I think I'll call him Horse.'

'That's not a cute name,' Jazz objected.

'That's not a cute cat. Cute cats rub against your leg and purr. They don't tear you apart like a hillbilly with a chainsaw from some crazed slasher movie.' Gemma held up her arm to show Jazz the long red scratches she'd earned from her good deed for the day.

'He didn't mean it. He was just frightened. Weren't you, kitty?' Jazz crooned, moving closer to the cat, who swivelled his head in the girls' direction mid-stalk.

Gemma bit back a smile as the animal hissed and Jazz withdrew her hand in alarm. 'Oh yeah, Jazz, he's a real cutie.'

'Well, you frightened him, what did you expect?'

Gemma rolled her eyes as her friend walked past her towards the door.

'Come on,' Jazz said. 'Let's get the stuff from the car.'

With one last wary glance over her shoulder at the angry feline, Gemma followed her friend from the shed.

●

Nash uttered a long string of expletives beneath his breath as he stormed into the house. Of all the stupid, immature things his sister had done lately, this took the bloody cake. Gone to the Gold Coast for a break? A *break*? Wouldn't that be nice. He couldn't even think of the last time he took a break. When you were solely responsible for a failing farm in the middle of a drought, holidays were unthinkable.

Grabbing his mobile, he hit his sister's number and listened to the phone ring a few times before her chirpy voice informed him she was unable to take his call but to leave a message. He did as instructed, and was pretty damn sure his message would leave her in no doubt of his feelings about her little surprise. Tossing the phone onto the bench, he bowed his head and took a deep breath.

Damn it, he needed an extra set of hands around the place, and even if he had been able to afford to hire someone, no one local was available. It was a busy time of the season and everyone was in the same position. Experienced labour was hard to find in a pinch.

Which brought him back to the two young women waiting outside to hear his decision. His mind instantly conjured up the memory of a shapely backside poking up from the stack of hay bales, and he gave a frustrated groan. He didn't have time for this. He didn't care how hot that brunette's body was, or how soft her moss-green eyes were. His life was falling down around him and he needed to focus on the problems at hand.

•

Gemma sat in the front seat of the ute and shut her eyes, listening to the gentle drone of insects and the sound of cattle calling in the distance. It was so peaceful. There was no traffic noise, no hustle and bustle, just a whole lot of quiet. Until Jazz started talking again, that was.

'Let me handle this, Gemma,' she said. 'I can convince him we're up for it. Don't worry, it'll be fine.'

'Jazz, it's not too late to turn around and go home,' Gemma said.

'Go home?' Jazz stared at her. 'You know how long I've wanted to do something like this—*we've* wanted to,' she amended. 'It was your dream too, remember?'

'Jazz, that was when we were, like, *eleven* and we'd just watched *The Thorn Birds* mini-series. We both had a crush on Bryan Brown and wanted to marry good-looking sheep shearers.'

'It could happen!'

'I don't want to marry a shearer. I don't even like sheep! Look, let's just explore the area for a few days and then go back to the city. You know, have a *real* holiday, one where you don't have to actually work?'

Jazz shook her head. 'That defeats the whole working-holiday thing.'

Gemma gritted her teeth. Why did Jazz have to be so stubborn?

'Please give it a chance, Gem. This is important to me. It's something I truly want to do. I want to make some outrageous memories while I'm young, and I want my best friend to be in them.' Jazz looked at Gemma pleadingly.

Damn it. Gemma had never been able to say no to Jazz when she got that look in her eyes. 'Fine. We'll stay if Brittany's brother says it's okay . . . But brace yourself for disappointment, he was really angry.'

A door squeaked open then closed with a bang as Nash strode out onto the verandah and down the steps towards them, his expression formidable. 'It seems I can't locate my sister at the moment, so *for now*,' he paused for emphasis, looking back and forth between them, 'you can stay here. But the minute I get hold of Brittany and sort out this mess you'll have to go. I don't have time for this.'

Gemma felt sorry for the poor guy. In his shoes, she probably wouldn't be too happy either, but she was grateful they wouldn't have to turn around immediately and go home. She just needed one night in a real bed before they got back into the rust bucket and headed home to the city.

'May as well grab your stuff and I'll show you where the rooms are before I go back out,' Nash said.

The girls retrieved their bags from the back of the ute. Gemma caught Nash's double take as he spotted her trendy suitcases, complete with wheels and pull-along handles. Maybe she should have listened to Jazz's advice and bought an ugly green duffle bag like hers from the camping supply store, but she loved her luggage, it had been a twenty-first birthday present from her parents. Although she hated to admit it, it did seem out of place here.

'Here, let me help.' Nash reached across to take the girls' bags, lifting them with ease and leaving Gemma and Jazz to follow with the rest.

Jazz elbowed Gemma and wiggled her eyebrows at the—admittedly impressive—view of denim-clad male butt walking just ahead of them. Gemma fought the urge to roll her eyes again. Looked like Jazz was getting more than her fill of rugged country boys lately.

Nash led them into the house and the girls looked about with interest. The high ceilings gave an elegance to the old house and Gemma noticed the fireplace in the lounge room as they walked past was blackened inside with generations of use. They continued down a hallway with two doors on each side and waited as Nash stopped and opened the first one.

Dropping Jazz's duffle bag in the room, Nash stood back to let her pass. 'You can have Brittany's room.' It was a large airy room, with pink walls and a delicate pink and white checked bedspread.

'There's a spare room just up the hall for you,' Nash said, glancing briefly at Gemma then away. 'But it hasn't been used in a while so the bed's not made up.' He took Gemma's suitcase down to the next room and put it just inside the door. Pausing, he ran a hand across his brow then hooked his thumb into his belt buckle as he took a step back. 'Check the cupboard in the hall for some sheets or whatever you need,' he finished vaguely. Gemma got the impression that overnight guests were not something he'd had a great deal of experience with.

'It's okay, we'll manage,' she assured him, still feeling bad about putting him out.

He gave her a slight nod before turning to walk away.

'Is there anything we can do to help out? I mean, we're here and all. We could do something . . .' Her voice trailed off as he turned back to look at her doubtfully. Their arrival had obviously blindsided him; he probably couldn't wait to get rid of them. Gemma had never been an unwanted guest before, and it wasn't a nice feeling.

He frowned. 'If you really want to make yourselves useful, the chooks need feeding and the eggs still need to be collected. I've got work to do and won't be back till late. You'll have to fend for yourselves for dinner—I haven't been shopping yet so I've got no idea what you'll find in the fridge.'

'Don't worry about us. We'll be fine,' Jazz called after him as he headed back outside, the door banging shut behind him. 'Our first job,' she said with a small clap of her hands.

Feed chooks and collect eggs. That didn't sound too hard, thought Gemma, feeling her spirits lift slightly. Maybe Jazz was right, maybe this wasn't going to be as tricky as she'd imagined.

She went to the doorway just as Nash reappeared from the back of the house and headed for the large white Land Cruiser parked next to the shed, circled by three excited dogs, one black and tan, the others brown and red. Gemma was relieved to see that they weren't the vicious-looking animals she'd been picturing. On the contrary, the way their tongues lolled to the side as they looked adoringly up at their master was kind of cute. The dogs jumped into the tray of the vehicle and Nash drove away, leaving a cloud of dust in his wake.

The girls headed through the house to a large sunny kitchen, then out the back door. Behind the sheds were dog kennels and a large fenced-off yard; inside it, half a dozen chooks of various colours scratched and pecked at the ground.

Gemma lifted the latch on the gate of the chook yard and pushed it open. Glancing over her shoulder, she saw Jazz hanging back. 'Are you coming?'

'Ah, I think I'll wait out here. I'm not really fond of birds.'

'*Now* you tell me?'

'I thought I'd be okay with chooks, but it seems not. You remember the rainbow lorikeet incident.' Jazz shuddered. 'I've never liked birds after that. There's something sinister about those beady little eyes.'

Gemma sighed. 'That was fifteen years ago and all it did was latch onto your finger. Anyway, I don't think chooks are into that kind of thing.'

'They're all the same. Trust me, they just know I don't like them and they love to come at me. If you do this I'll take over your share of something else tomorrow. I promise.' Jazz looked at her beseechingly.

'Fine. Stay here and guard the gate. If I'm not back in five minutes, run for help,' Gemma said dryly.

She picked her way across the dusty yard towards a tin shed at the back, trying to avoid the large smelly chook droppings. The first door led into a dark storage area with a container standing against the wall. Lifting the lid, she saw it was full of pellet-like grain and assumed that this was what the chooks were to be fed. A plastic scoop hung on the wall above the container, and Gemma used it to shovel out a heaped pile of pellets. As she carried it out into the yard, chooks came running from every direction and she yelped, throwing the feed on the ground in front of them.

'Do you think that's enough?' she called to Jazz, who stood watching from a safe distance behind the fence.

'Better give them some more, just in case,' Jazz called back.

Gemma threw the chooks two more scoops just to be sure, then replaced the lid on the container and went through the next doorway. A row of nesting boxes sat side by side; in some of them nestled brown and white eggs. Looking around, she realised she hadn't brought anything to put the eggs into, but on the ground she saw an old ice-cream carton. She went along the boxes, carefully placing the eggs in the container.

When she reached the last box, she discovered it was occupied by a large black chook. It shuffled uneasily on its nest, and she saw a flash of white beneath it.

'Come on, you've had all day to lay your egg. Shoo.'
Gemma waved her hand in the hope of moving it away, but
it just sat there.

Gemma eyed the bird irritably. She didn't want to come
back later just for one lousy egg. Frowning, she clapped her
hands loudly, but the chook just puffed out its feathers a
bit more and stared at her. Up close she had to admit that
Jazz was right—they *did* have evil-looking eyes. In fact, the
more she stared at the bird, the creepier the thing looked. It
seemed to be sizing her up, slowly tilting its head, its beady
little eyes cold and unblinking.

Would you stop! she told herself crossly. *It's just a chook.
You're twenty times bigger than it. Get a grip. Just stick
your hand under it and grab the egg.*

Taking a deep breath, she leaned forward and reached
towards the box. Instantly, the chook started flapping
madly, rising up in the air and seeming to double in size as
it pecked at her face with its sharp beak. Gemma screamed
and stumbled backwards, almost dropping the ice-cream
container as she ran through the doorway into the main
chook yard, yelling for Jazz to open the gate.

'What happened?' Jazz demanded, her eyes darting around
in terror.

'It attacked me,' Gemma panted as she slammed the gate
shut behind her, checking to make sure the chook hadn't
followed her.

'Oh my God! I told you they're psychotic!'

'It wouldn't let me have its egg,' Gemma said, catching
her breath. 'It can keep the stupid thing. I'm not going back
in there to get it.'

Jazz gave a shudder of revulsion and reached for the container of eggs. 'Come on. We need a drink. Nash better have some beers in that fridge.'

'*We* need a drink?'

'You scared the living daylights out of me when you came screeching out of that henhouse like a madwoman,' said Jazz, her hand over her heart as if to stop it pounding out of her chest.

'I don't think we're cut out for farm life, Jazz,' Gemma said wearily as they headed for the back door.

'Not everything is as scary as chooks. We'll be right.'

Gemma shook her head at Jazz's optimism. She had a horrible feeling there were a *lot* of things scarier than chooks out there waiting for them.

Four

'Well, he wasn't kidding about there not being any food,' Jazz declared with her head inside the refrigerator.

'I wonder how long he's going to be out there for?'

'Who knows. He's probably avoiding us like the plague.'

Who could blame him? Gemma thought. *They'd already subjected him to enough headaches for one afternoon.* 'Well, we have plenty of eggs,' she said. 'Maybe I should just make an omelette for dinner—or quiche if there's any pastry.' She opened the largest chest freezer she'd ever seen. Inside was nothing other than enormous clumps of ice stuck to the sides and a few unidentifiable plastic-wrapped lumps of what she assumed was some kind of meat. 'Omelette it is, then.'

While Gemma made dinner, Jazz searched websites and applied for cleaning jobs in nearby places that were advertising for seasonal workers. They had no idea what tomorrow would bring, but if Nash's mood earlier was any indication, it was highly likely they'd be leaving Dunoon. She knew Jazz would be disheartened to have to turn around and go home after a couple of days, and surprisingly, Gemma discovered that part of her would also.

After eating their meal, the girls sat up for a while watching television until Jazz yawned and said she was going to bed.

Taking the plates back out to the kitchen, Gemma ran some hot water into the sink and began washing up. It was a big job, washing not just their own dishes but the plates and cups that looked as though they'd been sitting in the sink for a few days. Thirty minutes later, she'd wiped down the bench tops and cleaned out the fridge as well. She found it soothing and surprisingly invigorating to potter around the quiet kitchen. Earlier she'd been exhausted and ready for bed, but now she was wide awake.

Her mother was a very traditional kind of woman who enjoyed her house and took pride in taking care of her family. If the business was Gemma's father's domain, then the house was definitely her mother's. As a child, Gemma had enjoyed helping her mother bake and cook for dinner parties, but when she reached the tumultuous teenage years, quality time in the kitchen with her mum was no longer cool. It wasn't until she went to university, when she moved out of home and into a tiny flat with Jazz, that she rediscovered her love of cooking. Now when she went home for weekends she enjoyed cooking with her mother again, learning from her expertise. Although Gemma had re-established her bond with her mother, there were still things she couldn't bring herself to talk about with her parents. Some things you just had to keep to yourself, like the fact that the mere thought of beginning her job in the family business made her feel like she was suffocating.

The back door squeaked open and Gemma jumped, startled out of her thoughts. She looked up to see Nash walking into the kitchen.

'I wasn't sure when you were coming back in for dinner, so I put your plate in the oven,' Gemma said nervously. There was something about his tall figure in the checked shirt and jeans that made her jittery.

He looked up as if surprised to see her there, but then his frown returned and he simply nodded before washing his hands in the sink. As he glanced around at the clean benches, his frown deepened. Gemma's heart sank. Maybe she'd overstepped some country boundary?

She retrieved his meal from the old oven, setting it on the scrubbed pine table in the centre of the room. 'There were a lot of eggs, so I hope you don't mind that I used some of them.'

'One thing we have plenty of around here is eggs,' he said, taking a seat at the table and immediately beginning to eat.

Gemma found herself wringing her hands anxiously. She wasn't sure if it was rude to leave him here by himself or if any attempt to sit down and make polite conversation would just irritate him further. 'Well, I guess I'll go to bed,' she said, easing towards the door.

'Thanks for making dinner and cleaning up,' he said, looking up. 'You didn't have to do that.'

'Oh, that's okay.' She smiled, relieved. 'I like cooking and I had nothing else to do anyway.'

'Half your luck.' He sighed and she saw how tired he looked. His eyes were slightly bloodshot and his hair, which was the colour of whisky and in need of a trim, was flattened to his forehead by sweat where his hat had rested all day. His stubble wasn't the designer type that was so fashionable with Hollywood heartthrobs. More than likely it was just because he'd been too tired or busy to have time to shave. He didn't look like the kind of man who'd bother with following trends.

'You look like you've had a long day,' she said. 'What time did you start?'

He gave a low chuckle. 'I haven't actually stopped since last week.' Gemma looked at him blankly. 'I have to finish windrowing, so I've been working pretty much around the clock. I'll try and get a few hours' sleep now and then start again.'

'That's insane,' she said, horrified. She had no idea what the hell windrowing was, but it was probably something important that she should know so she tried to look like she understood what he was talking about. However, it wasn't necessary to be an expert on farming to know that this man was working too hard.

'That's farming for you.'

'But surely you can't keep working at that kind of pace? How long will you have to do this for?'

He shrugged. 'Till it's done. It's not like I have much choice in the matter,' he added dryly.

'You're doing all this alone?'

'Yep.'

42

This was crazy. He was going to kill himself. 'You don't have anyone else to help you?'

'Well, I was counting on my sister coming back by today to take a little of the load off for a few months, but I guess that isn't going to happen now.'

Gemma felt terrible. Had she known that it was so vital that Brittany be here, she'd never have agreed to come. Brittany had grown up on this place. She knew how to *do stuff*. Her brother needed help from someone with experience, not a business graduate and an arts major who would only add to his workload. 'I'm really sorry about all this,' she said weakly. 'We honestly thought she'd spoken to you about it.'

Finishing his dinner, he picked up his plate and carried it to the sink. 'I'll try Brittany again first thing in the morning. Until then, don't worry about it. My sister has always been good at getting out of work and this has her name written all over it. I should have known better than to think she'd take her responsibilities seriously.'

'I can wash that up if you want to go get some sleep,' Gemma offered when he put the plate in the sink.

'Leave it until tomorrow. You should get to bed too. I imagine you had a long drive to get out here.'

She managed a wan smile. Compared to his day, theirs had been nothing, she thought as he ushered her firmly out of the kitchen and switched off the lights behind them. At the doorway of her room, Gemma stopped and looked over her shoulder to see Nash still watching her from the entrance to the kitchen. Heat crept up her face as she ducked inside the room, closing the door carefully behind her. As she changed into her pyjamas and slid under the covers of the bed, her heart was still doing an odd little dance.

•

'So what do you think about Mr Tall, Dark and Irritated?' Jazz asked as they cleared the table after breakfast the next morning.

'He's got every reason to be angry. He's working crazy hours.'

'I meant what do *you* think about *him*?' She cocked an eyebrow.

Gemma sent her friend a disapproving glance. 'I'm serious, Jazz. He's really struggling out here and we're only adding to his problems. He was counting on Brittany's help.'

'Exactly how long did you two sit out here last night and chat?'

'Not long, but I saw how tired he looked.'

'Well, I'll be!' Jazz said, a smug smile on her lips. 'You've got the hots for him!' She clapped her hands together gleefully. 'Little Miss I-have-my-future-all-mapped-out-including-the-perfect-man-I'm-going-to-marry-to-father-my-two-point-three-children.'

'Knock it off.' Honestly, Jazz could be the most annoying person sometimes. There were days when Gemma couldn't believe they had managed to stay friends for as long as they had. Although in truth they were more than friends; they were both only children who had somehow found each other and become the sibling each of them had been desperate for. They were often mistaken for sisters, not because they looked anything alike, but because most people listening to them bicker assumed they were siblings.

'I'll be accepting apologies anytime for all the arguing it took to make you agree to come along on this trip. Just so ya know.'

'Don't hold your breath,' Gemma muttered, walking out of the kitchen and towards the bedroom to get dressed. *Had the hots for him!* She gave a snort. As if. She'd only met the man yesterday. Anyway, he was *so* not her type. She'd always gone out with men who ran in the same circles as her family. What could she possibly have in common with Nash Whittaker?

Once dressed, Gemma went back out to the kitchen and began chipping the now softened ice off the sides of the freezer. She'd turned it off last night, planning to tackle the job today—quite possibly her last job here before they left.

Jazz came back into the room. 'I'm going for a drive into town. I want to grab some more internet credit and buy something decent to eat. Want to come?'

'I've started this now so I may as well finish it. Besides, I'm sick of sitting in a car. I can't believe you're ready to get back in one so soon.'

Jazz flashed a brilliant smile. 'Well, I figure since you've staked a claim on Mr Grumpy out there I'd better go and take a look around town and see what else they have to offer. Plus, we really do need some food.'

'I should have known there was an ulterior motive. Anyway, what happened to proving we're capable of helping out around here? What if he comes back to get us to do a job?'

'He said he was going to check with Brittany first, didn't he? I'm not sitting around here twiddling my thumbs while we wait for him to make up his mind.' Jazz shrugged, opening the back door.

Gemma knew it was pointless trying to talk Jazz out of anything once she'd made up her mind. And clearly she hadn't been joking when she'd said she was out to fulfil her cowboy fetish. Gemma wondered if she should be going along for the ride just to make sure Jazz didn't do anything stupid. 'Keep your phone on in case I need you to come back,' she called from the doorway as Jazz climbed into the rust bucket. *Like if they were kicked out once Nash got hold of his sister,* she thought, oddly unsettled by the idea.

'Yes, Mum!' floated back to her before the engine revved to life.

Gemma let out another sigh and went back to the freezer.

•

An hour later, she'd filled four buckets with ice she'd managed to dislodge from the sides of the freezer and was down to the last few big chunks on the bottom. Doubled over at the waist, her head and torso inside the large freezer box, she scraped her knuckle against a particularly stubborn piece of ice and let out a curse. She pushed herself back out of the freezer only to give a startled scream when she discovered Nash leaning against the sink, arms folded across his chest as though he had been there for some time.

'You scared me!' she gasped. 'I didn't hear you come in.'

'Apparently not. Do you make a habit of standing on your head?'

Crap! This was the second time he'd walked in on her with her bum up in the air. 'It's a new technique I'm trying,' she muttered, shaking her frozen hands to get some feeling back into them.

'Not that I'm complaining,' he said with an unexpected half-smile.

Damn her inability to remain cool under pressure! Gemma's face gave her away every time—right now she could feel a blush working its way most unattractively up her neck in big red blotches. 'Have you finished work for the day?' she asked, trying to change the subject.

'Nope. I need to do a quick repair job then get back out there. I just noticed your ute was gone and came in to check.'

'If all the family silver was still here?' Gemma asked.

'If your bags were gone,' Nash corrected expressionlessly.

'Jazz went into town to buy some groceries. I thought I'd stay and finish this.' She waved towards the freezer.

'You shouldn't have bothered with that. Your hands look like they're snap frozen. Here, put them under some warm water.'

'They'll warm up soon enough. Do you want a coffee or something before you go back out?' Suddenly remembering that she was the visitor—and an unwanted one at that—she felt herself blush again. 'Sorry, this is your house. I didn't mean to take over or anything.'

Nash looked as though her comment had distracted him momentarily before appearing to shake himself out of whatever he'd been thinking about. 'No worries. Make yourself at home while you're here. Actually, I have a better idea. I need to go into town and pick up some parts. We can get a cuppa in town if you want to come along? That freezer hasn't been defrosted in years, so a few more hours won't make any difference.'

'Oh. Um, okay. Yeah, that sounds good,' she stammered, surprised by the unexpected invitation, wondering why the offer to go for a drive into town with Nash sounded better than one from Jazz. Well, she told herself, Jazz was taking a very long time getting back with the food and she was getting a little hungry.

Nash's Land Cruiser felt huge compared to their little rust bucket. As they drove along the dusty track, Nash slid in a CD with a mix of country music and turned it down to a comfortable background level.

'How many acres do you have?' Gemma asked, looking out across the wide open space.

'We usually talk in hectares, not acres, and this place is just over sixteen hundred hectares.'

She didn't know how big sixteen hundred hectares was, but given that there were crops planted as far as the eye could see she suspected it was pretty large. 'You raise cattle as well?' she asked, thinking of the cattle she saw on the way in yesterday.

'I run cattle and a few head of sheep as well. Besides the canola, I've also got wheat and chickpeas, and I grow lucerne, which I harvest to store for feed. The rest is rotated for grazing.'

She wasn't sure which was wheat, canola or chickpeas, but the fields stretched around her like a vast ocean of textured green, brown and pale yellow. 'No wonder you're busy, with livestock and crops to juggle.' She really had no idea, but she imagined the two types of farming would require two totally different skill sets.

'You have to diversify nowadays if you want to get anywhere. We've had a couple of bad years in a row and it's knocked pretty much everyone around. We're due for a good turn.'

'It must be hard living with such uncertainty all the time.'

His shoulders moved in a resigned gesture. 'That's farming for you. You take the good with the bad.'

She wasn't sure she could cope with that. She liked to have a plan. A plan helped forestall any problems. It didn't help much with the unexpected ones though, she conceded as she thought about starting work back in Sydney and that niggling sensation of dread began to creep in once more. Stop it, she told herself firmly. She had a plan for her life, and if she stuck to it everything would be fine. But if she started thinking crazy thoughts about changing the plan then things would get messy, and she didn't *do* messy. She did *planned*.

Gemma turned her attention to the ploughed paddocks now passing her window. The rich red-brown soil stood out starkly against the tawny-coloured grasslands surrounding it. 'Is this what you've been out planting?'

'No, that's been in for a while. Right now I'm windrowing canola, further over the back.'

The openness of their conversation gave Gemma the courage to finally ask, 'What's windrowing?'

'It's cutting the crop and leaving it in rows to dry out.'

'So it's like harvesting?'

'No.' He shook his head and gave her a patient look. 'We do this before harvesting, because canola ripens at different stages, so if we cut it and dry it, it should all mature at the same time, ready for harvesting later.'

'And you've been doing all this on your own?'

'Yeah.' He glanced out his window and gave a ghost of what looked like a satisfied smile. For a moment, Gemma let her eyes linger on the small creases either side of his mouth.

Quickly turning away, she stared out her window and watched the scenery flash by. Although most of the land was cleared, there were still a lot of trees dotting the landscape. The area wasn't completely flat either, she saw now, but was a combination of gently undulating hills and gullies, with the lush bushland of a national park far off in the distance.

Nash lifted his hand at a passing vehicle, the fourth time he'd done that since turning onto the road to town.

'Do you know *everyone*?' Gemma asked.

He gave her an odd look. 'Pretty much. Why?'

'I don't think I've ever seen anyone who knew every single person they've passed on the road before.'

'You get used to it after a while. Although there are times when I reckon it'd be nice to have a little bit of anonymity.' After a pause, he added, 'Guess this place isn't quite what you're used to.' Gemma looked over to find that he was watching her.

'The town's smaller than I imagined,' she said carefully. 'Where do you go if you need to go shopping? There's not a lot here.'

'Most people head into Curranjuck once a month to get their dose of retail therapy. It's about an hour and a half from here.'

She tucked away that little piece of information. It never hurt to know where the nearest retail outlet was located.

'So what are you planning on doing after the holidays? More study?' Nash asked, again breaking the silence.

'Nope, no more studying for me. I'll be working alongside my dad, his brothers and two of my cousins in the family real-estate business.'

'So you'll be selling houses?'

'No, I'll be mainly handling the business side of stuff, paperwork.'

'Is that a good thing?' Nash looked at her narrowly, as if trying to gauge her tone.

'It's a secure job, which is nothing to sneeze at, especially since a lot of my friends are struggling to find work. Besides, my dad's been grooming me for this for as long as I can remember.'

'So how come you aren't excited about it?' he asked.

'I am,' she said quickly, then paused. *Aren't I?*

'Did you always want to go into the business?'

'It's what my family has always done,' she said evasively.

'You never wanted to do anything else? Ever?'

'Well, when I was five I wanted to be a ballerina.'

'Didn't work out?' he asked, smiling.

Gemma shook her head. 'Not once I realised you had to dance in front of people.'

'Yeah, that would be a big part of the job, I'd imagine. So you're not much of an extrovert then?'

'Never have been. That's Jazz's department.'

'What's her story, anyway?'

'Jazz?' Gemma asked, surprised.

'Yeah. She's a little . . . full on,' he said, choosing his words carefully.

'She can be.' Wondering where he was going with this, Gemma felt her defences rise. It was an automatic reaction. Some people could find Jazz a little too brash. Like Gemma's parents. During her teenage years they'd tried a number of times to get her to broaden her circle of friends, fearing that Jazz was a bad influence on her. Gemma was used to defending her friend; she knew the Jazz who hid behind that brazen exterior. If Jazz was sometimes a little self-centred, Gemma could usually forgive her; growing up with a mother like hers, it was surprising that she had turned out as normal as she had. When a child was desperate for a little attention from the people who were supposed to love them, they sometimes found strange ways of getting it. By the time she was a teenager, Jazz had worked out that she would never be able to win her mother's approval for anything she did, and so she simply did her own thing, rarely thinking about the consequences.

To Gemma's relief, Nash dropped the subject. 'Yeah, well, I can't say I'm a fan of crowds either, really. I think I've been living out here alone too long.'

'Do you ever get lonely?' Gemma asked. 'There's just so much . . . space.'

He laughed and shook his head. 'When I'm busy harvesting or drenching and marking stock, I'm too busy to get lonely. I miss having an extra set of hands, but I don't get lonely for company. I like the quiet. There's nothing like standing on top of a ridge and listening to nothing but the wind blowing through the trees. That's when I realise how lucky I am to be living this life.'

The simple sincerity in his words surprised her for a moment but she couldn't help but feel a little sad that he spent such a large amount of time on his own. 'So it's just you and your sister?' She'd seen a photo above the fireplace of a young couple standing in front of a church. Their outfits looked to be from the seventies and both bore a striking resemblance to both Nash and Brittany.

'Yep. Mum passed away when I was about thirteen and the old man just a few years back, so it's just Britt and me now.'

'That must have been hard, to lose both of them.' She couldn't imagine losing either of her parents, but to lose *both* of them . . . she couldn't even begin to fathom how she would feel.

'It's been hard,' he acknowledged. 'But I feel sorry for Britt. She was a lot younger when Mum died and it was pretty tough on her when she started getting older. Can't have been easy living with just Dad and me.'

Gemma felt a twinge of guilt as she thought about her past few, brief encounters with Brittany. Not that losing your mother was any excuse for being bitchy, but part of her was willing to make more of an exception for Brittany's attitude after discovering this piece of news.

'The property was named for the ridge you can see over there,' Nash said, pointing out through her window, effectively changing the subject. In the distance was a craggy peak overlooking the valley below. 'Dunoon is supposed to be the Aboriginal word, loosely translated, for ridge.'

Gemma knew from having driven out this way the day before that it was thirty kilometres into town, but it seemed to go faster this time, and before she knew it they were entering the town limits. As they drove along the main street, she caught sight of the rust bucket parked outside the old hotel.

Nash had spotted it too. 'I'll let you out here to go and find your friend. I'll drop back after I've picked up what I need and we could grab a counter lunch, if you want.'

'Sure. That'd be great. Thanks.' Gemma climbed out and waved as Nash pulled away.

As she pushed open the big doors and stepped inside, she was hit by that classic Australian pub aroma. There was nothing else quite like it. Although not a big drinker herself, she did frequent quite a few bars around Sydney, usually tagging along with Jazz. While she wasn't exactly a hermit, she had to admit that if it came to a choice between going out to a noisy pub or staying inside her nice warm apartment reading a good book, she'd prefer to be home. Only Jazz, using a combination of pleading and threats, could get her to choose the pub.

Finding Jazz was easy—she simply followed the laughter. Rounding the corner, she found her friend perched on a high barstool at a table with two men.

'Gem!' Jazz squealed, waving madly. 'Over here!'

Gemma gave the bartender an apologetic smile, as Jazz's sudden outburst had almost made him drop the beer he was pouring.

'What are you doing in here?' Jazz demanded. 'How did you get to town?'

'I got a lift.'

'Oh, never mind that. You remember our knight in shining armour, Mack? And this is his brother, Ben. Guys, this is Gemma, my best friend in the whole world,' she declared. 'I found some real cowboys. Aren't they hunky?' she added to Gemma in a fractionally quieter voice.

While the two men were certainly good looking, with similar builds and the same shade of dark brown hair, there was a stark difference between them. Mack had a friendly, outgoing nature that showed in his relaxed posture, and his hair was short but neatly trimmed; but the other man seemed wary, harder somehow. He wore his hair clipped short, so short you could see a scattering of scars beneath the stubble on his skull, and his jeans and old t-shirt were crumpled and on his arm she caught a glimpse of some kind of tattoo.

Gemma smiled weakly at the two men. 'Hi, Mack, nice to see you again,' she said before turning her attention back to her friend. 'Jazz, how much have you had to drink?'

'Don't be a downer, Gem. You just got here.'

Gemma frowned at her friend. Jazz drinking too much wasn't anything new, but drinking before lunchtime, alone in a strange town and driving their only form of transport, was irresponsible even for her. 'How were you planning on getting home?'

'Don't worry about your friend, sweetheart,' said the man who'd been introduced as Ben. 'We would have made sure she got home . . . eventually.' He winked. 'Let me get you a drink,' said Ben, rising to go to the bar.

'That won't be necessary,' came a voice from behind them. 'I believe these two were just about to head back to Dunoon.'

Gemma spun around to see a none-too-pleased Nash standing with his arms folded across his chest.

'No, we weren't,' said Jazz lightly. 'Come and join us, Nash. You work too hard.' She patted a spare stool beside her.

'Been a long time, Whittaker,' said Ben.

'Not long enough,' Nash snapped back.

'Not the time or place, boys,' said Mack quietly.

Gemma looked back and forth between the two men, wondering what was going on. Deciding it was none of her business, she reached for her friend's arm. 'Come on, Jazz. Time to go.'

'But I don't want to go yet, I just got here.'

'We're here to work, *remember*?' said Gemma, tugging on her arm.

Nash's scowl seemed to be deepening as the moments passed. 'If you want to stay and work you'll get your butt into that bomb of a car and let Gemma drive you home now.' His voice grated like steel and his gaze was fixed on Ben, who smiled drunkenly across at him.

'Oh, alright,' said Jazz. 'Well, I'll be seeing you two around, I guess. Thanks for the drinks.'

'Anytime, darling,' Ben drawled. 'Next time you should bring your friend here along and we can all get better acquainted.' He gave Gemma an approving once-over.

Seeing Nash's flinty expression, Gemma decided that the comment was aimed more at him than intended as a compliment to her; ignoring Ben, she hustled Jazz outside towards their ute.

Nash followed them out. As Gemma took the keys from Jazz and unlocked the door, he simply growled, 'I'll see you back there,' before reefing open his car door and climbing into the vehicle.

'What was up his bum?' Jazz mumbled as they trailed Nash out of town and back along the road to Dunoon.

'I don't know. He was okay on the drive in. Maybe he just doesn't like Mack and his brother.'

'You think?'

'At least I was thinking! You had no way of getting back out to the farm. What's wrong with you?'

'Hey! Don't get all parental on me. I was just having a bit of fun. Remember fun? Anyway, I was about to switch to water when you came in with Mr Party Pooper and ruined what was going to be a perfectly good afternoon.'

'You hardly know Mack, and his brother is scary. He could be a rapist or something.'

'God, you're so melodramatic, always thinking the worst of everyone. Chill out, Gemma. You'll be old soon enough. No need to get there before your time.' Jazz turned away and looked out her window.

Gemma shook her head and silently counted to ten. The problem was that someone had to be the adult, and it would never be Jazz. Gemma had faced the fact years ago that she would never have Jazz's devil-may-care attitude to life, and while Jazz might complain about it, Gemma knew she *needed* someone to look out for her. And whenever she got frustrated, Gemma reminded herself what Jazz's home life had been growing up.

Jazz's mother, Charlene Beadman, had moved to the city from Walgett in northwest New South Wales as a fresh-faced seventeen-year-old, looking for adventure. Within a week she'd found a job as an exotic dancer in a Kings Cross nightclub and changed her name to Bunny. What happened next could almost have been a fairytale: a young girl rescued from a life of debauchery by a rich older man. Except there really was no way of prettying up what had actually happened. Bunny had captivated a sixty-year-old man who frequented strip clubs, and they had married and soon had a daughter. Her father had died when she was just a baby, and Charlene had a short attention span and little patience for playing mother. She married again almost straight away and from then on a series of stepfathers had come and gone from Jazz's life in quick succession. Jazz made light of it all, but Gemma knew that deep inside she was still just a sad little girl who wanted to be loved. It didn't take a psychologist to work out that Jazz had issues. She hid her pain behind the party-girl persona, revelling in the attention she now got from strangers, attention that had been denied to her as a child.

Gemma had tried many times over the years to get Jazz to speak to a counsellor, but Jazz said she wasn't into 'that whole touchy-feely kind of thing'. It was hard at times to watch her friend's destructive behaviour, but Jazz was technically an adult and all Gemma could do was stay close and help pick up the pieces afterwards. That was the way it had always been.

As they followed Nash towards Dunoon, Gemma wondered what the fallout would be from her friend's latest escapade. What if Nash sent them away? Once she would have thought that a blessing in disguise, but now she only felt disappointment.

Five

Nash thumped the steering wheel and swore loudly. He'd already known Ben Henderson was back—God knows it had been the talk of the town for the last few weeks—but that was the first time in more than six years that Nash had actually seen him.

Flashes of loud music and sirens rang through his mind, accompanied by images of a bonfire, and he shook his head angrily to dispel them. The bastard shouldn't be here. What the hell did he think he was doing coming back to Bingorra?

His fingers gripped the steering wheel as he recalled the smirk on Ben's face as he'd ogled Gemma. He'd done it on purpose to get a rise out of Nash. It'd worked too; it was only by clenching his fists by his sides that he had restrained himself from dragging Ben across the table. Nash would not give him the satisfaction of seeing him lose his cool.

In his rage, he hadn't realised what he was saying when he'd told the girls to get back to Dunoon. Before then, he hadn't even been intending to let them stay. Great, he thought, fuming. Now he was stuck with two city slickers and no idea what the hell he was supposed to do with them.

•

Gemma parked beside Nash out near the sheds, and the girls followed him inside, feeling like a pair of delinquent teenagers.

'If you're serious about working here, then that means no slacking off and heading into town to sit around in the pub all day, understood?' Nash was looking at Jazz with an expression Gemma hoped to never find herself on the end of. 'I'm responsible for you both. In future, you don't just up and leave for town without telling me. If you're serious about working here, then I need one hundred per cent commitment. If I assign you a task, I have to know you're actually going to do it—if I then have to do it instead, it's a waste of time I don't have to spare. Understood?' he repeated.

'Understood,' Jazz replied, holding his gaze without flinching. 'But we have weekends off and you don't get a say in how we spend our personal time.'

'Fine,' he snapped.

'Then you, my friend, have yourself a deal.'

Nash stared at her grimly, no doubt wondering what he was letting himself in for. 'Well, now that we have that sorted, I need you to take some feed down to the weaners and make sure they have water.'

Once the back door had banged shut, Jazz grinned at Gemma like a Cheshire cat. 'See, I told you everything would work out.'

'But we still have no idea what we're doing!' Gemma protested. 'What the hell's a weaner and what on earth do we feed it?'

'That, my dear worrywart, is what Google is for.'

'I *can't* believe we're doing this,' Gemma groaned, following Jazz to her room to fire up the laptop.

'Here we go,' said Jazz, moments later, tapping on the keyboard. 'What is a weaner?'

Gemma shook her head and looked up at the ceiling as if for some kind of divine guidance.

'A weaner is a term used for a calf when it's been weaned off its mother's milk,' Jazz read out cheerfully.

'Okay, so what does it say we feed them?'

'What do weaners eat?' Jazz said as she typed and hit enter. 'A precondition ration for calves should include a mix of corn, sorghum, barley, wheat or oats and legume-hay, plus a concentrated supplement that includes protein.' She looked up at Gemma. 'Simple! Come on, let's go and see what we can find.' She got up to head out of the room, but stopped when she noticed Gemma's feet. 'You can't wear sandals out there.'

'Why not?' They weren't even her good pair. They were comfy leather ones she'd had for ages and it was hot. She didn't want to stuff her feet into boots on a hot day like this.

'Have you ever seen a jillaroo wearing sandals?'

'Again, yet another reason I've never had any desire to be a jillaroo.'

'Put your boots on and I'll meet you outside,' said Jazz.

Gemma grumbled all the way back to her room, where she rummaged through her suitcase and pulled out the long rubber boots she'd bought in a trendy little boutique down near The Rocks. *Hmm, not too shabby*, she thought, taking a moment to admire them in the mirror before rushing outside to find Jazz standing beside Nash's ute.

'So what the hell are we going to do about—?' Gemma stopped when she caught Jazz's warning glance. Just then Nash moved around the rear of the vehicle.

'About what?' he asked.

'About . . . global warming,' she said lamely.

'You have a plan?' He eyed her sceptically.

'No,' she hedged. 'Not really.'

'Nice boots,' he said in a neutral tone.

'Thanks. I like them.'

'What are you *wearing*?' Jazz gaped at Gemma's purple and pink heart-printed gumboots.

'My new gumboots,' said Gemma.

'I told you to pack *work* boots,' Jazz whispered.

'I didn't like those. I saw these and fell in love with them.'

'But they're not *work* boots,' said Jazz.

'They're *my* work boots. Do they *look* like something I'd wear anywhere else?'

'If you're both done with the fashion show,' said Nash tiredly, 'I've loaded the feed and shown Jazz where it's kept so you two can take over doing this for me each day. I'll have the rest of this seeding done by the end of the week and then I'll need you to help with ear tagging, vaccinating and drenching. I don't have time to take you out and show you around the place, so you'll have to make do with the mud map on the back of that list of jobs for today. Once I get this seed in, I'll have more time to show you where everything is. Think you can manage okay?'

'Of course we can!' Jazz gave him a reassuring wave before he walked away.

Gemma looked at her friend.

'What did I tell you?' Jazz said smugly. 'We can do this.'

'He's only letting us stay because he's run off his feet.'

Jazz shrugged before moving to climb up into the driver's side. 'Come on, get in before he changes his mind.'

'Ah, no. I'll drive,' Gemma said holding the door when Jazz went to close it.

'Oh come on, I'm not wasted, I only had a few drinks before you showed up.'

'Gemma will drive.' Nash's cold voice cut in from behind them, making both girls jump.

'I'm fine,' Jazz said, rolling her eyes sarcastically. 'It's not even a real road we're driving on.'

'Get out of the car.'

Gemma glanced anxiously between the two. Nash's tone was almost glacial as he held Jazz's mocking gaze in a silent stand-off until, finally, Jazz slowly slid from the driver's seat, making an overly grand gesture with her hand for Gemma to take her place.

Nash remained in place, unamused.

Gemma took a small step closer to him. 'It's okay, I won't let her drive,' Gemma said quietly, in an attempt to reassure him and saw something almost like indecision briefly flicker across his face, before his jaw unclenched and he seemed to relax slightly.

'Make sure she doesn't,' he snapped before turning away and disappearing into the depths of the shed.

'Is it just me or was that a little extreme and creepy?' Jazz said in a sing-song voice under her breath as Gemma shut the door, her gaze still on the shed entrance Nash had gone into.

'He was right. You could still be over the limit to drive. He was just being cautious.'

'Covering his own arse more like it.'

'What do you expect? He's technically your employer—if you totalled his work ute his insurance probably wouldn't cover it.' She had no idea if their unusual position here was covered under workplace health and safety but, nevertheless, Jazz needed to grow up and start taking some responsibility.

'Do you have any idea where we're going?' Gemma asked, taking her eyes off the dirt track briefly to glance at Jazz a little bit later as they drove along a rough dirt track away from the homestead.

'There's a set of stockyards around here somewhere and the weaners are in a yard nearby.'

Gemma was relieved when they found the yards after following the track for a few kilometres. The two girls unloaded the buckets of grain and dragged a small bale of hay across to the fence, then lifted it over the metal rails.

'They're so cute—look at those big brown eyes,' Gemma cooed as the half dozen calves munched on their grain and hay.

'Told you you'd like this farm work stuff.' Jazz smirked.

'I don't know about the work so much. You sure wouldn't need a gym membership if you did this all the time.' Just lifting the bale of lucerne over the rails had made Gemma's arms shake. 'What's next on the list?' she asked, wiping sweat from her forehead as she watched Jazz pull the piece of paper from her top pocket.

'Feed the dogs, clean out their cages, check the water in the troughs, feed the chooks and collect the eggs,' said Jazz.

'Oh, is that *all*?' Gemma gave her friend a desperate look.

'At least it's not too complicated. Even we should be able to work out how to do most of this stuff on our own.'

With the roughly drawn map in her lap, Jazz gave directions to where the water troughs were supposed to be located, and they bounced along the corrugated track.

'Look at all this,' Gemma said, looking out at the countryside. 'It's amazing to think we're the only two people for miles and miles.' For some reason this space that had intimidated her only yesterday now didn't seem so scary. Maybe it was the way Nash had described it so vividly in the car earlier. Seeing it from his perspective had made her look at it differently.

'Isn't it great?' said Jazz. 'Imagine living like this all the time.'

Gemma grinned. 'I know you're channelling *McLeod's Daughters* right now, Jazz, but can you *really* see yourself giving up the nightlife and shopping back in Sydney for this?'

'You sound just like my mother,' Jazz groaned. 'Is it so bad that I wanted to come out and experience it for a while? Do something I've always wanted to try?'

Gemma sighed. Jazz went into everything at full speed. There was never anything half-hearted about her, it was all the way or nothing, in life and in love, which was why

Gemma was so worried about her ridiculous plan of fulfilling her 'cowboy' dream. Knowing Jazz, she wouldn't be happy until she'd got it out of her system.

'No,' Gemma said. 'It's not a bad thing. But this is Nash's livelihood and it looks as though he's going through some pretty stressful times. I just don't think we should add to his problems.'

'Hello? We're *helping* him, not adding to his problems.'

Sure. How on earth could two inexperienced city girls pretending to be experienced farmhands possibly add to the man's problems? Gemma decided to keep her mouth shut and let Jazz enjoy her moment. She had a funny feeling this was going to blow up in their faces soon enough.

•

After dinner that night, Gemma carried a saucer and a bottle of milk outside and headed for the shed. She flicked on the torch she'd found next to the back door, and the narrow beam of light bounced merrily along the ground ahead of her. It was so quiet. She tried not to replay horror movie scenes in her head as she approached the large shed, its tin walls reflecting the small amount of moonlight. There was no sign of the cat, but earlier that day she'd caught sight of a flash of ginger fur disappearing into a corner, so she knew it was in here somewhere. She placed the saucer on the ground and poured in some milk. For some reason, the animal had been playing on her mind quite a bit. She felt kind of bad for yelling at it, but in her defence, rescuing an ungrateful cat after the stressful day she'd been having up to that point yesterday had not been what she'd needed.

'Here you go, kitty,' she said softly. 'Maybe this will improve your disposition,' she added under her breath, before replacing the lid on the milk bottle. There was something about its fierce 'I don't need any help' attitude that just didn't ring true. Not when she'd seen it watching them from the shadows on more than one occasion. She'd never had a pet—her mother didn't like animals in the house—so she might be wrong, but it was almost as if it wanted to come out of the shadows but fear kept it hidden, fear that it covered up with ferocity when it felt cornered. She wanted to see if she could crack that tough exterior, and had decided to try for a peace offering of milk.

The walk back was much less creepy. Lights glowed warmly from the windows and back verandah. She didn't see the dark form until it stepped out in front of her, when she let out a loud shriek.

'Out for an evening stroll?'

She recognised the voice straight away, but her heart still pounded violently in her chest. 'You scared me!'

'What are you doing wandering around in the dark?'

'I was—' She paused, somehow knowing Nash wasn't going to be too thrilled about her feeding feral cats. 'I was looking for my cardigan. I thought I left it out here earlier.' She slowly moved the bottle of milk behind her back, hoping he hadn't seen it.

'You should be careful walking around out here in the dark. Did you know most snakes do their hunting at night?'

Gemma's gaze flew around the ground, expecting to see a slithering mass of reptiles like the pit scene in *Indiana Jones*. She shivered involuntarily at the thought.

'Lucky for you I'm here to rescue you, should the need arise,' Nash added.

Her gaze returned to his face and she could just make out his grin. 'Very funny. Point taken. I will not be venturing outside in the dark again.'

He chuckled when he realised she was waiting for him to lead the way back. Gemma meekly followed behind, resisting the urge to grab a fistful of his shirt and jump on his broad back just in case there was a snake nearby.

•

The next day had been kept busy with a list of chores similar to the previous day. In the afternoon, Jazz took the ute out to check on the water levels in the troughs while Gemma made a start on dinner. Suddenly the radio on the bench crackled to life, startling her.

Earlier that day, Nash had shown the girls how to work the two-way radio located on the kitchen bench. He'd told them there was another one in the work ute if they ever needed to contact him and there was no phone reception.

'Gem, are you there?' came Jazz's voice.

Gemma quickly wiped her hands on a tea towel and snatched up the handset to answer.

'Press in the button before you talk, dummy,' said Jazz before she had a chance to speak.

'I know,' said Gemma crossly.

'Took you long enough to answer. What were you doing?'

'My hands were wet. What's wrong?' asked Gemma.

'Nothing. I'm bored and this is free, so I don't have to use up the credit on my mobile.'

'You said you were going out to check the water troughs.'

'I did,' said Jazz.

'Well, come back here and help me with dinner if you've got nothing to do,' said Gemma.

'You've got that all under control, and besides, you're too anal to let me help, Ms Control Freak.'

'I am not,' said Gemma, indignant. Okay, maybe she liked doing things a certain way, but that didn't make her a control freak.

'I think we're supposed to say "over" after we finish saying something,' said Jazz. 'Over,' she added, laughing.

'Jazz, I've got stuff on the stove.'

'You didn't say "over". How am I supposed to know you've finished talking if you don't say "over"? Over.'

Gemma closed her eyes. 'Why don't you call Nash and see if he has something else for you to do while you're out there?' she suggested. There was a deafening silence before she gave an irritated sigh and pressed the mic button again. 'Over.'

'That's better,' said Jazz. 'I'm not calling the boss man. God only knows what he'd think up for me to do. Now if *you* asked him I bet it'd be different. He *likes* you,' she added in a cheeky tone. 'Over.'

'Would you please knock it off? I'm pretty sure the last time I heard anyone say "over" on a radio was on reruns of *Skippy*. I'm getting off this thing. I have stuff to do—unlike some people.'

'Have you two finished messing around?' came Nash's deep voice.

There was a long, embarrassed silence before Jazz said, 'Sorry, boss. I didn't know you could hear.'

'The whole district can hear; it's an open radio frequency. Now get back to work.'

The whole district? Gemma felt as though she might actually sink to the floor in a mortified puddle.

'Roger that, ten-four, good buddy,' Jazz said in a very bad imitation of a trucker's voice. 'Over,' she added a few seconds later.

Gemma shook her head in despair. Why did she allow Jazz to keep getting them into these situations? The sizzling hiss of water bubbling over onto a hot stove snapped her out of her humiliation. As she hurried to attend to the pasta, she was grateful that sowing long into the night would keep Nash out of the house until she had gone to bed.

•

Nash was usually up and out on his tractor before the girls woke up, and unless he came back for something from the shed, they didn't see him until dark. Having noticed that he took out a thermos of coffee and a small esky of food when he left early in the morning, Gemma had begun making sandwiches for him while she cooked dinner. The two girls ate dinner by themselves once they'd finished all the jobs Nash had listed for them, and Gemma left Nash a plate either in the oven or in the fridge to reheat when he came in. Though Nash had told her she didn't need to cook for him, she had seen how tired he was when he came in at night—too tired to prepare a meal. And it wasn't as if it was a hassle to rustle up an extra portion when she was already cooking for two.

After that first night when Gemma had caught him coming into the kitchen, she'd fallen into the habit of having a cup of tea before bed, which always seemed to coincide with the time when he finished work. She was just being a polite guest, she'd told herself more than once.

Now she looked up as the back screen door squeaked open, and felt that strange little flutter in her stomach that his presence always triggered.

'Hi,' said Nash, looking bone weary.

'How'd it go out there?' asked Gemma. 'Getting closer to finishing?'

'I reckon by tomorrow I might have it all in,' he replied.

'That's great. Bet you'll be glad when that's over,' she said, smiling in genuine relief for him.

'You're not wrong. Then it'll be time to start on the cattle and sheep, then spray and then harvest, and start all over again with the winter crops,' he said with a tired smile.

'It doesn't end, does it?'

'Nope.'

Yet again Gemma tried to comprehend how farmers coped with the endless highs and lows they experienced. She was ashamed to realise just how much she had taken food for granted, rarely considering where it came from, not to mention the work that went into producing it. She knew farmers worked hard, but never in her wildest dreams could she have imagined what it must cost them.

Getting up, she took his plate out of the oven and brought it over to the table. She placed it down and took up her seat on the other side of the table, picking up her mug of tea.

'Tell you what, though,' he added in a brighter tone, 'it's been great to come home to a hot meal each night.'

'It's nothing special,' said Gemma, trying not to beam at his compliment.

'It's better than anything I could make, and I really appreciate it. Sorry I haven't thanked you properly before.'

That wasn't true, thought Gemma. *He always thanked her after he finished his meal.* 'It's nothing, really,' she said. 'I have to cook dinner for me and Jazz anyway.'

'It gives me something to look forward to each night,' he said quietly, his gaze holding hers.

Gemma swallowed nervously as her heart rate marked double time and her cheeks went warm. *Holy moley*, she thought a little breathlessly. With one look the man had her going all Mills and Boonie. How was this possible? She'd gone out with men, usually ones she'd grown up mixing with within her family's social network. Safe, well-mannered, scared-of-her-father kind of men, and none of them had ever made her feel the way she did when Nash was around her.

'Well, I feel bad that you're out there working long after we've finished for the day,' she said, trying to sound unflustered.

'It's my job.' He shrugged, dropping his gaze to the plate and picking up his cutlery. 'Besides, I feel bad enough giving you work to do when I don't even pay you. I still can't wrap my head around that. Why would anyone want to work as a holiday?'

'People *pay* to come and work on places like this. Technically we're getting a bargain. Maybe you should tap into that market?'

Nash gave a chuckle. 'Yeah, maybe I should before someone wakes up and realises it's the wrong way round.'

It did seem weird, but Gemma had seen the figures and they showed that farmstay/working holidays, particularly in the overseas tourist sector, were big business.

Over his meal the last few days they'd talked about a surprising range of things; he asked a lot of questions, and seemed genuinely interested in her life back in the city. She'd told him that she'd just finished her business degree and would be starting work when she returned to the city, but after that she always managed to change the subject so she didn't have to talk about taking up her role in the family business. Every time she thought about it she felt those now-familiar knots in her stomach.

'So your father was okay with you taking time off before you started work?' Nash asked tonight, seemingly out of the blue.

Gemma felt her stomach automatically tighten. 'Well, I think he'd have preferred that I started straight away, but my mum talked him into letting me have a bit of a sabbatical.'

'He's more understanding than I am with my sister.'

After several fruitless attempts by Nash to contact Brittany, Jazz had finally got hold of her, but she hadn't been too contrite about the missing details. The more Gemma heard about the girl, the more annoyed she felt on Nash's behalf. Jazz had convinced Brittany to call her brother, so at least he knew she was alive—whether she remained that way the next time he saw her, though, was another story.

'I guess she just wanted to hold on to her last remaining days of freedom. It's kind of hard to give up.' As she spoke, Gemma realised she was talking more about herself than his sister.

'But she knows she's got responsibilities here. She would never have got away with this kind of crap if Dad were still alive.' Nash frowned.

'Well, in fairness, once Jazz got the idea in her head she made it pretty hard for Brittany to turn down. Jazz can be very persuasive when she wants to be.'

Nash shook his head. 'I had more faith in my sister than that—or at least the sister I once knew. I thought she loved this place as much as I did. The last few years it seems like she's changed.'

'Maybe she just wants to spread her wings a little?' Gemma asked gently.

'Some of us didn't get that choice.'

Hearing the bitterness in his words, Gemma waited to see if he would elaborate.

He paused as he sliced through his steak and lifted his gaze to hers. 'Five years ago my dad got sick and couldn't handle this place on his own, so I came back to help out. It changed a lot of things around here.'

'Where were you before that?'

'In my third year of university.'

'You pulled out of school to come back and help your dad? Did you ever go back and finish?'

'Nah. Wasn't much point. Dad passed away about eight months later and by then I had too much to do here.'

'So you weren't always planning on being a farmer?' She knew she'd said the wrong thing when his face went stony, and he quickly finished the rest of his meal in silence.

'Thanks for dinner,' he said at last.

Gemma watched in confusion as he put his chair back under the table and gave her a brisk nod goodnight.

That was strange, she thought as she stared at the empty doorway through which he'd left. Given his dedication to the work, she'd pegged him as a die-hard farmer, so what should she make of tonight's revelation that he'd once lived in Sydney and gone to university? And why, for that matter, was he being so hard on his sister for not wanting to come back here when clearly it hadn't been in his plans either?

●

Nash tugged off his shirt and dropped it on the floor before collapsing onto his bed with a sigh. He shouldn't have given Gemma the cold shoulder just now. She'd only asked a simple question, but it was the one question that somehow still managed to set off an emotional avalanche inside him. *So you weren't always planning on being a farmer?*

The truth was that no, he hadn't been planning on it. It had been more or less thrust upon him. He'd wanted to be an engineer and create things—help build amazing projects and get well paid for his trouble—and he'd hoped to spend some time working overseas. Instead, at the age of twenty, he'd found himself back at home, looking after his sick father and working himself into the ground while still struggling to make ends meet.

Immediately after thinking these bitter thoughts, he felt bad. His dad had always hoped that Nash would come back and help keep the place running. And for most of his life, Nash had thought that too—after all, that was what the Whittakers had always done. But during his last year at high

75

school, everything had changed. All it took was one night and one wrong decision. After that, he'd wanted to leave this place as far behind him as he could. Guilt had a way of eating away at you.

Even before then, Nash had been fascinated by how someone could build massive high-rise buildings, and bridges that spanned astonishing distances. At eighteen, longing to escape Bingorra and all it now represented, he suddenly knew what he wanted to do with his life. He wanted to be an engineer and travel all over the world—with the added bonus that he would go as far away from this place as he could get.

It had broken the old man's heart when Nash finally told him he wanted to go away to uni and study engineering. He never said so, but Nash saw the sad look in his father's eye. He helped out around the place while he was home on uni breaks, but it wasn't the same—his father seemed to have lost his passion, and Nash knew that he was the cause of it. Why would his dad bother working his guts out to improve the place when he'd just have to sell up when he got too old to farm it himself? Nash blamed himself for the depression that had led up to his father's illness. He sometimes wondered if by adding to his dad's worries he'd helped hasten the stroke somehow.

At eighteen he hadn't had the same attachment to the land his father had. He was an impatient kid who wanted more from life than surviving from one bad season to the next and hoping to get a few good ones in between. Now that he was older, though, he understood his father's sentimentality. There were memories here, good and bad, and those roots grew up around your legs and planted you firmly to the ground. After his mother had died, his dad still saw her in every corner of the house. He'd refused to remove any of her clothes from their wardrobe; hairbrushes remained on the dressing table and her favourite perfume still lingered in their bedroom, clinging to her clothes and trapping his dad in the past. Looking back now, he realised the kid who had also missed his mother and who had been grieving had learned to grow up pretty fast. His dad had shut himself off from them and hadn't had the strength to deal with his kids' grief on top of his own. No amount of arguing or pleading could ever convince his old man to part with any of her things. The day after his father's funeral, Nash had cleaned out the room, removing all of his parents' clothes. Back then, he'd been angry at the world—angry at his father's miserable death, angry at his own situation. He was still angry, he acknowledged; all he knew was that his future had been sealed when his father died and left him to provide for his kid sister, who was only sixteen at the time.

Nash stared up at the ceiling, his eyes stinging. Christ, he was tired. He willed himself to get some sleep. Nothing good could come out of going over all this crap now. Maybe when he finished sowing—in between all the thousand and one other jobs that needed to be done—he would have time to give more thought to the future.

Six

It was mid-morning and Gemma had just finished hanging out a load of washing when she heard dogs barking and an engine approaching along the track. She dropped the laundry basket by the back door, went inside and quickly wrapped up two slices of freshly baked date loaf, then headed back outside.

Earlier Jazz had received a phone call and then left saying she would be back in a minute. Gemma suspected the call had something to do with a certain person named Mack. The two had been calling and texting almost constantly. Jazz assured her that she wasn't heading into town, just up the road for a bit. She didn't think Jazz would be stupid enough to repeat what happened the other day; she hated to think what might happen if she did.

The sun was warm on her shoulders as she walked towards the paddock where she could see Nash on a large four-wheeled bike, weaving in and out of a mob of sheep. Gemma set the plastic-wrapped cake on top of a post; leaning on the fence, she watched on quietly. Before now she'd only ever seen this kind of thing on television; in real life it was so much more vivid. Her senses were filled by the sounds of sheep bleating loudly and dogs barking, the smell of dust and wool and warm manure. Nash slowed down and surveyed the animals carefully, maybe counting them. Gemma didn't want to disturb him, and now she felt a bit silly for having come up here, though she couldn't very well walk away without at least saying hello. He'd think she was weird—well, weirder than he already did.

As he came closer he looked up and saw her standing there. He drove towards her and brought his bike to a halt on the other side of the gate. 'Everything okay?' he asked.

'Yeah. I . . . just came up to see what was going on,' she said, feeling foolish when he didn't return the friendly smile she'd plastered on her face. 'I, ah, brought you some morning tea,' she added, picking up the date loaf and holding it out.

He hesitated for a moment before reaching out to take it from her, his gaze still fixed on her face, his own expression unreadable. 'Thanks.'

'You're welcome. I hope you don't mind but I decided to do some baking. I like to keep busy . . .' Her voice fell away as he continued to look at her without speaking.

Finally, he dropped his other hand from the handlebar and unwrapped the date loaf. Gemma breathed a sigh of relief. 'So, what *are* you doing?' she asked, dragging her gaze away from him.

'Moving the sheep.'

'Oh.' Apparently that was that, thought Gemma, feeling at a loss. Thankfully the noise of the animals around them and the sight of the dogs as they took their cue from their master and sat down in the shade of the bike offered a distraction of sorts.

'This lot should have been sold weeks ago,' Nash said.

At his sudden offering of information, Gemma glanced up from the dogs. 'So why aren't they?'

'The bottom's fallen out of the market,' he said as he crushed the plastic wrapping in his fist and handed it over to her. 'Last year we were selling big numbers to the Saudi market at around a hundred and fifteen per head. At the moment you'd be lucky to get thirty bucks a head.'

'Wow, why? What happened?'

He sent her the look he reserved for those 'city girl' questions. 'You do watch the news sometimes, I take it?'

'Of course I watch the news,' she responded, offended.

'Then you may recall a small incident where live export trade was suddenly terminated?'

She did recall it, actually. She remembered watching on a news program the terrible footage of cattle being tortured, and then how animal activists and a general public outcry had brought about the sudden and immediate halt of livestock export out of Australia. 'But what's that got to do with the price of your sheep?'

'We had a massive livestock trade with countries all over the world and the government put a stop to the whole lot.

It wasn't just cattle either; it was sheep and pigs too. So now there's a flood of animals we can't get rid of. Butchers are naming their price, and livestock aren't selling at the market.'

'Can't you just wait till they need more meat and then sell them?'

Nash sent her a wry glance. 'And in the meantime we have to feed these animals somehow, and we haven't had decent rain in a while so the paddocks aren't going to last long, which means we'll have to handfeed, and that costs a lot of money—money we were counting on from contracts we can no longer fill because the government suddenly destroyed our industry.'

'So what will happen?' asked Gemma.

'On most places, animals are going to have to be destroyed because the cost of feeding them is more than they can be sold for. It costs us money to transport them to the sales too, and if they don't sell and we have to bring them home again, all we're left with is the bill from the transport company.'

'I didn't realise it was so big a deal,' Gemma said quietly.

'Not many people do. Once something else comes along to catch the media's attention, normal people lose interest. Then the farmers are left to try to pick up the pieces and deal with the fallout. This thing is ruining people's livelihoods. It's destroyed us as an industry. I'd hate to even try to count the personal damage it's already done, the rise in depression local GPs are going to have to deal with, not to mention the suicides that always follow.'

Gemma looked down, unable to meet Nash's level gaze. She was one of those people who'd promptly forgotten about the whole issue after the debate on news and current affairs shows had dried up. Yet now that she was faced with the personal side of the argument it was a lot harder to just shrug it off as nothing to do with her.

'Thanks for the cake.' He restarted the engine of his bike.

'It was date loaf,' she corrected lightly.

'Well, whatever it was, it was delicious,' he added, pulling away from the gate.

It was only a throwaway remark, but it instantly brightened her day. It felt good to have done something nice for him, even something as small as baking.

She turned away and headed back to the house. Behind her she heard the bike continue to move around as Nash worked the sheep.

As she walked back towards the house she noticed a trail of dust following their old ute as it headed towards the house. Maybe things were going to be okay after all, she thought, and found herself humming under her breath as she pushed open the house gate and went inside.

•

'This'll never work,' Gemma groaned as she and Jazz sat huddled in front of her computer late one night. Until now, life had fallen into a nice kind of rhythm. They did whatever chores Nash left for them to do and most of the time they had the afternoons to themselves when there was nothing else he trusted them to do. Then tonight, Nash had surprised them, with both his presence at dinner at a respectable hour, and the news that they would be drenching sheep the next day.

'Sure it will. Look, there's nothing to it,' Jazz said, her eyes fixed on the video of a group of young German backpackers on a five-day jackaroo course being taught how to work a mob of sheep. 'If they can learn to do all this stuff in five days then surely it can't be that hard!'

'Jazz, it's not a real course; it's like a holiday camp. You know, the kind we were supposed to be on until we got here and lied about having any sort of useful experience!'

Without lifting her gaze from the computer screen, Jazz waved away Gemma's concerns. 'It'll be fine.'

Gemma watched the German guy on the video try to force a long-hooked metal gun down a sheep's throat and sighed. This was *so* not going to be fine.

•

When the two girls came outside the next morning, ready for their first day's work with the sheep, the yards were hot and dusty and full of bleating sheep and barking dogs.

'Just remember the video,' Jazz whispered as she walked past. 'It'll be a piece of cake.'

Piece of cake! Gemma shook her head. Watching the video was one thing, coming face to face with a real live sheep was something else. Feeling Nash's gaze on her, she lifted her head and took a few deep breaths. You can do this, she told herself firmly. 'Side of the mouth, over the back of the tongue, and done,' she repeated quietly, reminding herself of the main message from the video footage they'd watched.

'So, you right with this?' Nash asked, dropping a container with the drenching solution at their feet.

'Of course.' Jazz nodded confidently.

'You *have* done this before, right?' he asked, looking at her narrowly.

'We can handle it,' said Jazz with a brilliant smile, refusing to give up the charade.

'You sure about that?' Gemma heard the challenge in his words.

'Absolutely.'

Nash looked sceptical, but there was no way Jazz was ever going to admit defeat—at least not until she got tired of the whole farce. However, Gemma wasn't going to risk harming an animal just to play along with Jazz's ridiculous scam. 'Actually,' she cut in, 'can you just run through it with us one time?'

Nash leaned down to retrieve the container, then carried it across to the yards. 'I'll start you off here, and then I'm going to begin on the drafting.' They watched as Nash stepped into the small enclosure and caught one of the sheep, easily inserting the gun and squirting the medication down its throat in one smooth action.

He climbed out of the yard and handed over the drenching pack, which Gemma slid on before cautiously climbing over the railing. Her first thought was that the sheep looked a lot bigger once you were in the yards with them. The second was that somehow she had to approach one of these animals and jam this gun thing down its throat. Swallowing her anxiety, she moved towards one of the sheep. It protested and backed away, making the one behind it bleat loudly.

'Just grab it and stick it down its throat,' Jazz called from the gate where she stood waiting to release the freshly drenched sheep into the larger holding pen beyond.

Gemma took another step forward and reached out to grab the animal's head. The sheep bleated louder and swung its head around wildly as Gemma tried to hold it steady enough to insert the gun.

'Just shove it in,' Jazz instructed.

'Easier said than done,' Gemma grunted as she tried to push the metal tip into the side of the sheep's mouth.

'Hand under its chin,' Nash called from across the yard.

Gemma wrestled the sheep with her spare hand and eventually managed to pin the animal across the chest, bracing her elbow against her knee, and somehow slide the gun between the disgruntled creature's lips. She heard the clink of teeth as she manoeuvred the gun into the corner of its mouth before pulling the trigger. When none of the liquid came back out, Gemma gave a small triumphant cheer before pushing the large animal behind her and out to where Jazz stood waiting to shoo it through the gate.

She glanced up, still grinning like a fool, and caught Nash watching her from across the yard, a slow smile spreading across his face. It was ridiculous to feel this much satisfaction over something Nash would consider mundane, but it filled her with a sense of pride none the less. She'd conquered her first sheep of the day. But as she looked back at the sheep packed into the run ahead of her, her smile wavered. *Only a few hundred more to go*, she thought with a sigh.

•

When they had finished drenching for the day, Nash took the dogs and the quad bike to move the younger sheep to the finishing paddock. Gemma almost didn't want to know what the finishing paddock was, and was relieved to hear it was where the animals were fed and fattened before sale, not finished, literally—at least, not here.

The older sheep Nash had drafted were left in the holding yards, awaiting transport the next day to the saleyards. Gemma tried not to think about how delicious she found a good lamb roast or chop on the barbecue, having now spent the day being *baa*ed at by her food. Her queasiness was slightly eased by the fact that she'd been trodden on and headbutted more times in one day than during her entire previous life. Right now, as she nursed her aching limbs, she had a decided lack of empathy for where the sheep ended up tomorrow.

They'd earned their drink that afternoon. Gemma wasn't normally a beer drinker, but when Nash handed her a cold can from the fridge in the shed, droplets of condensation beading on the aluminium, and she took a long gulp, she thought that nothing had ever tasted so damn good. Her mother would have a fit to see her sitting on an upturned esky, covered in dust and sheep poo and drinking beer out of a can. Right about now, Caroline Northcote would be sipping a nice crisp chardonnay on the back deck and probably listening to Gemma's father talk about his day at the office. Looking around her, Gemma had to admit that a week ago *she* probably wouldn't have believed she'd be sitting on an upturned esky, covered in sheep poo and drinking a beer.

'Well, I'm out of here, folks,' said Jazz, tossing her empty can into the bin like a pro basketball player. 'I have a date.'

'A date? With who?' This was the first Gemma had heard of it.

'Mack.' Jazz threw a resentful glance at Nash. 'You remember him from the time you two gatecrashed our lunch at the pub.'

'But—'

Jazz held up a hand impatiently. 'Don't even go there, Gem. I'm not going to drink, I'm just going to head into town for a quick bite and then come back home.' She got up and walked towards the house. 'See you later.'

Gemma watched her friend disappear into the house and shook her head. 'I don't know how she can be bothered to go anywhere. I don't think I can move after today.'

'Yep, you're gonna be sore tomorrow,' Nash agreed, not sounding particularly sympathetic.

They sat listening to the sounds of farm life and to the birds calling as they flew around the tall gum trees while the sun sank slowly below the horizon. Gemma shut her eyes and took a deep breath of the cooling evening air. First thing in the morning, the air out here smelled crisp and clean. In the middle of the day it was hot and dusty, smelling of sun-warmed earth and eucalyptus; but when the afternoon shadows stretched across the land, it changed, bringing a cool freshness. She liked this part of the day. By evening the sun's fierceness had given way to a gentle warmth, and the hills cast sheltering shadows across the wide open planes.

'I think I owe you an apology for the other night.'

Gemma opened her eyes and looked across at Nash. His gaze was fixed on something far off in the distance.

'I shouldn't have walked out on you like that,' he went on.

'It was none of my business.'

'You just caught me off guard. It was a pretty rough time around then.'

Gemma dropped her eyes to the can in her hand. 'Sorry, I wouldn't have asked if I'd known. I didn't mean to bring up bad memories.'

'You couldn't have known. It's all good.'

Feeling lighter, Gemma summoned up some energy and pushed herself to her feet. As she crossed the floor of the shed, she tossed her can at the bin and missed. *Typical*, she thought before she bent down and picked it up, then dropped it in.

'If you're headed inside, just grab some meat and I'll cook it on the barbie if you like.'

'That's okay. I found a slow cooker in the pantry. Dinner's sorted.' She glanced down at her filthy clothing. 'I'm going to clean up first though.'

'I've got a few things to finish up out here and then I'll be in,' Nash said, tossing his own can from twice the distance, slotting it neatly into the bin. She rolled her eyes at his cocky grin, but couldn't help smiling back.

Gemma stepped into her room a few moments later and let out an irritated huff as she saw Jazz had been rummaging through her stuff again. Gemma had refused to do Jazz's washing while they were here and had been warning her that she better put a load on soon if she didn't want to run out of clothes, but in typical Jazz fashion she kept putting it off until later. Clearly Jazz didn't have to worry about running out when she had a steady supply of Gemma's to choose from. Snatching up a pair of jeans and a t-shirt from the floor, she grabbed her towel from the back of the door and headed for the shower, every muscle aching. She had no idea how

Jazz did it: going out was the last thing she could imagine doing after the gruelling day they'd just had. She looked at herself in the bathroom mirror and cringed. Wisps of hair had escaped her ponytail—not in an attractive, designer fashion way—and sweat had left trails in the dust that had plastered her face. But her cheeks had a healthy glow and her eyes shone brightly in spite of her exhausting day.

After peeling off her dirty, sweaty clothing, Gemma stepped under the shower and gave a low moan. God bless hot water, she thought as she grabbed the shampoo and worked the lather through her thick hair, watching as a stream of muddy water circled the drain at her feet. She could never recall a time in her life before when she had been this dirty. Until now, she hadn't even believed a person was *capable* of getting this dirty. A slow grin tugged at her lips as she realised she was happy. Who would have thought? She hated sweating, she avoided the gym like the plague, and yet here she was—tired, filthy, and feeling as though she had accomplished something. Gemma shook her head in bewilderment before getting back to scrubbing.

●

'That smells amazing,' Nash said. 'I could eat the crotch out of a low-flying duck.' He'd finished up outside and had also taken a shower before dinner. His still-damp hair looked darker than usual and he was now dressed in a clean set of jeans and white t-shirt.

'Well, you're out of luck, it's beef, not duck,' Gemma told him, serving out the chilli she'd thrown together earlier that morning. 'And I'm pretty sure it's not the crotch, although I can't be a hundred per cent certain.'

'You're a great cook. Seriously. This is awesome.'

Gemma felt herself blushing. 'It's really nothing fancy.'

'Are you kidding? I've been eating like a king since you got here.'

'I like to cook.' She shrugged, but his compliment meant more to her than he could possibly know. Cooking was her passion, and she loved having the opportunity to try out different recipes. They'd come to an unspoken agreement that, as well as her jobs on the farm, she would take care of cooking and food shopping.' On her first trip into town to buy groceries, he'd told her to put it on his account at the store. She hadn't bothered, instead just using her credit card. She suspected that things were pretty tight in the cash department for Nash and the property and, in truth, she loved having free rein to buy whatever ingredients she wanted. Gemma knew she'd feel guilty buying so much stuff on the farm account, and she felt that paying for their food was the least she could do for Nash, considering that their arrival had caused him his fair share of headaches. She wanted to spoil him a little and at least feed him something decent while they were out here.

All this shopping meant that Gemma was getting to know Wendy, the owner of the grocery store in town. Early on, they'd both guiltily admitted to an addiction to reality TV cooking shows, and now enjoyed discussing each episode. Wendy was a cheerful round-faced woman in her mid-forties. From the first day they met, Gemma had been drawn to her friendly, laid-back manner. It was a new experience for Gemma to stop in the aisle to chat. A chore that usually took only a few minutes back home, nipping in to grab a few things, barely making eye contact with anyone, now took a good forty to fifty minutes each time.

'Are you sure you don't want to put this on Dunoon's account?' Wendy had asked on her last visit.

'Positive. I don't think the imported goat meat you ordered in for me would go over too well with Nash.'

'You must be a magician to be able to get him to eat anything with goat meat in it. Wish I knew your secret—my mob turn their nose up at anything more than meat, potato and peas.'

'What if you just cook what you want and tell them if they want anything else they have to make it themselves?'

'I don't think I could handle their moaning and whining. Anyway, I'm usually too buggered after working here all day to feel like getting creative,' Wendy admitted. 'Maybe when the boys leave home and it's just Darrell and me,' she added wistfully.

It was a shame, Gemma thought, that Wendy didn't get a chance to cook for enjoyment. Gemma found cooking relaxing, and the thought of it becoming a chore saddened her. Her thoughts turned automatically to life once she left Bingorra. Her father worked long hours and expected his employees to do the same. She hated to think that maybe she too would end up too tired to enjoy cooking. She supposed there were always weekends, but memories of her father locked away behind his study door all weekend dampened her optimism. After she left here, these carefree cooking days were sure to come to an end.

'Everything okay?'

Nash's words cut into Gemma's thoughts and she started guiltily. 'Sorry, I was just thinking.'

'It doesn't look like it was something very pleasant.'

Gemma shook off her mood. 'Wasn't important.' *Just my life*, she added silently.

'So where did you learn to cook like this?' asked Nash.

Gemma winced. 'You'll laugh if I tell you.'

'No, I won't,' he replied.

'I watch reality cooking shows. I'm kind of addicted to them, actually.'

'Yeah? You mean people actually watch that rubbish on telly?'

'It's not rubbish. And yes, lots of people watch them—they're very popular, in fact,' she said, then realised how defensive she sounded. She'd lived with her father's criticism of her cooking-show obsession through her last years of high school and hated having her passion dismissed. More than once her parents had told her that she had more important things to concentrate on than cooking. Then, one weekend during her first semester at uni, she'd gone home and announced that she wanted to drop out of her course and do a cooking apprenticeship. Her father had just about had a heart attack, and her mother had been upset by the tension in the air. There was never tension in the Northcote household. Everyone just agreed and got on with it. She'd learned her lesson that day and had never brought up the idea of a cooking apprenticeship again.

'See, I knew you wouldn't take it seriously,' she told Nash.

'Okay, sorry, you're right; I shouldn't knock something I haven't watched.' He looked genuinely remorseful, but

Gemma suspected he was just humouring her. 'So you learned to cook after watching a TV show?' he went on.

'Well, not exactly. I used to watch my mum. She loves entertaining, so she was always throwing dinner parties when I was growing up. But I guess the TV shows just made it cool again. I started watching them in high school, then when Jazz and I got our own flat I decided to experiment more.'

'You really love it, huh?' He sat back in his chair and looked at her curiously.

Gemma felt her cheeks redden slightly. 'Well, you know, it's just a hobby.' But as she said the words she felt as though she was betraying something deep down inside her.

'You know, you never really answered me that day when I asked if you always wanted to go into business.'

'Yes, I did.'

'No, you said it was what your family does. That's not exactly what I asked. I wanted to know if *you* always wanted to do a business degree.'

'It's been the plan for so long, I can't even remember wanting to do anything else,' Gemma hedged. This was dangerous territory, and she could feel her stomach tightening again.

'If you had a choice, would you have wanted to do business?' he probed.

'You make it sound like I was forced at gunpoint to do my degree.' She laughed nervously, toying with her fork.

'*Were* you?' he asked with a faint smile.

'My parents are firm believers in being realistic. They own a company where they expect me to work and they don't understand why I'd want to do anything else.'

'Maybe because you might be interested in something else—like cooking?'

'Yeah, well, cooking isn't a lucrative career,' she said mechanically. 'It's highly competitive and I know plenty of chefs who are out of work. Besides, a business degree is a useful thing to have. It doesn't mean I have to work for my father forever. I can use it for a lot of different things.'

She was grateful when he didn't ask any more questions. Soon after, she collected their plates and took them to the sink. She hated having to defend her decision. Even Jazz knew not to push her too hard on the subject. There were days when she felt as though she was a pushover when it came to her family, but there was also a side of her that liked not having to go out on a limb, venture into the unknown. She liked security and knowing where she was going in life; in this way, too, she was the opposite of Jazz, who liked to wing things.

After the dishes were done, Gemma waited until she heard Nash go into his office, before reaching into the cupboard under the sink for Horse's saucer. In the last fortnight she'd gradually managed to entice the cat further out of the shed. Now he came right up to the back door for his milk.

Gemma was proud of the progress they'd made. While he certainly wasn't a well-mannered housecat, he didn't hiss or run away anymore. Despite his new-found bravery, though, he still watched her suspiciously. It shouldn't matter so much, but it did. She hated that anything should live with such mistrust and fear in its life.

She poured the milk into the saucer and placed it at the bottom of the step, then sat down. A few seconds later, the ginger cat stalked from the shadows and cautiously approached the saucer.

'Hey there, Horse,' Gemma murmured, and saw one of his ears twitch at the sound of her voice. She eased down another step as he lapped at the milk. He watched her as he drank, and she smiled when he didn't move away. She was now on the second-lowest step—the closest she'd managed to get. A small thrill of victory went through her as she sat quietly and watched the animal drink until the saucer was empty. She held the cat's gaze as he raised his head, and waited for him to make his move. But he turned and disappeared back into the darkness; disappointed, she released the breath she'd been holding. One day she hoped he'd come up and let her stroke his fur, but clearly that wasn't going to be tonight.

'You've been feeding the cat all this time?'

She looked up to see Nash standing just inside the back door and felt like a kid being sprung eating from the biscuit tin before dinnertime.

'I just give it some milk at night.'

'It's feral. As in *wild*.' He pushed open the screen door and came to stand on the top step above her.

'I know that,' she countered.

'Then why are you feeding it milk?'

'Because I didn't want it to go hungry.'

'You named the cat *Horse*?' he asked, looking at her like she was some kind of dimwit.

'I thought about naming it Nash because you both have the same temperament,' she shot back, 'but then I thought that might be unfair to the cat.'

'Ouch.' He raised an eyebrow before a slow smile broke out across his face. 'And here I was thinking you were going to say you called him Horse after me because he had a big—'

'In your dreams,' Gemma cut him off quickly, her cheeks flaring again. 'It's after Horse from *Footrot Flats*—you know, the big mean cat who thinks he's the boss?'

'Oh, *that* Horse,' he said. 'You think I'm mean?'

'Maybe not mean, just . . . grumpy all the time.'

'I'm not grumpy all the time,' he protested.

'I'm not judging, just making an observation.' Gemma really wished she hadn't started this line of conversation.

'Well, your observational skills are clearly faulty.'

'Not that you don't have good reason to be grumpy,' she said quickly. 'I mean, we *were* kind of dumped on you, and it must be hard having your house invaded by strangers.' The more she considered it, the more Gemma realised he had every right to be annoyed.

'Yeah, well, the upside is I get fed regularly. Come to think of it, maybe me and Horse have more in common than I first thought.'

Maybe they did, she mused, eyeing him warily. There was something off limits about Nash that made her itch to figure him out, overcome his defences. 'Maybe I should start giving you milk too,' she said, slipping by him to head back inside.

Seven

Gemma met Jazz as she came out of the bathroom the next morning looking bleary-eyed, her blonde hair sticking up in all directions. Gemma had awoken to a low rumbling engine pulling up outside late last night and realised Mack must have driven Jazz home.

'Big night?'

A muffled grunt was her only reply.

'Here's a strange question: where's the ute?'

'I left it behind the pub. Mack's coming to pick me up later to go and get it. It's no big deal.'

Gemma shook her head as she went out to the kitchen to put on the jug. Too bad if she'd needed the car today!

'We're going to be marking today,' Nash said after he'd

finished his breakfast a little while later, and thanked Gemma as she handed him his coffee.

'Fine,' Jazz said with a bored sigh. She'd turned down breakfast and still looked a little pale, but Gemma refused to feel sorry for her. They were here to work, and yet Jazz seemed to think it was all a big joke—partying till all hours and drinking too much when she knew she had to get up early the next day.

'I suppose you've done it before?' Nash asked casually, taking a sip of his coffee.

Gemma busied herself with reaching for the sugar as Jazz shrugged and said, 'A few times.'

Nash stood up. 'Great. Then I'll see you outside in ten.' He held Gemma's gaze for a moment before picking up his coffee and heading out the door.

Gemma waited until the door had shut before giving Jazz a furious look. 'Would you *stop* doing that!' she whispered. 'Just tell him we don't know what we're doing. We don't have to keep pretending we can do stuff.'

'I'm not going to give him the satisfaction of thinking we're incompetent,' Jazz said grimly, looking at her coffee.

'We *are* incompetent, and I'm pretty sure he's figured that out by now,' said Gemma. 'How the hell are we going to do this, Jazz? We need to google—stat!' She heard the panic in her tone but didn't care. She could see this blowing up in their faces, big time.

'There's no time for that. We're just gonna have to wing it.'

Wing it? Was she insane? How were they supposed to do that with Nash out there watching them?

'Would you just relax? You're making my head throb worse than the hangover. How hard can it be to mark a cow? We just paint a number on its back or something . . . Right?'

•

By the time the two girls met Nash outside, the day was already beginning to heat up. The cattle milled around, stirring up dust and voicing their disapproval at being locked up in the yard overnight. Gemma was getting used to the dust in the air and the smell of cow manure. The smells were earthy and sometimes pungent, but not unpleasant. She couldn't help smiling to herself. Who would have thought Gemma Northcote would appreciate cow poo?

'Okay, so we need to separate the bulls from their mothers,' Nash began. 'We'll push them up through the race and into the cradle.'

'The what?' Gemma asked, confused.

'The race.' He pointed to the long narrow section of steelwork that ran down the side of the cattle yards. 'We push them down along there and into the cradle at the end.'

The girls followed him cautiously into the yard as the nervous cattle shifted around irritably and tossed their heads. While Nash moved between the cattle with confidence, throwing his hands about and sidestepping irate cows as they tried to protect their young, the girls did their best to shoo the young calves into the race. 'Only the bulls,' Nash yelled across at them, more than once.

'It's a bit hard to tell which ones've got dangly bits and which ones don't,' Jazz yelled back.

Gemma suspected that the job took longer with the two

girls helping than if Nash had been working alone, but finally they'd managed to separate the boys from the girls and the race was crammed with baby bulls, all bellowing for their mothers.

Nash swung himself up and over the side of the stockyard fence, and Gemma took a moment to appreciate the rugged grace of the man. God, he was hot. She was jolted back to reality when Jazz elbowed her and smirked having caught Gemma staring. With a sharp whistle, Nash called the dogs away from the cattle and they obediently trotted across to sit at his side, watching his every move.

Nash had backed the ute up to the end of the race and lowered the tailgate to act as a workbench, an assortment of equipment spread out neatly across it. Gemma eyed the objects with an anxious frown as Nash turned to the girls.

'So I need one of you to move the calves up the race and the other one out here to work the cradle while I do the marking. I'll do the first one and show you how it works.' He moved the loudly protesting calves up the race until the first one was secured between a set of gates. Nash pulled a lever and the gate locked behind the young male, separating it from the others behind it. He pushed another lever and the whole section fell sideways, trapping the calf on its side. He grabbed a scalpel and moved towards the animal.

'Whoa, wait!' Jazz screeched. 'What are you doing?'

'Marking. What's it look like I'm doing?' he asked, eyeing her strangely.

'It looks like you're about to cut off that bull's gonads.'

'Yes,' Nash said slowly. 'We're marking today.'

'Marking? *This* is marking?' Jazz demanded, a look of horror plastered across her face.

'What the hell did you think we were doing?'

'Marking!' she cried. 'You know, writing numbers or whatever the hell you do to mark them.'

Nash looked at her like she'd grown two heads, and gave a sceptical chuckle. 'You're not serious?'

'This is so not what I thought marking was. It's *nothing* like what I thought marking was supposed to be. Why would you even call it that, for God's sake?'

'Jazz,' Gemma said warningly, trying to calm her friend's rising hysteria, although truth be told she was also shocked at the idea of what Nash was about to do.

'Look, I don't have time for this.' Nash moved across to the animal and quickly sliced through one small testicle. The calf bellowed and tried to kick, while the dogs sat waiting patiently beside Nash, eyes eagerly glued to his hands.

'Oh my God,' Jazz gasped, slapping a hand across her mouth.

Gemma stared in mute horror as Nash cut through a long stringy cord, before tossing it to one of the dogs, who scoffed it down hungrily. Jazz ran past her, disappearing behind the yards, and the sound of violent retching soon followed.

Gemma was still in shock as she watched Nash repeat the procedure on the other side. He pushed the lever to return the calf to its feet, then released it from the cradle into the main yard, where it wobbled its way out to find its mother.

'That's all there is to it,' Nash said breezily, turning to Gemma. 'You okay?'

She wondered if she looked as white as she felt. 'Better than him,' she said, her eyes following the path the little bull—correction, steer—had taken.

'It looks worse than it is. There, he's back with his mum, having a drink,' Nash pointed out as he washed the scalpel in a bucket of disinfectant before placing it back on the equipment tray. Sure enough, the little guy was busily drinking while his mother gently nudged around him as though comforting him.

'It's just we weren't expecting . . . this,' Gemma said, waving at the equipment on the back of the ute.

'I thought you'd already done it a few times?' Nash said.

'We may have embellished the skills we actually have . . . a little.' Gemma grimaced, looking at the ground. She felt heat flaring in her face.

'No shit?'

Gemma couldn't bear to look up, stung by his tone. She thought she would have preferred an explosive outburst to sarcasm.

'Look, if you're up to it, I could really use a hand,' he said flatly. 'I need to get this done today.'

Gemma finally looked up. She didn't want to do this job. She wasn't even sure how she'd managed to keep down her own breakfast, but seeing the weary look on Nash's face and hearing the quiet desperation in his words, she squared her shoulders and pushed away her squeamishness. This situation was their fault, hers and Jazz's. Nash needed someone to help him and that was what they'd promised to do. Well, maybe not exactly this, she amended, not knowingly, but if it was part of farming duties then it was part of their role.

'Okay.' She nodded at him, squaring her jaw. 'Show me the levers again?' He nodded back wordlessly, and she listened closely while he repeated the instructions.

They moved the next calf into the cradle and she pushed the lever to tip him sideways. 'Be brave, little man,' she whispered, turning her head away while Nash made the quick incisions. After the first few, she gained a little more confidence in working the machinery, and the work eventually got into a rhythm of sorts. Focusing on the levers and Nash's movements helped to take her mind off the gruesome task.

They finished by midday, and she left Nash to go and make some lunch. She'd built up an appetite without even realising it. First, though, she poked her head into Jazz's room to check on her. Jazz was in bed, her face turned to the wall. 'You okay?'

'That was barbaric.' Jazz shuddered.

'You just got a shock, that's all,' Gemma said. 'It wasn't that bad after the first few times.'

'I can't believe you stuck around to help him butcher those poor little things.'

'It's not like you gave me a choice. He needed someone to help him.'

'This was not part of the deal.'

'This wouldn't have happened if you'd just told him we didn't have any idea what we were doing,' Gemma said evenly. 'He wouldn't have thrown us into it like that if he knew.'

'So it's all my fault as usual?' Jazz demanded, finally rolling over to glare at Gemma.

Well, yes, Gemma thought, but she knew it wouldn't help

the situation to point this out now. 'I'm making some lunch, are you coming out?'

'How can you even eat after watching that?'

'Alright, I'll leave you something in the fridge to have later,' she said, backing out of the room as Jazz rolled over again. She should be used to Jazz and her melodramatic ways by now; God knows she'd seen enough of them over the years. But as painful as she could be, Jazz was still her best friend. You didn't just throw away a best friend because they had their faults. And Gemma knew she wasn't perfect either.

Even with the heat it was too nice a day to be inside, so once she'd finished making some sandwiches, Gemma took them outside. By then Nash had packed away all the gear they'd used and the cattle were let out of the yards. He was washing his hands under the water tank beside the shed when she put the wrapped sandwiches and thermos of coffee down near a log close by.

'Have I mentioned I could get used to this?' he said, coming over to take a seat beside her.

'I need to stick to what I'm good at.' She'd been on edge waiting for him to bring up the earlier fiasco and call her out on lying to him, but he didn't seem as upset as she'd been expecting.

He unwrapped the plastic from his sandwiches. 'You know, I still can't get my head around this whole "work for a holiday" thing. I've tried, but I just don't get it.'

Gemma shrugged, taking her time unwrapping her own lunch. 'It was a chance to do something different. A seize-the-moment kind of thing.'

'You just don't seem like the kind of girl whose first choice of a holiday would be marking cattle.'

'I'm not . . . or rather, I wasn't. Jazz was always the one who thought wide open spaces and riding horses into the sunset would be romantic. I just came along for the ride. It's the last holiday we'll get to spend together before we both start work.'

'Hell of a way to spend a holiday.'

'Tell me about it,' she said dryly, and smiled when he chuckled. He really did have a nice laugh; it was a pity he didn't get to use it more often.

'Despite having no idea what you were doing, you actually did really well today.'

'So I guess you figured it out pretty early on, huh?'

'Pretty much,' he confirmed, lips twitching. 'I was curious to see how far you'd both go with it.'

'I think you just found out.'

'Maybe you should give farm work a second thought as a career?'

'Ah, no. I don't think so. I'm not really the outdoorsy type.'

'That's right, you're a working-in-an-office kinda girl,' he said without looking at her. Something about his tone made her bristle; she wasn't sure why, but somehow she felt as though he had made a dig at her. Gemma finished eating her sandwich in silence and packed up the rubbish without further comment.

'Thanks for lunch,' Nash said as she headed back to the house.

'Sure.' She shrugged, but didn't look at him. She didn't

know what had happened between them, but there had definitely been a shift in the mood.

•

As he watched Gemma walk back to the house, Nash cursed himself for ruining the easy working partnership they'd established during the morning. The woman was tying him up in knots. Never before had anyone confused him as much as Gemma Northcote. Just when he thought she couldn't surprise him any more she went and proved him wrong, leaving him dumbfounded. Today had been a prime example. When Jazz had stumbled away from the yards in disgust, Nash had expected Gemma to quickly follow suit, but instead she'd stepped up and done the job of two people, even though he knew she didn't like it. She'd surprised the hell outta him. But then he'd gone and opened his big mouth to talk about her career choice. And why? Because for the briefest of moments he'd allowed himself to imagine a completely different future for Gemma, and then reality had slapped him across the head and he'd felt some idiotic need to remind them both that she didn't belong here.

The truth was that since the very first time he'd set eyes on her delectable butt sticking up from behind that bale of lucerne, she'd had him in a spin, and he didn't like it. Even though she continued to prove to him that she could handle pretty much anything he threw her way, the fact still remained that she was as city as a freeway and he was as country as a dirt track. But somehow he kept forgetting the warning he repeated to himself each morning before he set eyes on her: *Don't get used to this*. Soon she'd be gone, with her beautiful smile and big green eyes, and with her would go the home-cooked meals and the clean house. Christ, the house even *smelled* different; there was a sweet, fresh scent around the place that he could only attribute to her. When she left, he'd go back to a quiet, messy house and no one to talk to. Cereal for dinner and a damn stray cat that would demand milk every night!

Eight

It was Friday night at last and Gemma was looking forward to a sleep-in the next morning. This week had been their busiest yet. Since Tuesday's marking debacle, life around the property became busier. Now that Nash wasn't out in the tractor day and night, he was freed up to show them how to help with a lot more work around the place. He was a patient teacher and the girls had a whole new range of jobs to keep them busy throughout the day. She was physically tired, but with it came a deep sense of satisfaction she had seldom known before. And she had noticed her body responding to the hard work. All the lifting was making muscles ache she'd never even known she had, and her arms and legs were already looking more toned. None of the magazines told you about the 'how to look fit and fabulous feeding weaners' workout.

She was even getting more confident with the chooks. Well, *most* of the chooks. She'd named the psycho bird from her first encounter Glennie, after Glenn Close's crazed character from *Fatal Attraction*. It still took a while to work up the nerve to move Glennie off the nest each day, but the unfriendly fowl had become Gemma's personal challenge. She vowed that she'd win the damn bird over if it was the last thing she did.

Jazz had never quite recovered from the whole marking fiasco; some of the romantic shine had definitely been taken off her jillarooing dream that day, but fortunately she'd snapped out of her indignation by the next day and they'd gotten on with it.

Tonight, though, Gemma was breaking her usual routine by accompanying Jazz on one of her regular trips into town after work.

'Do you want to come with us?'

Nash shook his head and pushed away his empty plate. 'I think I'll just catch up on some missed sleep.'

Initially Gemma had thought about turning down Jazz's invitation to the pub tonight, but then found that she was actually looking forward to it. She hoped that this would be a good chance to unwind and relax with her friend; and, truthfully, ever since this trip started their friendship had been under a lot more strain than usual. She had an uneasy feeling that things had changed since they came out here, and not only between her and Jazz but within herself. She felt an inner turmoil that she could barely articulate to herself, and part of it was the surprising realisation that as much as she'd dreaded this crazy working holiday adventure, she was happier here than she'd been in a long time. Maybe Jazz was right. Maybe all she needed was a night out to clear her head and have some fun, remind herself that she was just here on holiday.

Gemma stood up slowly. 'Well, I guess I'd better go get ready.'

'Have a good time,' Nash said as she left the room. She didn't bother looking back. No doubt he was already thinking about something else.

It irked her slightly that he hadn't seemed at least a little bit disappointed she was leaving him all alone tonight though. *What did you expect?* she scolded herself. The guy was only living with her and Jazz under sufferance. They had invited themselves into his house, invaded his privacy, and encroached on his hospitality—why should he want to spend his precious spare time with her too?

•

They pulled up in front of the hotel in the main street. Light and music spilled from the windows. As they walked inside, Gemma's ears were assaulted by shouted conversations vying with the live band playing in the far corner.

'I'm going to get a drink,' said Jazz. 'What do you want?'

'Lemon squash, thanks.'

'Come on, Gem, you can have a few drinks. We're not driving home until later.'

'Just a lemon squash, thanks.' Ignoring Jazz's impatient eye roll, she looked around the room. There were lots of younger people out tonight. The older crowd were either seated at the bar or in the lounge, visible through the archway, presumably to get away from the band. Gemma was surprised to see so many young people here, until Jazz explained that most of them were uni students home on holidays.

She shouldn't have been surprised at Jazz's knowledge, since she'd practically become a regular here over the last few weeks. Gemma took her drink and followed Jazz through the crowd towards a group of people seated at a table. Gemma recognised Mack and his brother from before. At least this time Ben seemed to have made a bit more of an effort with his clothes. His smart checked shirt wasn't wrinkled and he wore jeans without any rips in them that she could see.

'Gem, you remember Ben and Mack?' Jazz said, her smile lingering on Mackenzie. Gemma smiled and gave a small wave as she was introduced to the four other people seated at the table. Chad and Lucy were around the same age as Jazz and Gemma and high-school sweethearts, engaged to be married later in the year, and Lucy's younger sister, Bec, and her friend Kylie both seemed nice.

Ben jumped up and brought over a seat from another table. He placed it next to his own and indicated for Gemma to sit there. She thanked him and he grinned, his eyes sparkling as he finished one pint and immediately started another. She sipped her drink as she listened to the conversations going on around her. As usual, Jazz had taken centre stage, and was busy telling everyone at the table how she and Gemma came to be out here, albeit with lots of theatrical embellishments thrown in which the group found hysterical.

Gemma jumped slightly as something touched her shoulder, then realised that Ben had rested his arm along the back of her chair. She sat up a little straighter and tried not to lean back. He was probably just getting comfortable, she told herself, but it still made her feel self-conscious.

'So Brittany ditched Nash and you two came out in her place?' asked Lucy, looking perplexed. 'Why?'

Jazz shrugged. 'It was a great opportunity and it came at the perfect time, since we were planning on taking a bit of a break between uni and getting jobs.'

'You came out here for a *break*?' the girl persisted.

'Well, a *working* break,' Jazz clarified.

Their table mates all seemed to think it was a bit strange, but Mack pointed out that it was no stranger than the flood of backpackers who came through the area looking for work each year.

'You don't exactly look like the kind of girl who'd come out this way looking for a job,' Ben said quietly to Gemma when the conversation around the table moved on to something else.

Why did people keep saying that? 'What kind of girl do I look like?' she asked, actually interested to find out, but she inwardly cringed when she realised he may take it as flirting.

'Too classy for this place.'

Did she really stand out so much? Maybe she should come here straight from the yards one day, covered in dust and smelling like sheep, and see if he still thought that. She smiled at him neutrally to make sure he knew she *wasn't* flirting with him. 'Jazz wanted to do it, so I came along to keep her out of trouble.'

'And who's keeping you out of trouble?' he asked, and lightly traced his thumb across her bare shoulder.

'Apparently, that's been my job.'

Gemma turned her head at the deep voice and felt a rush of pleasure to see Nash standing there. But her pleasure soon turned to dismay as she realised how it must look with Ben's arm draped proprietorially across her chair. 'I thought you weren't coming in?' She blushed slightly when she realised how defensive she sounded. She had nothing to feel guilty about. It wasn't as if she'd asked the guy to put his arm there.

'This is a nice surprise,' said Bec, a smile spreading across her face as she looked Nash up and down.

Gemma felt her hackles rise, and frowned at her reaction. It wasn't like she had any claim on the man. *Even if I do make his dinner and pack his lunches*, another little voice huffed indignantly.

'We were starting to think you'd become a hermit or something,' Lucy put in.

Nash shrugged. 'No rest for the wicked.'

'Sit down and have a drink with us,' Mack said, standing up to head to the bar.

'Nah, mate, thanks. I'm not drinking.'

'Aw, come on. Just one.'

'No, thanks.'

'He's probably intimidated by the company. He never could handle his alcohol,' Ben announced, and Gemma noticed for the first time that his voice was slightly slurred.

'Some people know when they've had enough,' Nash said quietly, but a muscle pulsed in his cheek.

'Some people think they have the right to preach when they should know damn well they're no bloody saint!'

Gemma was trying to follow the conversation but it was obvious that she was missing a few vital pieces of information. Everyone else at the table had fallen tensely silent.

'Enjoy your evening,' Nash said, his gaze briefly falling on Gemma's face before he walked down to the end of the bar and disappeared into the crowd.

'Did you have to be such a dick, Ben?' Mack scowled.

'The guy's a jerk. Always has been. He goes out of his way to rub it in.'

'Bull crap. He was just coming over to say hi. You need to adjust your attitude, mate. You're back home now.'

'Oh? Where have you been?' Jazz asked brightly, trying to change the subject.

The faces around the table froze, and there was an uncomfortable silence. Gemma and Jazz exchanged a glance.

'You would have heard about it sooner or later,' Ben snarled without looking at anyone. 'I've been in prison. Yep, I'm an ex-con.' He pushed himself away from the table and strode off in the opposite direction to Nash.

'How was I supposed to know?' Jazz sighed into the awkwardness that followed.

'You weren't,' Mack assured her, giving her a hug. 'Come on, this is supposed to be a fun night out, not a damn wake. Who wants another drink?'

Gemma stood up too. 'I'm just going to the ladies'.' She needed to get away from the noise and the crowd for a while. The relative quiet of the hallway outside was a haven. Maybe there was something wrong with her, she thought. She'd never enjoyed socialising the way Jazz did. She was just a geeky homebody, she thought ruefully, and felt almost relieved that her uni days had come to an end. Maybe now she wouldn't stand out so much.

The ladies' toilets were located in the lounge. Over on this side of the bar there were a few people seated at tables chatting. The poker machines whirling in the background helped to drown out the band in the next room, but at least a person could hear themselves think.

She paused momentarily as she spotted Nash across the room; he was standing with a small group of older men, listening to their conversation. Then she pushed open the heavy door to the bathroom. The door closed behind her, and her ears almost rang in the near silence. The bathroom was old-fashioned, with a little carpeted foyer and two comfy-looking chairs. Beyond them were three stalls and a long sink. She took her time washing her hands and found she had butterflies in her stomach as she thought of Nash's sudden appearance. She resisted the urge to fix her makeup; she did however run her hands through her hair, but that wasn't for Nash's benefit she told herself firmly. On her way out a few minutes later she eyed the chairs a little longingly, and briefly contemplated waiting for Jazz in here. Then she forced herself to head back out, bracing herself for the noise as she opened the door.

She had only taken a few steps when Nash appeared in front of her. Gemma's gaze lingered on his jawline which was now freshly shaven and noted he'd changed into a button-up shirt and clean jeans for the occasion. 'Oh. Um, hi,' she stammered, then added, a little disingenuously, 'I figured you'd have left by now.'

'I was going to but I got caught up talking and didn't make it outside. I didn't have you pegged for Ben's type.' He slipped his comment in so smoothly it took a second for it to register.

'My type? How do you know what my type is?' she asked, curious. Was he jealous of her being with Ben?

'I guess I don't. But I wouldn't have thought you'd be into the party scene.'

'Actually, I'm not. I only came along tonight because of Jazz.'

'Did I hear my name?' Jazz said, coming up beside them. She gave Nash an irritated glance before turning to Gemma. 'Mack says they're all staying in town tonight at a friend's house and we're welcome to stay to save driving home.'

'You're staying?' Gemma asked.

'Well, yeah. I thought you might like to as well. That way you could drink and actually enjoy yourself for a change.' Jazz looked accusingly at Nash.

'No, I don't think I will,' Gemma said. 'I might just go home.'

'Please stay,' Jazz begged. 'It'll be fun, Gem.'

'I don't even *know* these people. *You* don't even know these people.'

'I know they're fun! Like the Gemma I *used* to know,' Jazz snapped. 'Well, I'm staying. I guess I'll see you back at Dunoon . . . eventually.' With an angry toss of her blonde head she turned on her heel and marched away.

'Keep your phone switched on,' Gemma called after her. Jazz didn't look back, and Gemma sighed as she watched her friend disappear into the crowd. What was happening to them? Lately all they seemed to do was argue.

'Mack's an alright guy. She'll be safe enough,' said Nash, and she looked up to see him still watching her.

'Maybe it's Mack I'm worried about! The poor fella won't know what's hit him once Cyclone Jazz strikes.' She smiled weakly, trying to make light of the disagreement he'd witnessed.

A smile touched Nash's lips. 'He's a big boy, he can take care of himself.' Slipping his keys from his pocket, he tossed them in his hand. 'Do you want me to wait for you? Or are you ready to go now?'

'No, I'm ready to go,' she said, and followed him outside.

'I had to park in the next street.' He stood waiting till she found her keys in her bag as they stopped beside her car parked in the main street outside the pub.

Realising he was waiting for her to get into her car, she waved him off. 'You go, I'm fine. I'll wait for you out along the road.'

Gemma muttered under her breath as she tried all three keys on the ring before finding the right one. She was just opening the door when a dark shadow fell across her, and she jumped. She looked up to see Ben standing beside her. 'You scared me,' she said, her voice no more than a whisper.

'Finding out I've done time put you off, huh?' He sounded more than a little drunk now.

'Ben, I wasn't interested in the first place. I'm only here for a few weeks. I'm not looking for whatever you think I'm looking for,' she finished lamely.

'Yeah, right, but you'll give it up for good old Nash,' he jeered.

'I'm not giving up anything to anyone,' she said coldly. 'You should just go back inside to your friends.'

'Let me tell you something about Nash Whittaker. He's not the stand-up guy everyone seems to think. You should be careful.' Ben took a step closer; Gemma automatically leaned back, which only seemed to increase his anger. 'I've done my time, you hear me? Everyone around here thinks I got off lightly, but I didn't. I paid more than they'll ever know.'

Wishing she hadn't sent Nash away, Gemma searched the street as unobtrusively as possible so as to avoid antagonising Ben further.

'He thinks he's so damn superior, but you know what? If he's such a goddamn hero he should have saved her that night.'

This statement caught Gemma's attention. She frowned as Ben looked at the footpath beneath his feet, swaying slightly. 'Should have saved who?' she asked, despite her better judgement.

'Kim . . .' His voice trailed off in a slurred mumble as he turned away and stepped heavily off the kerb. 'He should have saved her life,' he said quietly before walking away to disappear into the shadows beyond where the streetlights didn't reach.

Letting out a shaky breath, Gemma slid in behind the steering wheel, then locked the door behind her. *What the hell was that all about?* she wondered, turning the key in the ignition and carefully pulling out into the street. Up ahead she could see Nash waiting at the intersection. Once she'd driven past, he pulled out behind her and followed her home.

As she went back over in her mind her conversation with Ben, she sent a quick glance in her rear-view mirror at the twin headlights behind her. Who was Kim? How had she died, and why would Ben imply that Nash could have saved her? Was it just drunken talk or was it some kind of warning? Shrugging off Ben's outburst, she concentrated on the dark road ahead—the last thing she wanted to do was hit another kangaroo.

Parking the ute in its usual place near the shed, Gemma was glad that Nash was there to walk her inside. She hated the darkness out here. With no streetlights, it was just so . . . *dark*. It was something she found very hard to get used to.

'Were you alright back there?' Nash asked, falling into step with her as they headed for the house. 'I was just about to drive back down to the pub to see where you'd got to.'

'Ben stopped for a chat.'

Even in the dark, she felt Nash's reaction to the other man's name. 'You could have stayed longer if that's what you wanted,' he said stiffly.

'If that's what I'd wanted, yes, I could have,' she told him bluntly. She knew Nash's reaction had nothing to do with jealousy. The bad feeling between the two men had long preceded her arrival on the scene.

'What did he want?' he asked.

'Nothing, really. I think he was a bit put out that I was leaving so early.'

'I bet he was.' Gemma could hear the tension in Nash's voice.

'He told me to be careful of you,' she said as the security light on the verandah came on, the bright light making her blink. Turning to Nash, she caught the frown on his face.

'Why do you think he said that?' She stepped in front of him and stopped in the doorway, blocking his entrance.

Nash's lip curled and he looked away. 'I guess he's got his reasons. Who knows how the guy's mind works.'

'He mentioned Kim,' she said quickly, before she lost her nerve. She might as well get it all out in the open now before she went and did something really stupid like fall for him. She knew bringing this up wasn't going to endear her to him. Maybe that was why she was doing it now, before they went inside, just the two of them, alone together in the house. She didn't trust herself to say no if he made a move on her, it was pretty much that simple. And then where would she be? She'd told Ben the truth when she said she had no interest in a relationship that could only last at best a handful of weeks. What was the point? Her life was mapped out for her back home; she was unlikely to ever return to this place. It was Jazz's dream to sow her wild oats before she settled down and found a job. That had never been what Gemma was looking for. And yet Gemma hadn't counted on meeting someone like Nash. Someone she enjoyed being with. They didn't even have to talk; some days while they worked side by side she just enjoyed the fact he was just . . . there. But when they did talk, she found the topics they covered fascinating. She enjoyed his dry sense of humour, and the fact that he could raise her heart rate with just one look.

He didn't seem surprised to hear Kim's name. 'And what did he say about her?' he asked icily, his hand resting on the rail and his foot propped on the bottom step.

'Not much, nothing really. Just that . . .' She couldn't repeat what Ben had said, and suddenly she had a terrible feeling about this conversation. 'Why would he bring her up?' she asked instead.

'Probably because he likes you,' Nash said flatly.

Gemma frowned. 'What does that have to do with anything?'

'Because he also liked *Kim*.'

She gritted her teeth. When would someone tell her what was going on? 'Okay, so obviously I'm a bit slow on the uptake. I don't understand.'

'It was years ago, back in high school. She was my girl-friend. We broke up and she . . . It doesn't matter now, it was another lifetime,' Nash said quietly.

High school? So this was all over some stupid schoolyard jealousy, someone's injured pride? Ben really did have some major issues to deal with if he was holding a grudge against someone from high school.

'Or,' Nash said, taking another step up, standing so close she could smell the traces of the pub still lingering on his shirt and the heady masculine scent of the aftershave he wore. 'It could have something to do with the fact that I killed her.'

Gemma froze. Even if she had been capable of speaking, she didn't get the chance. Nash put his hands on her arms and gently moved her aside so he could walk past, leaving her alone on the steps outside.

Nine

She heard a door shut somewhere inside the house and blinked in shock. *Nash killed Kim?* she thought. *He killed her?* The next thought came immediately: Gemma was going to spend the night alone with him in the house. *Get a grip!* Some saner part of her brain kicked in and took charge of her hysterical thoughts. If he were a murderer, surely all those people he'd been chatting to earlier in the pub would have avoided him? They certainly hadn't treated him like a killer. On the contrary, it seemed that he was well respected in the town. Did murderers usually receive such a warm welcome?

She turned and made herself go inside. Rather than torturing herself with questions, she decided to find some answers. If she didn't, there was no way she was going to be able to sleep tonight.

She closed her bedroom door and opened her laptop, then connected to the wi-fi and typed in Nash's name. To her surprise, the search brought up several links to agriculture articles he'd written for various rural newspapers and magazines. She was briefly distracted by these, skimming through some of them, impressed that he had written such pieces. Then, on the second page of results, she found a link to the local newspaper from eight years earlier. Opening it, she saw a photo of a pretty blonde girl. The heading read: 'Local girl killed in car accident.'

Gemma's heart was pounding as she quickly read the article. She discovered that Kim Sweeney, seventeen, had been a passenger in a car that had hit a tree, killing her instantly. However, the person named as the driver wasn't Nash, as she'd expected, but Ben Henderson, then aged eighteen. He had walked away from the accident with only a few minor cuts and bruises; when breathalysed, he had been three times over the legal limit.

She searched for further reports on the accident; from an article dated around a year later she learned that Ben had received a ten-year prison sentence. After searching fruitlessly for any more information about the incident, she eventually gave up and shut down the computer. She frowned, baffled. Why would Nash say that he'd killed Kim when Ben was the one who had been charged with drink-driving and sent to prison? Was there something more to it? Had Nash been involved in the accident somehow? Had he been driving and for some reason Ben took the blame? But it didn't make any sense.

At least she felt reassured that she wasn't about to end the night buried in a shallow grave, but Gemma felt sad for the poor girl who had died in the accident. What a waste of such a young life.

She was distracted by the creak of the screen door opening at the front of the house. In the afternoons, Gemma and Jazz sometimes sat out on the verandah to catch a cool breeze. But tonight it could only be one person, and she decided to venture out and try to talk to him, although she was unsure what kind of reception she would get.

She took the seat next to his. 'Can't sleep?' she asked, when he didn't even look up.

'Nope.'

Well, this is going well, she thought as a silence settled once more between them. 'I read about what happened to Kim,' she said, and braced herself for an angry outburst. When none came, she risked looking at him; in the light falling out through the front door she saw that he was staring dully out across the dark paddocks. 'I don't understand how you had anything to do with it. Ben was charged with drink-driving.'

For a long time the only sound was the high-pitched chirping of crickets. Gemma waited.

'Ben may have been driving,' Nash said quietly at last. 'But I made her get in that car that night.'

Once more, Gemma waited for him to continue, but it seemed that he was finished. Was that the only explanation she would get?

'I'm sorry,' she said awkwardly.

'Not as sorry as I am.'

She had no idea what to say to him. Her first instinct was to reassure him that Kim herself must have decided to get into that car, and that if anyone was to blame it must be Ben;

but she didn't know anything more than what had been in the paper, so how could she presume to tell him? Still, she didn't like seeing him so silent and withdrawn.

'Do you want a cuppa?' she finally asked. 'I thought I might make one.'

'I'm right, thanks.'

She bit back a sigh and stood up. Obviously the man just wanted to be left alone and she had to respect that, but still it went against the grain to leave him out here alone with his grief.

She turned on the lights in the kitchen, then switched on the coffee machine and took down a mug. As she looked around the little kitchen, she couldn't help smiling. She'd grown attached to this little house. It had a homey feel to it. Her mother loved everything to be modern with clean edges, and their house had always been immaculate. This house was all mismatched fabrics and old furniture, and yet somehow it worked, in an old-fashioned, slightly shabby way. Almost the only modern thing in the kitchen was the sleek black coffee machine. Last week, after deciding she couldn't stomach another cup of instant coffee, Gemma had driven all the way to Curranjuck to pick it up.

'I changed my mind. Is it too late?'

Gemma jumped as Nash's deep voice cut through her thoughts. 'Too late?' she repeated dumbly.

'For that coffee?'

'Oh. No. Sure.' She quickly turned to grab down another mug. From the corner of her eye she saw him move further into the room and lean against the sink. He watched silently as she dropped in another pod and pushed a button.

'Tell me again why you needed to transform the kitchen into the flight deck of the *Enterprise*?' he asked, eyeing the flashing blue and green lights as the little machine made its robotic-sounding noises.

'Because life's too short for bad coffee,' she told him, and saw the corners of his eyes crinkle into a smile. When his expression almost instantly became solemn again, Gemma realised what she'd said. Her cheeks ablaze, she turned away from him, relieved to be able to focus on heating the milk.

'We were at a friend's eighteenth-birthday party,' he said suddenly, his voice soft.

Surprised, Gemma carefully placed the mug of coffee on the countertop beside him, then waited for him to go on.

'We had an argument, and she spent the rest of the night hanging out with Ben. She was only doing it to make me jealous. Anyway, trying to ignore the fact that Ben had his hands all over my girlfriend, I drank more than I usually would have. Later on I saw them leave the party. I was so pissed off at her for doing it in front of all our friends,' he said, looking up at Gemma. 'I should have dragged her away as soon as I saw her getting into Ben's car. We'd all been drinking, but Ben was completely smashed. But I was just so angry at her for making me look like a loser in front of everyone . . .' He trailed off, and Gemma could easily imagine the hot-headed teenager whose pride had taken a beating in front of his mates. 'I should have stopped her getting into that car.' He slumped back against the counter.

'Could you have, though?' Gemma asked timidly. When he looked up at her, she saw the heart-wrenching pain in the depths of his dark eyes. 'I mean, clearly she was angry too. If you'd told her not to get in the car, chances are she wouldn't have listened to you.'

'But that's the thing—I *did* tell her to get in the car,' he said quietly. 'I told her to go with him, Gem. She came over and told me she was leaving with him. I knew she wanted me to tell her not to, but I didn't. I yelled at her to go, then just stood there and let them drive away.' His voice was hollow, his expression so bleak and miserable it stabbed at her heart.

'I'm sure no one blames you for it, though. I mean, how could they? You weren't the one driving. Ben was. He was to blame.'

Nash dropped his head and stared at the floor. 'Her parents did.'

'I'm sure they couldn't—' Gemma began.

'They did,' he cut her off harshly. 'They asked me how I could let her get in the car with him. And I've been asking myself the same bloody thing all these years.'

'Oh, Nash.' Gemma felt tears pricking her eyelids as she bit her lip, picturing the whole horrible scene in her mind. The room was suddenly very quiet once more.

'Would you like me to make something to eat with this?' she asked at last, unable to think of anything to say that might comfort him.

He shook his head. 'No thanks,' he said, and gave a shaky laugh, finally moving to sit down at the kitchen table with his coffee. 'I'm becoming addicted to your cooking, you know.'

Gemma smiled. 'It's a treat for me to be able to cook for someone. It seems a waste to only cook for myself.'

'What about your Siamese twin? You don't cook for her too?' Gemma was relieved to hear the teasing note in his voice.

'Well, sometimes, but Jazz has more of a social life than I do. We lived in the same house for the first year of uni and then mutually decided we were not cut out to be flatmates,' she said dryly. 'Jazz moved in with some other kids from uni, so we actually don't spend that much time together.'

'I've been trying to work out how the two of you are even friends. You're so different.'

'Yeah, I know, it baffles a lot of people,' she said. 'Maybe we complement each other. She's the outgoing, popular girl I've always wanted to be.'

'And you're the smart, sensible one she's never been?' he added.

Gemma's smile faded slightly; she might consider strangling Jazz on a daily basis but no one else got to put her best friend down! Not even obscenely good-looking farmers with tortured souls. 'Jazz is smart; she just tends to hide it from most people.'

'I've never understood why people do that. There's nothing wrong with being smart.'

'I guess it's her way of coping with life. She's had a tough time herself, and she's always been there for me. I don't know what I would have done without her. It was kind of lonely growing up—my dad worked all the time, and my mum was pretty busy with committees and things. There was a lot of pressure on me to do well in school . . . Maybe it wouldn't have been so bad if I'd had brothers and sisters, you know? Someone else for them to focus on. Anyway, Jazz made things bearable. She saved my life.'

Nash looked at her sharply and she bit her lip. But she realised she'd come too far not to tell him the rest.

'Two days before I was due to sit my HSC exams, Jazz found me curled up in the corner of my room clutching an empty bottle of sleeping tablets.' It still made Gemma ill to think about that time in her life. The pressure she'd felt to get into the university she was expected to attend had pushed her to breaking point. She'd been a mess, exhausted and on the brink of a nervous breakdown. If Jazz hadn't been worried enough to come looking for her, she would have died that night. 'Jazz called an ambulance and stayed with me at the hospital till my parents got back from a business trip.'

She shuddered to remember how badly she'd disappointed her parents, how upset they'd been. She never wanted to put them through something like that again.

'So you see, I'm not *always* the smart, sensible one.' She'd never before told anyone about that night. It was something she was deeply ashamed of but since he'd been brave enough to tell her about his own painful past it seemed fitting that she should be equally as frank.

'I stand corrected. We could all use a friend like Jazz,' he said, making a toast with his mug.

They drank their coffee in silence after that, both lost to memories of things they would rather forget.

●

Later that night, Nash lay in bed with his hands linked behind his head as he stared up at the ceiling and listened to the house creaking and groaning, making the same noises it had been making his entire life. He hated thinking about the accident. He did his best to forget about it, but now and then something would set off a memory. Something like Ben's release from prison a few weeks ago, which was big news in the district. He'd often wondered what he'd say to the bastard if he ever saw him again. Well, from what happened tonight, it seemed that when it came to Ben Henderson he was still chicken shit. He'd seen Ben twice now and what had he done? Nothing.

For as long as Nash could remember, Henderson had been a thorn in his side. Ben was a year older than Nash and always a bully. He'd given Nash a black eye on his first day of school just because he didn't like the way Nash had looked at him. Over the years, Nash had learned to avoid Ben and his mates whenever possible, but they'd made his primary school days a nightmare. Once Nash went to high school and began to catch up to Ben in size and strength, the physical bullying had stopped, but he still gave Nash grief in any other way he could. It was on the footy field that Nash really enjoyed getting back at Ben. Many times they'd been pulled aside and reminded that they were on the same team. But their mutual dislike hadn't softened with time.

Now Nash thought back to the night of the party and the smug grin Ben had flashed him as he cupped Kim's arse in his hand and gave it a territorial squeeze. He was daring Nash to go over and do something about it. Right up until the end, when he'd held the door open for Kim to get into his car, his gaze had been locked on Nash's, silently telling him that he'd won. He'd managed to take Nash's girlfriend off him in front of everyone.

Part of Nash had wanted to race over and drag Kim from the car and wipe that grin off Ben's face once and for all. But another part just couldn't be bothered. He was tired of Henderson's constant provocation. It was like an annoying drip from a tap. It went on and on until it almost drove you insane. So instead of pulling Kim out of the car, he'd told her to go with Ben. *Good riddance to both of you*, he'd thought at the time, turning away from Kim's disappointed look. Deep down he knew she'd wanted him to take Ben on and fight for her. She wasn't a bad person, she was just young and maybe a little bit spoilt and bored. She'd used the boys' mutual hatred on and off over the last twelve months to play them off against each other, but Nash had finally had a gutful. He wasn't playing her game anymore. If she wanted excitement in her life she'd have to find it in Ben bloody Henderson.

Later, when the sirens of the local Volunteer Rescue Association truck had screamed past, everyone had known that something was very wrong. The ambulances weren't far behind. When someone finally came to the hall with word on what had happened, Nash called his father to come and get him so he could go up to the hospital.

As he walked through the front door of the hospital he saw Mrs Sweeney clutching at the doctor's shirt. Then she'd looked straight at Nash and just stared. He remembered taking a few steps towards her, even though his whole body screamed at him to run away. Mr Sweeney had gently detached his wife's hands from the doctor's shirt and wrapped her in his arms, but she continued to stare at Nash as he stood frozen to the spot. Then she'd begun to cry. Big, ugly, gut-wrenching sobs that tore at his very soul. 'Why did you let her get in that car? Where *were* you?' she'd screamed.

The words cut through him. They cut so deep they hit bone.

Nash thumped the pillow into a more comfortable position as he rolled over, trying uselessly to push away the memories.

Where were you? Kim's mother had demanded. He'd been right there, and what had he done? He'd told Kim to get into a car that minutes later would slam into a tree and obliterate her body and decimate her family forever. He *could* have saved her. He *should* have saved her, but instead he'd done nothing.

It was going to be another long night filled with the echo of crunching metal and Mrs Sweeney's cries and the endless, gut-churning guilt that hovered above him like a cloud.

Ten

The morning hadn't started out so well once she discovered that most of her clothes were either in the wash or had mysteriously disappeared—like perhaps into Jazz's overnight bag somewhere! Stomping down the hall to her friend's room, she dug through what looked like an entire wardrobe on the floor of Jazz's bedroom and pulled on the first two items she could find, angrily writing a threatening text in between to Jazz about bringing her clothes back in the same condition they left in.

Gemma walked into the kitchen to a surprising sight. Nash was standing at the stove, cooking breakfast.

'Morning,' he said, looking over at her.

'Morning,' Gemma said, moving across to put on the coffee.

'Sit. I'll get it,' he ordered before she could switch it on. He chuckled at her surprised expression. 'I'm not completely useless in the kitchen.'

'I didn't think you were,' she murmured.

'Okay, maybe I'm a little useless, but I think I can manage bacon and eggs.'

'I can make the coffee,' she suggested, desperate for her morning hit.

'No, no. I got it. Just sit. There's a paper there if you want to read it.'

She sat down, then reached across and unfolded the newspaper, keeping one eye on the pan spitting fat across the stovetop while Nash was at the other end of the kitchen gingerly going through the steps to set up the coffee machine. She bit back a smile as she saw him fumble with the pods, his big fingers carefully manoeuvring the round capsule into the little slot, a look of intense concentration on his face as he did so. Only the day before she'd seen those same hands rough-housing with his dogs and manhandling uncooperative sheep.

She read through the paper, taking note of the top stories in the district. Kids who'd won ribbons for various live-stock events; a proposal council was voting on for a new government-funded community centre; rumours that a coal seam gas company was sniffing around the area.

Nash finally placed the mug in front of her, almost sloshing its contents over the edge when he looked across and saw the bacon beginning to burn. He grabbed it off the heat, wincing as he burned his hand on the edge of the frypan. 'Ah . . . I hope you like your bacon crispy,' he said, shaking his hand.

'Do you want me to do the eggs?'

'No. I got it.'

'Okay,' she said, dropping her eyes back to the paper. She hadn't considered herself a control freak before, but during the last few weeks of having the kitchen to herself she'd clearly developed a kind of territorial feeling towards the place. She liked being in control of this one small aspect of her new situation. At least in here she didn't feel like a complete idiot, and it was a lot less scary than facing off with psychotic chooks and potentially being stampeded by man-eating cattle. And, in here, she knew Nash would at least appreciate her efforts.

They ate in silence, except for the crunching of crisp bacon, which in the end had them swapping grins across the table.

'Okay, so maybe I'll leave the cooking to you after all,' Nash said, looking a little sheepish.

'No, this is fine,' she hurried to reassure him. 'Really. I like bacon well cooked.'

He shook his head as he studied her. 'You don't have to do that, you know,' he finally said.

'Do what?'

'Always saying the right things to make sure you don't hurt anyone's feelings.' He put his cutlery down on his plate and pushed it away from him slightly.

'I'm not. I do like crunchy bacon,' she said defensively.

'Well, maybe you do. But you're also the first to jump in and smooth things over.' He shrugged. 'You don't like confrontation, do you?'

'I don't know many people who do,' said Gemma, dropping her gaze back to her almost empty plate.

'Jazz likes to stir up trouble,' Nash said calmly, taking a sip of his coffee as he watched her.

Gemma frowned at that. Her first instinct was to deny it, but then she realised he had a point. Jazz could be pretty obnoxious when she wanted to be, often saying things just to get a rise out of people. 'She doesn't mean anything by it.'

'Maybe, but you always rush in to try to fix everything, make sure no one's pride is hurt.'

'And that's a bad thing?'

'Not at all,' he said, shaking his head, 'but it just got me thinking about how you always try to head off disagreements.'

Nervously, she wondered where he was going with this observation. No, she didn't like confrontation. In the Northcote house you didn't argue or talk back. You just accepted the way things were and made the best of them. 'I'm a lover, not a fighter, I guess,' she muttered, standing up and reaching for his plate.

'You don't have to worry about hurting my feelings, that's all. You can tell me whatever's on your mind,' he finished almost self-consciously.

Gemma blinked uncertainly before summoning a faint smile and moving away from the table. It was obvious that Nash was not a man used to opening himself up to many people, and the fact that he had last night and then again this morning by initiating this whole breakfast thing told her he was trying to show her a side of himself usually kept private.

Together they cleared the table and packed the dishwasher. When they'd finished, Nash suddenly spoke up. 'Do you want to get out of here for a while? I'd like to show you something—a place. Want to come for a drive?'

Gemma bit back the leap of excitement she'd felt at his suggestion. 'Sure,' she said, trying to sound calm. 'Should I get changed?' She glanced down at her borrowed faded jeans and pink t-shirt with sparkly silver sequins that spelled out 'fabulicious' across the front.

'Nah, you'll be fine. Fabulicious, even,' he said, smirking and turning away. She made a face and followed him outside.

•

Gemma stepped out of the Land Cruiser, walked around to the front and watched as Nash climbed up onto the bonnet. They'd headed towards the ridge Nash had pointed out to her on her second day at Dunoon.

'Here, give me your hand,' he said. Hesitantly, she placed her hand in his much larger one and allowed him to pull her up to sit beside him.

'Just look at that view.' He indicated the valley below them and the rolling hills in the distance. 'Not many people get to look out their office window and see this.'

He was right, it was spectacular. Gum trees grew on the slopes of the ridge, and from here she could see the network of red dirt tracks they'd used to drive around the property. It still amazed her to look out over all this land and see no other sign of human occupation. There wasn't even a next-door neighbour in view.

'You're beautiful.'

His comment surprised her so much she would have slipped off the front of the bonnet if Nash's lightning reflexes hadn't saved her.

'You okay?' he asked, grinning.

'Yeah. Thanks.'

He still held her arm, and his hand was warm against her skin. His face was close to hers, and she noticed for the first time the flecks of green in his brown eyes. So caught up was she in this small but fascinating observation that she didn't realise he'd moved until warm lips touched her own. It was a tentative kiss, almost as though he were testing her reaction. It was such a contrast to the confident, often irritated Nash she'd known so far that it threw her off balance. He liked her? *Like* liked?

Her lips seemed to have a mind of their own, encouraging him to continue. The kiss deepened and, to avoid slipping off the bonnet again, Gemma wound her arms around his neck. The action drew a deep rumble from his chest, and a shiver of desire went through her. Never before had she made out on the bonnet of a vehicle—though of course his Land Cruiser was much larger than a normal car. The windscreen was cold against her back, but it failed to temper the heat she felt with her body pressed against Nash's. His hand had worked its way beneath her t-shirt, and the gentle soothing motion of his fingers sent another shiver through her. For all his gruffness there was something reassuringly gentle about him. No wonder his animals adored him.

His delicious scent—sweat and soap—and the warm smell of the bush that surrounded them mixed into a potent cocktail that set off a spontaneous explosion of lust and need so powerful she didn't feel as though she had any control over her actions. Never before had she had this kind of reaction to a man. The ferocity of it should have terrified her, but somehow with Nash it didn't. This felt so right, so good. She couldn't get enough of him.

Frustrated, wanting to feel him against her, she began to undo the buttons on his shirt, but he pushed her hands aside, reaching behind him to tug the shirt off. He broke their kiss only long enough to pull it over his head, and she found herself staring breathlessly up at him. Within seconds he was back, and she'd lost sight of his naked torso. What she'd managed to see had only made her heart beat faster. The skin on his chest was a couple of shades lighter than the darkly tanned skin of his forearms and neck. His chest was lightly covered in hair that narrowed to trail below his belt buckle, and his broad shoulders seemed even broader without clothing.

Gemma ran her hands across his back, feeling his muscles ripple as he eased her t-shirt higher. The sensation of the warm breeze on her skin and the trail of heat his hands left behind made her shudder in longing.

Suddenly, Nash froze. Then Gemma heard it too: the sound of an engine. He lifted his head and looked over his shoulder, then swore softly. Easing off her, he reached for his shirt. He pulled it quickly back over his head, slid off the front of the Land Cruiser and turned to help her down.

The sound of an approaching vehicle grew louder, and Gemma couldn't meet Nash's eyes as she slid off the bonnet down the length of his hard body. She felt him watching her, willing her to look at him, but the sudden invasion of their privacy was a rude awakening. What was she thinking? Had she really been just about to have sex on the front of a car in broad daylight? With her boss?

She tucked a few stray strands of hair behind her ear and tugged at the hem of her t-shirt to make sure she was respectable. Hoping that her cheeks weren't too flushed, she was grateful that Nash had moved away, already heading over to meet the quad bike that had appeared over the rise of the hill and now pulled to a stop in front of him.

'Mack,' she heard him say. Gemma looked up: on the back of the quad, sitting behind Mack, was Jazz, wearing a bright smile and looking none the worse for wear after her night out.

Feeling self-conscious, Gemma crossed to join them. She ignored Jazz's hitched eyebrow as she took in her dishevelled appearance and the familiar clothing she wore. The downside of having a best friend who knew you so well was that they could see through any front you tried to put up.

'What were you two up to?' asked Jazz with a grin.

'I was just showing Gemma some of the sights,' Nash answered smoothly.

'Oh, I bet you were,' Jazz said, her grin spreading even wider.

'What are you doing out here?' Gemma asked.

'Mack was taking me for a ride, after showing me some of *his* sights most of last night and this morning.' Jazz dropped her arm from Mack's waist to rest her hand on his thigh.

I will not let her embarrass me, Gemma told herself, determined not to turn bright red.

'We were just coming up to the ridge to take a look,' Mack said to Nash.

'No worries, you know you're always welcome here.' Nash shrugged.

'Yeah, look, sorry about Ben. It's taking him a while to fit back in. Don't take it personally. Mum and Dad are just about beside themselves trying to get through to him.'

'There's no need for you to apologise on your brother's behalf, Mack,' Nash said. 'There's never been any love lost between Ben and me. Can't see that changing anytime soon.'

Mack nodded in response, and a silence fell between the two men.

'Come on, let's leave these two to get back to *sightseeing*,' leered Jazz. 'I won't be home tonight, so don't wait up for me,' she called, moving her arms back up to Mack's waist as he kicked the bike into gear and pulled away.

Gemma stared after them, dreading having to face Nash after what had happened before Jazz and Mack had interrupted, and not sure if she should be frustrated or relieved they'd turned up when they had. 'Sorry about Jazz,' she said awkwardly. 'She tends to jump to conclusions.'

'Of all the times for her to be unduly observant,' he said, rubbing the back of his neck, and scuffing the toe of his boot into the dirt.

Gemma wasn't used to seeing Nash anything other than confident. To see him so unsure of himself made her forget her own nerves for a moment.

'Probably a good thing they came along when they did,' he went on, frowning. 'You could slap me with a sexual harassment suit.'

'I wouldn't do that,' she said, horrified he would even suggest it.

'Yeah, well, it would have complicated everything, I guess.'

Gemma's jaw had dropped and she stared at him in disbelief. What sort of person did he think she was?

He looked up at her, for the first time seeming to register that she was annoyed by his comment. 'I didn't mean to imply you would . . . I was just—'

'Forget it.'

An uncomfortable silence fell between them, with the cawing of two crows in the distance the only sound for miles around.

'I guess we should get back,' Nash said eventually, stalking to the Land Cruiser without looking to see if Gemma was following.

Had she overreacted? She didn't feel as though she had, but a small part of her had kind of hoped he'd pick up where they left off, only for him to be *relieved* that they'd been interrupted. And then to insinuate that he was concerned she'd hit him up for sexual harassment? That was really too much for her fragile ego to handle. *Maybe he'd been joking?* a little voice suggested hopefully, but she dismissed it quickly. He didn't want complications, she reminded herself bitterly, and nothing said a guy found you attractive quite like his relief at dodging a sexual harassment suit.

It was a silent drive back to the house.

Eleven

It was amazing how many things you could find to do around a property if you wanted to avoid someone. After they returned home from the ridge, Nash had dropped her back at the house and mumbled something about catching up on some work. He'd driven off in his four-wheel drive and she hadn't seen him again till late that night. Since then, Gemma had thrown herself into the chores with a vengeance that left Jazz scratching her head.

'What's got into you?' Jazz finally asked when she tracked Gemma down outside the chook pen.

'Nothing. Why?' Gemma said, pulling on a pair of long garden gloves.

'Well, for starters, you're volunteering to get the eggs from under a psychotic chook.'

'I think I figured out what's wrong with her. She's broody.'

'Broody? Or moody?'

'Broody. You know, clucky, *literally*. She wants to keep her eggs and sit on them.'

'How do you know that?'

'I googled it, of course.'

'So what are you going to do?'

'I'm going to catch her and put her in a cage for a few days.' Gemma set her shoulders back and took a deep breath. When Jazz was strangely silent, she turned her head to find her friend staring at her in horror. 'What?'

'You're going in there to *catch* her?'

'Unless you want to do it?'

'No way. That bird is possessed. And I told you, chooks freak me out.'

'That's what I figured,' Gemma said, pulling on the quad-bike helmet.

Jazz looked at her askance. 'Do you think the helmet is a touch of overkill?'

Gemma wasn't taking any chances. She picked up a sturdy, long-handled fishing net she'd uncovered in the shed behind the garden, then turned rather awkwardly and gave the thumbs-up. 'I'm going in,' she said, before snapping down the clear visor and opening the chook pen gate.

The website had said to isolate the chook in a separate pen in order to keep it out of the laying box. When Gemma had come outside to investigate, she'd found a smaller cage propped up against the back of the chook pen, and had decided that this would be the perfect place to keep Glennie away from the nesting boxes.

Approaching the door to the laying pen, she peeked inside cautiously. As usual, the other chooks had already laid their eggs and gone, leaving Glennie sitting in the last box. The evil beady eyes remained fixed on Gemma as she quickly collected the eggs in a bucket.

'This is for your own good, bird,' Gemma said softly as she edged closer. 'I'm pretty sure if Nash knew you were behaving like this you'd be tomorrow night's dinner, so you should be grateful it's me in here and not him. Easy now,' she said, praying there wouldn't be too much flapping and squawking involved.

Her prayers were not answered. When she'd got within arm's length, Glennie let loose with a terrible, almost human scream, flew at her and began pecking. Gemma screamed right along with her, but somehow held her ground. She lifted the net, dropped it over the frantically squawking bird and ran from the pen. Inserting the net into the cage, she gave it a shake and watched as Glennie tumbled out in a less than dignified manner.

As Gemma slammed the door shut she could hear Jazz cheering outside the chook pen. Turning, Gemma lifted the visor and pumped the air as though she'd just won a gold medal. Jogging triumphantly out through the gate, though, her grin slipped as she looked over and saw Nash leaning against the side of the machinery shed, arms folded across his chest, staring at her as though she'd lost her mind.

Jazz turned to see what had caught Gemma's eye. 'Oh, look, there's lover boy—I'd better make myself scarce in case he's got a thing for women dressed up like Evel Knievel.' She laughed at Gemma's mortified expression. 'Just act natural.

Maybe he won't say anything,' she said without bothering to hide her amusement as she sauntered away. 'Just off to check on the calves,' she told Nash as she passed him.

Gemma leaned the net against the wire of the pen and removed the helmet, then quickly gathered her hair into a ponytail. She wiped her arm across her face to mop off the worst of the sweat that had accumulated inside the headgear, and stifled a groan as Nash made his way towards her.

'Hi.' He came to a stop in front of her.

'Hi.' Had she not been sidetracked by her embarrassment, she may have been able to give this moment the significance it deserved, considering this was the first voluntary conversation they'd had in two days.

'Interesting technique you've got there,' he said with a completely straight face, looking over at the still squawking bird in the cage.

'She's broody,' Gemma said, trying to sound confident.

'I see. Had a lot to do with broody chooks in the past, have you?'

'Well, you know. A bit,' she said, then rolled her eyes. 'Oh okay, I googled it.' She glanced down at the motorbike helmet by her feet. 'What could possibly have given it away?'

'You used a guinea pig cage,' he told her matter-of-factly. For the first time since their breakfast the other morning, Gemma saw a hint of that carefree Nash she'd begun to like way too much.

'Well, where do you *usually* keep chooks when they're broody?'

'The freezer,' he said. 'But your way looks far more ... practical.'

Gemma smiled in spite of herself. It was just nice to be speaking with him again.

'Look, about the other day,' said Nash, his gaze shifting from her face to the ground. 'I know we said there was nothing to talk about. But I think we need to . . . clear the air.'

He looked so uncomfortable that, in the midst of her own hurt feelings, Gemma felt sorry for him. Clearly for him what had happened between them had been nothing more than a momentary impulse on his part, which he now regretted and was having trouble letting her down gently. 'It was a mistake,' she blurted to put him out of his misery. 'We were both tired from being up all night talking about some pretty deep stuff. It's okay, I understand.'

He looked at her silently, his eyes searching hers.

'It's not like it's going to happen again,' she said briskly. 'I mean, like you said, I'm basically your employee and that would be weird. So, you know, it's okay.' There, she'd cut the poor guy loose.

'Yeah,' he said at last, nodding and giving a relieved smile. 'I guess that's what it was. I just wanted to make sure you were okay. It feels as though you've been trying to avoid me since then.'

'I've just been busy doing . . . farm stuff.' *Oh yeah, way to go, Gem*, she thought, *impress him with all your big important jobs, like collecting the eggs and cleaning out the dog cages! It wasn't like he was doing anything super important around the place.*

'Right,' he said agreeably, moving his hands from his hips to his front pockets and then folding them across his chest, as though he wasn't quite sure what to do with them all of a sudden. It would have been kind of cute if it wasn't for the fact that he was inadvertently stomping all over her self-esteem by now regretting their close call on the bonnet of his car.

'Well, anyway. I better go and do something,' he finally said, throwing an arm out in the vague direction of the shed.

As Gemma watched him walk away, Glennie gave a loud, indignant squawk. 'Oh shut up, what would you know?' she muttered, picking up the bucket of eggs and heading back to the house.

●

'Hey, love, I thought I might see you in here today,' Wendy greeted Gemma as she walked into the grocery store bright and early the next day. 'Your quince paste turned up. So, what's on the menu this week?'

'Oh, good. I was hoping it would. It's for the lamb and quince tagine I'm making.' Gemma pulled out her shopping list. 'I could have used some other kind of jam, I guess, but I wanted it to be right.'

'Always the perfectionist.' Wendy shook her head. 'Darrell was talking to Nash the other day and he was raving about your cooking. You've certainly made an impression there.' She winked, looking at Gemma knowingly.

Gemma blushed. 'It's not like that, Wendy. I enjoy cooking and it's the least I can do to make up for the hassle it must be to have Jazz and me staying with him.'

'Trust me, if Nash Whittaker was feeling inconvenienced you'd know about it. He must have mellowed a little. Maybe it's your cooking,' Wendy said, chuckling when Gemma rolled her eyes.

An elderly couple arrived at the checkout and began unpacking their trolley and Gemma moved out of the way so Wendy could serve them.

'Gemma, this is Mavis and Fred Smith,' Wendy introduced as she began scanning their groceries. 'They're your neighbours. This is Gemma; she and her friend are helping out over at Nash's place for a few weeks,' Wendy went on to explain to the older pair eyeing Gemma curiously.

'Ah,' Fred said with a nod. 'So you're the young lass who has Nash all hot and bothered then?' he said with a chuckle.

Gemma felt a blush creeping not so subtly up her throat. 'I don't know about that,' she stammered, awkwardly.

'Fred, stop it. Leave the poor girl alone. Don't mind this silly old coot,' Mavis said, shaking her head at her husband. Despite the reprimand she was giving him, it was clear Mavis loved her husband by the tolerant glance they exchanged.

'I'm told you're a bit of an expert marker now?'

Oh God, Gemma thought in dismay. *Please don't tell me he's been telling everyone about that day?*

'Nash was very proud of the way you handled it, spoke very highly of you,' Mavis cut in, reaching over to give her a reassuring pat on the arm. 'It's not easy coming out here when you're not used to this life,' she went on. 'I know what it's like to be an outsider. I've been here almost fifty years now and I'm still not considered a local,' she said with a chuckle.

'Best thing I ever did was whisk this one away from the bright lights of the city and bring her out here,' Fred added.

'You're just lucky I decided to stay,' she shot back at him before looking back at Gemma. 'There was many a time I felt like turning around and going back, let me tell you.'

'But you stayed because you loved me,' Fred shrugged.

'Well, I must have,' Mavis said, sounding a little flustered at such a public declaration, but not altogether upset about it.

Gemma couldn't help but smile at the couple and hoped one day she would have a bond as strong as theirs with someone.

'Best cook in the district,' Fred went on with a wink at Gemma and Wendy.

'Oh, go on with ya,' Mavis said, pushing his arm and blushing slightly.

Gemma and Wendy exchanged a grin before Gemma said goodbye and got back to her shopping list.

The shop was quiet when Gemma had finished, and Wendy walked her out. 'It must be lovely to be able to eat out in some of those fancy restaurants in the city,' she sighed as she passed the plastic bags to Gemma at the ute.

'I have to admit, that's one thing I've been missing. Not that there's anything wrong with Bingorra,' Gemma added quickly.

Wendy waved a hand in the air. 'Don't feel bad. I don't know how you gave it all up to come out here in the first place.'

'I was wondering where everyone goes to eat out around here.'

'You've only got two choices—the pub or the twenty-four-hour servo up the road,' said Wendy. 'Don't get me wrong, the pub's nice, but Lyn's been cooking there for the last thirty years and I'm pretty sure the menu hasn't changed once in that whole time. Otherwise, you have to drive into Curranjuck, but most people can't be bothered driving that far late at night.'

'That must be hard,' Gemma said with a frown.

'So anyway, tell me what these fancy restaurants are like in Sydney. What's your favourite place?'

Gemma grinned as she placed the last bag in the back of the ute and dusted off her hands. 'There's a lot of seafood places down on the harbour. And the big-name chefs all have signature restaurants that are amazing to go to, even if it's just for the experience of dining in a celebrity chef's restaurant. If you ever get to the city you should try to do it. You usually have to book in well ahead of time, but it's so worth it.' Gemma realised she was gushing, but it wasn't often she got to talk about her passion with a fellow cooking enthusiast.

'But I guess my favourite place to eat,' she continued, 'would be this little place called Nirvana which serves European food, mainly French. On the weekends the chef, Micca, gives classes. I've taken quite a few of them and got to know him pretty well. That's another thing you should do one day. You can do guided cooking tours of the city and do all these amazing cooking classes and then eat what you create. That's how I've spent most of my free weekends over the last few years. You pick up all sorts of great tips.'

'You make me want to organise a trip to the city right now,' said Wendy longingly.

'You should,' Gemma urged her. 'Call me up any time you come to town and I'll go along with you. We'd have lots of fun.'

'That's a thought.' A smile lit up Wendy's face as she pondered the idea. 'I think I'll do it. I'll have to start saving now, though,' she added, stepping away from the back of the ute with a wave.

'I better get moving. I left Jazz and Nash alone. I hope they haven't killed each other.' Gemma opened the driver's side door and waved goodbye.

As she drove home past the endless fields of multicoloured crops, Gemma found herself thinking back over her conversation with Wendy. *Call me up any time you come to town.* It felt strange to think that sooner rather than later she'd be back in the city and all this would be a memory. Funny how she was the one who'd been reluctant to come out here, and now the thought of leaving made her sad.

The rest of the trip passed in a blur of paddocks and the sound of wind rushing through her open window as a strange melancholy settled on her.

Twelve

Gemma smiled as she locked the gate of the dog pen behind her, listening to the snuffles of dogs digging into their feed.

Her stomach rumbled, and she realised she'd been so busy today that she'd forgotten to have lunch. The night before she'd taken a frozen chook out of the freezer, intending to roast it for tonight's dinner. Automatically, she thought about Glennie, still in the guinea pig cage. She really hoped the angry bird got over her chook PMT soon; quite frankly, Gemma wasn't sure she was ready to cook someone she knew.

But she hadn't even reached the gate to the house yard when she smelled the tantalising aroma of barbecued meat wafting in the air. Following her nose, she discovered Nash standing in front of an old brick fireplace, turning steaks on a hotplate. She sniffed appreciatively.

'I know what you're thinking,' he said, holding up his tongs as he turned to face her. 'But I'm better at steak than eggs.'

'I wasn't thinking anything of the sort,' she denied.

He looked at her narrowly. 'Anyway, I feel a need to redeem myself, and everyone knows a male can't bugger up a barbecue, right?'

'Right,' she said keeping a straight face. 'Do you want me to make a salad?'

'I was thinking we could just whack it on some bread.'

'Oh, okay,' she stammered. *Whack it on a slice of bread? No salad?*

He shook his head and gave her a tolerant smile. 'But if you feel a need to add some rabbit food to it, then by all means go for it.'

'It's good for you,' she protested weakly.

'So's jogging, but I've survived this long without doing that.'

'I'll add some bacon to it,' she compromised.

He let out a long sigh, but she caught the smile on his face as he turned back to the sizzling meat on the hotplate. 'The deal clincher . . . bacon. You fight dirty.'

She smiled as she walked into the house. She could always cook the chook tomorrow night. She'd been wanting to try out that new bacon, fetta and spinach recipe, and now she could. She just hoped there was some bacon left in the freezer.

•

'Where are you going? Nash is cooking tonight,' Gemma said as Jazz walked past in a pair of Gemma's best jeans and wearing make-up.

'Into town.'

She'd been about to mention the fact Jazz was wearing *her* clothes again but her answer distracted her. 'Again?'

'Ah, yes, again. I'm young and single and I have *a life*.' Jazz shot Gemma a disapproving look. 'Why don't you go and get dressed and come with me?'

'No, thanks.'

'Your loss. Have a blast here with Mr Funbags.' Jazz waved her fingertips as she left the room.

She was having a good time, damn it!

'Jazz's gone into town, she won't be eating with us tonight,' she told Nash, coming back outside with a plate.

'She's quite the party animal,' he said, transferring the meat from the barbecue to the plate. 'You didn't want to go with her this time?'

'No. I don't go out that much, even in Sydney. I'm a bit of a homebody, I guess. I'm *boring*, according to Jazz.'

'I beg to differ,' Nash said with a grin.

Gemma sent Nash a wary glance. *What was he doing?* They'd just agreed that their last encounter had been a mistake, so why would he be flirting with her? Gemma cleared her throat and continued. 'Anyway, how could I pass up this feast?'

'You know what they say, the way to a woman's heart is through her—'

'Rib cage?'

'I don't think that's exactly the proverb I'm thinking of.'

'I don't think it's actually supposed to be the *woman's* heart. Isn't it usually the man's heart?'

'Well, men are easy. It doesn't take much to get us eating out of your hand.'

'As long as you add bacon.'

'Right.'

They decided to eat outside. The sun was sinking and the evening was still warm. Soon Gemma felt herself unwind and relax. She could really get used to this, she thought, then stopped herself in alarm; she knew damn well *this* was not something she would be getting used to.

'Everything alright?' Nash asked suddenly, and she looked up guiltily.

'Yep. Couldn't be better.' She smiled. 'This steak melts in your mouth.'

He ignored her compliment about the meat and continued to look at her closely. 'What were you thinking about just now? One minute you were smiling and the next you weren't. It's not about what happened the other day, is it? I know we agreed to forget about it . . . but I can't, and I don't know what you're thinking.'

Thank God for that, Gemma thought. He'd think she was an idiot if he knew what she was thinking half the time. *Wait a minute, did he just say he couldn't stop thinking about what had happened the other day?* She quickly tried to replay his words in her head, but he was talking again.

She watched in surprise as he got up and paced before her. 'Look, I think we get on pretty well, but every now and then I see you frowning, like you're remembering something bad. If it's about what happened, I want to know. I don't want you to feel weird around me.'

'I don't feel weird around you—well, not *that* weird.' If he only knew how heart-stoppingly strange he made her feel sometimes, she thought, hoping her cheeks wouldn't betray her. 'I mean, apart from the whole incident with the chook.' She shrugged, walking across to put her plate with the other things waiting to be carried inside.

'Okay, that *was* kinda weird,' he agreed with a smile. 'But I've got used to expecting the unexpected where you and Jazz are concerned.'

At least he was smiling about it.

'I really like being out here,' she said honestly. 'I didn't think I would. This was all Jazz's big dream, but I've grown to like it.'

'I'm glad. And I never thought I'd hear myself saying this, but it hasn't turned out to be altogether too much of a pain that you both turned up when you did,' he said, moving to stand beside her.

Gemma laughed at that. There were times when she knew he'd probably like to strangle them both, but clearly they were at least doing something right. 'So, does that translate into "You've been a huge help and I wouldn't have survived without you"?'

'Let's not get too carried away.'

Gemma glanced up, her smile slowly fading as she caught the look on his face. She felt pulled by an invisible magnet, unable to think straight. As she swayed forward, into his hard chest, she caught the smell of smoke from the barbecue mixed with Nash's unique, heady scent, and all her good intentions were swept away. A small groan escaped her at the first touch of his warm mouth against her own. She braced her hands on the edge of the bricked workbench behind her in order to hold herself upright as he cupped her face, holding her firmly in place while he proceeded to kiss her senseless.

The edge of the bricks pressed against the small of her back, but she liked it. It reminded her that this was real, not just some figment of her overstimulated mind.

Something brushed the back of her bare leg, and Gemma pulled away an instant before Nash let out a startled expletive and began shaking his leg as though doing some kind of demented dance move. It took a second for Gemma to look down and see that something large and furry had attached itself to Nash's leg. She gasped. 'Nash, stop! You'll hurt him.'

'Hurt *him*?' Nash paused momentarily in the midst of cursing the animal who still clung determinedly to his denim-clad leg, and gave Gemma a disbelieving glare.

'Stand still and stop yelling. You're scaring him.' She bent down to detach the feline from the stiff fabric. 'His claws are stuck,' she crooned.

'Yeah. You'll find them about two inches into my leg,' Nash told her through his gritted teeth.

'I'm working as fast as I can,' she told him, lifting the last claw from Nash's leg. Horse was gone as soon as his paws touched the ground, obviously warned off by Nash's tone.

'That cat's a menace,' Nash said huffily. 'That's not the first time he's jumped me, you know.'

'He was just looking for his milk. Anyway, it's your own fault,' she added. 'If you were nicer to him, he'd like you.'

'When I catch him he's going to kitty heaven.'

'If you lay one finger on that cat—' Gemma narrowed her eyes.

'What?'

'You might accidentally get a bad case of food poisoning,'

she told him with a haughty flick of her hair as she turned away to collect up the plates.

'You wouldn't dare.'

'Better not try me.'

'You better make sure your cat learns a few manners,' he warned, heading inside to clean up the scratches and leaving her alone in the dark.

It was a good thing Horse came along when he had. When would she stop falling for that sexy smile of his and those mind-numbing kisses? They only ever led to trouble! Didn't they work out last time it was a mistake to cross that line between employer and employee?

•

Nash was loading the last of the feed onto the back of the ute when Gemma walked into the shed the following afternoon.

'I'm just heading into town for a while. I'll be back for dinner,' she said as she manoeuvred a box onto the front passenger seat of her vehicle.

'What have you got there?' Nash asked, coming over to open the driver's door for her.

'It's beef bourguignon. I cooked dinner for Wendy and her family.'

'Wendy?'

'Wendy from the grocery store. When I went into the shop today, her husband said she'd been in hospital for a few days. I'm not sure why, he didn't go into any details, so I didn't like to ask. Anyway, one day she was telling me how much she loved to cook but that she was too tired after work to bother, so I thought I'd take her dinner.'

Nash didn't say anything, just considered her silently.

'Is that okay?' she asked, suddenly nervous.

'Sure. That's a good idea,' he said, 'but take the Land Cruiser. I have no idea how this damn thing of yours has managed to stay in one piece for so long; it's a deathtrap waiting to happen.' He eyed the old bomb in disbelief.

She couldn't very well argue with him on that, but it was the best they could do in a squeeze. 'Well, if you're sure?'

'I'm sure,' he said, reaching for the box while she switched vehicles before passing it back to her and stepping away to shut the door.

Gemma rolled down the window.

'It was a hysterectomy,' he said.

'Excuse me?' Gemma said with a frown.

'Wendy. That's what she went into hospital for.'

'How do you know that?'

'From Darrell, her husband. I was talking to him at the feed store the other day.'

'Oh.' Well, of course they would have been discussing Darrell's wife having a hysterectomy in the feed store.

'I've known them a long time,' Nash added dryly, as though reading her thoughts.

'Do you think Darrell will mind me dropping this off?'

'Nah, I think he'll appreciate it. But if it tastes as good as it smells it might not make it home. Maybe you should just drop it off at the house instead.'

'I don't know where she lives.'

'Can you wait about ten minutes? I'll just finish up here and come with you.'

'She might not appreciate having a stranger turn up on her doorstep unannounced,' Gemma said, worrying at her bottom lip. This wasn't what she'd planned. She'd intended to just drop the box at the shop and come back home.

'She'll be right,' he said, waving off her concern and heading back to the ute to finish loading.

Forty-five minutes later, they pulled up in front of a weatherboard house at the end of a quiet street. Nash opened his door and reached down to lift the box out of the car.

Gemma followed him through the gate and up to the front door. He opened the screen door and stuck his head inside to call out a hello. It had taken Gemma a little while to get used to the doors at Dunoon never being locked, and it surprised her that no one seemed to lock their doors in town either.

Wendy's voice floated through the house. 'I'm out the back.'

Gemma followed Nash down a hallway and out into a long galley kitchen. A glass sliding door opened up onto a timber deck outside. Wendy was resting on an outdoor lounge, reading a cookbook. The sight brought a smile to Gemma's face.

'Nash, Gemma! Well, this is a surprise.' Wendy smiled at them brightly as they stepped out onto the deck. 'Excuse the mess inside. I was told to rest up for a few days, and who am I to argue with the professionals?'

'Darrell reckons you were faking it just to get a few days off work,' said Nash, smiling and leaning over to kiss Wendy on the cheek.

'Faking it? If it wasn't for his damn giant genes and having to push out three enormous, watermelon-headed children I wouldn't be in this situation to start with,' she shot back with a twinkle in her eye. 'So he can damn well handle the shop on his own for a while. I've earned a break.'

Gemma's eyes widened as her mind filled with images of watermelons and she contemplated the anatomical contortions required. Catching her expression, Wendy started chuckling. 'I was exaggerating, Gem. It's not that bad.'

'Oh. Well, I suspect it'll be quite a while before I have to think about all that.' Aware of Nash's amused glance, Gemma felt herself blushing. 'We've brought you dinner,' she went on quickly.

'You didn't have to do that!' said Wendy. 'But thank you. That's a lovely thought.' She looked surprised and touched.

Gemma shrugged. 'I know you said your family didn't really like gourmet food so I made a stew that's really flavoursome but hasn't got too many spices. I hope that's okay.'

'It sounds divine. Thanks so much, love.'

'I wrote out the recipe and stuck it in the box, in case they liked it and you felt like making it when you're feeling better.'

'This one's a keeper, Nash,' said Wendy with a grin.

Gemma felt heat working its way up her throat and she wasn't game to look at Nash. An *employee*, she told herself firmly, that's what Wendy meant. She was a good employee.

They left shortly afterwards, since Wendy's watermelon-headed children were due home from school any minute. As curious as she was to see them for herself, Gemma wasn't sure she would be able to without wincing.

Thirteen

A few days later, Gemma came out of the house with some food and drinks for her and Jazz to take while they did their morning jobs, and froze as she spotted what was sitting in the back of the ute.

'What are *they* doing in there?' she asked, watching two of the chocolate-coloured dogs vying for Jazz's attention as she rubbed their heads affectionately.

'I can't see why they can't come out with us for a bit of a run. Look at them, they're on their best behaviour.'

'No, Jazz. We have to get them back into their pen.'

'Look at them, Gem.' Jazz turned one of the adorable hairy faces towards her. 'They're born to run, not stay locked up in a pen all day. What harm can it do to take them out with us? We'll have them back before his lordship even knows they were gone.'

Gemma eyed the three dogs. She had to admit they did look happy to be out of the pen, but she still couldn't shake the feeling that this was a very bad idea. Seeing that Jazz was determined, though, she gave up arguing and climbed into the ute. There was no talking to Jazz when she set her mind on something. 'It's on your head if this thing all goes wrong,' she muttered, staring ahead through the windscreen.

'Oh, lighten up. What could go wrong? They're the most well-behaved dogs I've ever seen in my life.'

Maybe she was right. They *were* incredibly well-behaved. Watching them with Nash, Gemma had noticed that it only took one word or hand signal from their master for the energetic, active little dogs to drop and wait for an order; it was as if they were completely in sync with Nash's every thought and movement.

The morning went smoothly, and by midday they'd nearly completed their work. The dogs were happy to sniff around fence posts and under fallen logs, chase lizards and snap at insects. Gemma, relieved, was beginning to think that Jazz was right: maybe she did worry too much.

They pulled up at the last trough for the day. As Gemma climbed the fence to check how much water was in the trough, she saw a flash of brown race past her. 'Jazz, the dogs!' she yelled, watching in alarm as the three streaks of lightning headed for a mob of cattle grazing at the far end of the paddock. The sound of alarmed mooing rose from the cows, who shifted uneasily as they saw the dogs approaching.

The dogs began circling and barking, moving the animals in a loud, protesting cluster. Then they started snapping at the cows' ankles, and soon the cattle had picked up their pace and were heading up through the paddock at a brisk trot.

Gemma heard Jazz calling the dogs and whistling for them to come back, but they ignored her, apparently too caught up in the excitement. They swung the herd around and chased them along the boundary fence.

'How do we stop them?' Gemma shouted at Jazz, who stared after the cattle in dismay.

'I don't know. They won't listen to me. What does Nash do to call them off?'

'I'm not sure, he just whistles or something, I think.' The cattle were now running full pelt, clouds of dust filling the air. And still the dogs worked together to keep them running and turning.

'Jazz, we've got to do something!' Gemma cried. 'The cows are freaking out. I'm going to radio Nash.'

Jazz climbed through the fence, setting off at a jog as she continued to call the dogs.

As Gemma leaned into the cabin of the ute to pick up the handset, she caught a movement from the corner of her eye and straightened, shading her eyes with her hand. A quad bike was heading their way; as it drew closer, she made out the rider, and the furious expression on his face. At least she wouldn't have to call him on the radio, she thought, watching as he roared along the last of the bumpy track towards them.

'What the hell happened?'

'We can't get the dogs to stop chasing the cattle. We've tried calling them but they won't listen.' Gemma followed him at a jog as he strode to the fence and swung himself through the barbed wire with practised ease.

Nash let out an ear-splitting whistle, and instantly the three dogs dropped to the ground. He turned and glared at Gemma. 'What the hell were the dogs doing out here in the first place?'

'W-we thought they looked sad locked in their cage and we figured we could take them out with us for some, um, exercise,' Gemma stammered.

'Exercise? Does this look like exercise to you?' Nash demanded. 'These are working animals. They're also fairly young, which means I'm still training them. They'd have run those cattle until they dropped. You have no idea how bloody lucky you were they found the cattle and not the sheep ready to drop lambs any day. I would have lost my entire income if I'd lost those sheep. This is not some game. This is my livelihood you're screwing with here.'

'We're sorry,' said Gemma, wishing she could sink into the ground and disappear. There were so many things that could go wrong out here, things she couldn't even begin to comprehend.

Nash gave another whistle and the dogs trotted quickly to his side, clearly sensing his anger, their tails between their legs and their heads drooping. Gemma stood by helplessly as Nash stalked to the rear of the ute, opened a large toolbox bolted to the floor, took out some chains and hooked them to more bolts on the tray. He called the dogs up into the back of the ute and secured each one to a chain before heading back to his quad bike. 'Get them home and give them water straight away. Think you can manage that? I'll speak to you both later,' he added over his shoulder. 'This isn't over.'

The two girls watched as the quad bike sped off. The dogs panted noisily in the rear of the ute behind them.

'Come on, they're thirsty,' said Gemma grimly.

'Why didn't he just water them here?' said Jazz.

'Jazz, get in the bloody ute,' Gemma snapped. 'And don't even think about undoing those leads.' The last thing they needed was for the dogs to pick up where they had left off, herding the exhausted-looking cattle.

'You're beginning to sound just like Nash.'

'We're in so much trouble, Jazz.'

'Nah. He'll have cooled off by the time we see him tonight,' Jazz said.

Gemma turned on her. 'Did you not hear what he said? We could have ruined him. We could have killed animals.'

'But we didn't,' Jazz said airily, climbing up into the driver's seat.

'How can you just brush this off?' Gemma looked at her in disbelief, reluctantly climbing in beside her.

'Because worrying about it will just give you ulcers. And where's the good in that? Okay, so he was pissed off at us. He'll go back to his nice air-conditioned tractor, listen to some music and calm down. Meanwhile, you'll fret all day about what he'll say tonight and worry yourself sick. Just stop it. He was angry. He'll get over it.'

Arrrghhh! thought Gemma. It should be legal to strangle someone if you had a good enough reason! Jazz was driving her insane, surely and not so slowly.

•

That afternoon, Gemma parked the rust bucket in front of the post office and locked the door, though more out of habit than any real worry that someone might steal it. She needed to get away from the farm for a while. Not only was Jazz driving her crazy, but she also had no desire to face Nash just now. She'd come into town to buy phone and internet credit as well as send a postcard back to her parents.

Inside the post office, she waited while an older lady chatted to the man behind the desk. Gemma didn't actually mind the wait; the air-conditioning was a welcome relief after the hot sun outside. She couldn't help overhearing the old woman's loud conversation.

'I saw that Henderson boy out with some girl on the weekend. Probably some foreign backpacker type, I'd imagine. What is the world coming to, Michael? Once, we knew everyone in this town, but nowadays people are blowing in from all over the place.'

Well, this is awkward, Gemma thought. She had just glanced at the door, wondering if she could surreptitiously sidle out before they realised she was there, when it opened and in walked Ben. The conversation stopped immediately, and the two people at the counter eyed her and Ben suspiciously before swapping a look that clearly said, *See! Blow-ins!*

'I thought I saw you heading in here,' Ben said, coming to a stop behind her.

With a nervous glance towards the pair at the counter, she managed a smile before replying. 'I just had a few things I wanted to do in town. I won't be staying long.'

'But you have time for a drink?'

'It's a bit early for a drink, isn't it?' She knew her tone was censorious, but she didn't care. Both times she'd seen Ben he'd been drinking and she wasn't too keen on repeating the performance of their previous encounter.

'Well, I guess we could go and have a coffee at the servo,' Ben said, although he looked as though he couldn't quite believe he was suggesting it.

'I really shouldn't be gone too long. I didn't tell anyone where I was going.'

Ben raised an eyebrow. 'Don't tell me Whittaker owns you? I thought you just worked for him?'

'Of course he doesn't *own* me,' Gemma snapped. 'But I do *work* for the man, so I can't sit around having coffee all day.'

'Relax. One quick coffee won't make any difference.'

'I don't know. I still have to finish what I came in here to do.' She was uncomfortably aware that the pair at the counter were hanging on every word of their conversation.

'I can wait.'

What was this guy's problem? From the two occasions they'd met, she already knew they had nothing in common. She thought Jazz was probably more his type, but unfortunately for Ben his younger brother had got in first. Turning her back on him, she gave the post office worker an irritated glance, wishing he'd stop gawking at her and finish serving his customer.

Eventually the woman completed her purchase, with much dramatic whispering and several meaningful looks. Gemma didn't much care what they said, she was just relieved to buy her credit and flee.

Ben gallantly held the door open for her and led the way back down the street towards the service station that also doubled as the town's only cafe. They found a table and ordered two coffees.

'I can't stay long,' Gemma told him again, firmly this time.

Two other tables were occupied, and Gemma knew she wasn't imagining the covert looks being slid their way. She really hoped the coffee wouldn't be too hot: she wanted to scull that sucker and get the hell out of here.

'So, did you ask Whittaker about Kim?'

The question surprised her; although he sounded calm, she saw that his jaw was tense.

'I did. It's very sad.' What was he waiting for? The way he watched her, as though looking for some kind of reaction, was unsettling.

'He acts like he was the victim in all this,' Ben went on, frowning. 'But if it wasn't for him I wouldn't have had to drive her home that night. Did he tell you he ditched her at that party after they had a blue, and told her to go home with me? What was I s'posed to do?' he demanded. 'Leave her out there? He wasn't going to take her home.'

Gemma didn't want to get into this with him, and especially not in front of an audience. Why was the coffee taking so long? she wondered irritably. Had they gone all the way to damn Colombia to hand-pick the stuff or what? 'Hindsight's a wonderful thing,' she said vaguely. She knew the words were completely inadequate and she felt angry that he was putting her in this position. Did he want her to somehow try to make him feel better about something she really had no business knowing in the first place?

'It's always been like this with him,' Ben went on. 'He's always making out that he's so hard done by. Don't let him fool you into believing any of his shit, okay? Kim made that mistake. I'd hate to see anyone else fall for it.'

'This is really none of my business, but maybe it's time that you let some of your anger go?' Impatience made Gemma speak more sharply than usual.

Ben gave a snort and leaned back in his chair, folding his arms across his chest as he studied her. 'So he's already got to you. That's what he does. Everyone thinks he's some kind of hero and I'm the big bad villain. I was a kid! I made a mistake. I wasn't the only one who used to drink and drive—only that one time it went wrong. Not a day goes by that I don't regret driving that night and that Kim died, but I did my time. What do they want from me, for Christ's sake? They want me hung or something? I did my bloody time. I deserve a second chance.'

Ben was cut short by the waitress finally appearing with their coffees. After she'd gone, an awkward silence settled between them and Gemma took a quick sip of her coffee to fill the gap. The sooner she drank it, the sooner she could get out of here.

'You know what the real kick in the guts is though?' he asked, although clearly not expecting an answer from her when he continued after barely a heartbeat. 'Seeing the look of disappointment in my parents' eyes. Every. Single. Day.'

Gemma swallowed painfully over a sudden lump in her throat that followed his gruff admission. 'I'm sure things will settle down soon,' she said at last, although of course she had no idea if they would. Looking around this town, it seemed not a lot had changed over the years; maybe they just hung on to things a lot longer out here.

'Ever feel like you just don't belong anywhere anymore?' he asked.

All too often, she thought to herself. She gave a small nod of her head. 'Sometimes.'

'Well, I feel it all the time. It sucks.'

Gemma felt some of her previous irritation lessen a little, and they drank their coffee in silence, listening to the chatter from the other tables. A wave of sympathy washed through her as looked across at Ben's downcast eyes and the glimmer of uncertainty she caught when he glanced up briefly. She couldn't imagine what it would be like to go to prison so young, to spend six years of your life there and then to find yourself back out in mainstream society—and not just any society but a small rural community where everyone knew exactly who you were and what you'd done. If the guilt you carried around inside yourself wasn't bad enough, the weight of those stares wherever you went would be unimaginable.

When they'd finished their coffees, Gemma dug in her purse for some money, but Ben waved her away. 'I got it. You didn't have to sit with me, but you did. Thanks.'

'Thanks for asking me,' she said quietly, and she meant it. She suspected he'd originally asked her for a drink to make trouble between her and Nash, but somewhere along the line he'd forgotten to be the aggressive jerk he usually was and she'd caught a glimpse of who he was inside: sad, a little scared, and very lonely.

'Maybe we could do it again sometime?' he said, and she

detected a hint of apprehension in his voice as he looked down at his boots.

'Maybe,' she said cautiously. 'But I'm here to work and then I'm heading back to the city,' she added, not wanting to give him the wrong impression.

'Yeah. I get it.' He looked away.

'Thanks again for the coffee. I hope things look up for you soon, Ben,' she said, impulsively kissing his cheek before heading outside.

As she made her way back to the ute, she passed a vacant shopfront she'd never noticed before, and stopped to take a closer look. A faded sign on the front window read *Giuseppe's Family Restaurant*; inside a lone chair remained in the centre of the room among the dust and peeling wallpaper. This must once have been somewhere the locals came for family outings or to meet friends, but all that remained now was an abandoned shell.

Feeling sad, she turned away and continued to the ute. Ben's words had resonated within her. She knew what it was like to see disappointment in the eyes of someone who had only ever looked at you with pride your entire life. As she walked she pulled out her phone and selected a number. She listened to it ring in her ear, almost hoping it would ring out.

No such luck. Her mother answered, sounding slightly out of breath.

'Hi, Mum. It's me. Did I catch you at a bad time?'

'Gemma! No, I was just out gardening. I'm glad you rang. It's about time we heard from you. Your father's been worried.'

'I've been texting you almost every day.' Gemma tried to keep the exasperation from her tone but suspected she'd failed when her mother's tone cooled a little.

'A phone call wouldn't have hurt.'

'Sorry, Mum. It's sometimes hard to get reception out here.' Technically it wasn't a fib. There were black spots here and there and it was dodgy in places back at Dunoon, but the real reason she hadn't called was that she found it draining trying to talk to her parents. They clearly had no idea why their once sensible daughter would decide to go off on some silly working holiday out of the blue when she could have been back in Sydney preparing for her exciting new role.

'So how are you?' Caroline asked.

'I'm great. I didn't think I'd like the work, but I'm actually enjoying it.'

'Really?'

'Yeah. I know, I've never been the outdoorsy type. It's really pretty country out here.'

'Well, it's very quiet here. I wish you'd change your mind about Christmas . . .'

'Mum,' said Gemma, sighing. They'd been through this before she went away. Yes, she knew Christmas was a big deal to her parents, and yes, she knew it was a time for family and being together, but just this once she wished her mother wouldn't lay a guilt trip on her. 'It's just too far to go for a few days and then travel back out here again. Next year it'll be back to normal.'

'It won't be the same,' said her mother, annoyed.

'So, I guess Dad's out playing golf?' Gemma said innocently.

'Of course. Where else would he be?'

Gemma bit back a smile as her mother launched into her well-rehearsed tirade. While golf was her father's passion, it was the bane of her mother's existence and the only topic Gemma knew for certain would be able to divert her mother's wrath. It was worth the five minutes of non-stop scathing commentary she had to listen to.

'I think it would put his mind at ease if you could show a little more enthusiasm about the business, though,' her mother said unexpectedly.

'The business?'

'We've both noticed that you haven't been overly excited about your new job. I think your father feels a bit hurt that you don't seem to appreciate this opportunity.'

'I do appreciate it,' Gemma said, feeling a familiar wave of guilt wash over her. 'I've just been busy with planning this trip and everything.'

'Well, maybe it wouldn't hurt to let your father know you're looking forward to it, and showing a bit of interest in the business when you speak to him.'

'Sure, Mum. I'll do that next time I talk to him,' Gemma agreed meekly, swallowing down her irritation. She hated to disappoint her parents, and she was truly grateful for everything they had done for her, but it really irked her to be rebuked like a naughty five-year-old. 'Well, I have to get back to work. Tell Dad I said hello and give him a hug for me. I'll call again in a day or so. Love you.'

She disconnected the call as quickly as possible and let out another long sigh as she climbed into the ute. Though she'd never admit it to Jazz, coming out here had been a good idea. It had given her an opportunity to put some distance between herself and her parents. Distance that was giving her thoughts a certain clarity. Out here, she felt as though she could finally breathe. It was also making her take a very long, hard look at her future. What she saw frightened her a little. Was she brave enough to tell her parents what she really wanted to do with her life? If not, what would be the costs of her cowardice? She leaned her head back against the headrest and stared out at the quiet main street.

Fourteen

'Have a nice trip into town?' Nash asked from where he was changing a tyre on the work ute when she pulled up.

'I needed a break,' she said, eyeing him a little warily. He seemed to have calmed down, but it was difficult to tell while he was concentrating so hard on tightening the wheel nuts, which he seemed to be doing with quite some force.

'From who?'

'Everyone, actually.' She hadn't forgotten how angry he'd been earlier, but it still stung that he'd refused to listen to her.

'How's Ben doing?'

Gemma snapped her head around to stare at Nash in shock. 'You followed me?'

'Didn't have to. Word travels out here like a grass fire.

Nothing happens around these parts without everyone knowing about it.'

'But I only just left town,' she said faintly.

'Jack from the produce store was out here delivering that,' Nash nodded towards a pile of bags stacked on the dirt floor beside his ute, 'when his missus called him and mentioned she'd just seen Henderson and a woman having coffee.'

'And you got me from "a woman"?'

'Described you to a tee,' he grunted as he tightened another wheel nut.

'Doesn't anyone around here have anything better to do with their time than gossip?'

'Not when there's something juicy to gossip about.'

'I had coffee.' She frowned at him, hands on her hips. It was totally wasted on him, however, as he turned away and continued working. 'I thought you might need a bit of space.'

'If anything had happened to that stock . . .' He closed his eyes as if striving for calm. 'It was dangerous and stupid.'

'If we'd known what could have happened we would never have done it. We just felt sorry for the dogs being tied up and everything . . .' she trailed off as he glanced up at her.

'I know it was Jazz's idea,' he said quietly. Gemma opened her mouth to speak, but he held up a hand. 'She came out and told me it was her idea to take the dogs and that you'd tried to talk her out of it.'

'I should have tried harder to stop her, so it's my fault too.'

'Why do you do that?' He sounded angry and baffled at the same time.

'Do what?' asked Gemma.

'Jump in to save her all the time. She's not a kid.'

'I don't.'

'You do. You're always covering for her impulsive, stupid ideas. She gets you into trouble and you take the blame.'

'I . . .' Did she? 'I should have made her leave them behind. I didn't. So, I'm just as much to blame as she is.'

He gave an irritated shake of his head as though it was no use arguing anymore. 'I need to hand feed the cattle.' He tossed the wheel brace aside and indicated with an irritated nod of his head at the bales in the back of the ute. 'If it's not interrupting your social life too much, could I get you to drive while I push these off?'

'I'd like to push *you* off,' Gemma muttered beneath her breath as she swung into the driver's seat and revved the engine. They didn't speak again, not for the entire trip out to the cattle and not on the way back in. Nash seemed lost in his thoughts as he stared out the window.

•

Dinner was a strained affair. Nash had declined to eat with them, choosing instead to stay in the office and finish his book work. So it was just Jazz and Gemma seated at the dinner table. Jazz chattered and ate with gusto, apparently unaffected by the day's events, but finally she noticed Gemma's unresponsiveness.

'For God's sake, would you snap out of it?'

'Out of what?'

'This whole "I got in trouble" thing. Big deal! We didn't hurt anything, all the animals are still alive, so stop moping around the place like you got sent to the naughty corner or something.'

'I wish you'd take things seriously for once.' Gemma said. 'We didn't have control over those dogs, and if Nash hadn't come along, something could have gone very badly wrong.'

'Well, it didn't. End of story.'

'Grow up, Jasmine!'

'Ruh roh,' Jazz said, imitating Scooby Doo. Usually Gemma found it amusing, but not tonight. 'You used my *whole* name so I *know* you're pissed off.'

'Yes, I am pissed off, as a matter of fact. You need to stop it.'

'Stop what?'

'This!' Gemma waved her arms around at the room. 'Your insane attempt to play out some weird fixation you have with country life. News flash, Jazz, shows like *McLeod's Daughters* aren't real. Real farm work is hard. It's not romantic; it's not fun. It's dangerous and there are no stunt men to take the fall. We're *not* country girls. We're from the *city*.'

'You had to go and spoil it, didn't you,' Jazz said, sliding her chair out from beneath the table and standing up.

'By pointing out the truth?'

'By raining on my parade! You know, if you just forgot to be perfect for five minutes, you might actually have some fun. You can't stand that I can enjoy life, can you? You can't stand that I get to be happy.'

'Oh, don't be ridiculous,' Gemma said, pushing away her plate.

'It's true. You're so miserable, stuck in your self-imposed prison, that you want everyone else to be just as miserable as you. *News flash*,' she spat Gemma's words back at her. '*You* are the only one keeping yourself trapped in your life. You've got a backbone—use it. Until you do you're going to be this uptight, pain-in-the-arse Dudley Do-Right who drives me up the wall!' Jazz exploded, before leaving the room in a huff.

The bedroom door down the hall slammed and Gemma stared at the empty spot in the kitchen where her best friend had just been. Later, as she was cleaning the kitchen, she heard the door open again and Jazz came storming down the hallway, carrying her bags.

'What are you doing?' Gemma asked.

'I'm going out.'

'With all your stuff?'

'No, not all of it. I need to get away from all this negativity. Maybe if you and *the arsehole in the office*—' Jazz turned towards the hallway and raised her voice— 'just jumped each other's bones, you'd get all this crap out of your system and people would want to be around you both.'

Gemma was too angry to be mortified. 'Fine. Go and be spontaneously happy somewhere else. See if I care.'

The screen door slammed shut behind Jazz as she lumbered out with her overstuffed bag.

'And keep your phone with you!' Gemma shouted from the back door as she watched Jazz throw the gear into the back of Mack's car which had just pulled up, clearly having been summoned by Jazz while she'd been furiously packing. Turning away, Gemma looked back up the hallway and saw Nash standing there, arms folded across his chest, raising his eyebrows in a silent question that looked a lot like, 'Do I really want to know what happened?' She didn't bother to answer. She hoped to goodness he hadn't heard Jazz's stupid statement, although it would have been hard not to hear her.

Just kill me now, Gemma thought with a frustrated groan before turning away to clean up the kitchen.

She sat down in the lounge room and flicked through TV stations without interest, then tried to read her book, but found it impossible to concentrate on the words. Finally, she gave up and decided to go to bed.

She walked past the office door, which was open. Looking in, she saw Nash staring at a spreadsheet on the computer screen. She knocked lightly on the doorframe, hovering uncertainly. 'It wasn't anything,' she said quietly from the doorway.

'What wasn't?' he asked without looking away from the screen.

'Today, with Ben. It was just coffee.'

'Nothing to do with me. You're free to pick your own friends.' He looked across at her then, pinning her with a look that made her feel cold inside.

Gemma backed out of the doorway, stung by his icy tone, and left him to stare at the computer.

•

Goddamn it, Nash thought as he stared sightlessly at the screen, twiddling with a pen. He'd been unable to concentrate all night. He felt like crap—had done ever since he'd ripped both girls a new one earlier today over the damn dogs. *Of all the stupid things to do*, he thought again. Everyone knew working dogs weren't pets. They were tied up for their own damn good, not to mention the good of anything else with four legs.

He threw the pen down on the desk in disgust. Who was

he kidding? There was no way he was going to get any work done tonight.

He needed a drink.

After turning off the computer, he hit the light switch and made his way towards the kitchen. When he opened the fridge, he felt like a dick all over again. Gemma had made his dinner.

Jazz had been right earlier when she'd called him an arsehole. He really was. Even after yelling at her and treating her like crap all day, Gemma had still saved him some dinner. He took the plate and put it in the microwave to heat up. As he watched the turntable spin round and round he knew exactly how it felt. He felt as though he was doing the same thing, turning in circles, getting nowhere. If it didn't rain soon, he was going to start having to make some pretty serious decisions, selling off his livestock at a fraction of their value and losing his prime breeding stock or continuing to gamble on rain, throwing thousands of dollars a day away in feed; money he didn't have to waste.

He took the plate over to the table, sat down and ate. Over the last few years he'd got used to being alone, but ever since the twin cyclones, Jazz and Gemma, had roared into his life he'd become accustomed to having company around. Damned if he didn't even look forward to sharing a meal each night and listening to the two girls nattering away. Half the time they lost him, talking about places he hadn't been, movies he hadn't had time to watch, and girl stuff he had no desire to know about.

What he really looked forward to, though, were the late-night conversations with Gemma, when she drank a cup of tea while he had his dinner. She didn't even have to talk much, he just liked her company.

After he'd finished eating, he sat back, wondering if he'd blown it. He rubbed his hands over his face and groaned. Yeah, he'd overreacted a little, he conceded. Not about the dogs, but he'd definitely gone too far tonight with giving her the cold shoulder. He hated to admit it, but he was jealous. He hadn't even been completely sure it was Gemma who Jack's wife had seen with Ben until she'd confirmed it herself. But as soon as Jack had told him the gossip, he'd immediately had a horrible feeling. He knew Henderson would be counting on word getting back to Nash; now he'd be laughing his arse off about it. He expected that from Henderson, but he hadn't thought Gemma would fall for Ben's bad-boy charm. Jazz, yes, but not Gemma.

It's not like you've made any claim on her, a little voice reminded him.

Maybe if you and the arsehole in the office just jumped each other's bones you'd get all this crap out of your system and people would want to be around you both. Jazz's words came back to him and he gave a small, reluctant chuckle. If only it were that easy. Recalling the day they'd gone up to the ridge, how Gemma had felt in his arms, he experienced a renewed rush of desire and shifted uncomfortably in his seat. He was just horny, that was all. It'd been a while and she was attractive. But the list of excuses wasn't helping his situation; if anything it was making it worse. Now he couldn't stop thinking about it. Christ, she'd felt good against him the other day. Damn Mack and his shitty timing.

They should have talked about it then and there. Instead, somehow they'd ended up getting their wires crossed and he'd found himself agreeing that they should keep things on a professional level.

Clearly he'd lost his touch with women. He wasn't a monk; the sad fact was that he was too exhausted by farm work to even bother trying to meet a woman. What little energy he had left nowadays he sure as hell didn't want to spend on playing games, and that was what most of the women out here were after. The ones who were barely over the legal age were too damn energetic for him, and the ones his age were either married and bored, or divorced and jaded.

Nope, it was safer to just keep his head down and stay out of trouble. In recent years his only concern had been to get the seed into the ground before the rain came, and hope that when the rain did come it didn't turn into a flood. There was always something to worry about, and now there was one more: a brunette with green eyes sleeping a few feet away from him, while his own head was full of ideas about what he'd like to be exploring with her in that bed.

Fifteen

Gemma was up before Nash the next morning. There was no point lying in bed when she'd spent most of the night tossing and turning. How dare Nash act as though she'd somehow betrayed him when all she'd done was have a cup of coffee with someone? Not to mention that it hadn't even been planned. It had just happened.

When he found her in the kitchen, he sat at the other end of the table and wolfed down his breakfast, not bothering to make eye contact with her once. Gemma sat there fuming, and when he pushed his chair away from the table with a loud screech her jangled nerves snapped. 'What *is* your problem?' she demanded.

'I don't have enough time to list them all right now,' he grumbled, drinking his coffee as he walked across to the sink.

'Then what can I do to help?' asked Gemma, deciding to take the moral high ground and ignore his bad mood. Obviously a night's sleep hadn't put him in a better frame of mind. If he wasn't going to accept her word that there was nothing going on between her and Ben, then he could just shove it up his ar—

'I have to start drenching in the next few days.' Unexpectedly, Nash interrupted her thoughts. 'And I've got a fence down in the back paddock that I have to get to at some point. With this rain on its way, that's going to put a few things back even further.'

'But isn't rain good?'

'Some rain is good, but if we get a flood I'll lose all that money I just paid out in seed and have to start again—*if* I can afford to buy more seed, which I'm not in a great position to do at the moment.' He braced his hands on the edge of the sink and stared out the window.

'Does the weather report say it's going to flood?' Gemma moved across to stand beside him. The sky was overcast but not, she thought, particularly threatening.

'No, not yet, but there's a storm cell coming this way— sometimes they can cause flash flooding.' His face creased with a worried frown, and she felt a sudden urge to reach out and smooth it away, or give him a hug, although she knew that a hug would make no difference whatsoever to the long list of jobs he had to do. It would also be an extremely inappropriate thing for an employee to do to her employer.

Who was she kidding? They'd been dancing around this thing ever since that day on the ridge. It was always there, hanging between them, and all it was going to take was for one of them to make a move. Catching her breath, she went to touch his shoulder, but just then he downed the last of his coffee before placing the cup in the sink. She quickly lowered her hand to her side.

'Is Jazz planning on coming back?'

Gemma dropped her gaze, feeling flustered and foolish. 'I have no idea. I'm not her keeper.'

'Looks like it's just you and me then,' he said, turning away.

Gemma followed him outside. Thanks to Jazz and her hissy fit of the night before, she was now stuck here alone with Nash.

'What are we doing?' she asked nervously as Nash rolled the quad bike out of the shed.

'You ever ridden one of these before?' He straightened up to tip his hat back from his face.

'No.'

'What about a motorbike?'

'No.'

'Never?' he asked incredulously.

'Ah, no. I hate to break this to you, but not everyone has a quad bike parked in their garage at home,' she told him as he went back into the shed and brought out a dirty-looking trail bike.

'Well, I guess you're going to have to do a crash course in quad-bike riding. I need a hand bringing the sheep up. I just got word there's an empty truck coming through later this afternoon that I can put a load on, which means we're gonna have to get them up in the yards ASAP.'

'So has the market improved then?' Gemma asked. 'You

said the other day that you couldn't sell any stock because the bottom had fallen out of the market.'

'No, it hasn't improved.'

'Then why are you selling them?'

'Because I can't afford to keep feeding them.'

'But didn't you say the rain was supposed to be coming?'

'It won't be here soon enough to make any difference. Every day I wait costs me more in feed. I don't have a few weeks up my sleeve to wait until the rain comes, *if* it comes, and then for any new feed to grow. I'm cutting my losses and selling them now.' He turned his back on her, which put a stop to any further discussion.

Gemma watched uneasily as he came back out of the shed with a helmet, which he handed to her.

'If we were headed into the back country, I'd take a day or so to run you through a bit more training, but it's all pretty flat where we're going so there shouldn't be any dramas.' He indicated for her to climb onto the quad bike. 'They're pretty easy to ride. This one's got an automatic clutch so you won't have to worry about changing gears and stuff.' He showed her where the foot brakes were before leaning across in front of her to push the starter. 'Alright, put it in drive and when you're ready to go, release the brake, slowly,' he said, raising his voice over the sound of the engine. 'Okay?'

Gemma nodded and moved her foot to the brake pedal, placing her hands tightly on the handlebars. The bike lurched a little as she released the brake and she bit back a startled squeal, but once she was moving, she realised she actually had a lot more control than she'd expected. She rode the bike in a circle, heading back to where Nash stood watching her, and pulled to a stop with a victorious grin spreading across her face.

'You'll do,' he said with a nod. Turning away, he climbed on his bike and kicked it into gear.

Her grin was soon replaced by a look of horror as twin flashes of brown and black appeared from nowhere. Nash's shout of warning came nanoseconds after two of his dogs launched themselves at her at full speed, somehow managing to pull up instantly and balance, one on the seat behind her and one on her lap.

'Sorry, I should have told you,' Nash said. 'They like to ride on the quad.'

'A little warning would have been nice,' she muttered once her heart had dislodged itself from her throat. She could feel the warm breath of the dog behind her; the one on her lap glanced up, his wide grin and long lolling tongue seeming to ask, 'Well? What are we waiting for?'

'Just follow me and take it steady,' Nash yelled over the loud roar of the two engines. He gave her one final look, waiting until she managed a facsimile of a confident nod, before heading down the dirt track leading away from the house.

Gemma was relieved to discover that Nash had been right when he'd assured her it wouldn't be too difficult to handle the quad out in the paddock. Most of the trip was on the dirt roads that ran along the fence lines of paddocks that seemed to stretch as far as the eye could see. After the first few kilometres, Gemma found herself beginning to relax, and a few more in she actually started to enjoy it. She knew Nash would probably prefer the brownish landscape to be a lot greener, but she found it rather striking; there was a harsh kind of beauty to the place.

The paddock where they found the sheep was familiar to Gemma as she and Jazz had been bringing out feed over the last few days, pushing the heavy bales of lucerne off the tray of the work ute to the mob of bleating sheep who trotted expectantly after them. Easing on the brake, she waited as Nash kicked down the stand of his bike and went to open the gate, then waved her through.

'Keep your eyes on me,' he called as she passed. 'We're going to push them through here and back the way we came. I just want you to stay at the back and push them forward. The dogs and I will do the rest.'

Well, that sounds easy enough, she thought, giving him a nod as he climbed back on his bike and took off again. *Stay at the back and push them forward,* she repeated to herself, pointing the quad in the direction Nash had gone. It sounded simple, until she saw that the sheep were scattered across the paddock and she had no idea where 'the back' actually started. However, it wasn't long before the dogs, sent with a series of whistles from Nash out into the paddock, began hunting the mob into a central group. Gemma marvelled at the dogs' skill and fluid grace as they became little more than blurs of colour streaking across the paddock, working almost like extensions of Nash's body as he whistled and called out commands from his bike, slowly circling as he watched his furry helpers work their magic. In no time at all the sheep and dogs had passed her, and Gemma carefully followed, keeping a distance and hoping she looked like she knew what she was doing.

As they moved along the dirt track, the steady pace gave Gemma time to think. Disturbed by what Nash had told her a couple of weeks ago about prices of livestock plummeting, she had looked up the market report. Scanning the number of sheep before her now, Gemma tried to work out how much Nash might make with this sale. Having seen the sharp drop in prices this year compared to last, she cringed at the deficits he faced. No business could afford to continue to run with such huge losses, and she wondered how much longer Nash would be able to do so.

Her gaze strayed to Nash riding on the right of the mob, towards the front, and she couldn't help but admire the broad expanse of his back beneath a navy-blue work shirt. Today he wore a baseball cap instead of his faded akubra. From this far back she couldn't make out his features as well as she'd have liked, but by now she didn't really need to see them. She'd spent enough time over the last few weeks memorising each and every angle. At some point she'd developed a rather perverse fondness for stubbled jawlines and sleep-deprived bloodshot eyes. It was unbelievable, but the man still looked hot even when he was exhausted. Talk about unfair.

As they approached the stockyards, Gemma dropped back and guarded the rear; at least that's what she was technically supposed to be doing, although she hoped the silly things didn't decide to turn around because she really wasn't confident she knew what to do to stop them if they did. The dogs seemed to have everything under control, zigzagging and wheeling, funnelling the unimpressed sheep through a narrow gate and into an ever narrower set of stockyards. It was sheer poetry in motion.

Gemma stopped and dismounted from the quad bike as Nash shut the gate to the yards. She stretched her legs, admiring their handiwork with a sense of pride. Even though she knew she really hadn't done much besides driving along behind, it still felt like an accomplishment.

But there was no time to stand around; Nash was already calling out the next task. For the rest of the day she didn't get a chance to do much more than run along behind him like one of his well-trained dogs.

The truck arrived late in the afternoon. Leaning against the rails of the stockyard, well out of the way, Gemma watched the men load the sheep into the double-decker trailer of the semi. The whole place was alive with the sound of sheep bleating, dogs barking and men shouting, the scene slightly hazy through the fine layer of dust kicked up from all the commotion. Watching on, she felt the pure excitement of a child. Everything was new to her, and totally outside anything she'd experienced before.

As she headed inside just on dark, Gemma was smiling. Although she was dusty and tired and smelled like sheep, she felt great. She chuckled at the thought of her parents seeing her now; they wouldn't believe their eyes. There was definitely no chance of mustering sheep or pushing feed from the back of an old ute when she returned to Sydney. Her smile slipped a little at the thought, which took a tiny bit of the shine off her happiness. Determinedly, she pushed it away and headed for the shower. There would be plenty of time later to think about her future. Right now all she had to worry about was getting the dust and sheep poo out of her hair.

•

Despite the pleasant tiredness that overwhelmed Gemma when she went to bed, she couldn't fall asleep. She was worried about Jazz. She sent her a text to check she was okay but it went unanswered. So did the phone calls she made early the next morning before she got out of bed. By now she was really worried, not to mention annoyed. She didn't need this kind of stress. She was too young to be playing mother to a delinquent!

Gemma found the usual note left on the kitchen table. Today, though, instead of a long list of jobs, Nash had told her she should just hang around the house or head into town if she liked. Driving into town really didn't hold much appeal when she looked out the window and saw that it was rather dismal-looking. The gloomy day made her think of chicken soup and movies. The clouds were a lot darker than yesterday, hanging heavy and low in the distance. 'The rains are comin', Ma,' she mimicked before turning away.

She had just finished feeding the dogs and chooks when the sky opened up and the rain started bucketing down. She ran back to the house and kicked off her boots at the door, rubbing her arms against the sudden, unseasonal chill in the air.

After she pottered around inside and tidied up, she decided to bake some biscuits. As she did so, she found herself frequently glancing out the window and wondering where Nash was. She hoped he was on his way back; it was really coming down hard out there.

Finally her phone beeped with a message, and she snatched

it off the bench. The text was from Jazz. *Gone out of town. Be back in a few days.*

Back in a few days? What the . . . ? Gemma quickly pressed the dial button, and with increasing frustration listened to the call ring out. They were supposed to be out here working together. Where did Jazz get off thinking she could just dump her without even telling her first? This wasn't part of the plan. Her fingers flew across the keypad. Obviously Jazz wasn't in the mood to explain anything further, though, and the phone remained silent.

Gemma tried to watch a movie but she was too restless and found her mind continued to drift. She needed to find a distraction and as usual she found it in the kitchen. There were two big pumpkins on the floor of the pantry, so she began chopping up one of them, throwing the chunks into a huge pot she'd found in one of the kitchen cupboards. Leaving the pumpkin to cook, she was cleaning up the scraps and about to flick on the coffee machine when the radio on the bench suddenly burst into life.

'Gemma, you there?'

She scrabbled for the handset. 'I'm here.'

'I've got the Cruiser bogged up to its axles. Can you come out this way and pick me up in the work ute?'

'Okay. I'll leave now. Where are you?'

'In the northeast paddock. You'll see me once you get close.'

'In English, Nash. Which way is northeast?'

The radio went silent and Gemma could picture him, eyes shut and head bent as he strove for patience. 'Head towards the stockyards, hang a right and keep driving until you see me.'

'Why didn't you just say that in the first place?'

'I need you to check the snatch strap's still in the toolbox before you leave.'

'Okay. What's a snatch strap look like?'

'It's an orange strap. Should be rolled up in the toolbox in the back of the ute. Be careful. It's raining pretty hard and the track's slippery.'

'Okay. I'll be there soon.' She hung up the handset and turned the soup down low before grabbing one of the long raincoats hanging on a hook in the laundry. Eyeing the rain outside with a reluctant sigh, she shrugged on the coat and pulled on gumboots.

She made a rather ungainly dash across the yard towards the large machinery shed where the work ute was parked. Leaning over the tray, she opened the grubby-looking toolbox lid to find equally grubby-looking tools and an assortment of other things. She riffled gingerly through the contents but couldn't see anything orange resembling a strap. Closing the lid again, she searched the rear of the ute, lifting a folded tarp before trying under an old hessian bag. There was a straplike thing rolled into a coil, but it had been a while since it was orange—or clean for that matter. She picked it up and held it away from her, hoping she didn't get any of the mud or cow poo on her clothes, and got in behind the wheel.

As always, the keys were in the ignition, something she still wasn't used to, but she had to admit it made life easier. She reversed out into the driving rain, the windscreen immediately streaming with water. As she set off away from the house she had to lean forward and peer through the rain to see the dirt track.

At the stockyards the well-worn track forked, and she veered to the right. The windscreen had already fogged up and the fast beat of the wipers against the glass drowned out the radio softly playing to itself. 'Great directions, Nash,' Gemma muttered, squinting out her window. She could barely see the track in front of her, let alone a speck in a paddock somewhere.

She'd slowed down to negotiate the deep puddles and places where the track had begun to erode when she saw a light up ahead, wavy through the rain. As she got closer she realised it was the headlights from the Land Cruiser. She pulled the ute to a stop on the track beside it, and waited while Nash jogged towards her. He tapped on the window and she wound it down a little, yelping as the cold rain hit her face.

'I need you to reverse back so I can hook up the snatch strap. I'll be back in a second.'

Gemma manoeuvred the ute so the rear of the vehicle was in front of the Cruiser and pulled on the handbrake. She watched in the rear-view mirror as Nash hooked up the strap to the front of the bogged Cruiser, losing sight of him as he bent down to connect it to the back of the ute. Moments later he was at her door and motioning for her to slide over.

'Are you sure this old thing can pull it out?' she asked doubtfully. The ute was only half the size of the big Cruiser and she had visions of them being dragged down into the boghole alongside the other vehicle and having to walk home in the rain.

'It's tricky but it can be done,' he said, releasing the handbrake, his eyes glued to the rear-view mirror as he put the ute into second gear. The ute lurched forward but didn't get far. Gemma glanced across at Nash and saw his jaw clench as he sent a look at her side mirror. He tried again; this time the ute revved and pulled for a few moments, until they lurched forward and promptly stalled. With a loud curse, Nash shoved open the door and went around to the back of the ute.

Gemma didn't need to ask what had happened; in the side mirror she saw Nash bend down and unhook the broken strap and toss it into the back of the ute. He came over to her window and she wound it down. 'I'll have to bring the tractor to pull it out,' he said wearily.

'Okay. I'll drive; your hands are probably blue by now.' She scooted across the seat, wincing as the rainwater he'd deposited soaked through her jeans. He didn't protest as she'd expected him to, but disappeared briefly to grab something from the Cruiser before returning and slamming the passenger's side door shut behind him.

The rhythmic sound of the windscreen wipers and the beat of the rain pounding on the roof was loud inside the cabin of the small vehicle. She tried to concentrate on the road but it was distracting trying to drive with him sitting so close. Rain dripped from his head and jacket onto the seat and floor of the ute. She really needed to concentrate, she chided herself, peering through the fogged-up windscreen. She didn't have to look at him to be distracted though. The scent of oilskin from his Driza-Bone, grass and rain all mixed with something uniquely Nash. She could feel his body heat radiating beside her and she squirmed uncomfortably in her seat.

'Wait. Stop. Pull up here a sec,' he said, breaking her already precarious concentration.

'What's wrong?'

'Stay here. I'll be right back.'

Gemma watched as Nash's large dark form merged into the gloom outside. She just made out his figure as he stopped near a fence and seemed to struggle with something. After a few minutes, she couldn't stand it anymore: clearly he was having trouble. She pushed open the door and stepped out, catching her breath at the cold slap of rain that instantly drenched her head.

Nash looked up as her door slammed shut. 'Grab the boltcutters from the back,' he yelled.

Gemma ran around to the back of the ute and reached into the big toolbox, digging through the bewildering assortment of tools until she found something with long handles that resembled what she thought would be boltcutters. Apparently she had guessed correctly; as she approached Nash he reached out and took them without comment.

Looking over his shoulder, Gemma saw a small huddled form, a calf who had got tangled in the fence. The poor little thing looked exhausted. She watched as Nash carefully cut through the barbed wire that had entrapped it. Then he scooped the limp, bedraggled creature up in his arms, carried it to the ute and laid it in the tray.

'Is it okay?' Gemma asked, throwing the small animal a concerned glance.

'Yeah, just a bit tired and wet. Get in out of the rain—I'll try and patch up this fence and then we can head home.'

'I can help, if you like.' She felt guilty sitting in the warm cab while he was outside in the rain.

'It'll be quicker on my own.' At least he slightly softened the blow with a crooked grin. He was probably right, she told herself dejectedly; by the time he told her what to do he could probably have done it himself twice as fast. He opened the passenger's side door for her to jump inside, then rummaged around in the toolbox in the back.

True to his word, a few minutes later he was heading back to the ute. He put the tools in the back and climbed into the driver's seat beside her.

Gemma looked through the windscreen as they drove back to the house, occasionally wiping away the fog their warm breath created inside the cabin. She stole a glance across at Nash, who was concentrating on the rough track ahead. Water dripped off his hair onto his oilskin coat. Droplets rolled down his sleeve and onto the floor, and the rain continued to pound noisily on the roof of the ute as they drove.

'I finally heard from Jazz,' she told him, breaking the silence. 'She won't be back for a few days.' She looked at him warily, but he didn't react as she'd expected.

'I know. I had a phone call from Grace Henderson. She's not too thrilled that her son has been led astray by one of my unsavoury workers—her words, not mine,' he added, looking at Gemma.

If she hadn't been so distracted by the fact that once again Nash seemed to be one step ahead of her she would have felt indignant at being lumped into the 'unsavoury' category along with Jazz. 'Where are they?'

He shrugged, returning his eyes to the track ahead. 'No idea. That's why she was calling me, to find out if I knew.'

His calm response puzzled her. 'Aren't you angry?'

Once again he took his eyes from the track to glance at her briefly. 'It's not as though she's the most reliable help around here. If anyone was going to be pissed off, I'd assume it would be you. She's your friend and she ditched you.'

'She hasn't ditched me,' Gemma snapped. She hoped.

'It's not my problem. And it's not as if I was paying her. Actually, I can't work out why *you're* still here.'

Why was she still here? 'We agreed to help,' she told him quietly.

The rain beating on the roof of the vehicle was the only sound for a few minutes until Nash spoke again, his face expressionless. 'You know, you're not obligated to stay on. If you want to take off, there's nothing stopping you.'

Gemma fought to keep her own tone as equally neutral as Nash's had been, despite the rush of confusing emotions the idea of leaving produced. 'I can't leave. When she comes back she won't have a car. Besides, I don't like leaving a job half done.'

Nash didn't speak or take his eyes off the track again for the remainder of the trip, but he seemed to relax slightly. She only hoped she hadn't promised something she couldn't deliver.

•

'You should go inside and get dry,' Nash said, pulling the ute into the shed. It was late and dark by the time they'd returned.

201

'What are you going to do with him?' Gemma turned to look through the window of the cab at the small bundle of misery in the tray.

'I'll give *her* a feed and put her in a pen until this rain eases off,' he said, correcting her lightly. 'Give her a chance to dry out for a bit. She'll be good as new in no time.'

As she headed outside, Gemma leaned over the side of the tray to give the tiny forehead a gentle rub before making a run for it across the clearing towards the house.

Inside, she kicked off her boots and slid her arms out of the raincoat, then held it over the laundry tub to shake off most of the water. It was so nice to be inside out of the cold; the house felt warm and cosy. In the bathroom, she caught a glimpse of herself in the mirror and grimaced. Her hair was hanging in limp tendrils around her face, and a streak of mud across one cheek added a particularly attractive dash of colour.

Her shirt was wet all down the back from the raincoat being at least five sizes too big for her, and she shivered as she pulled it up over her head and threw it on the floor, then peeled off her wet jeans. Cold water dripped from her hair onto her shoulders. Before stepping into the shower, she looked for her towel, swearing under her breath as she realised it was still in her room.

Glancing down at the wet pile of clothing on the floor, she decided against trying to wrestle her way back into them. She mentally calculated the distance between the bathroom and her bedroom. Dare she make a run for it in her underwear? No doubt Nash was still outside, seeing to the calf or distracted by some other job. How often did he actually come in when he said he would? 'Ten minutes' to him often meant an hour.

Opening the door a crack, she listened carefully. The house seemed quiet, so she opened the door wider and tiptoed down the hallway. She had no idea why she was creeping along like some kind of cat burglar. She just prayed Nash wouldn't come inside before she had a chance to get her towel. So far so good, she thought as she approached her bedroom door.

Grabbing the towel hanging inside on the doorknob, she gave a relieved sigh. She'd made it. Mentally high-fiving herself, she turned and hurried back up the dim hallway, clutching her towel. She let out a small grunt as she ran into something solid. She would have fallen backwards if it hadn't been for the strong arms holding her steady.

'Whoa,' Nash said, looking down at her in surprise.

Gemma stared up at him, momentarily stunned by his unexpected appearance, but quickly regained her senses enough to pull the towel up in front of her. She silently cursed herself, standing like a dill in the hallway in her underwear. 'I forgot my towel,' she mumbled.

Nash's amused grin slowly slipped away as he stared down at her. His hands tightened slightly on her arms as his gaze slipped down to her chest, only partly concealed by the towel. 'You were wearing that to work in?'

Gemma frowned at the question, and glanced down quickly, following his gaze. Hadn't the guy ever seen a red and black lace bra before? 'What's wrong with it?'

'I . . . nothing. I just didn't think that's what you'd be wearing.' He swallowed, and Gemma noted in surprise the blush spreading up his neck. She'd never seen Nash so flustered before.

'It's just a bra,' she pointed out. Admittedly, it was a bra she hadn't intended anyone—let alone Nash—to see. As he lifted his gaze, she felt her pulse quicken at the look in his eyes. If eyes were capable of smouldering, then that's exactly what his would have been doing, she thought, a tingling sensation running through her body. All those times she'd made fun of Jazz's trashy romance novels, who knew that one day she'd be experiencing a simpering heroine moment of her own.

Slowly his warm hands moved down her arms, goose bumps forming in their wake. She stared like a rabbit caught in headlights as his head lowered and his lips covered her own.

Liquid heat raced through her at his touch. She no longer felt the cold, even half naked and with her hair dripping. Her thoughts fell away too, extinguished by the touch of his mouth and his hands as they roamed across her back and down along her ribcage.

As he deepened the kiss, Nash pulled her harder against him. Gemma clutched at his wet shirt, her knees buckling with the intense need that swept through her. The towel fell unnoticed to the floor.

She felt the cold wall on her bare back and gasped. Nash lifted his head a fraction, just long enough to zero in on the side of her throat. *This couldn't be natural, surely?* Gemma wondered dazedly. Never before had she felt as though she were melting from the inside out. He moved back to her mouth and she gave a small moan, tugging at his shirt. She wanted to run her hands across his bare chest. She needed to feel more of him.

Wedging a knee between her thighs, pinning her against the wall with his body, he leaned back far enough to tug his shirt over his head, before picking up easily where he'd left off.

Her hands ran up his wide back, the skin cool beneath her fingers, before sliding up over his shoulders. Even moulding herself against him like a second skin, she still needed *more*. What the hell was happening to her?

Nash lifted his head and looked down at her, breathing harshly. For a long moment they just stared at one another. She couldn't have moved if she'd wanted to; his body still trapped her firmly against the wall. 'You're cold,' he said, his voice sounding gravelly and uneven, as though he hadn't used it in a long time.

Glancing down, she saw that she'd begun to shake slightly. She didn't feel cold though. She felt as though she were about to spontaneously combust.

He scooped her up in his arms and walked towards the bathroom, shouldering the door open, and then turned to kick it closed behind him. Lowering her to the floor, he didn't let go of her, but reached out a hand and turned on the shower, waiting until steam began to fill the small room before stepping back to undo his jeans. Gemma felt her heart rate increase as she returned his steady gaze. Slowly he reached behind her and unclasped her bra. Easing away from him a little, she slid her arms from the straps and let it fall to the floor, followed by the remainder of her clothing. Nash closed the remaining distance between them and led her into the shower.

He turned her around so that her back was against his chest, and she sighed as strong fingers massaged her scalp beneath the deliciously warm water. It was entirely possible she had just died and gone to heaven.

Sixteen

Drowsy and spent, Gemma lay listening to the rain as it fell on the tin roof. It was so peaceful. The steady thump of Nash's heart beneath her ear made her smile. His hand was draped across her hip, and his chest gently rose and fell as he slept. *Poor boy is tuckered out*, she thought, maybe just a little smug at the thought that she'd contributed to some of his exhaustion.

They both must have needed the rest; Gemma had fallen asleep not long after Nash. She'd lay awake for a while thinking about what had happened but was too pleasantly spent to worry about rehashing it all.

She couldn't help thinking about how surreal this whole situation was. Why had they wasted so much time when they could have been doing this for weeks? A ripple of unease went through her as she briefly wondered how this would change things between them—after all, they still had to work together. She was considering this, biting the inside of her lip, when she felt Nash begin to stir. As she slowly lifted her head, he stretched out his arms like a big, manly feline. The image made her smile again. She wondered how Nash would react to being called a cat. He was like a panther—all muscle and watchful intensity. *Watchful intensity?* she scoffed at herself. Someone had been reading too many Mills and Boons.

'Morning,' he said, his biceps bulging rather distractingly as he folded his arms behind his head and smiled lazily at her.

'Morning.' She ducked her head in embarrassment and shut her eyes tightly as a wave of heat began to spread up her neck. *Oh, for goodness sake, at least try to act like a sophisticated woman of the world!* she thought. It wasn't as if she was a virgin, for heaven's sake. On the other hand, she hadn't slept with that many guys either—certainly nothing like Jazz's tally. The first time was when she was seventeen, out of curiosity, and the other two had happened in the last couple of years. Mitch had been an on-again, off-again boyfriend, really more off than on, until she met Andy. Andy had been her wake-up call to two-timing bastards. It was just a shame she hadn't worked him out a few months sooner than she had.

'Stop it.'

Gemma's eyes snapped open. 'Stop what?'

'Thinking. Stop it,' Nash said again, half smiling. 'I can see the cogs spinning in your brain—you're about to make this into some kind of problem when it's not.'

'It's not?'

'Nope.'

'But—'

'Nothing,' he said, cutting her off. 'Are you sorry it happened?'

'No,' she admitted, dropping her gaze back to his chest.

'Then there's no problem.'

'So . . . what now?'

'I thought you'd never ask,' he said, taking his hands from behind his head and sliding them down over her bare back.

'I meant workwise . . . and stuff,' she said, smiling.

'You want special privileges for sleeping with the boss?' he asked teasingly, moving his hand lower on her back.

'Special privileges.' She snorted. 'As of yesterday I'm your *only* employee—and you don't even pay me.'

'Lucky you're getting paid in sexual favours then, huh?'

'*You're* lucky,' she muttered, hitting his chest lightly.

'Yeah, I am,' he said quietly, and the change in his tone from playful to almost solemn made her look up at him again. 'If you knew how many times I've lain here at night and thought about this, you'd probably slap me.'

'You did?'

'I'm male. Of course I did.'

Hearing his admission made her smirk a little. 'So you were lusting after me this whole time?'

'Pretty much.'

'Hold on a minute. Me or my cooking? Because I distinctly recall you drooling over my chilli more than once.' She eyed him suspiciously.

'You're the whole package—a good-looking woman who can cook.'

Some part of her should probably have felt indignant on behalf of women's liberation everywhere, but the fact that he enjoyed her cooking stroked her ego in all the right places and she was happy to accept the compliment without guilt. 'So, about these special privileges . . . ?' she prompted. Nash spent quite a long time outlining—then demonstrating—exactly what he had in mind.

When they finally got up, Gemma made pancakes for a late breakfast, and put on lamb shanks to cook slowly for dinner, the divine smell soon wafting through the house. As she pottered around happily in the kitchen, she wished that she could pause the whole day and make it last a little longer.

Except for a brief run by Nash to check on the livestock and get the Land Cruiser unbogged, they spent most of the day inside, warm and snug, while outside the rain poured down, wrapping them in a blanket of blissful isolation. It was the first time Gemma had seen him relax for more than a few minutes at a time. If he wasn't out late in the evening he usually worked in his office, and the only TV station he seemed interested in was the weather channel, so it was a pleasant surprise when he suggested they watch a movie together after dinner. Usually Hugh Jackman could hold her interest the entire length of a movie, but Nash's hands became far too distracting and they barely made it to the halfway mark before ending up back in bed.

•

Waking slowly the next morning, a warm sensation spread through Gemma as she registered the weight of Nash's arm across her hip and heard his deep even breathing. She opened her eyes, careful not to move in case she woke him. She wanted to enjoy studying this man who'd been such a mystery to her for so long, and who now lay beside her, his arm securing her to him even in sleep. That strong jawline was shadowed with stubble, and she smiled when she recalled its roughness on her soft skin. Her hand itched to reach up and stroke it, but she resisted, loath to disturb him when he looked so peaceful.

As her gaze roamed his features, she noticed that the frown between his eyebrows that had seemed a permanent fixture was nowhere to be seen. Without it, he looked younger, though no less handsome.

His eyelids flickered, and a few seconds later they opened to reveal two brown eyes flecked with jade staring back at her steadily. 'I thought maybe I dreamed the past two days,' he said in a low, husky voice. 'I didn't want to wake up this morning and find my bed empty.'

'Maybe we both dreamed it. Maybe we're still dreaming?' Gemma whispered, catching her breath as his hand slowly slid from her hip and down her thigh.

'I can't say I've had a dream that felt this good before. I'm pretty sure we're awake.'

Once again, it was almost mid-morning by the time they had breakfast. And Gemma couldn't take her eyes off the man never further than an arm's length away from her. He was like a different person—the smile she'd previously only glimpsed on occasion now hardly left his face. He seemed lighter, freer somehow. Deep down, Gemma knew these lazy few days together were merely a brief interlude. After today he'd have to go out there again and continue to work; livestock would still need to be looked after, rain or shine. But for one more day she and Nash could lock themselves away and at least pretend to have all the time in the world to spend getting to know one another.

•

The next day there was a short break in the rain, and Nash went back to work before the next low-pressure system rolled in. Finding herself alone in the house, Gemma decided to make a run into town and get some more supplies. Since Nash had left early that morning she'd been moping around inside, and was horrified to discover how soppy she'd become after barely forty-eight hours together as a couple. She mulled over this thought on the drive into town. *Were* they a couple?

She couldn't deny there'd been something between them almost from the first time they'd met. It was definitely more than a casual fling: she had real feelings for him, she just wasn't sure it could be something more. She respected him. She loved the quiet way he went about his work, despite the long back-breaking days. He just got out there and did it. She frowned slightly as her gaze took in the puddles on the side of the road and the grey skies on the horizon, knowing that Nash was still concerned about flooding, but her mind was focused on defining this thing between herself and Nash. Maybe there *was* no definition, she thought. Maybe she should take a leaf out of Jazz's book and just go with it and see where it led. But she wasn't good at throwing caution to the wind. And how on earth would she begin to explain it to her parents?

She pushed the thoughts to the back of her mind as she parked in front of the grocery store. It had to be the grey skies making her feel so gloomy. Perhaps making something nice for dinner would cheer her up, she thought, feeling her mood brighten as plans for a meal began to take shape.

'Hey there, stranger. You've been quiet lately,' Wendy greeted her as she walked into the store.

'Things have been a little hectic,' Gemma said. 'We've been a bit short-staffed since Jazz decided to run off.'

'Ah, yes. I heard about that.' Wendy nodded slowly. 'And she's shacked up with Mack somewhere? She's a bit of a whirlwind, that friend of yours. I'd like to be a fly on the wall at the Hendersons' place! Somehow I don't think your friend is the sort of girl Mrs Henderson pictured for her son.' Wendy's eyes twinkled, and Gemma felt a twinge of indignation at the thought of anyone looking down on Jazz.

'So how're things with you and Nash?' Wendy went on with a mischievous grin. 'All alone in that big old house. Just the two of you . . .'

Gemma shrugged, looking away. 'Business as usual.'

'Monkey business maybe,' Wendy scoffed.

'I don't know what you're talking about,' Gemma said, feeling the betraying heat spread up her cheeks.

'I knew it!' Wendy chortled. 'You two had sparks flying off you when you called in the other day. If one of you didn't make a move soon I thought I'd have to step in.'

'Would you keep your voice down?' Gemma said, looking around. 'It's not a big deal.'

'Yes, it is,' said Wendy. 'I've known Nash all his life and I can tell you this is a very big deal.'

'No. It's not,' Gemma said firmly, fighting a new wave of panic. Wendy had to be wrong. If this was serious it would complicate everything. *You mean it would force you to face your parents once and for all*, added that snide little voice. How would serious even work? Would she just stay out here forever? *Could* she do that? She'd enjoyed working alongside Nash over the last few weeks, doing things she'd never thought herself capable of, but was this really what she wanted to do with the rest of her life—live and work on a farm? Nash had certainly hinted that he'd welcome her staying and working beside him. It wasn't working in an office, that was for sure, but would she just be trading one person's vision for her life for another's?

What did *she* want to do with the rest of her life? That was the question she desperately wished she had an answer for.

•

Three days.

That was all it took for Nash to realise he'd lost his heart to a woman.

From the first day she'd arrived, he'd been fighting a losing battle to remain unaffected by Gemma. He'd got used to the hot meals and packed lunches. He'd adapted to sharing his bathroom with a benchful of hair products and make-up, hairdryers and straighteners; he'd even accepted the insanity of two city girls trying to fake their way through a list of chores. But he'd been totally unprepared for his life being invaded and rearranged, stripped bare and turned inside out by the sudden realisation that he was in love with Gemma Northcote.

He knew without a doubt that she held his happiness in the palm of her hand. Life would never be the same after this.

For the last three nights, holding her while she slept, just as he did now, Nash had found himself thinking about things he'd rarely let himself consider before. He thought about sharing his future with someone. He thought about spending years like this, holding Gemma in his arms as they slept, of days spent out in the paddock and coming home in the evening to her bright smile and warm body. He thought about the children they'd have down the track. Even though common sense told him it was far too soon to be thinking about the future, he allowed himself the luxury of it. This went beyond common sense—maybe it was insanity—but he didn't care what anyone else thought. He knew that this woman was meant to be in his life.

And Gemma was happy here. At least, she seemed happy, but he also knew she had responsibilities at home, a family who expected her to return and take up her role with them. The challenge would be to make her see how happy she was here during the few short weeks before she was due to go back to the city.

Gemma made a small noise in her sleep, a cross between a moan and a sigh. Wriggling closer to his warmth, she fell silent once more. He tightened his arms protectively around her. He now couldn't imagine coming back to this house each night to find it empty. Their future stretched before them, and yet he felt as though something waited just around the corner, ready to pounce when he let his guard down. It was late when he finally fell asleep.

Seventeen

Hearing a car approaching up the driveway, Gemma turned and shaded her eyes against the mid-morning sun. A large four-wheel drive, similar to the one Nash drove, rolled to a stop, and apprehension gripped her stomach as she recognised the driver. In the passenger seat next to him was Jazz. Gemma quickly scanned the area to make sure Nash was nowhere nearby, then put the container of eggs down on the top step and walked over.

'Gemma,' Ben greeted her with a lopsided grin as he followed Jazz towards the house, carrying her duffle bag.

The sarcastic welcome Gemma had been about to give her friend died on her lips as she caught sight of Jazz's red, puffy eyes. 'What happened?' she asked instead, as Jazz took the bag from Ben's hand with a mumbled thanks.

'It's over,' Jazz growled as she stormed past Gemma up the back steps and into the house. Gemma's spirits plummeted as she stared after Jazz's retreating back. This would change everything. In one fell swoop the little bubble of happiness she'd been living in for the last few days had been burst and she was being dragged back down to earth.

'Don't look at me.' Ben held up his hands as Gemma turned her confused gaze to his. 'I'm just the delivery guy. I try not to get involved in my brother's relationship problems.'

'Well, thanks for bringing her home,' Gemma said with a sigh.

'Your warden not here then?' asked Ben, casually leaning against the fence beside her.

'Do you mean Nash? You know he's not or you wouldn't be hanging around,' Gemma said, crossing her arms across her chest.

'I'm being neighbourly,' he protested.

'Sure you are.' She didn't want to be unfriendly, but she hoped Ben would leave now, before Nash saw him. She gestured towards the house. 'I'd better go and see if she's okay.'

'Yeah, I'll be off. Things should have calmed down by now back at home. You two certainly know how to liven up a dull place.' He tapped his hands on the fence and gave her another of his cocky grins before turning away. 'See ya round, Gem.'

Momentarily relieved, Gemma headed inside. As she went down the hallway she could hear Jazz slamming drawers and banging things in her room. Stopping by the bedroom door, Gemma watched as Jazz tossed clothing and belongings haphazardly into her duffle bag.

'What are you doing?'

'Packing the rest of my stuff. I'm leaving.'

'You can't just leave.'

'There's nothing keeping me here. It's over with Mack.' Jazz's voice broke on a sob.

Gemma watched as Jazz continued to gather up her belongings. 'What happened?'

'His mother finally got her way. The old cow gave him some kind of ultimatum and he crumbled. Spineless jerk!' Jazz muttered, throwing a shoe into the bag. 'Who the hell do these people think they are?'

Gemma knew the drill: she was supposed to stand there and insert the appropriate sympathetic noises when needed. But this time it was different. This time they were hundreds of kilometres from home and Jazz seemed determined to put as much distance between her and Mack as possible. 'So what? You're going to leave town over this?'

'He dumped me, Gemma. Do you not understand how humiliating that is?'

Gemma winced in sympathy, she could see her friend was truly hurt by the break-up, but right now she needed to calm Jazz down and work out a solution. She wasn't ready to leave Dunoon. Not yet. 'Maybe you just need to give this some time. Don't do anything you'll regret.'

'I already have. I can't stay here, Gem. I'm not like you. This place is boring. It'd drive me bonkers sitting out on that damn verandah every night. I need excitement in my life, and now I can't even go to the pub anymore. The news is probably all around town by now.' Jazz straightened up, scanning the room for more of her things.

'We're here to help Nash. He needs us, Jazz.'

'Come on, Gem,' Jazz scoffed. 'You don't seriously believe we're easing his workload, do you? All you are to him is a glorified housekeeper and cook. What he really needs are proper farm workers, people who know what they're doing.'

Gemma tried to ignore the pang of doubt she felt at Jazz's words. 'You were the one who talked him into letting us stay. Now you just want to up and leave?'

'That's right—and *you* didn't even want to come out here in the first place,' Jazz pointed out.

That may have been true, but that was then. Gemma had grown to like it out here. She looked forward to her chores now: she had collecting the eggs down to a fine art, and she'd even grown attached to Glennie. Maybe it was just her imagination, but lately the crazy chook didn't look at her with quite as much animosity as she had in the beginning. Gemma loved the quiet mornings sipping her coffee on the back verandah looking out over the paddocks, and the nights she fell asleep to the chirping of crickets. And then there was Nash . . . *She liked it here.* And now Jazz was going to take it away just as thoughtlessly as she'd pushed Gemma into it. 'Just for once, could you finish something?' she snapped.

As soon as she saw the flash of hurt cross Jazz's face, she regretted it. 'That's a low blow, Gem. I don't need this from you when I've been hearing it from my mother all my life.'

Gemma gave a small groan. 'I didn't mean . . . Would you just wait a minute?' she called as Jazz pushed past her and went into the bathroom, slamming the door.

'You were right, okay?' Jazz shouted. 'Happy?'

'What are you talking about?'

'You said this was a stupid idea. You warned me we were out of our depth and I didn't want to listen. You win, okay?'

Gemma went to stand outside the bathroom door. 'No, Jazz.'

'What do you mean, no?'

'We said we'd stay until the end of December. We can't leave him in the lurch like this.'

'Fine, you stay.'

'Just take a minute to think this through and cool down.'

'I'm done thinking. I'm out of here.'

Damn it. Gemma ran a hand through her hair and turned a slow circle, trying to think of a way to talk Jazz around. She knew her friend wasn't kidding. She'd up and leave in a heartbeat, without a goodbye. But there was no way Gemma could just leave without talking to Nash first.

'I'm not leaving without letting Nash know,' she said at last.

'I'll go tell him now.' Jazz opened the door.

'No!' Gemma said firmly. 'He deserves better than that, Jazz. I won't leave here without giving him a few days' notice. Don't even bother arguing,' she said when Jazz opened her mouth. 'You left me here alone to do everything while you went off to have your fun. Well, for the next day or so you can just pull your weight like you agreed.'

'You went and fell for him, didn't you?' Jazz said, eyeing Gemma more closely. Jazz shook her head sadly. 'City girls are just a novelty to these guys. In the end, they want one of their own kind. He'll toss you aside like leftovers.'

'I . . . We . . .' Gemma frowned, at a loss to put into words what she'd done. This was all happening too fast. She couldn't think straight; there was so much noise inside her head and so many things she needed to figure out and everyone seemed to want her to do something. 'I need a few days,' she said quietly.

To her surprise, Jazz's face softened slightly. Without saying anything more, she gave a resigned nod and closed the bathroom door again.

•

When Nash pulled up in the Land Cruiser late that evening, Gemma was sitting on the top of the steps at the backdoor waiting for him. The sun was sinking slowly, leaving in its wake a trail of fiery orange and pink that outlined the distant mountain range. Along the top of the mountains, the tall trees stood in a row like soldiers silhouetted against the sky. It was so beautiful it almost hurt her to look at it. When she'd first arrived out here, she'd taken photos of the sunset, trying to capture its rugged beauty to take home with her, but none of the photos ever did the sight justice. It was times like this she wished she could paint.

When he got close enough he held out a hand to pull her to her feet and into his arms for a welcome-home kiss. When he eventually pulled back, he frowned slightly. 'What's wrong?'

'Jazz is back.'

'Oh? Decided to grace us with her presence finally, huh?'

'She broke up with Mack.'

'There's a shocker.'

'She's really upset about it,' Gemma said defensively.

'Sorry, but you can't tell me that was ever going to work out.'

'Why couldn't it?'

'Because Jazz has the attention span of a gnat, and Mack's never going to do anything to risk upsetting his parents in case they refuse to hand over the property to him when they retire.'

'Well, if that was always going to happen, maybe *someone* should have mentioned that to Jazz,' Gemma said with a frown.

'You really think she'd have listened if I'd tried to talk to her? Look, Mack's an alright bloke, but he's a Henderson first and foremost, and Hendersons always look out for themselves. Mack likes to go out and party and have a good time, but when it comes down to it, he's working for his parents and they control the purse strings. Jazz was never going to fit in with that lot. She was just a bit of entertainment for a while.'

'Like me?' Gemma asked, trying to pull away from him.

'No,' he said, refusing to let go of her. 'Not like you. We're talking about the Hendersons, not me.'

'We're talking about my best friend.'

'It's got nothing to do with you and me.'

Gemma should have told him right then that it had everything to do with them, but that look in his eye, the firm set of his jaw, weakened her resolve.

She loved him. She'd been trying not to get ahead of herself and even think about the L word, but it was inescapable. He wasn't just some holiday fling. But she had no idea what to do with this knowledge. She was a practical, sensible person—or at least she had been. When she let herself imagine staying here, safe and isolated from the rest of the world, anything seemed possible. But she knew that one day real life would muscle its way in. Her parents would have to be told of her plans, and that would be the end of the peaceful little existence she and Nash had managed to carve out for themselves in the last few days. There was no way her father would let her walk away from the firm without a fight, and it made her deeply sad to imagine the hurt and anger a rift between her parents and herself would cause. Perhaps she could understand Mack's situation better than she liked to admit. She was a Northcote, and Northcotes never turned their backs on family obligations.

But as Nash's arms tightened around her and he smiled down into her face, she knew she wasn't ready to walk away from him just yet. It might be selfish, cowardly and stupid, but she would give herself one more night with him before she faced up to reality and remembered who she was and where her responsibilities lay.

Eighteen

Two days later, as Gemma was busying herself with preparing breakfast, she tried hard to ignore her friend's pointed looks. Jazz's patience had apparently reached its end. She'd relented and given Gemma an extra day to break the news to Nash that they were leaving, and Gemma knew she couldn't put it off any longer. Picking up on the undercurrents, Nash looked back and forth between them a couple of times but said nothing, evidently not wanting to get involved.

The sound of a car pulling up outside interrupted the awkward silence. Gemma sat back and breathed a sigh of relief, glad of the distraction. Nash got up and went to the screen door. A look of surprise crossed his face, and he pushed the door open and walked outside.

Gemma went across to the back door in time to see Nash open his arms to the young woman who had climbed out of the small car. From where she stood, Gemma caught a glimpse of the girl's face and felt her heart drop to the floor.

'Who is it?' Jazz asked from behind her.

'His sister,' Gemma said quietly.

'It's about time.'

Gemma frowned and turned to her friend. 'What do you mean?'

'I called her. When you kicked up such a stink about leaving him in the lurch, I called Brittany and told her she needed to get her butt back here right now and take some responsibility.'

Gemma stared at Jazz in disbelief. *Responsibility?* 'You were the one who convinced her to go on that holiday in the first place, remember?'

Jazz shrugged, turning away from the door. 'She had her break, we had ours. Everyone's happy.'

'No. Everyone's *not* happy, Jazz. You can't just play with people's lives like that!' Why had she not realised before how destructive Jazz's fickle nature could be? Maybe because in the past it had only been the guys she sporadically dated and dumped who had been really hurt by her. Gemma herself had never before been drawn into the fallout, but this time it wasn't something she could shrug off. This time it affected more people than just Jazz and Mack.

'You can take the car, Jazz,' she said quietly. 'I'm staying.'

'What?'

'I'm not leaving.'

Jazz stared at her. 'You're not needed here anymore. Brittany's here. You think he'll want to babysit you when he's finally got someone here who knows what to do?'

Gemma shrugged. 'So I'll be an extra set of hands.'

'You'll be in the way is what you'll be. I'm telling you, it may seem like fun now, but eventually he's going to want someone who knows how to drive harvesters and mark cattle without supervision; this place will always come first.'

Jazz's words hit an insecure chord inside her. What if Jazz was right and Nash would be glad to see the back of her now his sister was here to help out? Gemma shook her head, no. Nash wasn't like that. He felt something for her, she knew he did. He'd more or less told her that what they had was nothing like what Jazz and Mack had and, yet, it was too soon for it to be something serious enough to risk either of them making major life changes for . . . surely? God, this was ridiculous! The uncertainty was doing her head in. That was it: she'd just have to come out and ask him what the hell this thing was between them so she knew where she stood. Only, she wasn't sure what she hoped the answer would be. If it was serious, was she prepared to make such big changes in her life? And if it wasn't, was she prepared to walk away from him and never look back?

•

Nash carried his sister's suitcases into the house and found the three girls standing in the kitchen.

'So, I decided to come back and let you two go home to Sydney,' Brittany was saying.

Nash looked across at Gemma, who glanced at him briefly before turning away to switch on the coffee machine. Home? No one had said anything about going home. 'There's no need for you two to leave,' he said, waiting for Gemma to look at him. 'Three sets of hands will be more help than one.'

'Our work here is done,' Jazz said dramatically in true superhero fashion. 'I'm happy to hand over the work gloves to their rightful owner.'

'You said you were here till the end of December.' Nash's gaze remained fixed on Gemma, whose face was still averted.

'Of course you don't have to hurry off just because I'm back,' said Brittany, looking uncertainly between her brother and the two girls.

'There's not much point sticking around now,' said Jazz briskly. 'If you like we can hang around today and help out while you settle back in, but I think we should leave first thing tomorrow morning. Get an early start for the long drive home.'

It was all happening too fast for Nash to keep up. First his sister had turned up out of the blue, then suddenly Gemma was *leaving*. What the hell was going on? He seemed to be the only one who hadn't got the damn memo around here.

Gemma turned back from the bench. Her face was pale as she looked at her friend. 'We haven't made any firm decision, Jazz.' Without looking at Nash, she went on, 'If you need us to help out, we'll stay. We *did* have an agreement, after all. Jazz, you should go and make a start on today's jobs and I'll catch up in a minute.'

He saw Jazz stare at Gemma and blink in confusion. Looking as surprised as he felt at Gemma's newly assertive tone, she turned on her heel and left the kitchen without a word.

'I'm just going to dump my stuff in my room,' said Brittany, taking her bags from where Nash had put them down, raising an eyebrow at her brother on the way past.

'When was all this arranged?' he asked Gemma, striving for calm. He'd been with her all night and hadn't left her side all morning, for Christ's sake.

Gemma bit her lip guiltily. 'I had no idea Brittany was coming. Apparently Jazz called her. She wants to go home.'

'And you?' Nash watched with growing panic as she silently took down some cups and searched in the drawer for a spoon. Finally he crossed the room and turned her around to face him. 'Do *you* want to leave, Gem?'

'We made a deal. I want to honour it. But I don't like Jazz driving all that way alone in that old ute, and I'm not sure what I . . .' Gemma paused and searched his gaze with a desperate look. 'I don't know what to do.'

'I want you to stay,' he said quietly.

Her look turned sad and his heart kicked painfully in his chest. Damn it, he'd just found her. It was too soon to let her go. He dipped his head and kissed her. He'd only meant it to be a soft kiss, a gentle attempt to convince her to stay, but the minute his mouth touched hers, desire hit him hard and fast as Gemma kissed him back with equal ferocity. Memories of their last few days and nights together rushed to fill him with a need so powerful he felt lightheaded.

The sound of someone clearing their throat made him pull back slightly, and he saw Gemma's startled gaze dart to the doorway. Turning, he saw Brittany standing there, a faint smirk on her lips. He muttered a soft curse under his breath at his sister's impeccable timing. He didn't want to let Gemma go, but reluctantly stepped away when she pushed at his chest.

'Well, I guess *that* answers a few questions,' Brittany said.

'I should go and help Jazz. I'll see you later.' Gemma practically ran from the kitchen, leaving brother and sister to stare at the doorway through which she'd fled.

'Don't say a word,' Nash said before Brittany could make a smartarse comment. He wasn't in the mood.

'I wasn't going to say a thing.' She grinned.

He turned on her, suddenly furious. 'You've got a lot to answer for. This whole mess is your fault. If you'd just come back when you were supposed to none of this would have happened.'

'And you wouldn't have been getting laid either, so *you're welcome*, big brother.'

He clenched his jaw and counted to ten, trying to remember the kid sister who used to be such a joy to be around. 'So why did you come back? Run out of money?'

'Actually, I did. So you see we're now *both* stuck here. Isn't this going to be so much fun,' she gushed sarcastically.

'Well, for both our sakes, you'd better go out there and convince them to stick around, or you'll be doing the work of two people.'

'I'm surprised they stuck around this long.' She pushed past him to take over where Gemma had left off with the coffee.

'What do you mean?'

'Well, Jazz isn't exactly what you'd call reliable. She goes through guys on campus like hot dinners. And, anyway, I figured you'd probably scare them off within the first week.'

'I was desperate, thanks to you not turning up.'

Brittany went on as if he hadn't spoken. 'You and Miss Goody Two-Shoes, though, that's a shocker. I never would have picked that scenario. How the hell did that come about?'

'Mind your own damn business.'

'Actually, it's a pretty smart move,' she said thoughtfully. 'With her backing you might actually get this place up and running.'

'What's that supposed to mean?'

'You know she's loaded, right?' Brittany stopped stirring sugar into her cup to glance over at her brother.

Nash frowned at her impatiently.

'You didn't know? Dude, her father's Max Northcote of Northcote & Sons—only the biggest property development and investment company in Australasia. How did you *not* know that?'

'It never came up,' he said defensively. Holy crap, her family weren't just well off, they were *filthy rich*.

Brittany sniggered. 'I guess you two had better things to do than talk.'

Nash had stopped listening. He was too busy trying to get his head around the fact that he'd thought he knew who Gemma was when in reality he had no clue. Why hadn't she told him? He thought back over their conversations about Dunoon in which he'd revealed how he stood financially, which was pretty much broke. Just the other day he'd actually shown her the figures, thinking he owed it to her to tell her the truth. He couldn't help comparing it to her family's financial position. What must she think of his situation? Was he nothing more than a project for her? Why the hell else would she hang around here? He felt like an idiot. How had he not suspected who she was?

Over the last few days he'd been turning over in his mind possible scenarios of how this thing between them was going to work. He'd tried to tell himself to slow down, but there were times when he watched her working alongside him and found himself thinking how easily he could get used to sharing his life with her. What a bloody joke that was. As if someone like her could be happy living here like this, always worrying about the next season, going to bed each night with an overdraft hanging over your head which you had no idea how you could repay if the crop was washed away.

Had she been playing him? What the hell was her angle? Was it some kind of rite of passage: the rich city girl slumming it with some country hick before she goes on to marry someone of her own kind? The more he thought about it, the angrier he got. She and Jazz must have been having a good old laugh at his expense, he thought bitterly. He turned his back on his sister and pushed open the screen door, hearing it slam against the wall as he stormed across to the shed where the two girls were standing, deep in intense conversation.

They stopped to look at him. 'I think you should leave today,' he said without preamble.

Gemma's eyes widened and a flash of something that looked like panic crossed her face. She stepped towards him. 'We've talked it over and decided we'll hang around and help,' she said, cutting off Jazz before she could speak.

'That won't be necessary,' he rasped. 'Britt and I can handle things. You should go.' He turned away, but not before he saw the hurt expression that settled on her face.

'Nash,' she called, but he didn't stop. He had to get away from her before he said something to make an even bigger fool of himself. He swore as she caught up to him and grabbed his arm.

'Would you just wait up a minute?' she cried. 'What's wrong? Why are you so angry?'

'I don't know. Why don't you tell me, Gemma?' He turned to glare at her. As she shook her head in confusion he pushed away his weakening resolve. She'd lied to him, or at the very least misled him. *Had she taken pleasure in fooling him?* he wondered, his ego smarting. At the same time he couldn't help wishing he could go back in time to a few days earlier when he'd begun to think life was good. His weakness disgusted him.

'Tell you *what*? I don't understand. A few minutes ago you were asking me to stay. What happened?'

'I'll tell you what happened,' he snarled, leaning towards her. 'I found out who you *really* are.' She searched his gaze, her expression so perplexed and alarmed that he almost relented, until he remembered the figures on his spreadsheet and how pathetic he must seem to her. 'I have a business to try and run here. I don't have time to pander to spoilt little rich girls and satisfy some weird lifestyle exchange or whatever the hell you thought you were doing. I've wasted enough time already. I know, *alright*? I know who your father is.' A flicker of understanding passed across her face and he shook his head. 'Why the hell didn't you tell me who you were?'

'I wasn't hiding it.'

'I'm pretty sure if you'd mentioned the fact that your father appears in the financial section of the newspaper on a regular basis, I'd have remembered it.'

'But I don't understand how who my father is changes anything between us,' she said blankly. 'Why does it suddenly matter now?'

'Why does it matter? You let me believe we could—' He stopped abruptly. *Have a future*, he had been about to say, but the words lodged painfully in his throat.

'Believe what? It doesn't change a thing about who I am.'

'It changes everything.'

'Oh, please!' she scoffed, her confusion replaced by growing anger. 'It changes nothing. I've worked my butt off to prove to you I could help. Are you seriously going to stand there now and tell me that I'm somehow unable to have done all the things I've done because I'm supposed to be some spoilt rich girl? Are you serious? You're going to throw in my face the fact that I come from money and treat me like I'm some kind of princess, too precious for hard work? How bloody dare you!'

Nash felt her outrage like a slap across the face and it made him pause for a moment. But it changed nothing, he reminded himself. She might think all this new-found independence was exciting now, but a year or so down the track it would no longer be new and interesting. Instead she'd be thinking about how much easier she could have had it back in the city, with her cushy job, living in a fancy house, and she'd resent everything about this life, including him. He needed to end this now before it was too late and it hurt even more.

He took a step back and plastered a sneer on his face. 'Look, it was fun. The sex was a bonus I hadn't been expecting, but I need someone around here who knows what they're doing. Go home, Gemma. You don't belong out here. I have work to do.' He turned his back on her shocked expression and walked away. 'Make sure you're gone by the time I get back,' he added over his shoulder. He hoped to God she would be; he knew he couldn't do this again.

•

Gemma packed her clothes in her suitcases, she couldn't even cry. She was numb. She could feel the pain lurking though, waiting for the shock which protected her now to wear off so it could pounce, but she wouldn't let it happen here. She wanted to be far away from this place when the dam burst. For once, Jazz didn't say a word. She'd taken one look at Gemma and led her silently back to the house, where she helped her gather her things, then started carrying their bags out to the ute.

He didn't want her.

She couldn't bring herself to look out the window as they drove along the road towards town. She couldn't risk catching sight of him somewhere on the property, so she shut her eyes and pretended to sleep. She could feel Jazz glancing anxiously at her from time to time, but she didn't bother trying to ease her friend's concern. She couldn't. For once in her life, Jazz would have to look after things by herself. Gemma didn't care where they stopped to eat and she didn't care where they stayed the night. She simply didn't care. Once they were far enough from Dunoon, she opened her eyes and stared at the scenery flashing by, fighting now to keep the threatening tears at bay, because she knew that once she started crying she wouldn't be able to stop.

Nineteen

The house was empty when Nash arrived home late that afternoon. There was nothing obvious to tell him that they had left; he just knew. The house seemed dead. Lifeless. The same way he felt inside.

He wasn't hungry and he couldn't bear to go into the kitchen knowing she wouldn't be in there waiting for him tonight—or any night from now on. Memories of all the long evenings he'd spent eating alone before Gemma barged into his life sent a knife through his heart. *Better to face it now than a year down the track when she'd dug in even deeper and the pain would probably kill you*, he told himself, but it did nothing to make him feel better. All he knew was that the ache he was carrying around hurt like a bastard and he wasn't sure how it could possibly *be* any worse.

He was sitting at his desk in the office when he heard Brittany's car pull up, followed soon after by light footsteps up the hallway.

'What are you doing still up?' she asked, sticking her head around the office door.

He could smell the lingering odour of the pub on her clothing and sent her a frown. 'First night home and you had to go to the pub?'

She shrugged one bare shoulder and Nash frowned more fiercely as he took in what his sister was wearing—or rather *not* wearing. The dress was strapless and barely reached mid-thigh. He'd always tried not to acknowledge the fact that his little sister was growing up but it was indisputable with her showing off the amount of cleavage she had on display in that dress. 'You're not in the bloody city now, Britt. Next time wear some damn clothes when you go out.'

'How old are you again? You sound like my grandfather instead of my brother.'

That stung, but he was in no frame of mind to go gentle at the moment. Maybe he shouldn't be taking his mood out on his sister, but then again this conversation had probably been a long time coming. 'I'm trying to look out for you—as usual. God knows someone has to.'

'It always comes back to this, doesn't it?' she said, raising her voice and stepping further into the room. 'I'm so sick of you making me sound like I'm some huge burden on you. I'm sorry you got stuck with all the responsibilities when Dad died, alright? But I didn't ask you to keep the farm. You could have sold at any time, Nash, but you didn't. You're holding this place over my head and using it as an excuse to stay angry at everyone. Get over it! Sell the place and move on. Stop hiding behind the shitty hand life dealt you.'

'Because it's just so easy, right?' he snarled. 'This place has been in our family for years! Dad would freak out if he heard you talking about selling the place.'

'Dad's gone, Nash,' said Brittany, her voice dropping and the fire going out of her tone. 'Nothing you do can hurt him. But holding onto this place and blaming him—*and me*—for you being stuck here isn't fair. You need to either get over it or do something about it, because I'm not staying here to watch you grow into a bitter old man. I'm going to go out and live my life *for me*, and you should do the same.'

'Do you have any idea how spoilt and ungrateful you sound?'

Brittany shook her head. 'I *am* grateful to you for taking care of me all these years, but I'm not going to give up my entire future to come back here and work on this place with you. That was never my dream—and at one time it wasn't yours either,' she added pointedly before turning away and heading to her bedroom.

Damn it, he wasn't being some kind of martyr! It was called being responsible and doing what needed to be done; and yet some of what Brittany said made him stop and think. Maybe he did need to start looking at things from a different angle. But not tonight. Tonight he just wanted to be left the hell alone.

•

Gemma stood at the end of the dock and stared out over the harbour. She'd needed some fresh air. Despite the size and opulence of her parents' house, she'd begun to feel almost claustrophobic indoors and needed to get outside. The view was breathtaking, but she was oblivious to the ferries and the sparkling blue of the water. Her mind was far away, picturing wide open spaces and gently waving fields of wheat. She'd been home a day and already she knew she didn't belong here anymore.

Her parents were both relieved that she was back. They hadn't asked any questions about why she'd come home early, and within half an hour of her return her father had suggested she might like to bring her start date forward and go in to work on Monday. As her parents watched her expectantly, she had felt everything closing in on her. She didn't know what to do. Should she just ignore her own feelings, agree to their suggestion and keep the peace like she always did? Somehow it wasn't that simple anymore.

Over the last few weeks she'd discovered she could do anything she set her mind to. During that time, she'd felt herself changing, becoming someone who would no longer sacrifice her own needs in order to make others happy. For a long time she'd had no idea what she wanted to do, but in the last few days before she left Dunoon, ideas had begun forming in the back of her mind, and she'd found herself daydreaming about opening a small restaurant in a quiet little rural town.

It was pointless now, she told herself sternly. Everything had changed. She knew Bingorra wasn't the only place where she could start a business, but it was the place she'd been imagining when she'd pictured it in her mind. Already, too, her earlier excitement had begun to wither as old fears undermined her new-found confidence. It was one thing to feel empowered to stand up to her father while she was hundreds of kilometres away, but since she'd been back here she could feel old habits reasserting themselves. Her parents were so happy that she was back home, and in time for Christmas after all; how could she extinguish their joy by telling them she didn't want to stay? And anyway, what choice did she have? There was no way she could fund her own restaurant. She shook her head at the irony—she was a business graduate and yet she hadn't earned a single dollar in her entire life. What was more, she was unlikely to do so until she started work for her father, which in the grand scheme of things was really the same as taking his money! With a sigh, Gemma realised that she didn't have much choice in the matter. Nash didn't want her, so where else could she go?

●

Nash took a beer outside and sat down on the back steps. Usually he liked summer nights. Cicadas filled the air with their loud, shrill mating calls and the breeze carried the scent of thunderstorms. But he wasn't thinking about any of that as he sat in the dark and stared at his beer can. Over the last few weeks he'd thrown himself into work to try to forget how much he missed Gemma. It had been harder than he wanted to admit. He knew he had no one to blame but himself for the way he felt; after all, he had all but kicked her out of his house. He'd been hurting, but he realised now it was his pride that was most wounded. He still felt sick when he recalled the evening he'd shown her the spreadsheets and explained where he stood financially. He'd done so reluctantly, but he thought that if she was going to stick around she deserved to know exactly what she was getting herself into. She knew now alright—just how pathetic his financial situation was. He cringed when he remembered thinking that she could put her business degree to use and maybe take over the office work for him. Working for her father she'd be dealing with multimillion-dollar businesses; his piddly little farm account must have looked like a joke. He was surprised she hadn't laughed in his face.

He shook his head irritably and swore. He'd been stupid to think she'd have fitted in out here. One look at the goddamn food bill he'd found in the rubbish after she left was enough to show him how different their worlds were. Who the hell spent that much on food? Imported goat meat? Was she crazy? Life on the land was often hard. He would never be able to give Gemma the kind of life she'd known growing up, or the job security she would have working for her father. There were no guarantees in farming.

One thing had changed for the better though. He'd thought about Brittany's words a lot since the night they'd argued. Had he been holding onto his anger and using the farm as an excuse to stay mad at everything that went wrong in his life? Maybe somehow it made dealing with bad years easier to swallow if he could shift the blame onto the fact he'd never wanted to be a farmer in the first place. But the truth was that the only reason he went off to uni in the first place was to escape the guilt and constant reminder of Kim's death which had hovered over him so dark and threateningly when he was eighteen. Being called home when his dad got sick had felt like this town's way of dragging him back to be held accountable and forcing him to deal with his guilt.

It wasn't until Brittany had thrown the challenge in his face to 'sell up or deal with it' that he knew beyond the shadow of a doubt he was doing something he loved. Try as he might, he couldn't imagine himself doing anything else. Already, since coming to terms with everything she'd said that night, he felt freer somehow.

A movement in the shadows caught his eye, and he glanced over just as Horse stepped out onto the path at the foot of the steps.

'No milk today,' Nash muttered, shaking his head at the size of the animal. He looked more like a dog than a cat. Nash wondered if the scratches he'd noticed last week on the dogs' noses had been the result of pushing Horse a little too far. He gave a dry chuckle at the thought.

The big cat stood there and fixed him with an unblinking stare, almost as though he was demanding to know where Gemma was.

'She's gone, mate,' Nash said sadly. He tipped some beer into the saucer by the step and watched as the cat moved closer to sniff at it suspiciously. 'Here you are. Get some of that into ya, big fella. You don't want those dogs finding out you're drinking *milk*, do you?'

Nash leaned back on his elbows and let out a long sigh as he looked up into the black sky above him. Gemma had given him a glimpse of a life he could have had. It depressed him to even think about it, so he didn't. He grabbed another beer instead and tried to forget the image of a brunette beauty with big green eyes and a smile that melted his heart.

Twenty

'Gemma? Did you hear me?'

Gemma jumped in her chair and blinked as she brought her mind back to what she was supposed to be focusing on. The meeting.

'I'm sorry, I was a bit distracted. You were saying?'

Her father was frowning from the end of the boardroom table; across from Gemma, her cousin Philip sniggered and her uncles were busy shuffling papers and sending sidelong glances at the clients. A blush crept up her neck as she realised that every set of eyes was now fixed on her curiously.

She'd been working in the firm for six weeks, comforting herself by making a plan to give it six months and then leave if she didn't like it. But she knew that Northcotes didn't simply tide themselves over in the business *for a while*; they pretty much had to be carried out of there in a coffin!

And so much for her father's argument that she should join the business so he could finally retire. Other than a few days a week when he knocked off early or came in late after a round of golf, there was no sign of him actually reducing his workload—much to her mother's dismay. Apparently Northcotes didn't simply retire either! An image popped into her mind of herself forty or fifty years from now, with her hair in a big grey bun, both herself and her desk covered in cobwebs.

Her Uncle James cleared his throat and repeated his question and Gemma took a deep breath and did her best to concentrate.

The truth was, she already hated the job. Each morning she forced herself out of bed and into the office, dreading every second of the day ahead. She felt uncomfortable in the tailored skirt suits and fitted blouses she had to wear, as well as the high heels that hurt her feet. She missed jumping out of bed, dragging on jeans and a t-shirt and pulling her hair back in a ponytail before starting her day. She resented the time she had to spend every morning putting on make-up and doing her hair. And she especially loathed being stuck behind these big glass windows, even if they overlooked a spectacular harbour view.

She missed Dunoon.

She felt like a square peg in a round hole. Although she had known them all her life, she felt as though she had nothing in common with the people she worked with. Her cousins were both married and played golf on weekends—they were like miniature versions of her father and uncles, something she hadn't questioned before but now found a little creepy. More than anything, she didn't belong in this job. She knew she couldn't put off telling her father much longer. Some big changes had to be made, for the sake of her sanity if nothing else, but right now she felt as though she was perched on the edge of a building with one foot up on the rail, waiting for the final push that would send her flying.

•

Gemma had tried to snap herself out of her low spirits. Even six weeks on she was still on farm time, waking up early every day, and she had taken to getting up and going for a walk. She'd read somewhere that endorphins produced by exercise were good for depression. She wondered if a broken heart was in the same class as depression. At least it couldn't hurt. So she went walking most days, enjoying the crisp morning air. It wasn't the same kind of crispness that she'd grown to love out at Dunoon, but it was as close as she was going to get in the heart of the city.

Jazz had settled back into city life easily, getting a part-time job waiting tables at the local cafe while she awaited news on the many job applications she'd sent out since they came back. Gemma had offered her the spare room until she found a better paying job. Most evenings Jazz went out for drinks, and was seldom home on the weekends. Sometimes Gemma reflected a little sourly that she should probably take encouragement from Jazz's ability to bounce back from heartbreak.

This Friday night, Gemma was meeting her parents for dinner. Even though making the effort to dress up and go out was the last thing she felt like after a long week of work, she knew that declining the invitation would only cause a huge fuss that she didn't feel like dealing with. Going out would be the lesser of two evils, and she made a deal with herself as she locked her car and headed for the restaurant: if she smiled enough through dinner, she could have an extra slice of the lemon and lime cheesecake she'd made last night and put in the freezer.

Walking into the restaurant, she couldn't help admiring the tastefully outfitted room. The crisp white linen on every table, secluded areas set aside for those wanting a more intimate dining experience and the tasteful yet unpretentious artworks that were scattered throughout the room—it all created an atmosphere which gave diners a truly unique and memorable experience. It also didn't hurt that the restaurant was owned by a celebrity chef, but she admired the way they'd put the place together.

Her parents were already seated at a table, and her heart sank as she saw they weren't alone. She plastered a polite smile on her face and leaned down to kiss them both in greeting. Their guest stood up and put out his hand as her father introduced him. 'This is Nathan Dupoint. You remember, I went to university with his father. He dropped by to say hello while he was in town and we invited him to dinner with us. Nathan, my daughter, Gemma.'

'It's nice to see you again, Gemma. I believe we met once before, many years ago.'

She did remember. 'You pulled my plaits and teased me about wearing braces.'

Her mother cleared her throat pointedly from across the table, but Nathan seemed amused and held her hand just a fraction too long. Dinner with her parents was one thing, but being polite to a stranger was a whole other kettle of fish; it was going to take more than one piece of cheesecake to get through this. When the waiter came by to ask if she wanted a drink she quickly ordered a glass of wine, and took a hasty sip when it arrived.

She hadn't planned on ordering a second glass, but Nathan was turning out to be a drag and she was desperately trying to catch the drinks waiter for a refill. In the last half hour they'd already heard no less than three times that Nathan was the youngest manager in his field, and Gemma suspected they'd hear it a few more times if he could possibly find a way to slip it into the conversation. He waved his hands about languidly while he spoke, and Gemma couldn't help noticing the immaculately manicured nails. When he'd shook her hand earlier she'd felt how soft his skin was. Somehow it just wasn't right that a guy could have a better manicure than her. An image of strong, work-hardened hands flashed before her eyes and she quickly pushed it aside before the familiar wave of longing had a chance to take hold.

'Your father tells me you've just joined the company. How are you finding it?' Nathan asked, sitting back in his seat as he sipped his wine and considered her.

Gemma opened her mouth to speak, but her father cut in briskly. 'She's got a bit to learn, but I think she'll be fine.'

The abrupt dismissal in her father's tone hit a nerve and suddenly Jazz's words played back through her head: '*You are the only one keeping yourself trapped in your life. You've got a backbone—use it.*'

'So, have you always wanted to go into the family business, Gemma?' Nathan asked, his gaze slipping a little to hover somewhere between her chest and neck.

'Actually, no,' Gemma found herself saying. 'I wanted to be a chef when I finished high school.'

'I wanted to be a train driver, but that was never going to happen, now, was it?' her father interjected sarcastically.

'Why not? Why couldn't you have been a train driver?' Gemma demanded, surprising herself and her parents.

Her father stared at her for a moment, then sighed. 'Because I had responsibilities. My father expected me to take over the company he and his father had built from the ground up, that's why. You think I would have been able to bring you up in the lifestyle you take for granted if I'd been a train driver?'

'Surely if you wanted to do something else, your father would have supported your decision,' Gemma said, staring at her father almost pleadingly. 'Isn't that what parents are supposed to do? Encourage their kids to be whatever they want to be?'

'I think you've had enough to drink,' her father muttered.

'I've barely finished my first one,' she said loudly. 'It's *not* the wine talking; it's me finally telling you what I've wanted to tell you for years. Dad, I don't want to work for you. I want to be a chef.'

'Don't be ridiculous.' He took a hasty sip of his wine, scowling at her to indicate she'd gone too far.

Gemma couldn't back down now. 'It's not ridiculous. I'm sorry, Dad, but I just can't see myself working in the office for the rest of my life. I don't love what I'm doing, not the way you love it. I love cooking.'

'Darling, this isn't really the time or place to be having this conversation,' her mother put in, glancing anxiously across at their dinner guest who looked like he wished he was sitting at any one of the *other* tables in the room right now.

'When *is* the right time, Mum? There's never a right time. I'm sorry but I can't do this anymore. Before I went out to Bingorra, I had no idea what I was capable of. Once I stepped out of my comfort zone, I discovered I could do amazing things. I drenched sheep and helped castrate cattle, for goodness sake.' From the corner of her eye she saw Nathan covering his mouth with his hand, and her mother's mouth dropped open in horror. 'I could never imagine doing that before, and yet I did. I *need* to do this, Dad.'

'You can't be serious!' her father blustered.

'I *am*,' she said slowly, as the enormity of what she was saying hit her. Holy cow, she was really doing this. A surge of panic threatened to choke her as she realised that she was actually telling her parents she was quitting her job so she could be a chef. She wondered for a moment whether she was dreaming; but if it were a dream, why would Nathan the metrosexual be sitting at the table with them, wearing a confused expression on his undoubtedly freshly moisturised face?

Dinner wrapped up pretty quickly after that, as her father was fuming silently and her mother looked like she was about to burst into tears. Gemma almost felt sorry for Nathan, who looked distinctly uncomfortable at finding himself inadvertently caught up in their family domestic. She slipped away after a hasty goodnight to her parents. She knew that further unpleasant discussions were inevitable, but this time she was determined not to buckle under pressure. She just needed to remember that she was so much stronger than she used to be; even if the magnitude of the risk she was taking terrified her, she was ready to give it a try. Nothing and no one could get in the way of her dream now.

•

Two weeks later, Gemma stared at her bedroom wall in disbelief.

This wasn't happening.

It couldn't be happening.

She dropped her eyes to her lap once more and realised with a sinking sensation that this was indeed happening.

Once again she saw herself on top of that building she'd pictured earlier; now, though, her foot slipped from the edge and she began to freefall.

According to the two bright blue lines on a small plastic stick, Gemma Northcote, heir to a mini dynasty and soon to be unemployed, was about to become a single mother.

Fan-freakin-tastic.

Part 2

Twenty-one

Gemma glanced in the rear-view mirror and smiled at the sight of the dark-haired child asleep in his car seat, surrounded by bags and boxes. They were on the last leg of their journey and she was grateful that he'd turned out to be such a great little traveller.

It had been just over fourteen months since she'd last been out this way. There were a lot of things she blamed the placenta for sucking out of her brain during pregnancy, but the day she left Bingorra was unfortunately not one of them: it was as fixed in her mind as her baby's date of birth.

Shifting tiredly in her seat, she focused once more on the road ahead. Had she made the right decision in coming back here? It had been anything but rash. The idea that had started to develop while she was first out here had never really left her. All this time it had been brewing in the back of her mind until the time was right for it to blossom from an idea into a reality.

She'd worked hard in the last fourteen months, harder than she'd ever thought possible. Her parents' initial reaction to her pregnancy had been understandably negative. She didn't blame them. She'd been in denial herself for the first three months. Automatically she glanced in the mirror again, feeling guilty for her earlier, less-than-maternal feelings at the discovery that she was pregnant. Now she couldn't imagine her life without little Finn in it. He was her entire world.

The early months of her pregnancy had not been a happy time. Just before doing the home pregnancy test, she'd accepted a job with Micca at Nirvana, his boutique restaurant. In the shock of her discovery, she hadn't told her parents or anyone else about the baby for the first few months, until it became a little difficult to hide. It was a big enough step resigning from her father's company without also dumping on them the fact that they were soon to become grandparents. If she was honest, she'd also been trying to avoid thinking about the baby herself—maybe in some delusional hope that it would all just go away and she wouldn't have to deal with this enormous change to her life. If she stopped to think about it for too long she started hyperventilating, so she just didn't think about it until it became too hard to ignore.

After resigning from her old job, Gemma moved out of her comfortable apartment and found a small one-bedroom flat near the restaurant. It didn't feel right to remain living in her parents' apartment when she'd more or less thrown a secure job and future in their faces in order to follow her dream. She knew it wouldn't be easy, and it wasn't, but she needed to do this on her own if for no other reason than to prove to herself that she could. She missed her parents. Leaving the company had hurt her father tremendously and they had made it clear to her that they would not be supporting her—quote—*foolish endeavour,* but it still hurt to know they had turned their backs on her.

In spite of her sadness over her parents, and the shock of her pregnancy, she was excited to be working as unofficial apprentice to Micca. It was just as well she didn't suffer from morning sickness, as she found herself working extra hard—partly to avoid having too much time to think, but mainly because she wanted to learn as much as she could. She also wanted to prove herself to everyone who thought she was nuts for throwing away a secure, well-paid career to work long hours for low pay in the restaurant industry.

Her parents' response she understood: they had a right to feel blindsided by her sudden decision and apparent personality change. It was Jazz's initial reaction that had upset her the most. Gemma had expected a little support from her best friend—after all, for years Jazz had been telling her she needed to stand up for herself and choose her own path in life. But Jazz had stared at her as though she'd lost her mind.

'You've done *what*?'

'I resigned and I'm taking an apprenticeship with Micca,' Gemma repeated.

'You're giving up a ninety-thousand-dollar-a-year job to work in a restaurant for twelve dollars an hour?'

'It's not about the money, Jazz. I'm doing something I love.'

'Well, I hope you love it a lot, because you won't be able to afford to do anything else *but* work.'

'Why are you being so judgemental all of a sudden? I thought you'd be happy.'

'When I told you to stand up for yourself I didn't mean you should work for minimum wage! I thought you'd just get a job with another firm.'

A few months later when Gemma finally broke down and told Jazz about the baby, her friend had been speechless, for probably the first time in her entire life. 'You're pregnant?' she'd finally said in a flat tone, unsure she was hearing right. Then it sunk in. 'You're pregnant to Nash!' she'd gasped.

'Of course to Nash. Who else would it be?'

'Oh my God,' she whispered before raising her voice, 'Oh. My. God, Gemma! What are you going to do?'

'I don't know. Have it, I guess.'

'You guess?'

'I don't have much choice, do I? I can't bring myself to . . .' She couldn't really even say the words out loud. In fact she had considered getting rid of it—the thought had gone through her head moments after the initial shock of realising she was pregnant—but she'd immediately dismissed the idea. She'd never imagined herself ever being in this position and now that she was, she found it strange that everything inside her was telling her to protect this child, even though it could not have possibly come at a worst time in her entire life.

Gemma had allowed herself one self-indulgent moment to cry and, all the while, Jazz had held her and told her everything would be alright.

'Have you told Nash?'

'No.'

'You know you have to, right?'

'Yes, I know,' Gemma said wearily. 'I tried calling him last night but he wasn't answering. I've left him a message to call me. I don't want you to say anything to Brittany about this,' she said, turning her head to look Jazz in the eye.

'How could you even think I would?' Jazz said and Gemma felt bad when she heard the injured tone in her voice.

'I'm sorry, it's just that I know you two are friends and I didn't want it to slip out and have her telling Nash before I do.'

'I haven't even seen her since we got back,' Jazz shrugged. 'I don't really have a lot in common with them anymore.' She'd been spending a lot of time with her new workmates. 'I can't believe I'm going to be an aunty,' she said, shaking her head. 'Aunty Jazz,' she said slowly, testing the name out loud. After that there was no stopping her. Jazz would drop by with baby clothes she'd seen at markets, and toys she just couldn't resist buying while out shopping; anyone would think she was the one who was having a baby instead of Gemma.

•

Her parents, too, had eventually come around once they'd gotten over the shock of discovering she was pregnant. They doted on Finn, and Jazz had melted at her first glimpse of him, twenty minutes after his birth, when she'd come to after passing out in the delivery room. So much for Jazz being her support person during labour, Gemma thought wryly. Indeed, Jazz's own life had taken an unexpected turn that day: having hit her head when she passed out, she'd spent a few hours under observation and ended up dating Gemma's doctor. They were engaged and due to be married at the end of the year.

Oh, how the tables had turned. Everyone had always thought Jazz was the ditsy one who would end up doing something stupid like falling pregnant, and yet here she was about to marry a doctor while 'good girl' Gemma had thrown in a promising career and was about to start a business from scratch with a five-month-old baby . . . alone!

The thought triggered a twinge of guilt, which she quickly brushed aside. Nash Whittaker was *not* the reason she was coming out here. Well, he wasn't her only reason for coming out here. She was still hurt and angry that he'd sent her packing in the first place, but she was also furious that he'd refused to return any of the phone calls she'd made when she first found out she was pregnant. She'd left multiple messages on his phone asking him to call her back, although not mentioning the reason why; there was no way she was leaving a voicemail message saying that she was having his baby. However, he'd made it more than clear he didn't want to have anything to do with her. Maybe knowing he'd fathered a baby would have made him call her back, but at the time she wasn't thinking very logically. In any case, after those first few weeks of jumping each time her phone rang only to be disappointed when it wasn't him, her heart had hardened and she'd stopped calling. His feelings about her were crystal clear. She'd rather raise the child alone than with someone who felt trapped into being part of her life. A girl had her pride, after all.

Until a few months ago, her emotions had still been too fragile and her life too shambolic for her to think about Nash and his feelings, but recently she had started to think about the situation more rationally and had realised that she couldn't in all decency keep Finn a secret from him for much longer. No matter how cruelly he might have treated her, it was his right to have the opportunity to see Finn grow up. And Finn had the right to know his father. If Nash still wanted nothing to do with Gemma, then so be it—she was stronger now and she knew she could handle it—but he needed the chance to be part of his son's life. And deep down she knew Nash would never turn his back on his child.

•

Nash parked the ute and sat quietly for a minute, closing his eyes and enjoying the sun through the windscreen. It had been a while since he'd taken time out to just sit and do nothing. He'd been working hard the last few months, and it was starting to pay off, thank God. Prices were up this season and his crop looked good. He'd been doing well enough to hire an offsider, and having an extra person around—particularly one who didn't need to look up YouTube to work out how to do things—made a big difference. He gave a small snort of amusement at the thought, but as quickly as it came it was gone again, replaced with a dull kind of pain. He hadn't thought about Gemma Northcote for *two whole days*. It was hard to forget someone when everywhere you looked she'd left some kind of mark.

The kitchen wasn't as clean as when she'd lived at Dunoon, but it still had the little touches she'd brought to it—the bright placemats in the centre of the table, the blue-winged stained-glass butterfly she'd bought one day in town and hung from the curtain rod. In her haste to leave on that last day, she'd left behind a hairbrush and a bottle of perfume on his dressing table, and he couldn't bring himself to move them. He was no better than his father. He'd turned into a real-life, love-gone-wrong country song. He couldn't even escape her memory outside; everywhere he went he still saw her.

Shaking himself out of his doldrums, he pushed open the door. Passing the back of the ute, he gave the three dogs a quick rough pat and told them to stay, then headed towards the hardware store. Since Gemma had left, he avoided town as much as possible. Unfortunately he still had to eat, and on his rare trips to the grocery store he dreaded having to face Wendy and her knowing, silent disappointment. He'd prefer it if she actually yelled at him—anything but that look in her eye that suggested she thought he was the world's biggest dickhead for letting Gemma walk out of his life. Like he needed anyone to tell him what he already knew. But it still didn't change anything. You couldn't make certain things fit where they didn't belong. It was as simple as that.

It hadn't helped that, early on, Wendy had tried to talk to him about it. He'd almost snapped her head off, which he felt bad about now, but he hadn't been in a good place those first few weeks after Gemma had left. He'd thrown himself even harder into his work and refused to talk to anyone. Britt had left again not long after the girls, heading back to Sydney. He didn't blame her—he'd been such a walking ball of pain and fury that even *he* hadn't wanted to be around himself.

He'd slowly eased himself out of the initial mood, but inside he still felt broken and bruised. Then coming in from work one day, a few weeks after Gemma had left Dunoon, he'd found two missed calls from her on his phone. Seeing her name on the screen, his heart had briefly pounded with hope, then sunk again. His thumb had hovered above the keypad for a moment as he waged an internal war with himself, and, although it hurt like hell to do so, he deleted the calls without listening to them. He didn't know why she was calling, but he knew there was no way he could hear her voice and not go tearing down to the city to beg her to come back. He wanted to with every fibre of his being, but he kept remembering those hard years he'd lived through with his father when they'd been so deeply in debt that they had barely managed to hang onto the place. He knew he couldn't make Gemma live that kind of unpredictable life with all its stresses.

He did a double take as he reached the old Giuseppe's restaurant and noticed that the faded 'For Lease' sign was gone. He made a note to ask around and see what was going on. Clearly he'd been doing too well at avoiding everyone. That'd teach him to stay away so long. He wondered what other news he'd missed. It was time to stop licking his wounds and get back to life.

•

Gemma slowed the car to a crawl as she drove through the main street. There was no traffic to worry about, so she double-parked in front of the old restaurant and squinted, trying to make out anything behind the frosted glass.

In his baby seat, Finn was beginning to get restless. He'd been so well behaved, only getting squirmy the last twenty minutes or so before hitting town. Gemma drove on a few metres, parked her car in front of the estate agent's office, and unclipped her seatbelt with a weary sigh.

The real estate agent was a happy round-faced man, short and stocky and with a wide-brimmed bush hat in pristine condition. Gemma signed the final papers on the lease of the shop and small apartment above, then climbed back into the car for the short drive up the street. A narrow laneway ran behind the main street; Gemma parked her compact Mazda in the carport attached to the rear of the shop. For now she grabbed only the basics, deciding to wait until Finn was asleep later that evening to get the rest.

As far as homes went, it wasn't fantastic, but it would do just fine until she got her business up and running. She was pretty sure the decor hadn't been updated since the late seventies, but given that retro was coming back into fashion it was probably trendy again.

By the time she sat down at the small kitchen table and unpacked the esky bag with Finn's snacks inside, she was exhausted. What she'd really like to do right now was sit and relax, but she knew that wasn't going to happen just yet. She needed to go to the grocery store and grab some food before it closed, and she wanted to check out the progress on the restaurant downstairs. She'd been lucky to find such a helpful builder who had been sending her updates regularly by email, attaching photos here and there, but she still couldn't wait to see it for herself.

She hadn't told anyone she was coming back to Bingorra—and by anyone she meant Wendy. Everything had happened so fast the day they left town that she didn't realise she hadn't said goodbye to her friend till she was already back in Sydney. She wasn't sure of the reception she would receive when she eventually went into the grocery store, but she'd be finding out soon enough.

Carrying Finn, she unlocked the back door of the restaurant and pushed it open. She did a quick walk-through, inhaling the strong scent of freshly cut timber, and running her hands over the white tabletops and the bright red upholstery of the booths. They looked fresh and new—in stark contrast to the dirty, scuffed walls, which she'd asked the builders to leave so she could paint them herself. She couldn't afford to pay for everything to be done, and she'd have to put in a lot of elbow grease herself in order to get the place ready for opening, but she had budgeted for a new kitchen and new booth tables and flooring. Which left the painting, cleaning and decorating for Gemma to take care of.

Her parents had offered to fund the entire business outright, given that they couldn't talk her out of her plan, but Gemma didn't want a handout. She also wasn't going so far as to turn them down either. She wasn't naïve—getting a loan from a bank with her limited experience and a child to support wasn't going to be an easy feat—so she had a solicitor draw up a loan document with her parents and borrowed the money from them. Had she wanted to, her parents would have lent her more than enough to have the place looking state-of-the-art, but she knew that the majority of new businesses went bust within the first year or so because they had too much debt hanging over them. She was expecting the first few months to be lean until she got the place up and running and established a regular clientele, so she was happy to keep the loan to a minimum and see how things went before investing too much money in fittings and decorating.

'What do you reckon, Finn? You think Mummy can pull this thing off?'

Finn looked up at her and grinned. Despite her fatigue she couldn't resist his smile and did a twirl around the centre of the room.

No one was at the counter when she walked into the grocery store a little while later. Gemma sat Finn in the baby seat in the trolley and clipped the belt around his middle before digging out a rusk for him to chew on while she raced through the store and grabbed the essentials.

As she rounded the first aisle she saw a figure stacking the shelves. She met Wendy's surprised gaze and stopped. 'Here we go,' she breathed softly. This had been one of the moments she'd been dreading since making her plans to come back but it had to happen eventually.

'Gemma? What ... ?' Wendy's face had lit up in a big smile, which faltered when she saw Finn, who beamed at her from his seat in the front of the trolley.

Gemma squared her shoulders. 'Hi, Wendy.'

'What are you doing out here?'

'I've just moved into town. I'm opening a cafe in the old restaurant premises.'

'You're what?' Wendy gaped. 'You're the new owner?'

Gemma shrugged. 'Well, I'm only renting it—but yes, I guess so. Surprise!' she said, rather weakly.

'Why didn't you ring and tell me?' Wendy demanded after a pause. 'I could have helped you with everything.' Then her eyes dropped back to Finn. She looked at him more closely, and surprise then understanding flashed across her face. 'Oh. I see. You thought I'd tell Nash.'

Put like that it sounded awful. 'It's not that I didn't trust you, I just didn't want you to be in the middle of it all. It's complicated, Wendy. I just wanted to do this by myself in my own time.'

'You're going to tell him you're here, though, right?'

'Eventually.'

'Eventually? You have to tell him, Gemma, especially . . .' Wendy paused and looked down again at Finn. 'I don't even have to ask. He looks just like Nash. He doesn't know about any of this, does he?'

Gemma shook her head. 'He made it clear he didn't want anything to do with me, Wendy.' No matter how much time had passed, it still hurt to remember that. 'I'll tell him once I get things sorted with the cafe.'

'You think you'll have that much time? Sweetheart, you're in Bingorra now. I'll be surprised if he doesn't already know you're back in town.'

Gemma felt a flutter of panic at Wendy's words. No! She wasn't ready yet. She'd been trying to prepare herself ever since she'd made the decision to come back, and she was under no illusion as to what Nash's reaction would be. She just wasn't ready to deal with it *this minute*. 'I'll handle Nash if and when he turns up,' she said firmly. 'Right now, though, I have a business to set up, and I'd really appreciate having a little more time to settle in before I have to talk to Nash.'

Even as she said it, she felt bad. This was why she hadn't told Wendy in the first place. The last thing she wanted to do was put her in an awkward position, but she didn't have much choice.

Wendy looked at her levelly. 'I'm not going to call him, but there's no way you're going to be able to keep it hidden from him for long. Not here. Sooner or later you're going to have to deal with it. And Nash has a right to know about his son.'

It irked Gemma to hear this from Wendy. Hadn't she already decided that Nash was going to be part of Finn's life? That's why she was here. 'I'm giving him the chance to get to know his son,' Gemma snapped. 'I didn't have to do this after the way he refused to return my phone calls when I tried to tell him I was pregnant. So now I do this on my terms.'

'Fine. But I hope you know you're stirring up a wasps' nest by going about it like this. If he doesn't find out directly from you you're going to have one mighty pissed-off man on your hands.'

Gemma nodded abruptly, and turned away. Whichever way she did it, Nash wasn't going to be happy. But right now she had too many other things on her mind, and priority number one was in desperate need of a bath and dinner.

Twenty-two

Over the next few days, life slowly began to fall into place. Before she'd left Sydney she'd contacted the day care in town and enrolled Finn. She was relieved to find the small but clean centre every bit as welcoming as the manager had been on the phone. Finn was used to day care. He'd been going to one since he was six weeks old. Her mother had offered to have him part of the time which at first Gemma had hesitated to accept, but once she saw how happy it made both her mother and her son to have that quality time together, she realised it was good for all of them.

By the end of the first week she'd finished painting the walls, and had the menus printed. The suppliers had been dealt with and stock ordered, and today the floor coverings would be finally going down. The little restaurant looked bright and cheerful. She loved her new kitchen and couldn't wait to start cooking, which she'd need to do the next day in order to have her display case stocked with cakes and muffins. Everything else she would make off the menu from scratch. She'd finally mastered the large stainless-steel coffee machine she'd ordered and had installed, and the smell of fresh coffee wafting through the small cafe filled her with joy. This was so much better than she had ever imagined, she thought, taking one final look around at the freshly painted walls and gleaming tables she'd spent all day cleaning. She switched off the lights and locked the door before heading outside to climb the stairs to her apartment.

•

The cafe was empty, and she'd just finished wiping down the tables for the third time this morning, completely unnecessarily, when the door opened with a jingle of bells. Gemma looked up and smiled hesitantly as she recognised the man who had just walked in.

'Hello, Ben. How are you?'

'I heard a rumour about some city chick who'd opened a cafe, so I came down to check the place out,' he said, grinning as he came up to the counter. 'I had no idea it was you.'

His cheerful mood drew a genuine smile from her. 'Coming to check out the place?' Gemma teased. 'Or coming to check out the chick?'

'I have no idea what you're implying,' he replied, trying for a haughty tone.

Gemma rolled her eyes. 'Sure you don't. Anyway, how've you been?'

'Good. You know, working with the old man, trying to stay outta trouble, that kind of thing.'

'How's your brother?'

'Perfect as always,' he said with a sarcastic drawl. 'Keeping Mum and Dad happy by marrying some sheila from Melbourne. Just what we need, more city chicks moving to the country.' He leaned on the counter and gave her a lopsided grin. 'Whatever happened to your friend, that blonde bit of dynamite?'

'Jazz is engaged as well. To a doctor,' Gemma added, and hoped *that* bit of news got back to his mother as Gemma recalled Mrs Henderson hadn't considered Jazz good enough for her family.

Ben let out a small grunt. 'That was the only time I came close to being the favourite son, when Mack lost it for a while and took off with your friend.' His tone was blasé, but Gemma saw the shadow behind his grin. 'So what brings *you* back to this hellhole?' he went on.

She frowned. 'I like Bingorra. Plus I wanted a bit of a change and I knew there was a real need for a decent place to eat around here, so I thought I'd try my luck at opening a business.'

'Does Whittaker know you're back in town?'

Gemma looked away and grabbed a laminated menu from beside the till. 'I have no idea. Are you staying for something to eat?' She ignored the knowing gleam in Ben's eye. He was the last person she wanted to get into all that with.

'Sure, I could eat something.' He slid into the nearest booth. After giving the menu the briefest once-over, he ordered a burger. 'So how's it been so far?' he asked.

'Slow and steady,' Gemma said, managing a smile. The truth was it had been more slow than steady. 'But it's only the first week and a lot of people in the area don't come to town every day, so I'm expecting it to take a little while for word to get around that the place is open.'

'I wouldn't worry about word getting around, it's already starting to spread. Pretty soon everyone in the district will know you're here,' he added pointedly. 'You ready for that?'

Her smile didn't falter. 'Sure. If I was worried about who knew I was back in town, I'd hardly have come back here, would I?'

'I heard he was pretty cut up about you leaving,' said Ben.

'That was a long time ago,' she said dismissively. 'I'm sure we're both well and truly over it all by now.'

'Well, that's good to hear.' Ben leaned back in the booth as he looked at her. Gemma felt herself blush slightly at the open attraction she read in Ben's expression, and felt a flicker of something run through her. She couldn't say it was excitement, but it certainly wasn't disgust. It had been a long time since she'd been looked at like that by a man. When she was pregnant with Finn, she had become invisible to men—not that she minded. Even after Finn's birth, she was so busy and so intent on learning everything she could and making plans for her own business that men were the last thing on her mind.

'I'll just go and get your order ready,' she said now, escaping into the kitchen.

The next day, business began to pick up. Two people came in for breakfast, and then six for coffee and cake before midday. She suspected they had come in mainly out of curiosity, to see what had happened to the old Giuseppe's, but they all seemed impressed by the transformation she'd wrought, and she basked shamelessly in their approval. She figured it didn't matter what had brought them in, as long as they came back again and spread the word.

She was looking forward to unveiling phase two of her plan—opening the restaurant she would run on the same site—but she had to wait until she'd gained a reputation through the cafe and the business began earning a decent income so she could hire some extra staff to work alongside her. Tamping down her impatience, she decided to simply enjoy her first taste of success. She needed to learn to savour the small achievements when they came around. Besides, she'd come too far to blow things by being overeager.

•

Nash put the last of his groceries on the checkout belt and dug his wallet from his back pocket. Wendy seemed a little preoccupied today, he thought. As he looked at her, she glanced away almost guiltily. Okay, something was definitely up. 'What?' he asked, putting his hand over the bag of chips she was about to lift and scan.

Wendy shook her head, not meeting his eyes. 'Nothing.'

'I know something's going on. You're not tearing strips off me for filling the trolley with junk food. What is it? Is something wrong?'

Without looking up, she brushed his hand away and scanned the rest of his purchases. Only then did she speak. 'Have you been up to the new cafe yet?'

Nash frowned. 'Don't change the subject.'

'I'm not.'

His frown deepened. What the hell? 'No, I haven't. Why?' He stared at her, baffled, as she chewed her bottom lip. 'Wendy, for God's sake, what's got into you?'

'You need to go up there,' she said quietly.

'Okay then,' he said, watching his old friend warily. 'I'll be sure to check it out soon.'

'No. You *need* to go up there. Today,' she added, a little more firmly.

There was obviously something very wrong with her, Nash reflected with dismay. Not that he had much experience with women's health issues but maybe Wendy was going through menopause. Didn't women go a little haywire and get those hot flushes? He eyed her carefully but didn't see any sign of profuse sweating. 'Okay. I'll go up and check it out before I head home,' he promised, keen to finish the transaction and get the hell out of there. Waving away her offer to charge the food to his account, he handed across an array of twenty- and fifty-dollar notes.

'I'm sorry,' said Wendy, looking at him with a worried expression.

'For what?'

'Th-that I didn't have any bigger change,' she stammered, dropping the coins in his hand and closing the register.

Nash threaded his fingers through the plastic bags and hurried outside, genuinely concerned. It was frightening to see how quickly someone could lose their marbles. After he'd placed the groceries in the back of the Land Cruiser, he hesitated, looking up the street towards the old restaurant.

Just then his stomach growled impatiently. With a sigh, Nash headed along the footpath to see what all the fuss was about.

•

Gemma pushed open the front door of the day care centre and rushed to the counter. She'd received a call to come and collect Finn after he'd come down with a sudden temperature. Fortunately there hadn't been any customers in the cafe at the time as she'd had to close it to come and get him. However, this had clarified how tenuous her situation was. Whether she liked it or not, she was going to have to hire someone to help. She would have preferred to wait a bit longer before having to pay wages; there were still some quiet times during the day when she'd be paying an employee to just stand around. But hopefully that wouldn't last much longer. Each day seemed to be bringing in more customers, and so far all the feedback had been positive.

She had begun to suspect that Ben had something to do with her growing success. More than a few people had told her that Ben had strongly recommended the food, and she would always be grateful to him for that. As it was, Ben himself came in most days for lunch. While Gemma appreciated his friendship and support, she was growing increasingly aware that he was hoping for more than just friendship. She'd dropped several hints that she wasn't interested in romance, but each time the subject came up he just smiled and told her he would wait her out. She really didn't want to hurt him, and it troubled her that he was refusing to take her seriously.

When she walked into the centre, her poor little man was lying in the crib looking flushed and miserable. She picked him up and held him close, feeling love surge through her. Before Finn, she hadn't realised that she could love anyone so fiercely. Motherhood had opened her up to a whole new range of emotions and she found it hard now to think back to a time when she didn't have this precious little person in her life.

'Come on, mister, let's get you home and to bed,' she whispered, kissing his forehead. She took his backpack from the kindly centre operator with a grateful smile.

Juggling her sleeping baby and the keys, Gemma unlocked the door at the rear of the cafe and climbed the staircase to the apartment. After dropping her handbag, Finn's backpack and the keys on the small dining table, she settled Finn into his bed and put the jug on. There was no way she could reopen the cafe again this afternoon with Finn sick, but closing again tomorrow was out of the question: all the hard work she'd put into building up her reputation would go down the drain if people turned up only to find it closed. There was no longer any question about it: first thing tomorrow she was going to hire herself a helper.

•

Nash reached over and irritably turned up the volume on the CD player. Damn Wendy. He hadn't even been hungry until she'd started banging on about the cafe. Then he was suddenly starving, but when he reached the new cafe he'd found it closed.

Whatever was going on with Wendy, he hoped she got over it fast. And who the hell opened a new business and then closed whenever it suited them? It was only three o'clock in the afternoon! He suspected that the cafe owner, whoever they were, wouldn't be in business for long.

Twenty-three

Finn was a little better in the morning, but Gemma didn't want to risk sending him back to day care, so she put him in a playpen in a small space between the kitchen and the front counter. He was quiet for most of the morning, but by lunchtime he'd had enough and was beginning to get restless.

As Gemma delivered coffees to an elderly couple, then brought over their toasted sandwiches, she crooned to Finn as calmly as possible, 'Mummy will pick you up as soon as I finish doing this, baby. I promise.'

It was then that she looked up to see Ben standing in the doorway, his eyebrows almost disappearing into his hairline. *'Mummy?'*

Crap. Gemma managed a weak smile, then cringed as Finn's grumbles grew in volume.

'Hey, little fella. What's all the noise about?' Ben walked around the counter to scoop her son up into his arms. He picked up a well-loved teddy bear and waved it in front of Finn's face.

'Ah, you don't have to do that,' said Gemma, her hands full and her eyes darting madly between her son and the man who held him.

'It's okay. You finish what you're doing, and me and the big guy here will get to know each other.' Without waiting for Gemma's response, he carried Finn across to an empty booth.

Gemma hesitated, but she had another order to get out. She quickly set about delivering the food, a forced smile on her face. Just as she was about to head back to rescue Ben, the doorbell tinkled and another set of customers walked in. *Double crap,* she thought. She was a little reassured by a glance at Finn, who seemed quite content to be sitting on a complete stranger's lap, grinning as Ben played peekaboo. Making herself breathe out, Gemma headed over to the newcomers, smiled and handed out menus.

Half an hour later, with all the customers eating and seemingly content, Gemma finally went over to Ben. 'I'm so sorry, this is the busiest day I've had,' she said, shaking her head. 'Let me take him so you can get going.' She reached for Finn, automatically feeling his head and noting he was starting to feel warm again. A quick glance at her watch told her he was almost due for another dose of paracetamol.

Ben looked up and grinned. 'It's alright. We're having a great time.'

'You didn't come in here to babysit,' Gemma protested

weakly, before adding, 'But I'm so glad you were here, I don't know what I would have done otherwise.'

'Happy to help out. Came as a bit of a surprise though,' he said, eyeing her curiously.

'Oh? I didn't mention Finn before?' she asked innocently.

He raised an eyebrow. 'I think I would've remembered if you'd told me you had a kid.'

'Oh. Well, this is my son, Finn.'

'And he'd be . . . how old?' Ben asked.

Gemma pursed her lips. 'You're pretty good with babies. Where did you get all your practice?' She scooped Finn up into her arms and took him out the back to give him his next dose of paracetamol.

'My cousin has a tribe of kids,' Ben called after her. 'She's always over at our place. What can I say, kids love me.'

Gemma came back out a minute later, Finn on her hip. 'Well, you certainly have a knack for it. Thanks for taking care of him. I'm a bit stuck with him not feeling too well. I was supposed to be finding time to place an ad for a part-time waitress.'

'Like after-school work or something?'

'Well, I was actually hoping to get an older person with a bit of experience so I can leave them alone here when I have to.'

Ben looked thoughtful. 'I might be able to help you out there. Give me a sec. I'll be right back.' He got up, pulling out his mobile as he went outside.

Gemma stared after him mutely, then shook herself out of her abstraction and got a bottle for Finn, who still didn't have much of an appetite. She put him in his pram to lie down with his drink and hopefully go to sleep.

She was clearing a table, balancing plates and cutlery, when Ben came back in, grinning broadly.

'What are you looking so pleased with yourself for?' Gemma asked, although his smile was contagious.

'I think I may have just solved one of your problems.' He crossed his arms across his chest and rocked back on his heels slightly. Gemma tried not to let her gaze rest on the head of the dragon tattoo that poked out of one sleeve of his t-shirt or the tail on the other arm, or on the muscles that bulged beneath them. The last thing she needed right now was to give the man the wrong signal.

'Which problem would that be, exactly?' she asked, moving back towards the kitchen with the dishes.

'Your staffing problem.'

'Oh?'

'There'll be someone coming in to see you this afternoon. It's my Aunt Corrine. She lost her old man a few months back and Mum was only saying the other day that she needs something to keep her busy. And I know for a fact she could use the extra income.'

'Really?' Gemma didn't want to get her hopes up, but this sounded promising.

'I think you'll like her. She's not a bad old stick.'

Old stick? Gemma frowned. 'Er, Ben, just how old *is* your aunt?'

'Buggered if I know. She's older than Mum, but.'

Well, this could be interesting, Gemma thought wryly,

picturing an old woman hobbling around cafe on a walking stick, trying to balance a tray of coffees in one hand.

Later that afternoon, the door opened and a tall, slim woman in her late fifties came in and introduced herself as Corrine. For a moment, Gemma could only stare at her in surprised relief.

'Benjamin did tell you I was coming in, didn't he?' Corrine said hesitantly.

'Oh. Yes! I'm sorry, he did mention you'd be in today,' Gemma gabbled, feeling like an idiot. 'Please take a seat and I'll bring coffee.' She showed Corrine to a booth and hurried away to make two coffees, shaking her head and smiling. Imagine Ben describing this elegant woman as an old stick! Sometimes being in Bingorra was like learning a whole other language.

Corrine was perfect. She was quiet but had a friendly smile, and although sadness hovered behind her eyes she seemed excited by the prospect of working again. 'Terry was a lot older than I was,' she told Gemma quietly. 'We'd been travelling around Australia and were only home a few weeks before he had his heart attack. It was a big shock to everyone. I still can't believe it's happened. Since we sold our business I haven't had anything to do during the day. And now that Terry's gone . . .'

'I'm so sorry for your loss,' Gemma said, feeling the inadequacy of the words. Her heart went out to the woman. How horrible to be looking forward to retirement with your husband only for him to pass away before you'd really begun to enjoy it. 'If you'd like the job it's yours,' she went on. 'We can work out the hours that suit you. So far it's usually busier in the mornings, but I hope to get more people in for lunch as well.'

'I've been hearing wonderful things about the cafe,' Corrine said warmly. 'I don't think you'll have to worry about it being quiet for much longer.'

Gemma hoped Corrine's prediction was correct. They agreed on a starting date, and Gemma felt a weight lift from her shoulders as she went back to check on her sleeping son. She gently smoothed his hair from his forehead, glad to note the temperature had finally disappeared. He looked so much like his father it sometimes caught her off guard, like now. Some of the relief she'd felt moments before faded and that familiar heaviness settled once more in her stomach. The time was coming when she'd no longer be able to put off telling Nash about his son. She turned away and left the room quietly, her heart heavy and her nerves jumpy.

Twenty-four

Nash pushed open the door of the servo, tucking his wallet into his back pocket as he walked towards his ute, sitting beside the diesel bowser. He tossed his hat into the cabin and slid in behind the steering wheel. As he was pulling out of the driveway he caught a brief glimpse of a woman hurrying along the main street, her arms laden with plastic bags from the grocery store, and felt the colour drain from his face.

It couldn't be. He had to be seeing things. His gaze darted to his rear-view mirror and he swore softly as he swung the ute into a U-turn. Up ahead he could still make out the brunette, her long ponytail swinging jauntily in time with her movements, moments before she disappeared into the new cafe. Without stopping to think, he veered to the kerb, threw off his seatbelt and jumped out of the ute. He broke into a long-legged jog, then came to an abrupt halt as he reached the cafe. He hesitated only briefly before opening the old-fashioned screen door. A little bell announced his arrival. The brunette was nowhere to be seen, but he could hear someone moving around beyond the half door that presumably led to the kitchen.

'Won't be a minute,' a singsong voice called, and he felt the ground shift beneath his feet. He didn't need to get a good look at her now, he'd know that voice anywhere. He'd spent almost a year and a half wishing he could hear it again.

'Sorry about that, I was—' Gemma stepped out through the door from the kitchen, and the friendly smile dropped from her face. 'Nash.'

All he could do was stare at her dumbly. How was this possible? Was he hallucinating? What the hell was Gemma Northcote doing back in Bingorra? And why was she working in the cafe?

They stared at each other, neither of them speaking. Nash saw that she didn't seem as shocked to see him as he was at seeing her—well, she wouldn't be, would she? After all, she knew he lived here. He, on the other hand, could have used a little forewarning.

'What are you doing here?' Nash finally asked.

'I've started up a business,' she said carefully.

'But why here?' he insisted.

Gemma forced a smile. 'Why *not* here? There's a need for a service in town—so I'm providing it.'

'What happened to working for your father?'

'I decided it wasn't for me. I want to cook.'

'And you couldn't do that in Sydney?' He probably looked

as ferocious as he sounded, but he didn't care. Why the hell didn't anyone tell him she was here?

'I'd started thinking about it—not very seriously, but I had the idea while I was out here, but then . . . everything changed.' She shrugged a little awkwardly and looked away. 'But after I got back to Sydney it was all I could think about. I wanted to come back, to start my business here.'

'Why now? Why after all this time? You could have told me this was what you wanted to do before you left.' He raked a hand through his hair irritably. *Christ*, this changed everything!

Her expression changed in an instant to one of incredulity. 'You sent me away!' she cried, colour rushing into her cheeks.

'It was for your own good!'

'How? How was sending me away for my own good?'

'You would have realised sooner or later that you didn't belong here. You would have left,' he said, his voice quieter and his shoulders slumping.

'You had no right to make that decision for me.' She glared at him. A multitude of emotions floated in the space between them, all too painful and confusing to try to identify at the moment.

'You shouldn't have come back.'

'You don't get to tell me what I should or shouldn't be doing,' Gemma said angrily. 'I'm here and I'm not going anywhere. You'd better get used to it.'

He fought the little spark of hope that had lit up inside him at her words. He needed to regroup and think this through. It was too dangerous to believe anything this good could be true. 'You won't last out here,' he said helplessly.

Gemma's face hardened. 'Don't bet on it,' she snapped, her eyes flashing. 'Now, unless you're going to order something you can get out of my way. I'm working.'

Blinking, still in shock, he turned away and pushed open the door with an angry shove before vanishing out onto the street.

●

You should have told him. Gemma groaned, trying to drown out the nagging thought. She had done the right thing, she insisted; this was so *not* the time. There was no way she was calling him back today, when he was still in shock, to mention the fact that he had a son. Better to let the first shock sink in before she dropped the second one on him.

She made herself head back into the kitchen to continue unpacking her shopping. As she began chopping some parsley, she realised that her hand was shaking, and she put the knife down and took a deep, calming breath before picking it up again. *Focus, Gemma,* she told herself angrily. She tipped her head back and stared at the ceiling, drawing on whatever inner resources she had left. At least that particular unpleasantness was over and done with. She always knew the first meeting was going to be the worst. On reflection, it probably *would* have been better had she been able to combine it with the 'And by the way, you're a daddy' talk. Then it would have all been out of the way.

With a tired sigh, she resumed chopping methodically, replaying their conversation in her head. She wasn't going to last out here? Seriously? And then there was his explanation for the 'real' reason he'd sent her packing: because he expected her to go running back to the city when things got too tough.

She shook her head angrily as it sunk in. He'd chosen to push her away based on the possibility that she might eventually leave him. He'd devastated both their lives because of a stupid, irrational insecurity. Now she was more than angry with him—she was furious. Where did he get off thinking he had the right to make such a huge decision for both of them?

Well, she thought, scraping the now well-chopped parsley into a mixing bowl, he was going to have to live with that decision. She hoped he thought it was worth throwing away what they'd had. Now they'd never know what could have been. Instead of starting life as a family, they would be living as a two-house, two-family unit with their child in the middle. But as long as he did the right thing by Finn she would force herself to remain civil.

•

Nash strode into the grocery store. He was shaken up and a whole lot of pissed off right now and he needed some answers.

While he was standing at the front of the store, looking around, Wendy came out of the coldroom. Seeing him, she stopped. Judging from her expression she had instantly guessed why he was there.

She put out her hands in a placating gesture. 'Before you say anything, I didn't know she was coming back either,' she said.

'But you knew she was here!' he shouted. 'That was why you kept telling me the other day to check out the damn cafe.'

'Yes, but—' she started.

'You're my friend, Wendy! Why the hell didn't you just tell me she was back? Instead I had to see her walking up the damn street. I thought I was losing my bloody mind!'

'I'm sorry, Nash. I really am. She didn't want me to tell you.' Wendy frowned in frustration. 'What was I supposed to do? I tried to get you to go and see her.'

'You could have just told me outright.'

Wendy pursed her lips. 'Or maybe you two could just do everyone else a huge favour and get yourselves sorted out.'

'Sorted out? I didn't even know she was here.' Nash let out a long sigh and closed his eyes. 'Why the hell would she come back?'

When Wendy didn't answer, he opened his eyes and looked at her narrowly. It wasn't like her to just clam up. 'Tell me what you know, Wendy,' he said coldly. He didn't know how he knew, but something told him there was more to the story.

She shook her head, backing away. 'Oh no. I am not going to be the sacrificial lamb. You guys can sort out your own problems. If you want answers, then go ask Gemma. I'm done being agony aunt for everyone around here.'

Go ask her, he thought, rolling his eyes. Yeah, right, like he was calm enough to be having that conversation right now. He needed to take a step back and let everything settle in his mind before he even thought about talking to Gemma again. Even now he could see that Wendy had been put in a difficult position. He was still pissed off that he'd been left in the dark, but he knew it wasn't fair to take his anger out on her. If he was going to be angry at anyone it should be himself. Gemma was right, he *had* sent her away. He'd made it clear it was over between them and he'd let her walk out of his life. Why was it that something he truly believed to be in both their best interests suddenly seemed like the worst mistake of his life?

Twenty-five

After the first two days, Gemma had stopped jumping every time the doorbell tinkled. It was now almost a week since their first unpleasant meeting in the cafe, and Nash had obviously decided he had better things to do than think about her. The first few days she'd been a nervous wreck, convinced he'd be back once he'd had time to cool off, but thankfully the business was continuing to pick up and she'd been kept too busy to think about anything but making coffee and cooking enough scones, cheesecakes and muffins to keep the display shelf stocked.

The lunchtime crowd was also growing, and Gemma had begun to experiment with a few gourmet hamburgers. She didn't want to scare off her new clientele with anything too outrageous—dishes that would be fine in an inner-city sidewalk cafe would not necessarily go down as well in a rural, more traditional kind of place—but she didn't want to become just another hamburger joint either. Fast food had its place, but she was determined it wouldn't be the main focus of her cafe. Just because Bingorra was in the sticks didn't mean its population might not enjoy broadening their culinary experiences. It was her ambition to eventually include a gourmet section on her menu, and she hoped people might even discover something new and exciting through her cooking. After all, that's why she'd been determined to study under Micca before opening her own business. She didn't have to be a qualified chef to open her own cafe, but she wanted to at least learn everything she could from a top chef and know that she had the confidence to do it well before she risked her money and reputation on a business venture of her own.

To her relief and satisfaction, with each passing day the number of happy customers was growing. And with each compliment and promise to return, she felt her own confidence growing too.

One customer with a very set view of what constituted good food was Ben. Every day at lunchtime he came into the cafe and ordered what he called a *real* hamburger, one with as much beef, bacon, cheese, egg and pineapple as would physically fit on the biggest hamburger bun she had.

This afternoon he came in later than usual, just as Gemma was handing Finn over to his new babysitter, Bess, after picking him up from day care.

'Hey there,' Ben greeted Finn and received a big grin in return. 'You should bring him out home one day. Mum's got some new lambs she's bottlefeeding. I reckon Finn would get a kick outta seeing 'em.'

Gemma smiled gratefully. 'Thanks, Ben, Finn would like that.'

'Just Finn?' he asked, his gaze dropping to hers while Finn gripped his finger playfully. 'What about his mum? Would she like that too?'

'I like sheep,' she conceded lightly. She knew that wasn't what he was asking, but she really didn't want to get into this with him right now. Sooner or later she would need to have the 'talk' with him and make sure he was under no illusion that there was anything more than friendship between them.

'Fair enough. Then we'll make it a date,' he said with a cheeky grin before taking his seat in a booth and waiting for his hamburger.

•

Heading upstairs later that afternoon after locking up the cafe, Gemma was tired, but it was a good tired. It had been another busy day, and she was growing steadily more confident that the business would be a success. At any rate, she was proud of what she'd accomplished so far.

She smiled as she walked into the tiny apartment and saw Finn sitting on Bess's lap as she read him a book. Bess was perfect. Once again, Wendy had come through for Gemma in spectacular fashion. A couple of weeks ago, Gemma had asked her if she knew of anyone who might like a babysitting job that involved weird hours. It turned out that the hours would suit a year twelve student who lived next door to Wendy. When Gemma eventually opened the cafe at night she'd need someone to stay with Finn while she worked. That would be great for Bess, who was the eldest of four children at home. Finn would be asleep by seven and Bess would have the rest of the time to study for her HSC in peace without the distraction of her younger siblings. For now, though, she spent a few hours with Finn after school until Gemma shut the cafe.

'Thanks, Bess,' Gemma said now, reaching for Finn. 'Any problems?'

'There're never any problems,' said Bess, smiling and running a finger along his cheek. 'He's always a good boy.'

'I think you have the magic touch. He's always good for *you*,' said Gemma. In actual fact, Finn *was* a good baby. She was incredibly lucky; he rarely cried unless he was tired or hungry.

She waved Bess off before starting the nightly routine of dinner, bath and Finn's bedtime. During that time she was completely focused on her son, and no one and nothing else existed for her. It was only once Finn was in bed, in those few hours of quietness and solitude before she went to sleep herself, that her mind would turn again to Nash and the inevitable day of reckoning that was approaching. She'd picked up the phone on more than one occasion but always chickened out before she could dial his number. She knew she was running out of time to tell him about Finn herself, but she kept finding excuses and putting it off. And they weren't just excuses: her life was busier than she could once have imagined. But the fact was that she was terrified of the confrontation she knew would follow when she told him the truth. And once that happened, life would change for all of them.

•

The next day, Nash found himself pacing up and down the main street like a teenager working up the courage to ask a girl out on a date. It had been almost a week since his encounter with Gemma. He'd wanted to come back before now, but every time he'd thought about coming into town he'd talked himself out of it. He was still too confused and a little angry.

Part of what had thrown him was the change he'd seen in Gemma. Unlike the girl he'd known before, she'd been confident and composed. She also seemed to have hardened up a little, and he felt sad to think that his actions had probably contributed to this change in her. She had every right to be furious with him. Still, he couldn't *not* go back to see her. He wanted to apologise for the way he'd spoken to her the other day, and for the way he'd made her leave Dunoon. If he was honest with himself, though, more than anything he wanted to see her smile again. He didn't feel too hopeful about that last one, given her angry reaction the last time they'd spoken. But the thing that kept nagging at him was that even after everything he'd done, how badly he'd behaved, she'd moved back here. That had to mean something, though he wasn't sure exactly what.

He squared his shoulders and headed back towards the cafe. Before he did anything else, he needed to apologise for how badly he'd treated her fourteen months ago. As he walked past the window of the cafe he saw Gemma standing beside a booth and smiling, and the sight made him stop in his tracks, his breath hitching in his chest. Christ, he missed that smile. Then his gaze moved down to take in the person she was talking to, and his jaw clenched tightly. What the hell was Henderson doing in there?

But then he noticed something else, something that made him stare in confusion. Gemma was holding a baby. He knew it wasn't Henderson's, and there was no one else in the cafe. And there was something about the way she was holding him—relaxed and confident.

Nash stared at the kid in her arms and knew there was no way it could belong to anyone else. For the second time in less than a week he felt the colour drain from his face.

Gemma had a child.

He turned on his heel and headed numbly back along the road. A few moments later, barely aware of how he had got there, he found himself sitting on a stool at the bar, a pint in front of him.

Gemma wasn't here for him. She'd come to start a new life with her kid. Somewhere along the line she'd moved on from him and met someone else. Whatever her reasons for coming back to Bingorra, they didn't include him.

It was quiet in the pub, though he knew that wouldn't last long. After finishing one beer and ordering another, Nash was staring into his glass, ignoring the muted conversation going on at the other end of the bar, when he heard someone come in.

'What'll you have, Ben?' said the bartender, the unwelcome name jarring Nash out of his thoughts.

'Just a lemon squash, thanks, mate.'

Nash kept his head down, willing Henderson to walk away, not to start anything. No such luck.

'This is a bit of a role reversal,' said Ben, taking the seat next to Nash.

'What is?' Nash ground out.

'You drinking and me not.'

Nash didn't bother replying. Ben didn't seem deterred by his lack of civility. 'I saw you earlier, you know,' he went on, after sipping his lemon squash. 'Outside the cafe.'

Nash gritted his teeth.

'Must have been a shock seeing Gemma again.'

'What is it you want, Henderson?' said Nash in a low growl.

'I don't want anything, mate. Just making an observation, that's all.'

'Well, take your observation and shove it. *Mate*,' Nash snapped.

Ben let out a soft whistle through his teeth and shook his head. 'Guess it sucks to be on the outside for a change, huh.'

Nash picked up his glass and drained the contents in one long swallow, before placing the glass back onto the bar with a firm *thunk*.

'You never could take coming off second best, could ya, Nash?' said Ben. 'But it must hurt like hell this time to lose the woman *and* the kid.'

'What the fuck are you talking about?' Nash finally looked across at him.

Ben took a long swig of his drink, apparently fascinated by the horseracing on the television above the bar. 'Oh? Didn't you know?'

Nash was up off his stool and at Ben's side in one smooth movement. He grabbed Ben's shirt in his fist, snapping the man's eyes from the television to his. 'Know what?' he demanded. But somewhere in the back of his mind he knew exactly what Henderson was talking about. Ever since clapping eyes on the baby in Gemma's arms he'd felt something he couldn't quite bring himself to acknowledge. He was no expert on kids' ages but he could sure as hell make a rough guess. He'd been sitting here quietly doing the maths in his head, but his mind kept stumbling at what it revealed.

Ben's smirk grew wider and Nash's fist itched to pound it right off his arrogant face. 'You just keep doing what you're doing, arsehole,' Ben shot back. 'Keep pissing her off and driving her away. That suits me just fine.'

'Didn't. Know. What?' Nash repeated, shaking the man roughly.

'That the kid's yours, you prick. Any moron can see that.' Ben took advantage of Nash's slackening hold to push his hands away. Getting off the stool, he stood in front of him. 'Who's the arsehole now? I may be a bastard, but even I wouldn't leave a woman to have my kid all by herself.'

The words cut deep, snapping Nash out of his stupor. His arm whipped back and he swung wildly. But Ben had obviously been expecting it—more than that, Nash realised, too late, he had been trying to force this confrontation and he ducked just in time, bobbing back up with a sly, knowing look. Nash knew that look: it was the same one he'd worn the night he drove away with Kim in the car.

A veil of rage dropped over Nash's eyes and he was once

again standing in the hospital hallway, staring at Mrs Sweeney as she screamed at him, over and over again, '*Why?*'

Barely aware of what he was doing, he threw punch after punch, his fists connecting with Ben's cheek, stomach and nose. He felt Ben returning the blows but he didn't feel any pain. He tasted blood in his mouth and felt something warm trickling down his forehead, but he didn't care. All he wanted to do was inflict the same kind of pain on Henderson that he'd been carrying around inside him all these years.

They'd moved away from the bar and into the middle of the floor, and Nash lunged forward, wrapping his arms around Ben's middle and ramming him back against a bearer beam that supported the exposed roof beam above. Ben gave a loud grunt at the impact, briefly going limp, but as Nash staggered backwards, Ben recovered and drove his shoulder into Nash's chest.

They fell to the floor and wrestled. Nash threw a few punches and tried to roll Ben's heavy frame off him, but you don't spend six years in prison and not learn a few dirty tricks; Nash had to give up his advantage in order to prise Ben's fingers away from gouging at his eyes.

'Not so self-righteous now, are ya, Whittaker?'

'It should have been you, not her,' Nash snarled, finding the leverage to push Ben off him, raising his fist, ready to smack it down square in the centre of the other man's face.

'You think I don't know that?' Ben yelled. 'Everyone wishes it was me who died that night. You think I don't know that? Go ahead. Do it,' he said, his gaze holding Nash's unwaveringly.

Nash felt something shift inside him at the words. Maybe it was something about the deadness of Ben's eyes, or maybe he'd just needed to get this burning hatred out of his system. Whatever it was, the urge to hurt and punish went out as quickly as it had ignited.

'Every goddamn day I wake up, I wish it had been me instead of her,' Ben muttered in a broken voice.

Nash let his hand drop to his side and he lowered his head in defeat. Suddenly the fight just went out of him. He was tired, not just physically, but emotionally. This thing between them had been eating at him for too many years and now he was just . . . done.

Slowly their surroundings began to register, the smell of sweat and stale beer, and the annoying computerised chortle of the poker machines above the quiet voices of the few other men in the pub, who had stood back and let them belt each other.

Placing his grazed knuckles on the multicoloured carpet, Nash slowly pushed himself up, then rolled onto his back to stare at the ceiling. Now that the entertainment was over, the small crowd of onlookers quickly dispersed and went back to their drinking and gambling, leaving the two men breathing heavily and beginning to feel the effects of their fight.

For Nash, something had changed during the last few minutes. A weight had been lifted somehow. It hadn't absolved him of his guilt over Kim's death, but the burning need to take it out on the man who was responsible had gone. He and Ben Henderson would never be friends, but somehow he suspected that Ben had been needing a similar violent catharsis. He wondered if, like him, Henderson always carried around the same numb kind of pain that nothing seemed to touch. Maybe he, too, had just wanted to erase that numbness and *feel* something for a change.

Twenty-six

'What happened to you?'

'Is it true?'

Gemma couldn't take her eyes off the battered face before her. She'd opened the back door of her apartment to loud knocking, only to find Nash bracing himself against the doorframe, his face cut and bruised.

'Is it?'

'Is what true?'

'The kid. Is it mine?'

Gemma reeled. She'd imagined this moment a thousand times but she still wasn't ready. She opened her mouth to give him the detailed explanation she'd rehearsed, fine-tuning to a perfect, concise answer, but, really, none of that was important now. 'Yes. He's your son.'

He closed his eyes briefly, then opened them again and held her gaze with a steely determination. 'When were you going to tell me?'

'When it was the right time.'

'When was that supposed to be? At his twenty-first?'

'Nash, what happened to you?' She didn't like the way he seemed to be holding himself up with the aid of the doorframe, or the swelling around his eyes.

He waved off her question but then winced and clutched at his rib cage. Breaking out her most authoritative voice, Gemma ordered him upstairs, steadying him as they slowly climbed the steps to her apartment. Inside, she helped him sit down at the kitchen table.

'Can I . . . see him?'

The vulnerability she detected in his voice was so unexpected that it took her a moment to speak. 'I think you need to go to the hospital.'

'Nothing's broken, just bruised,' he said quietly. 'Please? Just for a minute. I only caught a glimpse earlier.'

Gemma hesitated before giving a slight nod. 'He's asleep, so you'll have to be quiet.' She led the way up the hall towards the second bedroom and gently pushed the door further open for Nash to walk in ahead of her. 'His name's Finn.'

She saw him stop beside the timber cot and look down on the sleeping baby. With the heavy curtains pulled, the soft lump in the centre of the mattress was just visible in the gentle glow of the night light. Gemma stood beside Nash and smiled at the sight of the small child beneath the blankets, one hand tucked beneath his chin, the other thrown up above his head.

Nash looked up and held her gaze. Despite the dimness of the room, she saw the emotion in his eyes. He was clearly deeply moved by the realisation that this child was his son. Feeling guilt well up in her, Gemma reminded herself that she'd done nothing wrong. If he had only returned her phone calls he would have known about his son much sooner. She quickly turned away, not bothering to see if he followed her out of the room.

'Are you going to tell me what happened?' she asked once they were back in the kitchen. Briskly she took out a bowl and filled it with warm water, adding antiseptic from the medicine cupboard above the sink.

'Are you going to tell me why the hell you didn't tell me I had a son?' he countered. He kept his voice even but she detected the anger which simmered just below the surface.

'It was a little hard to tell you when you refused to return my calls.'

'You don't think the fact that you were pregnant might warrant a little more effort to get in touch with me?'

'You made it pretty clear you didn't want to speak to me. I didn't much feel like setting myself up for rejection twice,' Gemma said, trying to keep her voice neutral. She glanced up just as a flicker of something that looked like regret crossed his face.

'I was wrong,' he said finally, and so softly she almost didn't hear him.

'It doesn't matter now,' she said, dunking a cotton ball in the antiseptic solution. 'I got on with my life, just like you did.'

'Really? It was that easy to forget what we had?'

She lifted the cotton ball and held his gaze. 'I didn't say it was easy. I said I moved on.'

He sat quietly while she cleaned the grazes on his cheek and across his nose, only wincing a couple of times.

When she'd tended to the cuts on his face, she noticed a bloodied rip in the side of his shirt. 'Take your shirt off,' she instructed.

'It's not that bad, really,' he protested.

'Take it off, or I will.' She placed her hands on her hips and gave him a fierce stare, before brushing his hands aside and taking over to do it herself. For the briefest of moments her gaze roamed the wide expanse of naked skin and muscle, her breath catching in her lungs, before she let it out in a rush when she caught sight of his injuries, reminding her of what she was supposed to be doing. 'Oh my God, Nash.' She gasped at the ugly red mark that ran across his ribs and ended at his chest. 'You need to go to hospital.'

'No, I don't. It's just bruised.' He looked away as if uncomfortable to be sitting in front of her with no shirt on.

'How can you tell? Are you suddenly a doctor?' She reached out to gently touch the inflamed skin. He flinched at the first touch of her fingers and she quickly pulled away.

'Cold hands,' he muttered.

'Sorry.'

'I know it's not broken. I've been kicked by a cow before, and trust me, once you've had a broken rib you never forget what it feels like.'

'Who did this to you? And don't say no one, because this isn't a hoof mark.'

'Henderson made a point of filling me in on the happy news,' Nash told her, his jaw clenching.

'*Ben* did this?' she asked, horrified.

'Well, he looks just as bad.' There was an edge of smugness in his tone.

Gemma stared at him in disbelief. 'So Ben told you about Finn and you *attacked* him?'

'You're not seriously sticking up for that bastard, are you?'

'I'm not sticking up for anyone, but do you expect me to congratulate you on taking the news so well?'

'Henderson and I had old business to take care of. It had nothing to do with . . . this.' He indicated the two of them.

'Well, that's a relief,' she muttered.

Nash looked up at her, his brow creasing. 'I don't get it. Why did you only come back now? Why not before?'

'I needed to get my life together first,' she told him evenly. 'I *was* always planning on telling you, but I needed to be able to provide for my son first.'

'He's my son too,' said Nash.

Gemma went on in the same distant tone. 'What I told you the other day was true. Bingorra was the perfect location for the sort of cafe I wanted to open. It needed an alternative to the pub, providing a different kind of menu. And this way Finn gets to have his father in his life—if you *want* to be in his life,' she added.

'Of course I do,' he said angrily, struggling back into his shirt and fastening the buttons.

'I had hoped so. But I wasn't sure.'

'How could you think I'd turn my back on my child?'

'I don't know, Nash,' she said, getting to her feet and carrying the bowl to the sink. 'Last time I saw you, you were telling me to get lost. Call it a wild guess.'

'That was different,' he said.

'Yeah, I guess you're right. That was just me.' It hurt, damn it. It wasn't supposed to hurt this much after all this time. But it did. She continued coldly, 'Anyway, the main thing is that you and Finn will get to have a relationship, and that's all that matters.'

'Gemma—' he started, but she cut him off.

'So we'll have to work out some kind of schedule. I think you'll understand when I say I'd rather he got to know you slowly, and I'd prefer he didn't go out to your place alone until he's a bit older, but you can see him here as often as you want—with prior notice, of course, so I can make arrangements.'

'Wait a minute.' Nash frowned. 'Supervised visits? You're making me sound like I'm some parolee on detention or something.'

'He's a baby, not a puppy. Until now it's only been me and him, and I'm not going to freak him out by letting some stranger take him away by himself.'

'I'm not some stranger. I'm his father,' Nash growled.

'*He* doesn't know that,' Gemma pointed out.

'And whose fault is that?'

'Really? You seriously want to bring this up again?'

'I didn't know you were pregnant! It would have been different if I'd known. Christ!' He pushed the chair back as he stood up. The movement made him double over slightly, and Gemma resisted her immediate impulse to reach out and help.

'Yeah, I know, you've made that clear. It was just me you couldn't stand having around. Excuse me if I didn't want to force someone to have me in their life.' She turned away and stood by the door. 'I have things to do. You should go.'

'Damn it, Gemma. That's not how it was supposed to come out. It's not what I meant.'

'Goodnight, Nash,' she said, refusing to look at him.

After a tense pause he headed across the room and made his way down the stairs. He stopped halfway down and turned to look up at her. 'I'll be back tomorrow.'

'Fine,' she replied.

Gemma waited until the door shut before she sank down on the top step. Dropping her head on her knees she gave in to the hot sting of tears, just this once. Maybe if she got it out of her system now she would be able to move on and pretend it wasn't killing her every time he looked right through her.

Twenty-seven

Gemma watched Finn crawl around on the grass in Wendy's backyard as the two women sat and enjoyed a rare quiet moment together. It was Sunday afternoon; Wendy had the day off, and Gemma shut the cafe at one on weekends.

'Sounds like he took it better than I expected,' Wendy said, sipping her coffee.

'I guess. It probably helped that he'd taken most of his aggression out on Ben before he came over,' Gemma told her dryly, watching as Finn kicked his legs and gurgled to himself.

'That particular storm has been brewing for a long time. I'm surprised it's taken this long to finally come to a head.'

'They must have loved her an awful lot,' said Gemma.

'Who?'

305

'Nash and Ben. They must have both really loved Kim to still be so angry after all this time.'

'I don't think it's about that. Kim was a lovely girl. It was very sad, and a terrible waste of a young life,' said Wendy, staring off into the distance. 'But I don't think it's love for her that keeps those two hating each other. They were all teenagers. Nash and Ben had spent most of their lives fighting over one thing or the other. Kim was just the latest thing to get between them. Nope, those boys have been letting that night fester inside them for years. Both of them feel guilt. On the surface of it, Ben was the guilty party, and he paid dearly for it. He went to jail and served his time. I know some people around here think he got off too lightly, but I'm not so sure. They were kids. I have boys that age now and they do things all the time without stopping to think them through. I can't bear to imagine one of my boys making one stupid mistake at eighteen and paying for it for the rest of his life.'

'I guess Kim's parents wonder why he should get to have a life when their daughter won't,' said Gemma. She could see both sides with painful clarity.

'If he'd also died then he wouldn't. But he didn't die in the crash. I guess my point is that he was a teenager, and teenagers' brains don't work like an adult's. I'm not excusing the choice he made. He should have known better than to drive after he'd been drinking. But it was one of those stupid, *stupid* decisions that an eighteen-year-old *kid* makes. I just don't think it's black and white when it comes to teenagers. And so they've come full circle with you.'

Gemma frowned at that. 'I suppose Ben enjoyed getting

on Nash's nerves by being my friend. But Nash and I . . .'
She paused. 'I don't know what we are now.'

'You need to give him some time to get used to the fact
that he has a son.'

Gemma shrugged, her gaze on Finn. 'I've got time. I'm
not planning on going anywhere.'

'He'll come around, you'll see,' Wendy said comfortingly.
'Things will work out.'

Gemma shook her head. 'I didn't come back for Nash.
I came back for Finn. We couldn't go back to the way it was
before. It's been too long. We're both different now.'

'Rubbish. You may be able to lie to yourself, but it's clear
to me that nothing has changed that much. He still loves
you. He never stopped.'

'He did a pretty good impersonation of someone who fell
out of love, the day I left.'

'I think he's convinced himself he was doing you a favour.'

Gemma laughed shortly. 'Nash was doing what he thought
was right for Nash. He pushed me away before I could do
anything to hurt *him*.'

'Pride's a pretty big thing around here. Sometimes that's
all a person has left when Mother Nature's taken everything
else. Sometimes they hide behind pride, out of habit.'

Gemma was sure Wendy was getting her hopes up over
nothing. She was fairly sure Nash wasn't thinking about
anything other than his new role as a father.

•

Nash couldn't concentrate. He was meant to be nailing a loose
wire to a fence post, a simple enough job, but he swore as

he hit his thumb for the fifth time that morning. It had been three weeks since he'd suddenly discovered he was a father. Three of the most confusing weeks of his life. His emotions had gone haywire: one minute he was walking around in a daze, the next he'd be grinning like a damn idiot when he pictured the little smiling face that greeted him each visit. Then he was plagued by insecurities: what the hell did he know about being a father? What if he did something wrong, messed up in some way?

He'd been dropping in to Gemma's most afternoons, spending time getting to know his son. Gemma usually made herself scarce to give them time alone. He both appreciated and hated it. He knew she was trying to be fair to him, give him and Finn a chance to get to know each other, but he liked it more when they were all together. That confused him as well. He found himself thinking about it as he worked. He didn't understand what Gemma wanted. She'd returned to Bingorra, brought his son out to be close to him, and yet she kept her distance.

He frowned and brought the hammer down hard on the nail as he recalled the sight of Henderson laughing with her that afternoon when he'd first learned about Finn. They'd looked close, and he suspected that Ben would like to be a hell of a lot closer to Gemma. But Nash hadn't seen him since the afternoon at the pub, and so far he'd never seen any sign of him at Gemma's place.

He knew he had a lot to make up to Gemma after pushing her away in the first place, but he was terrified that if he made the wrong move it would ruin this fragile truce they had made. He hated that she'd been in Sydney this whole time alone, having his baby. That stung more than anything. At first the thought of the time he'd wasted when he could have been involved in Finn's life made him angry. But after the initial shock wore off, he began to see things from her point of view. Maybe she hadn't tried hard enough to get hold of him, but given his treatment of her, he couldn't really blame her. She'd never know how hard it had been for him not to contact her or how many times he'd dialled her number only to hang up before it began ringing.

He'd thought he was doing her a favour. He gritted his teeth as he slammed another nail in. The truth was he'd been protecting himself, and he'd almost paid the ultimate price for it. If Gemma hadn't come to Bingorra, he might never have known he had a son at all. She could have married someone else and moved on with her life, and his son would have been brought up by another man. The fact that that thought felt like a punch to the stomach made him realise how much his world had changed in just a few short weeks. One tiny baby now had the power to drop him to his knees. *His* baby. *Their* baby.

He stopped hammering and looked across the paddock, lost in thought. Somehow he had to win Gemma back. He wanted a family—his family—and he'd do whatever it took to fix what he'd all but destroyed by sending her away.

•

Gemma turned off the road and into the driveway to Dunoon. Memories filled her mind as she forced herself to focus on the dirt track. 'This is where silly Aunty Jazz brought Mummy on a working holiday,' she said, glancing into the mirror at the small face of her son, who was staring out the window, his eyes wide. 'Look, Finn, can you see the cow?'

A bubble of excitement began to float in her stomach as she neared the house. She hadn't realised just how much she'd missed this place until now. Her time out here had changed her life forever in so many ways.

As she drew in beside the house, Nash came out of the shed, wiping his hands on a rag before throwing it into the back of the work ute. A smile spread across his face as he walked towards them, and her stomach flipped over. She remembered when his *brooding* looks had been enough to turn her knees to jelly, but when he smiled, the man was lethal.

The whole drive out, Gemma had been telling herself to be calm and courteous and nothing more. She was not going to put her son in the middle of something that had gone so badly wrong last time. That wasn't fair to Finn. She and Nash needed to remain on purely friendly terms. No sex, no strings, no emotions. Just two mature adults who both loved their child.

The minute the car came to a stop, Nash had the door open and was unbuckling Finn from his baby seat. 'Hey there, big fella. I've missed you.'

Gemma smiled a little at the sight of father and son grinning at each other. Nash's big tanned hands gently cradled the small overall-clad bundle in his arms as Finn reached up chubby little hands and tugged inquisitively at the wide-brimmed hat.

Gemma reached into the back of the car to grab the nappy bag before shutting the door.

'You remembered how to get here, then?' Nash said, taking the bag from her and stepping back to allow her to go ahead of him.

'It hasn't been that long since I was here.'

'Feels like forever,' he said quietly, and Gemma briefly met his steady gaze before turning away to head inside. It did feel like forever. It felt like a lifetime ago, and it was. It was from a life before she'd become a mother. Life before she'd grown up. Life before her heart had been broken by the man who walked behind her now, carrying their child in one strong arm.

Pushing open the screen door, Gemma inhaled the familiar scent of the old farmhouse. Her parents' house with its ultra-modern furnishings and scented candles and bamboo sticks always smelled like a homeware store. By contrast, this old place smelled comfortable and lived-in, and had a welcoming feel to it, like a warm hug from an old friend. Today, too, there was a scent of something else in the air, something delicious that had her mouth watering.

Gemma's gaze slid across to the kitchen table set with a tablecloth and cutlery, a vase of flowers sitting in the centre. The kitchen was tidy, not a dirty plate or coffee cup to be seen anywhere, so different to the first day she'd walked in here.

'I've become a bit more domesticated,' Nash said with a crooked grin as he watched her surveying the room.

'So I see.'

'I put on a roast.' He dropped the nappy bag on the floor and walked across the kitchen to open the oven door and peek inside. 'Should be another half hour or so.'

'I'm impressed,' Gemma admitted as she watched him cross back towards her, Finn balanced expertly on his hip. His grin was infectious and they stood for a moment sharing a smile, until Finn became restless and Gemma reached for him. 'I might give him something to eat first, he's hungry.'

'Make yourself at home.' Nash passed the baby across to her but didn't step back. Gemma looked up and swallowed nervously at the look she saw in his eyes. She'd almost forgotten the dark, smouldering intensity of his gaze and the power it had to make her knees go weak. Only now there was something more. Something deeper. Beyond the hunger there was something else, something more serious, a promise.

Gemma moved Finn to her hip and stepped away. She lifted the bag by her feet to the benchtop, then withdrew a small container of puréed fruit. Nash moved around the bench and brought out a highchair, unfolding it.

'You bought a highchair?' Gemma asked, surprised.

'Wendy gave me a heap of baby stuff. I set up one of the bedrooms as a nursery. It's just the basics, but if there's anything you need, I can get it.'

Gemma wasn't sure what to say. He'd obviously gone to a lot of trouble to set up his house for a small child, and it touched her deeply. He was being so incredibly generous about the whole thing. He could just as easily have brought in lawyers and court orders and made her give him complete access if he'd really wanted to, but he hadn't. 'I'm sure what you've got will be just fine. Thanks.'

Her reply seemed to set him at ease; he stopped shuffling his feet and smiled again. Gemma busied herself feeding Finn in his highchair while Nash moved around the kitchen like a pro, stirring gravy and chopping veggies. Gemma smiled to herself at how homey the whole situation felt. Everything would have been perfect if she could just ignore that prickling sensation of awareness that flowed between them. The only thing that could mess up this situation now would be if one of them did something stupid . . . like acted on it.

•

Dinner hadn't been as uncomfortable as she'd expected; in fact, it was almost like old times. Nash talked about the farm and filled her in on the local gossip she'd missed since she'd been gone and Gemma told him stories about some of the regulars that stopped by at the cafe. By the end of dinner, though, Finn was ready for bed, and Gemma began packing up their things to leave.

Nash stroked his grizzling son's head gently. 'Why don't you stay?' he said quietly. Gemma looked up in surprise and he went on, 'It's a bit of a drive back to town and I hate thinking of you trying to drive with him crying in the back. And this has been . . . nice. Don't go yet.'

'I don't—' Gemma started, but Nash quickly cut in.

'Your room's still there for you to use if you want and Finn would be right next door so you'll hear him if he cries,' he said calmly. 'I've been thinking . . . I know you don't want him to stay out here alone, but I thought maybe you could come out with him and stay . . . like on a weekend or something.'

Although Gemma knew she should just decline politely but firmly and drive away, her heart had jumped at his suggestion that she stay the night, and she felt the rush of something suspiciously like excitement. She'd enjoyed spending the afternoon and evening out here, and it would be a taxing drive back into town at night with a tired, irritable child in the back. 'I'd have to leave early in the morning to open the shop in time,' she hedged. She wouldn't need an alarm out here, Nash would be up before sunrise. But more than anything it was the look on Nash's face that made her accept his offer, that new, surprising mix of hope and vulnerability.

Any final twinges of uncertainty were washed away by his delighted smile when she agreed. Gemma turned away quickly from the look in his eyes. She had a feeling she was fighting a losing battle with herself. Deep down, she knew she was kidding herself if she thought she could remain immune to this man forever. She just wished she could trust that the risk would be worth it.

Nash hovered by the doorway of the nursery as she began to dress Finn after his bath. 'Can I do it?' he asked tentatively.

Gemma's first impulse was to say no, but then she realised she needed to step back and let him help more. *This is why you came out here, remember*, she told herself.

'I'm sorry, I didn't think you'd want to do the nappy thing.' She stood back awkwardly. 'Do you want me to show you how?'

'Nah, I've got it,' he said, stepping into her place at the foot of the change table, sliding a disposable nappy under Finn's backside and quickly securing the tabs on either side. He glanced up with a look of pride on his face and her eyes narrowed.

'How did you know how to do that?' On her first attempt, in hospital, she'd put the nappy on upside down, and it had definitely taken more than one attempt to perfect.

Nash looked offended. 'Gem, I drive high-tech machinery for a living. I analyse the weather and soil, I think I can manage putting a nappy on a kid.'

'You got help,' she said, her eyes suddenly widening. 'You googled it, didn't you?' she crowed, and when he blushed she knew she had him. 'Ha!'

'What, you think you're the only one who can fake your way through something?'

Gemma continued to laugh. She'd have to call Jazz and tell her about this.

'Well, it worked, didn't it?' he said in a huffy tone.

With difficulty, Gemma forced her face back into a serious expression, clearing her throat.

'Shut up,' he muttered, going back to dressing his son.

'You shut up,' she said, pushing his arm.

'See what Mummy's doing? We don't disrespect Daddy, do we, Finn?'

'Pfft,' Gemma said, her smile breaking through again as she watched the scene before her. If you didn't know any better they looked like a happy little family. As Nash's head bent close to Finn's she had to blink away a sudden sheen of moisture from her eyes.

Later, as they stood silently beside the cot looking down at Finn, now fast asleep, she felt Nash's hand reach for her own and then hold it. Gemma turned to look at him and caught her breath. She wasn't sure who moved first, but suddenly his face was close to hers and his other hand came up and gently cupped the back of her head as their lips met and clung. At the first touch she knew she was lost. It was a deep, slow kiss, as both of them savoured the other, clinging and devouring, reluctant to let go. When they eventually pulled apart, they were both breathing unevenly.

Gemma searched the eyes before her, those brown eyes with green flecks that she'd seen too many times in her dreams. Her whole body craved his touch, but her brain was yelling at her to stop now, before there was no turning back. Resisting all her instincts, she stepped away, fighting to get her breathing and thoughts back under control. Nash reluctantly released her hand, letting her move back towards the doorway.

•

Gemma stood leaning against the verandah post, her arms wrapped around her. God, she'd missed this, she thought as she looked out over the darkened paddocks. It was so quiet. So peaceful.

She heard the squeak of the screen door opening and then felt Nash come to stand behind her. She didn't turn around or acknowledge him, but her body had reacted immediately and was attuned to his, waiting for the moment when he touched her. She pushed away the stupid thought and frowned into the shadows. *Not. Helping*, she told herself angrily.

'I'm sorry,' he said at last.

Gemma shook her head slightly. 'It was my fault.'

He gave a loud, aggravated sigh and she could imagine him running a hand through his hair as he usually did when he was frustrated about something. 'I don't get it, Gem,' he said. 'I can't see what would be the problem if we acted on what we're both feeling.'

'It's complicated, Nash. There's Finn to think about now. It's not just about us anymore.'

'It's got nothing to do with Finn and everything to do with us,' he countered impatiently. He took a step closer and turned her so she had no choice but to meet his frowning gaze. 'It's still there. What we had before. It's still there, as strong as ever.'

'No, it's not,' Gemma said, hoping he couldn't see her cheeks burning at the lie. 'It's just being back here like this. We're confused.'

'I'm a lot of things right now but confused sure as hell isn't one of them,' he growled.

'We can't just pick up where we left off. Things have changed. *We've* changed.'

'Yeah, things have changed, but that doesn't mean we can't give it another try. We have a son now—'

'Yes,' Gemma interrupted. 'We have a son now. And when you decide to send us packing again because you're afraid that one day down the track we'll leave you for some reason, I'll have him to worry about.'

'It's not like that. Damn it, Gemma, are you going to hold that over my head forever?' He let go of her arms and turned away, swearing as he threw his shoulder against the post beside her. 'I made a mistake. I admit that. I acted like a complete arsehole, okay?' Agitated, he pushed himself away from the post to stand in front of her once more. 'But you're the one who came back here. You decided to give me another chance. You can't keep throwing the past in my face every time *you* get scared.'

Gemma tried to speak calmly. 'I know what it felt like and I won't let my son go through it.'

'*Our* son,' he said, raising his voice. 'And I know exactly how bad it hurt you, because I went through it too. Every goddamn day you weren't here, Gemma. I kicked myself for letting pride ruin the only good thing in my life. Every. Damn. Day.'

Gemma swallowed painfully past the lump in her throat as she saw the torment etched across his features.

'It won't happen again,' he went on, with quiet conviction. 'This time it's different.'

Gemma wanted so badly to believe him. She wanted nothing more than to throw herself into his arms and let him promise her the world, but it was too soon. They needed more time to get to know each other again. They needed to make sure that her being back here was the right thing, for both of them and for their son.

'Let's just concentrate on Finn for now. I don't want to confuse things with whatever's going on between us.'

Nash bit his lip. 'I'm not giving up on this, Gemma. You can try to deny it to yourself all you like, but I know that what we had is still there. I'm a patient man, I'll wait until you accept it too.'

He held her gaze until she turned away and said a hurried goodnight, slipping inside before her traitorous heart could override her brain. She would not rush this. She was a mother now, and she couldn't afford to make a mistake that could affect her child as well. This was too important to mess up just because her libido was having a meltdown.

•

Gemma blinked awake, slowly moving her arm off her face. For a moment, looking around the dim room, she forgot where she was. Then she heard the far-off sound of a cow bellowing, and sat up quickly.

She listened for Finn but could hear nothing. She stepped out of bed and quickly dragged on her clothes from yesterday before heading down the hallway to check the nursery, finding the cot empty. There was no one in the kitchen either, so she pushed open the screen door to check outside.

She spotted Nash over by the fence; his back was towards her as he pointed to something in the distance. As she drew closer, she saw him cradling Finn in one arm, talking quietly. The sight made her heart contract. It looked so *right*.

He glanced up and caught sight of her. 'Look who's finally decided to get out of bed?' he said to Finn, turning him to face her.

She flashed him a sardonic smile, but it melted into a genuine one the moment her gaze met the beaming face of her child. Was it wrong to think yours was the most beautiful baby on earth? She was pretty sure it wasn't just maternal bias, either. Finn was gorgeous—he looked just like his father.

'What have you two been up to?'

'Just checking stuff out,' said Nash, rocking his arm so Finn's chubby little legs swung back and forth, making him grin. 'He's an early riser like his old man.'

'Yes. He's usually up bright and early. I must have overslept. Well, I guess we better get ready to go. I have to open the shop.'

Nash's smile vanished instantly, and she felt bad for ruining the moment. 'I don't want you to.'

Seeing the pain in his face, Gemma decided to tell him the decision she'd made the night before. 'I know I said I didn't want Finn out here without me, but that was before I saw that you obviously know what you're doing. You can have him to stay here whenever you want.'

Nash continued to hold her eyes with his own. 'I want you *both* to stay. Permanently.'

'Out here?' She shook her head in confusion. 'That wouldn't work. I've got the cafe, and Finn goes to day care. We're set up in a flat and the cafe's starting to make money. I know you think you're helping by offering us a place to stay, but honestly, we're doing fine.'

Nash's face twitched in frustration. 'I'm not offering this to help you out. I want us to be a family. I want us to get married, Gemma.'

She stood frozen in front of him. She knew she should speak, but she couldn't seem to form a single coherent sentence.

Nash looked down at the baby, who was gazing up at him. 'Finn and I have been talking and we think it's a great idea.'

'I . . .' She didn't know what to say. While part of her wanted to scream 'Yes!', a small part of her stunned brain urged caution. She scrabbled for a rational response. 'Look, you've had him out here and he's been on his best behaviour, but it's not always like this.'

'Like what?'

'Like a TV commercial for nappies or something.' Gemma threw her hands up in the air. 'What happens when you're tired and cranky after working all day and he's teething and irritable and I've had a long day at the cafe? What happens when all you want is your peace and quiet back?'

'Do you hear yourself?'

'Yes—do *you*? I know you think I'm being ridiculous, but I have to think about these things.'

'Does any other new dad get a choice in this? No, they don't. So why am I any different?'

'Because you weren't there from the beginning,' she snapped, and instantly regretted it when she saw him flinch. 'What I meant was, most new fathers get nine months to prepare.'

He looked back at her with a determined expression. 'Wouldn't be the first time I've been thrown in the deep end. I'm serious, Gem, and I'm not taking it back. I want us to be a family. Just think about it.'

As Gemma drove back into town later that morning she did think about it. In fact, there was very little else she *could* think about.

She just wasn't sure she could make that leap of faith so soon.

Glancing in the rear-view mirror at her son's happy, trusting face, she felt overwhelmed by the responsibility of the decisions she was going to have to make. Every choice she made now would affect not only her and Nash, but also their son. Did she have a right to put her emotions first? Or should she ignore the concern she still had about Nash's motivation behind his proposal in order to give her child a life with a complete family?

Twenty-eight

Almost the sole topic of conversation in the cafe for the last few days had been the weather—or, more precisely, the rain that was forecast. In the weeks Gemma had been back in Bingorra, chatting with customers and overhearing their conversations, she had begun to pick up on the community's concerns, and now she always tuned in to the regular weather forecasts on the radio.

The bell tinkled, and Gemma looked up from where she was finishing the cappuccino she'd just made and hoped her smile didn't give away the surprise she felt as Grace Henderson walked into the cafe. Gemma had only ever seen her around town from a distance but there was no mistaking who she was. She bit back a smile as she remembered Wendy calling her Bingorra royalty as she'd swanned past the store once.

She was a stylish woman in a classical, understated way, and the epitome of less is more, dressed in black pants and a cream-coloured blouse. A thin gold necklace and slimline gold watch was the only jewellery she wore.

Gemma picked up the mug in its saucer and delivered the order, coming back to the counter where Mrs Henderson stood looking around curiously. 'Can I get you something?'

Mrs Henderson gave Gemma a keen-eyed once-over. 'I've heard so much about your little cafe,' she said graciously. 'I thought it was time I came down for a look.'

'It's nice to finally meet you, Mrs Henderson,' Gemma said with a polite smile. 'I'm Gemma.'

'Yes, I know who you are, dear, and please call me Grace. My son's a big advocate of your cooking skills, Gemma. He hardly eats at home anymore.' Grace gave a small smile that didn't quite reach her eyes, and Gemma wasn't sure how to reply. Fortunately, just then the back door opened and Bess came to the kitchen door with Finn on her hip.

'Please excuse me for a moment, Mrs . . . ah, Grace,' said Gemma, hurrying to the door. She reached out for Finn and buried her face in his sweet-smelling neck. She talked to Bess about how his day had gone before passing him back to her and returning to Grace's table.

'Ben mentioned you had a son. He's adorable,' Grace said, and Gemma wondered if that had labelled her somehow in the older woman's eyes, although her comment suggested she wasn't put off by the fact.

'I remember when my boys were that little. So precious, and they can break your heart so very easily,' she added softly, before clearing her throat and returning her gaze to the menu. 'I actually came in here today to offer you a catering job, if you're interested.'

'Oh,' said Gemma, surprised.

'It's my fortieth wedding anniversary in a fortnight and my husband and I are having a small gathering out at Bullowa—just seventy or so close friends and family. Do you think you could handle something like that?'

Gemma did a quick calculation in her head. A job this big would be fantastic for business and the added bonus to her income wouldn't hurt either. 'Sure. I can do that. I'll figure out a menu and a quote and get it out to you tomorrow. How does that sound?'

'That would be fine, dear,' Grace said with a nod.

Gemma quickly took down the details of the date and time and a contact number.

'Lovely. I look forward to working with you,' Grace said before walking out of the cafe.

After the older woman had gone, Gemma stared at the empty doorway, a million things running through her head. Already she was thinking about recipes and ingredients, working out the logistics of transporting food, and itching to grab her calculator and begin costing out a quote.

•

Nothing had gone right today. Finn, who was teething, had woken up three times during the night, uncomfortable and grizzling, and by morning Gemma had felt like a zombie. She had a thousand things to do while she finished cooking for the Hendersons' party later that afternoon. It had been raining almost non-stop for the last three days and the dreary weather wasn't helping her mood. Thank goodness the Hendersons had organised a large marquee so at least it wouldn't affect the arrangements for the party.

The cafe had been very busy lately, but she hoped today would be a little slower; she'd hired a friend of Corrine's as extra help and was confident they could manage most of the orders without her so she could devote herself to preparing the party food. She had also arranged for Bess to come in all day to babysit Finn.

But while Gemma was feeding Finn his breakfast, Bess's mother called to tell her Bess was sick and wouldn't be able to babysit after all. After thanking her for calling, and wishing Bess a speedy recovery, Gemma hung up the phone and dropped her head onto the table. Bess had proven herself entirely reliable and Gemma knew she would have to be pretty unwell not to come to work, but of all the days she could have called in sick, today was the worst. It would be so nice to just take Finn and go back to bed, but she knew that was out of the question today. Straightening up, she eyed the phone briefly before picking it up again. It was a long shot, as he was probably already out working, but she dialled Nash's mobile and waited, listening to it ring.

When, unexpectedly, he answered, Gemma pushed away the irritating little flutter of nerves at the sound of his voice on the other end of the line. It had been almost two weeks since she and Finn had spent the night at Dunoon. Nash hadn't pressured her about the discussion they'd had, in fact he hadn't brought it up again, but she knew he was waiting for an answer. Maybe he could see how stressed she was with the upcoming catering job and had given her a reprieve.

Everything had to be perfect for this party—her reputation was hinging on it.

'Hi. Sorry to bother you, you're probably busy,' she said in a rush.

'No worries. What's up?'

'I, ah, have a bit of a problem. Bess's sick and I was counting on her to look after Finn today. I've got Grace Henderson's party to cater for later this afternoon and I have to make the food. And Finn's teething and irritable and won't sleep, and I can't really have him in the shop because all he wants is to be picked up—'

'Calm down,' Nash interjected. 'I'm on my way. I'll bring him back here.'

'Are you sure?'

'Gemma. It's fine.'

'I have to go out to Bullowa at about two thirty to set up and I'll be finished around six. I'll drop by after that and pick him up.'

'Why don't you just stay here tonight?'

'Ah, I'm not sure . . .'

'You'll be exhausted by then and you probably won't feel like driving back into town,' Nash pointed out.

She knew he was right; by the evening she'd be dead on her feet. But after the last time she'd stayed at Dunoon she knew she had next to no willpower when it came to being alone with him, and there was still the matter of finishing their 'talk'. He'd be expecting some kind of answer and the truth was, she was no closer to knowing what to do than she had been a fortnight ago. Yet even as her brain was listing all the excellent reasons why she should decline, she heard herself saying, 'Thanks. That sounds like a good idea.'

'Great,' Nash said warmly.

After she'd hung up, Gemma let out a shaky breath and looked down at Finn, who chewed furiously on a cold teething ring on her lap. 'Well, kiddo, looks like we're having another sleepover at Daddy's house tonight.' She stroked her son's soft dark hair, so much like his father's, and felt nervous excitement begin to build inside her.

Forty minutes later, in the cafe kitchen, Gemma gently rocked a sobbing Finn against her shoulder and looked around in despair. She'd burned the first lot of hors d'oeuvre cases she'd baked and there was no point starting again while Finn remained so clingy. Every time she put him down he cried, and while she was pretty sure all the parenting books would frown at giving in to his demands, today she had no other option.

She was on the verge of bursting into tears herself when there was a knock at the kitchen door, followed immediately by Ben's head poking into the room. Gemma swallowed down her mini breakdown and summoned a weak smile.

'Whoa, what's going on in here?' Stepping inside, Ben gazed around the usually clean kitchen, now a chaotic mess with flour spilled on the floor and dirty bakeware stacked in the sink. On the bench were the still-smoking burnt offerings she'd just pulled from the oven.

'I'm having a bad day.'

'So I see,' Ben said. 'I came over to let you know Mum's invited a few extras to the party, so the numbers have gone up by another ten . . .' He paused at the sight of her face. 'I'm guessing that's the last thing you want to hear right now?'

'Ten more guests?' said Gemma in disbelief. The original seventy friends and family had grown to seventy-seven only the day before, and now another ten? Where the hell were these people coming from? That mini breakdown was threatening to turn into a major event.

Picking up on her stress, Finn began to cry again. Gemma jiggled him absently on one hip as she tried to calculate how many more batches she'd need to make.

'Here, why don't I take this guy for a bit and give you some space.' Without waiting for an answer, Ben reached over to take Finn from her arms and sat down on the chair Gemma had dragged from the front of the shop earlier.

'Oh, thanks. Actually, Nash will be here soon to take him, but if I can just tidy up some of this mess so I can see what I'm doing, that would be great.'

It helped that Finn seemed happy to sit calmly on Ben's lap and play with Ben's hat while Gemma cleaned up and then gathered what she needed to start a new batch of pastry.

'Are you looking forward to the party?' she asked as she mixed the ingredients.

'Forty years is a pretty impressive milestone.' Ben looked away. 'Can't say I'm thrilled about mingling with the guests, though. Most of them think I should still be rotting away in prison.'

Gemma glanced up at him, frowning. His expression was neutral but when he met her eye she saw a brief flash of pain. 'Surely no one thinks that,' she said gently. 'Not after all this time?'

'You still don't get the people out here, do you?' he said. 'It's black or white. There's no in between.'

'So why stay here? Why not move to some other place where no one knows you?'

'And do what? I don't have a diploma, I dropped out of high school after year eleven and I don't have a trade. I don't have any work or credit history . . . As soon as I apply for a job they want to know what I've been doing since high school. At least here I can work on the farm and earn some money.'

'Maybe in time people will think differently,' she said.

'I doubt it. This place has a long memory.' He fell silent for a moment, then went on in a brighter tone, 'I need to do a few errands up the street. Do you want me to take this little guy for a walk?'

'That won't be necessary.'

At the deep growl from the kitchen doorway, Gemma dropped the tray she'd just picked up. The clatter startled Finn and set him crying again, and Gemma quickly bent down to retrieve the fallen tray. Nash's sudden appearance had left her feeling unaccountably flustered and somehow guilty.

As Nash took Finn from Ben's arms, Gemma saw the glare the men exchanged, and hoped it wouldn't escalate into anything here in her tiny kitchen.

'Is he ready to go?' Nash asked grimly.

Gemma fumed, too angry to speak as she went through the back door of the kitchen and picked up the nappy bag, then handed it to Nash. He swung it up on his shoulder and turned away. 'I'll see you tonight,' was all he said, before shoving open the front door, leaving the usually serene bell jingling like a crowd of irritated pixies.

'I see why you like him so much,' Ben mused. 'It's his pleasant personality, isn't it?'

Gemma sighed and shook her head. 'You two wear me out.'

'Hey, I wasn't the one who stormed in here like a bear with a sore head.'

'Don't act like the innocent party in all this, Ben,' she snapped. 'You know damn well you provoke him whenever you get the chance. I wish you'd both just knock it off.'

Unfortunately, it seemed that the fight at the pub hadn't been a miracle turning point in their relationship. Well, Gemma was sick of being in the middle of their drama. 'I have to get all this finished,' she said, going back to her pastry. Ben left with a promise to drop in later and pick up most of the food, then finally she was left in relative peace and quiet to tackle the troublesome hors d'oeuvres.

•

It was only when she was making her second sweep of the party guests with her tray of salmon and smoked ham pinwheels, bocconcini with ricotta and smoked salmon, and ratatouille tarts that Gemma was able to relax and smile properly. Initially afraid that her food wouldn't be up to scratch, she was now actually enjoying herself as she carried the canapés through the crowd, accepting the enthusiastic compliments with quiet pride. She'd been asked several times for the recipe for her beetroot dip, and had secured two new catering jobs for the upcoming month. This made it all worthwhile, she thought as she headed back to the kitchen to restock her trays. All those bone-weary nights when her feet ached after working all day in Micca's kitchen and she

330

could barely think straight, juggling a newborn baby and shiftwork, had finally paid off. She was happy. She had her own business, a beautiful baby boy she adored, and she was doing something she loved. It made everything she'd gone through to reach this point worth it.

'Thank you, my dear. The food was absolutely divine,' said Grace a few hours later, handing Gemma a cheque for the catering.

'It was my pleasure,' said Gemma, smiling as she packed the last of her equipment into the back of her car parked under the shelter of the Hendersons' large carport off the side of the house.

'I've been hearing nothing but raves about your food all afternoon. I think you're going to be a very busy young lady.'

Gemma looked at her with profound gratitude. 'Thank you so much for giving me this opportunity, Grace.'

The older woman waved one elegantly manicured hand. 'I should be thanking you,' she said, smiling. 'Being the one who discovered you has made me the envy of the district.'

Gemma watched as Grace walked away to farewell the last of her guests. While Gemma was growing up, her parents were always either hosting or attending parties and charity events with the cream of Sydney's society. She hadn't realised that even a little place like Bingorra had a distinct social hierarchy, but tonight she'd seen that the women were every bit as well-dressed and dignified as their city counterparts. Who would have thought?

'Sounds like you were a big hit, Ms Northcote,' said Ben, emerging from the shadows of the stately verandah.

'Thank you, Ben.'

'For what?'

'You know for what. I know it was you who got your mother to hire me for this event. So thank you for introducing me to a whole new line of business.'

'I didn't do anything, really.' Ben shrugged. 'My mother never does anything she doesn't want to do. She must have been impressed when she came to see you or you wouldn't have got the gig.'

'Well, thank you,' Gemma said again. 'I don't know what I'd have done without all your help since I've been back.' Her smile faltered a little as a strange look crossed Ben's face and he suddenly stepped closer. He leaned forward and his lips brushed gently against her own. Startled, she returned his kiss for a moment until she realised what she was doing and pulled away, stepping back. 'Ben—'

'You don't have to say anything,' he said with a sigh. 'I know you've still got a thing for Whittaker. Can't blame a bloke for trying though, can you?'

Gemma wasn't fooled by his bravado; she knew Ben had real feelings for her and it hurt that she couldn't return them. 'I'm sorry, Ben. I really am.'

'Yeah. I know.' He dropped his gaze to the ground between them. 'Don't worry, I won't try anything again. I just figured I'd give it one more shot.'

Gemma laid a hand on his arm. 'You're a good friend, Ben. I hope that doesn't change.'

He winced, then summoned a weak smile. 'You sure know how to wound a guy. Don't you know using the "friend" word is the equivalent of castration?'

'My bad.' She grinned, grateful that he was handling the situation so calmly. The Ben she'd met when she first came out here wouldn't have been so gracious. He'd come a long way since then.

'You need a hand with anything else?' he asked when the silence between them threatened to get awkward.

'Nope, I'm all done. I'll take this stuff back to the cafe tomorrow.' She'd washed most of the trays and serving dishes inside before packing up.

'I guess I'll see you around then . . . *friend*.'

Gemma couldn't help but laugh and shake her head at his deliberately rueful expression. 'You shall indeed. 'Night.' She stepped into her car and started the engine, waving to him as she drove away.

As she left the lights of Bullowa behind and drove along the dark road towards Dunoon, a thrill of nervous anticipation went through her. A long night stretched ahead. Another night spent under Nash's roof, and with only Finn as chaperone.

Twenty-nine

She parked the car behind the house, next to Nash's big four-wheel drive, and made a dash to the back door. The house was quiet when she closed the screen door behind her. She walked through the empty kitchen to the lounge room, which was lit by the soft glow of lamplight, but there was still no sign of Nash or Finn.

A movement caught her eye as she stepped into the hallway, and she stopped as she saw Nash easing out of the baby's room, gently pulling the door closed behind him. He looked up at her and put his finger to his lips. Gemma closed her eyes briefly as tiredness washed over her, then opened them quickly when she heard Nash approach. But he only leaned against the hallway wall beside her, and she noticed that he looked almost as tired as she felt.

'Big day?' she asked.

'It's kinda full on, isn't it?'

'You could say that.' She smiled.

'But it was good. I really enjoyed having him here the whole day and putting him to bed. I'd really like to do it more often.'

Her smile wavered slightly. 'Well, it seems I'll be kept busy with more of these catering events, so I guess you'll get your wish,' she said, trying to keep her tone light.

'I take it tonight went well?'

'It did. I have the Hendersons to thank for introducing me to a whole new sideline for the business.'

Nash gave a snort and turned his head away. 'Yeah, they like it when people are in debt to them,' he said mockingly.

Gemma bridled. 'You know, I'm getting sick of this attitude of yours. I get you're not a huge fan of anything Henderson, but you really need to start letting go of all this hostility. You live in the same community as them and sooner or later you're going to have to get over it.'

'Wow, look who's an expert on the community after, what, two months?' he said.

'At least I'm not rude to people. The way you acted towards Ben this morning was terrible, Nash.'

'You think I like walking in there and seeing Henderson playing with my kid?'

'He was just entertaining him while I prepared the food for his parents' party,' she told him, exasperated.

'I don't want him near my son.'

'Well, that's too bad. You don't get to tell me who I can and can't have around my own place.'

'Don't push me, Gem,' he warned.

'What's that supposed to mean?' Things were rapidly getting out of hand, but in her exhausted state she couldn't hide her anger at Nash's tone.

'He's my son.'

'No one's disputing that, but it doesn't give you the right to throw your weight around.'

'Are you saying you and Henderson have something going on?'

'I'm not saying anything of the kind. Ben's a friend. You don't have to like that, but you do have to respect it.'

'You know what he did,' Nash bit out.

Gemma shook her head sadly. It always came back to this. 'I know what he did when he was a stupid teenager. A lot of people do stupid things as teenagers. It was a sad and tragic thing, Nash. He didn't murder her. He made a stupid decision to drive a car when he'd been drinking—a decision he probably wouldn't have made had he been older and wiser. But he'll live with that accident for the rest of his life. It happened and it can't be changed, but this town needs to stop being so judgemental and leave the guy alone.'

'You don't know him like the rest of us do.'

'I know the person he is now, which is more than most people in this town can say. Look, you don't have to like him. But you can't tell me who I can and can't see. You need to deal with your own guilt and then maybe you'll be able to get past this thing with Ben.'

'Right, 'cause it's that easy,' he said angrily.

'I didn't say it was easy. But it's time to let it go. You weren't to blame for Kim getting into that car. She got in of her own free will. I'm sorry she died, but everyone seems to be forgetting her part in all this.'

'You don't know anything about her.' He pushed himself away from the wall irritably.

Gemma tried to speak evenly. 'I know she was a typical teenage girl who had no idea that the choice she was making might kill her and destroy the lives she left behind. It's not her fault either, but you keep acting as though you forced her into that car by telling her to get in with Ben. But she didn't have to. She knew he'd been drinking. *She* made a bad decision. It wasn't *your* decision.'

'Her parents would disagree.' The pain she saw in his eyes sliced through her. The wound he carried around was still so raw.

'They'd just lost a child,' she said, taking a step closer to him. 'They had no idea what they were saying. They probably would have lashed out at anyone who was there. It just happened to be you. You were not to blame, Nash.'

He shook his head, but she reached up and clasped his face in her hands and forced him to look at her. 'It wasn't your fault,' she repeated more firmly.

'I should have—'

'It wasn't your fault.' She couldn't let him shake this off. Not this time. He needed to confront it once and for all. He clung to her gaze, and for the first time she saw in his eyes a glimmer of something other than guilt and pain.

'Say it, Nash,' she whispered, her own eyes filling with tears as she saw the battle raging inside him. She couldn't stand seeing him tormented like this. 'It wasn't your fault.'

'She died.'

'Yes. But it *wasn't your fault*. She'd tell you that if she could. You have to let this go. It's been long enough.'

He seemed to search her gaze, and she was relieved that at least he wasn't denying it, at least he seemed to be listening to her at last. That was something.

'Gem . . .' he started, then lowered his head to hers. His kiss was filled with anger and frustration. She didn't pull away; instead she accepted the onslaught, allowing him to take out on her whatever emotions were raging within him. Gradually his lips softened, became less desperate, and his kiss grew deeper and gentler. Her hands slid to the back of his neck and her fingers threaded through his hair as she tried to drag him closer. Fire leapt between them, swift and powerful.

A low moan escaped Nash's lips, sending her already erratic pulse skittering as they moved wordlessly from the hallway to the bedroom, still entwined. Standing in the dark room, Gemma pulled away slightly and tugged at Nash's shirt, her hands seeking the warmth of his skin. They undressed hurriedly, clothing landing in a pile on the bedroom floor. Gemma didn't allow herself to think, instead losing herself in Nash's clever hands and sensations she'd been missing for far too long.

The shrill sound of the phone ringing made her jump. Nash swore, not so softly, and rested his forehead against hers for a moment, fighting to get his breathing back under control before he went to answer it.

As soon as he left, Gemma let out a shaky breath. She quickly pulled on her clothes again and headed outside to cool her overheated skin. The rain had stopped for now, but she

knew it was only a brief reprieve; the weather forecast was
for more rain for at least another day or two. Her emotions
were all over the place. She knew Nash had been hurting—
supressing that hurt and anger and guilt for far too long and
had needed to let it out. Their lovemaking had always been
powerful, but what they'd almost experienced just now had
been . . . intense. Part of her was relieved the phone had rang,
while another part felt abandoned and frustrated.

She sank to the top step. Immediately a shape detached
itself from the shadows and moved towards her.

'Hello, you. I wondered when you'd make an appearance,'
Gemma said as the big feline made its way cautiously to her
side. 'Goodness, look how much you've grown.' Living up
to the promise of his name, he was enormous.

She held out her hand to the cat before gently running her
fingers along the soft fur of his back. Soon she was rewarded
with loud purring, as Horse rubbed his head around her
legs and nudged her for more stroking. 'Did you miss me?'
Gemma asked. Many times she'd thought about him and
wondered if he was still at Dunoon. There was a lot she'd
missed about this place.

The door squeaked open and she heard Nash's footsteps
behind her on the verandah. 'I've got to head next door for
a bit. Old Fred's got his tractor bogged out on the property,
and Mavis is worried about him.' He paused, waiting till she
looked at him. 'Will you be okay here for a while?'

'Sure.'

'I hope it won't take too long,' he said softly, holding her
gaze. 'We need to talk when I get back.'

KARLY LANE

When the lights of his ute had disappeared into the night, Gemma got up and went inside. She'd missed this old kitchen. She'd often thought about it during her time away. She couldn't pinpoint exactly what it was about it she loved so much. There certainly wasn't anything state-of-the-art about it, but it felt . . . like home. The thought echoed inside her and she blinked away the sudden sting of tears from her eyes quickly. She finished cleaning the kitchen and made a cup of tea, but an hour later he still hadn't returned.

Her phone ringing had her leaping to her feet and rummaging through her handbag to retrieve it before it woke up Finn. Nash didn't waste any time with hellos, and instantly she knew something was wrong.

'I need help finding Fred, and Mavis shouldn't be alone while she waits for news. Can you call the Hendersons and get someone to come over here?'

'Oh my God, what's happened?'

'I don't have time to talk now, Gem. Just call Bullowa and get someone over here. Grace will know what to do.' He hung up before she could ask anything else.

Her heart racing, Gemma scrolled through her phone and found Ben's number. It would be quicker to call him directly than ring directory for the Hendersons' number. As she waited for the call to connect she heard Finn wake up and quickly headed to his bedroom. She breathed a sigh of relief when Ben answered.

'I knew it, you couldn't resist my charms,' he drawled. 'You've changed your mind, haven't you?'

'Ben, this is serious,' she said, then told him what little detail Nash had given her.

Ben's jovial mood was gone in a flash, and he assured her that he and his mother would head straight to the Smiths'.

'Look, I'm up and dressed,' Gemma said. 'I can go over to sit with Mavis. Finn's awake now, so I can just take him with me. You don't have to bother your mother.'

'If Whittaker said he needed my mother out there then things must be bad, Gem. And Mum will want to come. The neighbours out this way are pretty close, especially in times like these.' Ben hung up with a promise to call and fill her in when he knew more.

Half an hour passed, and Gemma found herself becoming more and more tightly wound with each passing minute. She had to do something. Finn seemed to have picked up on her agitated state. She'd tried giving him a bottle, tried singing to him, and nothing was working. Finally, she wrapped him up warmly and carried him out to the car, then buckled him into his car seat and headed away from the house. The driveway was muddy and she drove carefully, trying to avoid the worst of the potholes.

When she pulled up in front of Fred and Mavis's house, it was lit up as if for a party, with several vehicles parked outside. But when she knocked on the door the mood inside was anything but festive. Grace greeted her with a worried frown, her gaze dropping to Finn as Gemma shifted him to her other hip.

'I hope I'm not intruding,' Gemma rushed in, 'but I couldn't get this fella to sleep and it was driving me crazy sitting at Nash's waiting to hear what was going on. I thought I'd come over and see if I could be any help here?'

'Come on in, I'm just making some tea.' Grace held the door open and Gemma walked in, noticing an older woman standing by the window, her arms folded tightly across her chest, a scrunched-up hanky in her hand. She didn't glance over, and Gemma suddenly felt like an outsider. Gemma recognised Ben's father, Harold, talking on the phone in the corner of the room.

'What's going on?' she asked Grace in a whisper when they reached the kitchen. 'Nash didn't have time to fill me in.'

'Ben's gone out to join Nash in the search. They found the tractor near the creek, but they can't find Fred.'

Gemma sent a quick glance through the kitchen doorway to where Mavis was still standing by the window. 'Oh no.'

'Nash called in the police, and Harold and I have been doing the ring-around of neighbours to come out and help.'

Gemma gently swayed her body, trying to soothe Finn, who was now rubbing his eyes and crying irritably.

'Would you mind if I . . . ?' Grace put her hands out to Finn, her voice a little uncertain.

'Oh sure. He's a bit grumpy though. He's tired but he keeps fighting it.'

'I remember when my boys were like that. Would you mind terribly making Mavis a cuppa? She said she didn't want one earlier but I think she needs something.'

Gemma touched her son's head lightly then went to find cups, milk and sugar. As she busied herself in the kitchen she watched Grace holding Finn and softly crooning a song. Though still every inch the stylish matriarch, as Grace looked down at Finn there was a gentleness in her that Gemma hadn't seen in their earlier meetings.

Gemma carried a cup of hot tea out to the old woman and placed it on the coffee table below the window. 'Thank you, dear,' Mavis said with only the most fleeting of glances at Gemma before returning to her silent vigil, staring out the window.

'They'll find him,' Gemma said, hoping her tone sounded reassuring.

Mavis only smiled sadly and nodded her head.

Gemma didn't know what else to say, so she kept her mouth shut and went back to the kitchen to find Finn fast asleep in Grace's arms.

'I've still got it,' Grace whispered, glancing up at Gemma with a smile.

'You sure do,' Gemma said, impressed. 'Do you want me to take him?'

'No, he's fine. I'm enjoying being clucky again after all this time.'

Gemma heard cars approaching and soon there were doors opening and closing and men's voices murmuring outside. 'More volunteers,' Grace said quietly as her husband headed outside to greet them. Within minutes engines roared to life again as the men set off across the paddocks.

A little while later a police four-wheel drive arrived. Gemma opened the door for the two officers and led them inside to talk to Mavis.

The radio provided a constant background chatter with men calling in to report they'd found nothing in their designated search areas and checking in for more instructions. Occasionally Gemma heard Nash's voice among the others';

in spite of her anxiety, the sound of his voice set off a little glow of warmth inside her each time.

'How can they not have found him yet?' she asked Grace in a whisper.

'It's a big area to cover, and the bad weather is hindering things.' After a short silence, Grace added, 'They're all going to be cold and miserable out there.'

'Should I make up some coffee for them?'

'Good idea. If they don't come back soon, we might have to take it out to them.'

'There's an urn in the laundry.' Gemma turned to see that Mavis had moved from her place by the window and was now standing in the kitchen doorway. 'I've got plenty of bread in the freezer out there too if you feel like making up some sandwiches.'

While Mavis and Grace took Finn into one of the spare bedrooms and made him up a little bed, Gemma collected the urn and a couple of loaves of bread. Then all three women worked in the kitchen side by side, trying to keep busy and not think about the men outside late at night in this horrible weather or the fact that somewhere out there was an elderly man, all alone.

'If you don't mind keeping an ear out for Finn, I'll take these out to the men,' Gemma said to Grace once they'd made up the last of the sandwiches.

'I can call one of the men to come back for them,' Grace suggested.

'Actually, if it's okay I'd like to go out there.' Gemma wanted to see what was going on and make sure Nash was okay. For the last hour or so she'd had a strange feeling in the pit of her stomach that wouldn't go away. Maybe it was seeing Mavis so worried that her husband of more than fifty years was out there, possibly injured, that had made Gemma realise she needed to tell Nash she'd made a decision. Life was so very fragile. Maybe it was time to take that leap of faith and trust him.

One of the police officers was about to join in the search, so Gemma got a lift with him out to where a circle of cars, all with their headlights on, made a makeshift meeting point a few kilometres from the house. The rain was coming down steadily, and as they drove across the bumpy paddocks, Gemma finally understood why it was taking so long to find Fred. There was no moonlight due to the heavy cloud, and the only light came from the police car's headlights, two thin beams in the rain and fog.

At the meeting point, a blue tarp had been strung up between two vehicles to provide temporary shelter from the rain, and Gemma unloaded the platters of sandwiches she'd brought from the house and a laundry basket full of cups, spoons and coffee.

As she offered the coffee to grateful farmers, who wrapped their hands around the cups for warmth, she hoped for a glimpse of Nash but couldn't see him anywhere. The men drank their coffee quickly and then were gone again. For a long while Gemma was left standing huddled beneath the tarp while the police officer manned a radio, following with his finger a map spread out on the bonnet of a four-wheel drive.

Then the radio burst into life again, and three words echoed in the darkness: 'We found him.'

Thirty

Nash was soaked through. He wore his long oilskin coat and his hat was pulled down as low as it would go, rain running off the edges as he sloshed his way through the soft ground alongside the creek bed.

When he first arrived at the Smiths' place, his mind had still been on Gemma, the feeling of her warm naked body in his arms, but once he found Fred's tractor bogged up to its axles and no sight of the old fella, his thoughts had been single-mindedly focused on finding his elderly neighbour as soon as possible. The radio in the tractor was dead and there were massive black spots out here for mobile phone coverage. His relief at the sound of an engine had been swiftly replaced by irritation when he saw who it was, but his concern for Fred outweighed any reluctance to work with Henderson, and he was happy to hear that more neighbours were being called in to help.

The creek had risen considerably over the last few hours, and as they searched along the banks, Nash saw that it was moving fast. Logs and branches were being swept downstream at a good pace.

The rain began falling more heavily, and more than once Nash lost his footing in the mud along the bank. Visibility was next to nothing, and his torch, although powerful, could barely penetrate the fog and rain for him to see more than a few feet ahead.

'This is bloody useless,' he heard Ben yell from behind him.

'Then go back,' Nash yelled over his shoulder.

'What makes you think he'd have come down here anyway?'

'Nothing, but I'm not leaving it unsearched.'

'Silly old bastard. He should have known better than to come out in this weather,' Ben grumbled.

'Guess he was too stubborn to ask for help.'

'Sounds like ninety per cent of the population out here,' Ben snorted.

'Over there,' Nash said, stopping and pointing to something on the far bank. The two men squinted at the dark shape on the opposite side of the creek.

'I'll go over and have a look,' Ben said, already shrugging off his jacket.

'Just wait a sec. We need to call it in, get some rope down here.'

'Bugger that, it'll just waste time if it turns out to be a dead sheep.'

'The current's running too strong to go in without a rope.'

Nash grabbed Ben's arm as the other man moved towards the edge of the creek.

Ben shook him off and glared. 'I said, I've got this, *mate*,' he snarled.

Nash's jaw clenched as Ben turned away and began wading into the swollen creek. 'Bloody idiot,' he muttered under his breath, watching Ben's slow progress through the water. It wasn't very wide, maybe fifteen feet, but it was much higher than usual and the current was pushing a lot of debris downstream.

Just before he reached the other side of the creek, Ben turned and called back, 'It's him. Get on the radio.'

Nash grabbed the portable radio from his pocket and held down the button on the side. 'We found him,' he said, then lifted his head as Ben yelled something else.

'He's alive, but barely. We need to get him out of here.'

Nash pressed the button again and repeated Ben's message, then gave the location, dropping the radio as he saw Ben lift Fred and position the old man's arm across his shoulders. Nash cursed and shrugged off his coat as he watched Ben stagger with the dead weight of the unconscious man and head back into the water. 'Just bloody wait!' he yelled, running into the water. 'I'm coming over.'

The water was now at mid-thigh on Ben, but the added weight of Fred and the strong current meant he was making little progress. When Nash finally reached him, the water was waist high and Ben was struggling to keep his balance. Nash ducked beneath Fred's other arm and anchored his own arm around the old man's waist.

They'd just passed the midway point when Nash looked up and saw a tree trunk rushing towards them. He shouted a warning, but it was already too late. There was nowhere for them to go, the current was too strong, and in seconds the branch had collected the three men, sweeping them along on its mad dash downstream.

Nash's feet were knocked from under him and the murky depths swallowed him, filling his ears with the turbulent, muted noise of a furious river. Once the trunk had passed overhead, he pushed back up to the surface, shaking the water from his eyes as he searched frantically for the others. He ducked back under several times and scrabbled around blindly, finally grasping a fistful of fabric. Heaving up the sodden weight, he saw Fred's pale face. He struggled to the bank, fighting the current, dragging Fred's lifeless form. As he went he continued to scan the water for Ben. Where the hell was he?

Torch beams appeared and he heard men shouting. He helped haul Fred up to the waiting hands on the bank, then immediately turned and dived back into the current, ignoring the shouts from the other men.

Beneath the water was a disorientating maze of branches, logs and mud. Surfacing again, he yelled out Ben's name over the roar of the water. Unseen objects smashed against his legs as he waded through the floodwater, and he was knocked over more than once and floated for a short way before regaining his feet. He saw that the large tree trunk that had swept them downstream had become lodged close to the bank. Fighting against the strong current, Nash waded towards it. His teeth chattering in the cold, and his eyes trying to pick out shapes in the dark, he called back for some light, and saw that the men were rigging up a safety rope.

'Ben!' Nash called out again. 'Where the hell are you, you bastard?'

Two other volunteers soon reached him and Nash took a torch someone handed him. Struggling to grip it in his frozen hands, he aimed it at the tree trunk, while others moved further downstream, calling out.

Then suddenly his torch picked out a hunched shape on the other side of the tree trunk, and he shouted for help.

•

Gemma heard Nash's words on the radio and let out a long unsteady breath. Thank God they'd found him. She shared a relieved smile with the policeman beside her, but within minutes more radio chatter started up as men converged on the location Nash had hurriedly rattled off.

'They're in the water.'

'We need ropes.'

'We need an ambulance. Get those guys down here!'

'We've lost one. I need more light down here, now!'

Gemma clutched her jacket tightly around her body. The urgency in the voices on the radio terrified her. Who had they lost? Where the hell was Nash? Why hadn't she heard his voice again since he'd first called in that Fred was found?

Following the burst of voices, the radio fell silent again. The rain continued to fall as Gemma stood next to the radio and waited anxiously for someone to speak. What was happening down there? She looked out over the paddock and wished she could see the creek but it was too dark. She might as well be in a different part of the country for all the good it did her.

The radio attached to the police officer's belt crackled to life. Gemma watched as he answered his partner, who was down with the others near the creek.

'We're on our way back,' the other officer reported. 'I've told the men to stay off the main frequency. We've got at least one fatality.'

Gemma felt pain slice through her chest as she fought to take a breath. *At least one fatality.* Was it Fred? The instantaneous surge of relief she felt at the thought was quickly followed by guilt. Poor Mavis. Gemma found herself staring blankly at the policeman, who had sent her a sharp glance after his partner delivered the news. He moved away to make some phone calls while Gemma stood stunned, unable to move from the spot. A little while later, he returned and guided her into the front seat of his vehicle. They headed back to the house in silence.

By the time Gemma went back inside she was shivering and her clothes were damp. Grace was instantly beside her, wrapping her in a warm blanket. The policeman made his way across the lounge room to where Mavis sat. Gemma heard the low murmur of his voice but couldn't make out any words. It was clear from the slump of the older woman's shoulders that she'd been given the news. Grace left Gemma and went to sit next to Mavis, wrapping a supportive arm around her shoulders.

Not long later, cars could be heard outside, and the lights of a slowly moving procession of vehicles approached the house. Gemma stood up, shrugging off the blanket, and ran to the door. Anxiously she scoured the dirty, wet faces of the weary-looking men as they climbed out of cars and trucks, then went into the big machinery shed, out of the rain. She couldn't see him. *Where the hell was Nash?*

The second police officer moved away from the group of men and climbed the stairs to the house. Gemma held her breath as he walked past her and into the lounge room. He stopped in front of Mavis and confirmed his partner's news, now giving her a more detailed report. In a quiet but authoritative voice he told her that they'd found her husband but hadn't been able to revive him. A small sound escaped Mavis's throat as she squeezed her eyes shut and nodded her head. The scene was heartbreaking. Her husband of nearly fifty years had gone out that morning and never returned. Gemma felt a tear slide down her face in sympathy and quickly wiped it away.

'Mrs Henderson.' The policeman, his face drawn, had now turned to Grace. 'I'm very sorry, but there was a second fatality tonight. Unfortunately, while your son Ben was trying to bring Fred back across the creek, he was swept downstream. It appears he became entangled in the debris and drowned before our volunteers could reach him. I'm very sorry.'

Gemma felt the remaining air in her lungs leave her body in a rush. Ben? Ben was *dead*? She searched blindly behind her and sank down on a chair.

'No! You must be mistaken,' said Grace, staring at the policeman.

A woman who had been out in the kitchen crossed the room and knelt beside Mavis as Grace stood up and clung to her husband's arm, shaking her head. 'Tell them, Harold. They must be mistaken, Ben can't be . . . No, it's a mistake,' she said, then slumped against her husband's chest.

Gemma couldn't watch any longer. She stumbled out of the room and made her way up the hallway towards the room where Finn was sleeping. As she paused outside the door, grief suddenly bent her in two. She closed her eyes and the tears spilled out, running down her face. Ben was dead? It just didn't make any sense.

She wasn't sure how long she stood there for, time suddenly had no meaning. Then strong arms closed around her. She lifted her head and gave a sob of relief as Nash held her while she cried.

'Ben's dead?' she said, struggling to force the words out of her throat.

Nash's face crumpled as he gave a jerky nod of his head. In his eyes she read final confirmation that Ben was gone. For a long time they didn't speak, just held one another, until Gemma's sobs eased and some awareness of where they were began to penetrate her sadness.

'Oh my God, poor Grace,' she said, wiping her eyes. 'I should go out there.'

'They've given her a sedative.'

'What about Mavis?'

'Her sister-in-law just arrived and the rest of the family are on their way. We should probably let them grieve in peace. I'll get Finn,' he said, letting her go, and she instantly missed the warmth of his arms. The sight a few moments later of Nash holding their sleeping child in his arms brought on a fresh wave of tears. She wasn't sure if she was crying for Ben or if, in her fragile state, a sight so beautiful was enough to trigger tears which were all too close to the surface.

They left the house with a few quiet farewells to the neighbours who were still there, and climbed into Nash's four-wheel drive. As they drove away, Gemma caught sight of the vehicle that held the bodies. The police and a few volunteers remained to keep watch over them until they could be transported back into town.

She rested her forehead against the cold glass of the window and shut her eyes, which felt gritty and sore. It was just past midnight. The road was dark beyond their headlights and the rain continued to fall. They didn't speak for the entire trip home. When they got to Dunoon, Nash gently lifted the sleeping Finn from the car seat and carried him into his room.

When he came back out into the lit hallway, Gemma saw how terrible he looked; his eyes were bloodshot, his face was scratched and a bruise was beginning to form on his cheekbone. He was still wearing the same wet and muddy clothes he went out in. Gemma swallowed back fresh tears; she didn't want to cry anymore. She took his hand and led him into the bathroom, where she helped him undress and put him under the warm spray of the shower.

'I'll go and make some tea for when you get out,' she said, turning to leave, but his hand shot out and caught her upper arm.

'No. I don't want tea. I need you.'

She searched his tortured eyes for a moment. Then, without a word, she undressed and stepped into the shower with him.

Wrapping her arms around him, she held him as the warm water fell down upon them.

•

Hearing a happy gurgle, Gemma opened her eyes to see her son lying beside her, staring up at Nash, who crooned soft baby talk.

Nash met her gaze, and for a long time they didn't speak, just shared a look that relived the sadness of the previous night.

Nash looked back down at Finn and spoke quietly. 'All the time I blamed myself for not telling Kim to get out of the car, I was always assuming that she would have done what I said and I'd have saved her . . . Last night I told Ben to wait, but he wouldn't listen to me. Now I realise that Kim wouldn't have got out of that car even if I'd told her to. I couldn't have changed things that night either.'

Gemma swallowed hard to keep from crying. He had to be ready to hear it before it sunk in. No matter how many times people had told him he wasn't to blame, he needed to reach this point before it made sense to him.

'I'm sorry about Ben,' Nash went on gently, meeting her eyes. 'I know he meant a lot to you. We didn't get along, but I didn't want him dead. I just wanted you to know that.'

Gemma nodded. 'You two were polar opposites of each other.'

For a moment they were both lost in their own thoughts. The sound of rain on the roof made Gemma feel warm and snug in Nash's big bed. It felt right for all three of them to be together here.

'Yes,' she said, her voice still husky from sleep.

Lying propped up on one arm, Nash quirked an eyebrow. 'Yes what?'

'Yes, I'll marry you,' she said quietly.

For a long time he simply stared at her, maybe searching her gaze for a hint that she wasn't serious, before a slow smile spread across his face and he nodded, looking down to where Finn held his finger tightly. When he lifted his gaze once more, she saw the fresh sheen of moisture in his eyes. 'I love you, Gemma.'

'I love you too.' She knew that if they could survive everything they'd been through so far, they could face anything together as a family.

'Where are you going?' Nash asked as she threw back the covers and slid out of bed.

'To call Jazz and get my laptop. We need to google "How to plan a wedding".'

'Gem . . .'

Gemma hit speaker and smiled at Jazz's irritable hello as she answered the phone. 'Guess what!'

'Gemma. This had better be good. It's still dark outside.'

'I'm getting married.'

For a moment the phone went silent and Gemma glanced at the screen to make sure she was still connected before Jazz let out a loud whoop of excitement. 'Well, it's about time! What is that guy's problem anyway? You'd think considering he knocked you up and then—' Gemma quickly took Jazz off speaker and sent an apologetic wince across to Nash. 'Ah, Jazz, I need to make some other phone calls, so I'll call you back in a bit, okay?'

'Same old Jazz,' Nash said drolly.

'You'll learn to love her. She grows on you after a while.'

'Yeah,' he chuckled darkly, tickling his son, 'like fungus.'

She'd probably always need to be the referee between those two, Gemma conceded, but deep down she knew that they both loved her enough not to take things too far. They'd just have to learn how to deal with each other . . . in small doses.

'Now what are you doing?' Nash asked as she opened her laptop.

'I'm googling how to make our own wedding invitations,' she said, as her fingers glided across the keyboard.

'Seriously?'

'Oh, and I heard about these really cute wedding-cake toppers you can get made to look like the bride and groom. We could get you one with an Akubra, and maybe for me we can find one holding a wooden spoon or something.'

Nash looked down at his son and shook his head. 'What are we going to do with her, mate?'

Gemma ignored him and started to type. 'And I need to work out a menu for the reception . . .'

Acknowledgements

Thank you to my lovely editors, Christa Munns and Clara Finlay, who always make sure my books are the best they can be. Thank you so much for all the time and care you've both put into this.

Thanks to my Facebook fans: I love being able to connect with you on such a regular basis. I love that you guys are always there to offer advice or help with any random questions I might throw out there ... like beer-drinking cats! (*Disclaimer: No cats were actually fed alcohol in the making of this book ... the same CANNOT be said for the author.*)

Thank you to my family who love and support me and who have been known to approach complete strangers in bookstores all over Australia to tell them that they really should read a Karly Lane book. I'm so lucky to have you all helping me.

Thanks to my two early readers, Catherine Finnegan and Karin Bridle, for great feedback and encouragement on this book.

A big thanks to Allen & Unwin who continue to publish my books and to give me these amazing opportunities to share my stories with you all.